Damnation of the Realm

Freedom or the Fire, Volume One
A Fantasy Tale

Joshua T. Calkins-Treworgy

BooksForABuck.com

2008

Damnation of the Realm

Freedom or the Fire, Volume One

Joshua T. Calkins-Treworgy

Published by **BooksForABuck.com**

ISBN: 978-1-60215-071-3

Dedication

I'd first like to thank my wife, Audrey, and my daughters, Cassandra and Celina, for supporting me in my endeavors and remaining a constant pleasure in my life. I'd like to thank my mother and father, who have never discouraged my desires to be an author, or my fascinations with all things fantasy.

I'd like to thank Christopher Edison, John Leonard, and Sean Salatka, my constant role-playing friends. Without their enthusiasm for the fantasy world of Tamalaria in which their pen-and-paper adventures took place, there would have come no format for this tale and the future Tamalarian Tales that I shall endeavor to produce.

To Mr. and Mrs. McDonald, my junior and senior year English instructors, I'd like to say thanks for the criticisms, the notes you gave me, and the encouragement you gave me back when the very idea of writing professionally was only a pipe dream for me. It's still a bit of a dream, but here you have it.

And of course, my thanks to Mr. Robert Preece, a true professional and gentleman who helped me flesh out a number of components throughout the story. I am very thankful to you, sir.

Joshua Calkins-Treworgy

Damnation of the Realm

Prologue

His armored fist slammed heavily into the guard's stomach, pushing undigested foodstuffs and body acids around in an uncomfortable fashion. "Please, forgive me for this," he rasped as the Human guard fell easily into his bracing arms.

"You know, nobody'd miss him," a small, high-pitched voice chimed in next to the dark traveler's ear. "Chances are he'll be able to find you if he gets within a hundred yards of you. He'll feel your presence. Just take care of that little problem." The shadow-wrapped creature harrumphed softly.

"Tempting, little one. Very tempting," the traveler said. Visions of violence danced through his mind. In the first, he slammed his fist through the guard's chest and ripped his spinal column straight out through the gaping hole. In the second vision, well, it involved his broadsword and an orifice not normally associated with the word 'entry'. The old fury, once so familiar, so easy to use, now tried to infringe upon his actions. "But no. This man has done us no wrong. Hopefully, that will continue to hold true until we figure out what to do next."

The traveler waved his left hand vaguely around in a circle. Smoke and shadows extended from the fog and darkness around the traveler's own body, and encased the guard completely within moments. Though the creature had managed to restrain his darkest impulses, he could not stop himself from tossing the unconscious body carelessly toward the bushes along the city wall. The heavy impact signaled to him that no effort had been made by the guard to soften the landing. He would stay asleep for a while.

"You there," shouted another guard, this one from a way off to the traveler's left.

Damnation, he thought. *Should have known there'd be more than one guard at the gates.* The cloaked stranger spun on his heel to face the second guard, a brown furred Werewolf in full hybrid form, as had become custom for the lycanthropes. This, the stranger thought, is going to be more difficult than dealing with the Human.

"Hold your position," the Werewolf shouted as he sped up to get in front of the stranger.

"I am in a hurry to get to the inn," rasped the cloaked creature, as dust plumed from his throat. "I do not wish to tarry here any longer than is necessary." Silver, he thought desperately. Why don't I ever carry silver?

"And you won't have to," said the Werewolf. His rough, gnarled left hand moved slowly toward the hilt of a longsword. "So long as you provide your papers and state your business." The guard's words would normally have put a traveler at ease to hear such simple requirements for entrance, especially in the lands of Tamalaria. The traveler moved his right hand into his cloak slowly, but obviously. As before, a comforting sign, this time for the guard. People didn't make such obvious motions if they intended anything harmful, most times. The traveler's body language spoke clearly to the Werewolf guard, and it said 'I'm getting those papers now'.

"This had better be the only other guard," the cloaked creature said to himself as he brought his hand out, releasing a thin bolt of purple energy into the Werewolf's chest. The magic struck with such accuracy and sudden force that the lycanthrope's entire body hit the ground without pause.

"Hmm. Nice fall," said a high-pitched voice near the traveler's ear. "No sissy attempt to soften it by bending the knees."

"Yes, well, I did hit him rather hard," grumbled the traveler as he darted down the main street. "Not sure he was conscious to make the attempt at saving himself." Keeping a flow of magical shadows wrapped around his body, the traveler moved seamlessly from the street, to the innkeeper's front desk, to a rented room. Tossing off the shadows that concealed his form, the traveler looked in the full-length mirror next to his dingy, two-gold-pieces-a-night bed.

"Looking good, boss," the little voice said. The traveler's head bore on its surface no trace of hair, feature, or flesh. Smoke billowed slowly from the half-rotted throat.

"Shut up, Alex." The traveler looked in the mirror at his ravaged, armored body. He lay down on the bed, staring at the ceiling until sleep took him, until dreams washed away the image in the mirror. He dreamed of how it came to this, how he became that which he had once hated, hunted, destroyed.

He dreamed the memory of his life as Byron Aixler, and how a warlock destroyed that life.

Chapter One
Memory of Birth

He dreamed, and found himself in the past. The sun remained behind clouds in the sky over the land of Tamalaria, casting a gray haze over the hundreds of men and women encamped at the foot of Mount Toane. Byron Aixler observed the overall effect the atmosphere had on his fellow Paladins and the other assembled combatants. As he strode from group to group, he caught sight of almost every Race and Class to be found in Tamalaria.

Lycanthropes played roughly with one another in their animal forms away from the main camps. Cuyotai, or rather Werecoyotes, numbered highest among the shape-shifters. Byron didn't see a problem with this. After all, the Cuyotai were the easiest lycanthropes to get along with. Though tribal, they were an easy-going bunch. Elves and Dwarves also walked about the camp, anxious and worried about the small army's purpose in coming to Mount Toane.

All manner of magic wielder sat in the clear patches of scrub grass, meditating and gathering spiritual strength. They would be pivotal in this final stand against the evil that lurked in Mount Toane. Byron Aixler looked at the furrowed brow of one Pyromancer, the caster's eyes squeezed shut, balls of fire circling his body in a protective barrier. The heat that came off the man wrapped about Byron's body and caused fresh beads of sweat to drip down his rugged, wind-worn face.

At a little over six and a half feet in height, Byron was intimidating at first glance. His silver, full plate armor shone in the brief glimpses of sunlight the clouds allowed, and his fluid movement even in such restricting armor only made him more frightening. That is, if you didn't know him. Byron Aixler was a holy warrior, a Paladin. His handsome smile flashed frequently when among his companions or when he was among the common people he sought to protect. To these people, comfort and ease of mind settled like blankets on their hearts and minds when Byron came near. But to the wicked, the unjust, and those consumed by darkness, his was a terrifying visage.

White light, the holy power granted to him by his faith, wrapped itself about his body. His blade would appear in his hand as if by magic, a servant of chaos or evil generally had as long to live as he had tricks up your sleeve. In Byron's time, only two such persons had eluded him—the warlock, Tanarak of Sidius, and Tanarak's apprentice, whose name no one knew.

And now those foul servants of the Pit sat in Mount Toane, coiled vipers waiting to strike. The mountain fortress was the central command for Tanarak's forces. For years, the warlock had influenced Tamalaria in subtle ways, taking control and wreaking havoc slowly but surely. Recently, Tanarak's tactics had changed, however. Now the warlock sent waves of undead creatures and assorted Orcs, Ogres, and Lizardmen to assault major cities and Order of Oun outposts. The damage caused had mounted quickly, and the number of innocent lives lost skyrocketed.

No Race was exempt, no group, no Class. The Order of Oun, an organized militia of Paladins to which Byron belonged, had stood against Tanarak since the warlock began his reign of terror, but could never seem to do enough. The free creatures of the land were attacked from all sides at all times. Tamalaria had quickly fallen under Tanarak's shadow.

The warlock had even manipulated political leaders over the years, and his forces met no resistance from these men of power. Entire platoons of warriors were told to hold their position, not to resist what passed them. By the time the Order of Oun had learned of the danger, it was almost too late. Tanarak had spread his evil to many places in the lands of Tamalaria, and few civilized cities or kingdoms stood against his new world order.

Ultimately, Tanarak's rise to power had brought Byron Aixler to the spot where he stood. For two years, he led the resistance against Tanarak and his apprentice, gathering together all who sought to destroy the evil that had enslaved the land. Most who joined the resistance were Werewolves, Cuyotai, Humans, Elves, and Dwarves. A small handful of Gnomes also joined, bringing their natural knack for strategy and magic to bear. Almost every Class was represented in the resistance.

By the year 824 A.F., the resistance encompassed nearly every Race as well, including some that were less than nice or, Byron thought, trustworthy. He didn't particularly care for the Minotaurs, but their brute strength and willingness to fight to the death gave him good reason to keep a few in his own battalion.

Lost in thought, Byron didn't realize someone trying to address him until the squat Gnome kicked him in the shin-guard.

The little white-haired man jumped around, holding his foot and cursing loudly. It was Lee Toren, a Gnome Pickpocket and informant to Byron. Lee only stood about three and a half feet in height, as did most of his Race. His hair stood out in wild, unkempt white tufts on his head, and his bright green eyes squinted shut as he held his injured foot in his hand, leaning against Byron's thickly built body and armor for support.

Byron's brilliant blue eyes bored into the back of Lee's head, waiting for the Gnome to speak. After all, he had kicked Byron to get his attention, or so the Human Paladin had assumed. When Lee finally looked up, he cleared his throat in a most uncomfortable and awkward fashion, as if to apologize without saying so.

"Sorry abou' that there, Byron," he muttered. "Some o' the gents in the third battalion just want to know when, exactly, you all are going in."

"Soon enough, Lee Toren," Byron said, patting the little man amiably on the head. "Tell them, soon enough. The Final Push cannot be rushed, for we enter into our enemy's home territory. None among us knows the layout of the inside of Mount Toane as well as does its masters. We must be properly prepared, my friend. Go tell them that. Especially Christopher Gray, as I know he is becoming impatient." Byron turned brusquely away from the thief, his thoughts shifting from his own comrades to questions about the dark warlock they all sought to defeat here. Would he be able to do his duty when the time came?

Byron regretted taking life but knew that sometimes it was necessary. If he had the chance to grant mercy to the warlock and his apprentice, would he grant it? He thought of his wife and son, left behind in a city safe from Tanarak and his minions. Would Tanarak grant his family mercy, if he were given the chance? Byron knew the answer even before he asked himself the question. It would have to be the answer to his first question.

* * * *

On the fields of Tamalaria and in the peaked colossus of Mount Toane, events occurred to which the Dread Knight Byron of Sidius had not been witness.

In the shadows of a deep and lofty chamber within Mount Toane, Tanarak of Sidius prepared traps for the impending assault on his mountain spire fortress. Serpentine shadows coiled around pillars of rock as they jutted toward the ceiling from the floor. The spikes of stone were set in the tunnel leading to the throne room through the use of dark Gaiamancy, a form of earth-based magic that Tanarak twisted to his own ends. Around these pillars, his apprentice had meticulously laid pockets of deadly Pyromancy, fire magic. As Byron Aixler's companions approached, the magic would unlock, releasing a devastating cone of flames, shooting fire like a column to the ceiling of the tunnel totally engulfing its victim.

Yet, the magic would leave Byron Aixler himself unaffected. The apprentice smiled smugly to himself. *The Master has other designs for that Paladin. A thorn in our sides he has been and for too long.* The apprentice crept along the tunnel, further and further from the throne room and closer to the hubs and corridors that led throughout the rest of Mount Toane.

Into the center of the first large chamber he crept, pooling massive amount of magical energy, manna, into himself for use. The apprentice threw back his hood to reveal a gruff, hard-lined face to the empty chamber. *Empty*, he thought with the slightest hint of humor. *Not so much so.* There were the skeletal remains of scores of warriors from ages gone by strewn about. Mount Toane glowed with evil energy from without, and it had attracted many a hero to their deaths over the centuries.

The light in the chamber dimmed as the apprentice chanted in a low hiss and drew runes in the air. The symbols lit up in the air and seemed to solidify. He chanted on, speaking in a strange tongue, long since dead to the world, but very alive to Necromancers. With a final rune drawn, the apprentice threw up his arms, shouting as loudly as he could, "Arise! Ye fallen ones, you are mine to command now in death!"

As the magic took hold, the mountain shook. Each of the remains pulled themselves into vaguely human forms. Some creaked, some smoked, and some others laughed. All had a single purpose now. The viper of satisfaction drew itself across the apprentice's face. That purpose was to kill all intruders except for Byron Aixler. Not that they would be any match for Byron, but they would be useful against the other troops.

The day would be theirs.

* * * *

Byron Aixler looked out over the crowd of assembled warriors. Paladins, Knights, sorcerers, mercenaries—it was an impressive force. But, Byron felt the skittering, festering vermin known as doubt crawl around his heart and soul. Even with the magic at their disposal and the skills and technique of skilled warriors, Tanarak had the advantage.

"Edgar," he yelled, summoning his second-in-command. Edgar Cesar was a Human Knight, well experienced in mass combat. A rough-edged fellow, he had served for years as a Commander of the Parun Kingdom armies. When war came to the Kingdom's doorstep, courtesy of Tanarak's forces, Cesar took his men and women to the battlefront with a fury and strategy that had been unrivaled in the war against Tanarak. The warlock's Orcs and Ogres numbered two thousand strong when they attacked the capital. Cesar led only eight hundred. After six hours of battle, no Greenskin remained, and Cesar's forces numbered five and a half hundred.

But spies throughout the capital had spent months doing the warlock's bidding. Some were in a position of power, and some were just assassins working as servants. While the Commander defended the crown, those spies had killed all of the ruling nobles in shadows and silence. Tired and fearful of a second attack wave of Orcs, Cesar had his troops fall back into the capital itself. There they were ambushed by all manner of sorcerer and creature, and many fell in the assault. Cesar had removed himself from the carnage and ran to his king. He expected to find his majesty surrounded by his Elite Guard. What he found were butchered men and a dead king.

Now the battle-scarred and war-hardened veteran stood before a man of even greater experience in personal combat. But Byron had little tactical expertise. For that, he relied on Cesar in the large-scale battles against Tanarak's forces. Once again, he would need the tactical skills of the Commander.

"You called for me, Lord Byron?"

"Indeed, Edgar. I fear the situation looks easier than it should. Any thoughts?"

"Well," said the Commander, looking off to the entrance of Mount Toane. "The warlock Tanarak and his apprentice have the advantage insofar as position. There is only one known way in or out of the mountain, and the path immediately bottlenecks once inside. Our men will be forced to advance at a maximum of three abreast. Of course, for the lycanthropes, the going shall be even tighter. Once inside, we will have to assess the situation further. I know little or nothing of the inside of the mountain, so we shall have to feel it as we go."

Byron looked into the stony countenance of the Commander, whose eyes said everything with a look. This is going to be a massacre, they said.

"What of the mages? How is the magic at our disposal divided," Byron asked, looking at the legion once more. Some were fathers, mothers, brothers,

10

sisters. All of them were someone's children. Some were close with their parents, others not so. Many would never be heard from again. None would be the same. That, alone, was certain.

"Well, my lord, we have a host of Pyromancers, some Gaiamancers, a small handful of Aquamancers, and a few Q Mages. Also, we have a single Summoner."

"Is she well guarded?" asked Byron, raising an eyebrow. He didn't care much for Summoners. Their Guardians seldom cooperated to the fullest measure and often didn't give heed to their master's allies.

"Actually, sir, it is a man. And yes, he is well guarded." Byron gave this detail considerable thought. A Guardian could be a useful tool in the fight, but inside Mount Toane, the creature might do more harm than good.

"Have him removed, Edgar. A Summoner is devastating out on the field, but the risk to our own men is too great. Bring him a horse, and send him on his way." Edgar Cesar gave a mute nod and salute. Within minutes, he had returned.

"The Summoner has gone, sir. Also, some of the mercenaries are complaining that they want better pay for this assignment. How shall I deal with them?"

Byron smiled broadly. Most mercenaries rated fairly low, but Lee Toren had given these men a high recommendation. They were little more than bandits and rogues. Wanted fliers hung in many a province and kingdom, each depicting a separate member of this group. Which made them especially valuable for his plans.

"Give them some coin from my personal tent. Whatever they ask, supply it."

The Commander winced ever so slightly. "Are these Black Vultures really worth so much, sire? They are asking for a hefty pay increase. Mightn't it be best to reserve any payment until the battle is over?"

Byron caught the sign of a serpent's smile creeping across Cesar's lips.

"Don't worry, Edgar. You know what they say; 'Gold is easiest earned when taken from a dead man.' Besides, it will raise their morale. Now see to it."

"Of course, sire." His face returned to the stony, stoic gaze of a soldier. Cesar went about the business of paying the mercenaries. Byron gazed at the gap in the mountain that made the only entrance and exit to Mount Toane. Strange lights and noises flashed on and off from that cold, dark, forbidding archway. It was time. Byron strode towards the Generals' tent, stepping into the center of the assembled leaders under his direct command.

"Gentlemen, ladies," he added with a slight bow to the two female Generals. "It is time for the Final Push. Rally your men and women, break down camp, and make final preparations. I shall speak with our soldiers once they are in formation, before we begin the siege." Byron looked from face to face.

Stern, taciturn countenances met his gaze, and each said roughly the same thing: *so this is it*. These Generals had come together for the same purpose—to dispose of the warlock who had the realm of Tamalaria in his grip. All were prepared to die for the freedom of their lands and peoples.

Revenge was the order of the day, and everyone wanted a heaping plateful.

"Lord Byron," said Morek Rockmight, the leader of the Dwarven city of Traithrock in the Western Mountains. "I don't mind telling you that I've a bad feeling about this whole thing."

Byron turned to the Dwarf and took a good look at him. Morek was tall for a Dwarf, standing four and half feet in height, and the traditional beard and chain mail of his race hung on his person like trophies. The only thing missing was the great iron war axe. There was a good reason for this: Morek preferred the Trade of Boxing. Silver gloves wrapped his hands, deadly heavy when striking, but light as a feather to the Dwarf.

"I know you don't like it. Few of us do. But we are here, and the time to strike is now. I expect you will be ready shortly."

A silent group nod and salute met him, and he walked out of the tent. Already messengers were running about, giving the word to break camp and prepare for the battle ahead.

The Werewolves, Cuyotai, and Dwarves were the quickest to prepare. They did not observe the ages-old tradition of using tents. Cooking pits and some blankets were well enough. Since they hunted for their food on a day-to-day basis, they had no need to pack foodstuffs.

Most of the camp was broken down and ranks formed within an hour and half's time. The army stood before Byron and his officers at the ready, a mix of fear, rage, and anticipation flowing from every pore in every body like a miasma. The time of truth was at hand.

Byron strode up to the front of the lines, inspecting the men and women for any signs of weakness. Everywhere he looked, he sensed fear, dread, and panic. But he also sensed courage, determination, and a sense of acceptance. Those who knew they had seen their last sunrise had come to terms with the truth of it. A good sign, if Byron was any judge of character. There would be no deserters.

He strode up to the top of a hill twenty or so yards away from the legion. With a whip-like motion, he drew his sword, raising it towards the heavens.

A mighty war cry went up from the masses. The earth trembled, and the air took on an expectant atmosphere. The smells of sweat and earthen loam rose up to meet the Paladin on the hilltop.

"Men and women of Tamalaria," he shouted, starting his speech.

All went silent around him, even the birds that had been happily hooting meaningless sing-songs hushed up. Even they could sense something grand about to begin.

"We are banded here together today, for a single purpose." He lowered his sword to his side and paced back and forth. "Men and women of all Races and Trades have come together under a single banner, under a single goal. I see before me Elves, Humans, Dwarves, several breeds of Lycanthrope, Minotaurs, even a Dragon-kin Draconus or two! Some of your Races and Trades have made war with each other before, and I know this is especially true between the Knights and the thief Trades," he said, to which laughter met him as a response. "But no matter your profession, you are here, wielding your tools, weapons, and skills not at each other, but at a common enemy!

"I am proud to be leader of a motley bunch such as this. As a Paladin, I have come to see the usefulness of some of those individuals I formerly jailed or silently disliked. We shall need everything that every person here can offer us to win this battle!"

Another cheer went up from the legion, and Byron remained silent until it was over.

"I will not lie to you or sugarcoat the truth. Many of you will die today. Some will die swiftly, some slowly. Some will fall to the sword, and some will undoubtedly fall to magic. But you know that already, don't you? You will go on to see your chosen deity, for truly you serve a good and noble purpose in being here.

"Some of you have families who shall never see you again, but you are here to ensure they are safe and free for the rest of their lives. When the warlock falls, this land shall once more be free. Now," he said, clearing his throat. This would be the final part of his speech, and it was familiar to him and all of the Paladins who belonged to the Order of Oun. "I want you all to repeat my words after me. This statement is used by us of the Order of Oun, and I believe it applies to you all today.

"We, who stand against the darkness, shall see it banished by our holy light. No matter the cost!"

The legion repeated this, and slowly, one small group at a time, began to chant the last four words as a battle mantra. *No matter the cost, no matter the cost, no matter the cost.*

"Stand by your comrades, carry out the orders of your officers, and if you should have to die, take your enemy with you!" With a final thrust of his sword towards the sky, Byron turned and charged towards Mount Toane.

The rumble of a thousand pairs of feet sent a wave through the earth from behind him. He rode that wave all the way to the entrance.

The peak stood silent, the mountain spire in the midst of the northeastern plains would forever be a grim monument to the free peoples of Tamalaria of the price of freedom.

* * * *

Tanarak and his apprentice gazed into the bowl in the center of the throne room, watching Byron Aixler lead his armies into the entrance of Mount Toane. From under his hood, the apprentice looked into the face of his master and saw something he'd never imagined, doubt. He looked back to the image and watched as the legion broke ranks and flowed into the mountain with surgical precision and speed. The assault appeared to be quite organized. This came as little surprise, now that he thought about it. After all, Tanarak had made many powerful enemies, men of experience in the arts of war. Many of them likely ran behind the mighty Paladin. "What is your wish, master," he inquired of the warlock.

Tanarak turned and stalked towards the entrance to the tunnel that would lead to the chamber that held Byron's fate.

"Unleash the Shadowbeasts," he hissed.

"But, my lord," complained the apprentice, taking a few steps toward his master. "We were going to reserve them for the second stage."

"We cannot afford to dally around with the Greenskins and slaves, my pupil. You have seen the determination in those men. Orcs, Ogres, and Goblins would stand no chance against their onslaught. Give the order and call to the undead warriors you have raised. They are to show mercy only to the Paladin. The rest must die, my apprentice. When you are done," he said, turning away from the pupil. "Meet me in the chamber. Let the fools come."

* * * *

The first wave of skeleton warriors met the full force of Byron's legion. Despite their otherworldly presence, they powdered and flaked into dust swiftly, the mortals' weapons destroying them utterly.

Little else could be done to slow the progress of the mighty legion, until the Paladin Byron Aixler led them into the first large chamber. At nearly a thousand men strong, the cave allowed many of the fighters into its expanse. Edgar Cesar moved to the front, and he and Byron walked a short distance from the foremost ranks of their army.

"Sire," Cesar began, his face flushed from the exertion of running and charging, but not, curiously, from battle. "There are four ways to go from this chamber. Shall we send scouts? There are Hunters to be put to use, sir." As he panted, Byron looked his right-hand-man up and down, thinking over the situation.

"What is our head count, General Cesar," Byron asked, casting about at the entrances to the tunnels that lay on all sides. For just a moment, he thought he spied a suspicious movement just off to his right. That would be the tunnel he took, he decided, as he spotted a black cloak whipping up as someone ran away.

"We are nearly one thousand strong, sire," said Cesar, his eyes going cold and steely again. Only the heat of a real challenge would break that sometimes-disconcerting look, Byron knew. He would give the General a chance. It was only a matter of finding Tanarak, and thus, his more worthy creatures. Byron's mind returned to the matter of splitting the army into smaller legions. Though it stood to reason that dividing forces would be the more logical and time-efficient way of dealing with the battle, Byron didn't care for it one bit. Cesar had been correct about one thing above all else: Mount Toane was home to Tanarak and his apprentice. Therefore, it could be assumed that the advantage lay with the warlock and his lackey.

"One thousand, you say?" he asked, looking sidelong at Cesar. "Very well. Divide the men into five forces of roughly two hundred each with a General at the lead. One group to each tunnel." Cesar looked at Byron curiously, his hand on his helmet visor.

"Sire? You seem to have miscounted. There are four tunnels, sire, and five groups. What is the purpose of the fifth group?"

Byron set his teeth and his gaze. Once again, he saw movement in the tunnel to his right. There was something about that figure that suggested leadership, power, and wickedness. It poured from the creature in waves, and Byron knew without a doubt what it was.

"The last group will hold this chamber for one full day's time," Byron announced aloud. "If we do not return by then, they will retreat to the nearest city and report to that area's leader that we have failed." Byron slowly turned his head, his eyes boring into those of Edgar Cesar. "Is that understood, General?"

For the briefest of moments, there was a flicker of an emotion present in those cold, coal-like eyes: doubt. It festered for a moment in the back of Cesar's mind, dank and pungent. With an effort, the Knight submerged it under the waves of duty, honor, and courage that he had fostered for so many years.

"It is perfectly understood, sire. Shall I prepare the divisions personally?"

"Yes," said Byron, taking a measured step back from Cesar. "And, assign one to your command, one to mine, one to Morek Rockmight, one to Ugin Moag. The division that remains behind will consist of the youngest fighters, and will be led by our young friend Christopher Gray."

"He is Rimzan's son, is he not?" asked Cesar, referring to Rimzan of Gray. Rimzan was well known as one of the mightiest Paladins the lands of Tamalaria had ever known. Presently, however, Rimzan was engaged with creatures on the Isle of K'aolu. But that is another story for another time.

"Yes," said Byron. "I think he would be most displeased with you and me, if he returned and found that his first born child had not been protected during this final fight against the dark warlock Tanarak. Of course, if we were to die too, we wouldn't be too worried about it, would we now," he added with a chuckle.

Edgar's face had pinched up into the look of someone who is both confused and horrified, usually in that order. Byron often spoke in this manner when he felt the odds were against him. Yet somehow, this time seemed more, well, final.

"Yes, sire," Cesar croaked. He cleared his throat, and said, "I imagine the worst he could do is curse our eternal souls, or some such thing as Paladins are prone to doing. No offense meant, of course, sire," he added a bit sarcastically. If Death had ordained to come for him that day, then the least he could do was be something other than a soldier for a few minutes.

"Why, none taken, thou blasphemous heathen," shot Byron with a grin. The two warriors smiled at one another for a minute or so, and then nodded, their faces blurring for a moment as they turned from each other. A collage of feelings ran their course over both men, but as they faced their legion, their faces were once again cast in stone. Cesar moved about, informing the Generals of their posts and assignments, and then assigning squadrons to their leaders. Once the commotion settled, Cesar returned to Byron.

"Sire, the formations are complete. When you are ready, give the word, and we shall set out." Cesar seemed to hesitate, that worm of doubt crawling into his voice and eyes once again as he looked deep into Byron's eyes. "And sire?"

"Yes," asked Byron, a hint of a smile on his lips.

"If we do not see each other again, I should like you to know that it has been an honor serving with you." The stoic soldier extended one gauntlet towards the Paladin, placing the other on his helmet visor.

"The same can be said for you, Edgar. Let us go into battle, then, with clear conscious and ready body. And may the Great God Oun protect you as he does me," Byron finished, shaking the offered hand. With a snap, Cesar shut the visor of his helmet and turned away from the Paladin. It would be the last time they would see each other alive.

* * * *

"Byron leads a separate battalion our way, my lord," rasped the apprentice into a small black orb. Smoke plumed from the surface of the object, and he could hear Tanarak's reply.

"Good, my apprentice. Are the other battalions near their demise?"

"Indeed, my lord," cooed the apprentice to the orb. "They shall meet their dooms soon enough. But there are a few who disturb me, lord."

"Oh," asked the voice inside the orb.

"Indeed, my lord. There is a Dwarven Boxer by the name of Morek Rockmight. He is mighty, and from what I have seen in my mirrors, he is also very thorough. Even the Shadowbeasts fall before him easily."

Silence hung in the air.

"Are there others," asked Tanarak via the orb, sounding the slightest bit testy.

"Also, there is a Human Knight by the name of Edgar Cesar. He is quite skilled, but unlike the Dwarf, there is fear in him. I can smell it as one can smell sweat in a brothel. It is very evident. Lastly, lord, there is a Cuyotai by the name of Ugin Moag. He seems to have some sort of enchanted bow and arrows."

"A Hunter, hmm?"

"Yes, lord. And like any other Hunter, he is making some poorly judged movement on his own. He commands a battalion, but they are having quite the time trying to keep up with him."

"Good," echoed Tanarak's voice through the misty sphere. "Get him alone, separated, and finish him off. The others will follow as our forces are able to converge. When the other Generals are dealt with, inform me. I shall be waiting."

The pools of fog swirled once more in the orb before dissipating into nothing. The apprentice smiled a knowing smile, and crept off into the tunnels once again.

* * * *

There seemed to be no end to the waves of undead creatures and Shadowbeasts, the black, humanoid-shaped demons from the upper layers of Hell. Though considered minor demons, Shadowbeasts tore through dozens of Byron's men at a time. With mounting anger Byron realized that the creatures taunted and leered at him, but only struck his comrades.

The pattern had become more apparent as his battalion pressed forward. There would be a tunnel filled with skeleton warriors and zombies, and then a tunnel filled with Shadowbeasts. In several of the chambers there was an amalgamation of both. He and his legion cut through the warlock's minions like a scythe through a field of wheat. Because of the number of creatures, it seemed an awfully large field with a quickly dulling blade.

Their lack of knowledge regarding directions inside of Mount Toane conspired against the battalion. Not even Byron *knew* which way to go next; his instincts called softly out to him from the void, giving him directions and insight. How much he could trust said instinct he knew not, but he wasn't being presented with any other options.

Once or twice, he thought he saw movement at the entrances to other tunnels that led further down into the mountain. *Something* observed the battle he and his battalion fought, but remained hidden by shadows and the flashing of steel. Byron had a hunch what, or rather who, had been spying on him. But why spy on him, he wondered. Why not simply attack? He blocked a blow from a Shadowbeast and plunged his blade into its skull.

As demons, Shadowbeasts do not bleed when struck. Instead, they ooze shadows and turn to ashes. As a result, the chamber became enveloped in a black fog. The few remaining creatures under Tanarak's rule fled the battle, leaving only Byron and his battalion in the fog. A soft, rhythmic beating flowed through the air, and Byron spun about to find its source. Magic, he thought. Something is using magic on the entire chamber, but what? "Brothers," he shouted to the chamber at large. "Prepare yourselves! There is a wicked magic being used against us!"

A flash of orange light erupted from the passageway where Byron had spied movement during the fight in the high chamber. Banshee wails rose from the ground itself, screeching and moaning at such volumes that Byron was forced to his knees. A great billowing wind rose as well, swirling the ashes of the fallen Shadowbeasts into a black wall through which the Paladin could see nothing.

Despite the ear-splitting wails, the cone-wall of blackness, and the sudden shaking of the ground underfoot, Byron stalked towards the tiny shine of orange light coming from his enemy. He did not know that every member of his battalion was seeing the same thing, from a different direction. Before anyone knew it, Byron had been cut off from his allies.

From somewhere deep in the mountain, a dry, whispery voice uttered a single sentence: "We have you now, Byron Aixler."

* * * *

The Cuyotai Hunter with the mystic bow and arrows had not been as foolish as he seemed, thought the apprentice bitterly. Upon his fiery demise in a deep pit, which had been ingeniously disguised as a good sniper point, the magical weapon had unlocked some other spell. This had sent the weapon hurling out of the pit, and indeed, out of the mountain, back to his village.

No matter, thought the apprentice. That's one less magical weapon for us to deal with, at any rate.

The Human Knight, the one called Edgar Cesar, had been a bit more of a challenge. His battalion had consisted almost entirely of mercenaries and fellow Knights. The creatures in the chambers they entered stood little chance against their onslaught. So the apprentice arranged Illusion spells to guide them into a trap-laden passageway.

"Temis," called Cesar to one of the mercenaries. "Move ahead and check that our path is clear."

The mercenary gave a brief, obligatory nod before moving off. He hadn't gone fifteen paces before he made a misstep, and triggered a Blasting Furnace spell.

Cesar watched a dragon's head made of smoke blast up from around the unsuspecting mercenary's feet, coiling about the small tunnel until it was face-to-face with Temis.

The stunned mercenary drew his sword and swung, but the spell could not be defeated so easily. The mouth of the great smoke dragon opened, and a wave of blistering, searing heat washed down the tunnel, turning Temis and twenty more Knights into smoking heaps of seared muscle and organs in armor.

Cesar had seen the spell once before and knew to run back through the tunnel. When the damage had been done, he returned to the front, and continued on, leading his battalion over the charred, mangled corpses the spell's victims. Rarely had Cesar seen so many warriors killed by a single spell, but there seemed to be a great deal of magical power spent on making the Blazing Furnace spell work so well, and quickly. A warlock of great power could cast such spells during battle, but there didn't seem to be any enemy present.

The spell, Cesar realized, too late, had been locked. Locking a spell was a process by which a magic user could expend extra manna in order to leave a spell on an object or surface. The spell would have a trigger condition, like someone stepping on a particular tile, or saying a certain phrase— "Or walking down a certain tunnel," he whispered to himself in horror, drawing his steps up short. Before he could think to act, someone ahead of him stepped between two oddly shaped stalagmites, and a whole host of Pyromancy spells scoured down the length of the tunnel, feasting upon the flesh of the nearly one hundred men who remained in Cesar's group. Shouts turned into blood-garbled squeals of pain, heavy plates of armor became heating plates, and for one or two men, helmets became cooking pots in which their skulls bubbled and congealed into a fine, pasty stew.

As his left eye erupted in a shower of pus and blood, Edgar Cesar could barely squeak out the words, "Good-bye, Byron."

A few minutes later, the only sound that could be heard in the tunnel was the hissing and steaming of burnt flesh. Among the smoke, a shadowy form crept toward the fallen Knight.

Clean up, thought the Knight with his last moments. As the creature reached him, he plunged into a cold, empty darkness. *We have failed.*

* * * *

Morek Rockmight wasn't having the sort of trouble the other captains had run into. Any Dwarf worth his weight in salt (which would have been a lot of salt) could see an ambush from a mile off. Morek could see one from further than that. And Dwarves are noted for their keen ability to detect magic in almost all of its forms. As a result, Dwarves are the most difficult Race to pass off an Illusion spell on.

When Morek and his battalion entered a chamber with two passages, one of which had a strong Illusion spell trying to make it look like barren rock, he led nearly two hundred men through a wall. At least, that was how the non-Dwarven soldiers saw it.

His battalion had fought for a good while against the warlock's forces, and showed little or no sign of letting up.

While this troubled the apprentice, he found he could adapt to the situation quite nicely. With a minimum of effort, he used a few simple Gaiamancy spells to shape a new tunnel in the mountain—one that led outside of Mount Toane. Morek followed the tunnel, thinking the throne room to be at the end, where the light was. But as he got outside, he saw that he had led his men straight out of the Mountain.

When he turned around to lead them back in, the mountain had closed up. "Blasted sorcerer," he muttered under his breath. But there was no help for it. His battalion would meet up with Gray's group, and they would in turn wait for Byron and his men.

All that remained for the apprentice was luring Byron Aixler into his master's trap. *It wouldn't take much to bait the Paladin*, thought the apprentice. *Just something to kick up his rage.*

The apprentice ran through the catacombs of Mount Toane like a rat in a maze—one that knows exactly where the cheese is. *Bait*, he thought as he hustled along. *What would make good bait for the Paladin?*

As he stepped over the charred, blackened remains of one of the legion's members, he sniffed the air. The putrid scent of burned flesh lingered in the air, hovering about in an invisible fog. Despite the obvious method of death, a chill wrapped around the tunnel's walls, much as some snakes coiled around their victims.

There came a sudden movement from the floor at the apprentice's feet, and he leapt back, cat-like, from a single outreached arm. Said arm was the color of used coals from a military cooking fire, and appeared to contain all the strength of the average domesticated house cat. Was this creature one of his? he wondered. Had something survived this magical trap that none of the others had? If so, how? Curious, the apprentice cautiously approached the outstretched arm.

As he came to a halt over the body, the apprentice threw back his head and cackled with maddened glee. Edgar Cesar, the Knight! Though the man's eyes were no longer in his own head, he clung to life. "Wh, wh-, who's there," whispered Cesar to the invisible world around him.

"I am the humble servant of Lord Tanarak," said the apprentice in his best 'I'm just the butler' tone of voice. A strangled gargling noise escaped Cesar's mouth, and what little blood was left to his body slowly dripped over the edge of the man's lips.

"And you appear to be a very unfortunate little soldier who has been rather nastily injured, my good man. Would you like me to make the pain go away," the apprentice asked, cooing sweetly and sarcastically. The pain and suffering Cesar experienced filled the apprentice's mouth with the taste of his own saliva; he savored every bit of agony the Human Knight lived through. It would be worth keeping the man alive, he thought, if just to feed his own dark powers and tastes with the pure torture of the man's mind, body and soul.

Something had grabbed his leg, tightly. The apprentice looked down to see that Cesar had managed a good grip on him and on a short, curvy sort of dagger.

"There, will be, justice," moaned Cesar as he swung the blade around.

The apprentice deftly grabbed the offending limb by the wrist and twisted, breaking the bones and disarming the Knight. He stood to full height, muttering words of the oldest tongues, used only for dark magic. A ripple like a shock wave distorted the air, and the faintest sound of breaking glass echoed out in the tunnel before a single bolt of Toane magic blasted from the apprentice's hand down through the already-ravaged body of the Knight.

"Such heroic nonsense," the apprentice growled, a sadistic smile curling the corners of his mouth. *This body*, he thought. *I'll drag it along. Surely Byron Aixler will come after his friend and ally!*

There comes a moment in every great game of chess, when the winning player realizes, quite clearly, that they have the game set and won. For the apprentice, that time was now.

* * * *

Throngs of undead creatures and Shadowbeasts assailed Byron from all sides as he chased after the shadowy figure that remained always a little ahead of him. But these creatures fell aside like so much hacked brush as the Paladin charged ahead, a single task burning in his head and in his heart. *I must catch him,* thought Byron. *The apprentice will know where the master is, and when I have found the master, this shall all be over.* His course of action set, Byron allowed nothing to get in his way.

He'd begun to despair that he was running a wild goose chase when he entered into a high, empty chamber. The distinguishing features were a throne hewn from the mountainous rock itself, and what appeared to be bones. On the far side of the chamber, he finally saw the apprentice.

Shadows wrapped about the man's face, a sort of magic Byron realized was used to conceal his true identity.

As the blue-cloaked figure stepped forward, Byron saw he'd hidden a man behind him. It was Edgar Cesar, scorched and blasted beyond hope of survival.

"Byron Aixler," the apprentice hissed softly across the chamber. "Do you recognize this man?"

The question mocked him, for Byron could tell by the tone of voice that the apprentice already knew the answer.

"His fate has been decided, as you can see. The Grim Reaper waits with bated breath for this man to give up the fight. Do you see how his chest still rises and falls," the apprentice asked.

Byron squinted hard, and could see the slightest movement of Edgar's chest. *He's alive*, Byron thought. *There may be a chance to save him yet.* "Yes, I see this, foul servant. Unhand him, and I shall spare you your miserable life!" Byron brandished his sword, mentally preparing a host of Paladin spells in his mind. He would have to be swift about this.

"If you want him that badly, come and get him!" With a single motion, the apprentice darted down the tunnel he stood in front of, Edgar Cesar's body following behind on a wave of magic.

Surely this is a trap, Byron reasoned. *But I cannot leave him to his fate.* No Paladin, regardless of their chosen God, would allow an ally and friend to be dragged to certain death. Sword in hand, Byron chased after the apprentice.

Several minutes earlier, the apprentice had informed Tanarak that his task had been completed, and he would be arriving with Byron Aixler in tow. As the warlock's right-hand man charged towards the chamber his master had prepared for this, he felt the rush of adrenaline stampede through his body, an unstoppable bull trampling over his fears and doubts. The master's plan had worked; but then again, if it hadn't, he would already be dead

For twenty solid minutes they ran, the Paladin chasing his quarry with unrelenting purpose. When he could, Byron sent bolts of holy energy hurling towards his prey, but each time the spell was nimbly avoided.

Finally, as the apprentice and Cesar passed through a narrow doorway of a sort, Byron stepped into a chamber filled with all manner of alchemical devices. Tomes of dark lore lay open on a bench off to his right, and as he took his first full step into the chamber, a dozen bolts of magical lightning surged into his body. Pain swept through him, the power of Toane magic coiling through his muscles and seeping through his veins like venom.

His body twitched and cavorted, wracked with pain that few men could withstand. As the last bolt released its grip on him, Byron fell flat to his chest, his weapon dropping from his hand. He hit the stone floor with a thud of metal armor and the sound of his forehead connecting with the floor. Darkness crept in on the corners of his vision, and spread, plague-like, to cover all he could see.

When he awoke, Byron found himself strapped to a wall, facing a mirror. The bonds that held him appeared to be simple shackles, but he sensed dark magic lying dormant, waiting for a trigger. The sweet scent of wild flowers lingered in the air, warring with the metallic taste of blood in his mouth. Just as he felt ready to test the limits of his bonds, two shapes stalked out from the shadows across from him.

The first he knew already to be the apprentice, for he had confronted and chased the man. The second he knew by process of elimination. "Tanarak of Sidius." He spit at the warlock's feet.

"Byron Aixler." The warlock pulled back his hood. The face that action revealed was as pale as a sheet of parchment, the flesh sullen and waxy. Blue lines laced the framework of a pitiless face, with eyes so dark and devoid of mercy that they seemed depthless. "You have been a thorn in our sides for some time, young Paladin. I wonder, how shall we punish you for your insolence?" The warlock took a step forward, and reached a hand out to caress Byron's cheek.

The contact made Byron's mind shriek with rage and his skin crawled at the chill of Tanarak's touch.

"You may torture or kill me if you like, warlock, but there shall always be someone to resist you." Byron tried to maintain his calm. "And the next time, they may not be so foolish as I. I allowed myself to be lured into your trap, but the next warrior may be possessed of less heart than I. Your apprentice has served you well."

Tanarak smiled widely, revealing a set of razors in his mouth where teeth should have been.

"Indeed, he has." Tanarak stepped back and patted the apprentice on the shoulder. "And so shall you, Byron Aixler."

Byron looked around the chamber, a cold sweat breaking on his brow. Was that what these two had had in mind all along? To use Alchemy to bend Byron's mind and spirit to their ends? He would die first, he decided. The Great God Oun would greet him in Heaven, and there he would be able to take rest and refuge in the holy light of his being. *Yes,* he thought, *I shall die before I serve one such as him.*

"My lord," said the apprentice, as he reached for one of the tomes. "Shall we begin?"

Tanarak said nothing, but instead began directing a coil of purple energy into Byron's chest.

Strangely, there was no pain, only a spreading sensation of wet coolness, like a river in midwinter.

"What do you intend, warlock." Byron surged forward against his restraints. "Do you hope to turn my body into one of your monstrosities? Ha! My soul shall ascend into the Heavens of the Great God Oun, and from that height I shall watch as your pathetic and corrupt essence is dragged kicking and screaming into the fiery pits of the Hells!"

Tanarak, not moving to disrupt his ritual, smiled a mirthless grin.

"Byron Aixler, you are wrong. With this spell I shall imprison your very soul in the thing I make of you. You shall watch for all time as I command your new being to lead my forces, and crush all who oppose me."

For a fleeting moment, Byron panicked. *But no such magic exists,* he thought. *I shall die, and my body shall be used as his puppet, nothing more.*

At this point, the apprentice began channeling mystic force into Byron's body.

Now the sensations of pain and agony spilled into him with the weight of a war hammer. Never before had the Paladin experienced such a feeling. But the pain only lasted a moment, and as he watched, Byron felt himself being locked inside of his own mind. He could still see the warlocks, the chamber around him, he could still smell the stench of burning flesh and black magic. Yet he felt detached from it all.

Without willing it, Byron's view became locked on the mirror across from him. His breastplate was blacked. Where the sign of Oun should have rested in the center sat the crest of Sidius. Also, he saw now why he smelled burning flesh; his head had become a bare skull, his eyes two red pinpoints of light in their sockets. He appeared to have physically grown as well, and spikes of bone shot forth from his shoulder plates. Byron watched with mounting dread as he saw himself, or rather the thing he had become, lurch forward once the shackles were removed. Try as he might, he could not get his body to do anything he wanted it to. He wanted to thrust his sword, placed in his hand by the apprentice, into said man's stomach and twist. Yet, he could not. All he could do was watch and listen.

"Now," Tanarak's voice was edged with pride. "You are Byron Aixler no longer. What then, is your name, my newest General?" Byron mentally refused to answer, but though he had no ears to hear with, he nonetheless heard the response.

"I am Byron of Sidius, master. General of Tanarak's armies, and servant to he and his apprentice." In his mind, Byron screamed a banshee wail. *How could this happen? Such magic should not exist!* And yet here it was, staring back at him through a mirror, evidence that Tanarak possessed the blackest soul on the whole of the land.

"And remember this." The apprentice stepped forward just a bit. "*Our* life force is tied to yours. Even if you gain the slightest control of your body, Byron, you cannot raise your hand against us. To do so will mean your death. Now, be a good little boy, and go take care of the ones who await your return at the foot of Mount Toane. When you are done, return here to us. Do you understand?"

"Yes," growled Byron of Sidius. "I understand." Weapon in hand, the creature that Byron Aixler had become set off into Mount Toane—to kill his former allies.

Chapter Two
Thus It Begins

Byron of Sidius awoke with a sudden start, shooting upright in his rented bed as he tried to shake off the memory called up in his dreams. That had been the way of things in the land of Tamalaria for fifteen years. But Rimzan of Grey, the Paladin supreme, returned to his homeland. Shortly after arriving, he hunted down and destroyed Tanarak in his lair of Mount Toane, thus ending his long, harsh reign of doom. The apprentice had vanished, but the peoples of all the lands of Tamalaria rose up and crushed what was left of Tanarak's forces. Only a few creatures had survived, hiding in the darkness.

And Byron of Sidius was one of those. When Tanarak died, the former Paladin had regained control of his body. Unfortunately, his body was still that of the creature he had been turned into. So now he half-sat, five years later, brooding, looking out of the window of a dingy inn room in the plains city of Koreindar, in the year 844 A.F. The dream left him feeling violated, unclean. His body and mind reeled, the remembered experiences so vivid that he could not shake the feeling that he had been temporarily taken back in time. Byron's mind wandered through hazy memories of the months that had passed since he had regained his freedom. He had regained mastery of himself, but what he had regained mastery of was a thing more violent and corrupt than any evil he had long since encountered. It had its own impulses, and these had merged with and, with so little time in control of himself once again, taken over those of the man himself.

During the initial flight from Mount Toane, Byron had come upon several of Rimzan's followers. Unable to master his own dark impulses, Byron had slain nearly a dozen powerful men effortlessly and rapidly. He got up off of the bed, and seated himself instead at the hotel room's lone table.

Shortly thereafter, brooding in the darkness of his chamber, he gazed at the blade with which he had slain those men. Their blood still soiled the blade's surface, coating the metal in dull crimson stains. The weapon seemed to speak to Byron, as if it were taunting him. *Go ahead, pick me up*, it urged. *Reclaim the bloody glory that is yours!*

"No," Byron shouted, dust pluming up out of his skinless face. In his service to Tanarak, other parts of his body decayed or became putrid with desecration and wickedness. The air from his lungs blew like smoke through a closed room, and more than once he thought his heart had stopped entirely. Yet still there was a gruff timbre to his tone, like the sound of bears growling in his chest. That voice had once terrified legions of men and women of all Races and Classes; now he spoke with that tone to a weapon.

Where will you go, Byron? What will you do, the weapon asked, seductively yet accusingly. *You cannot hide forever.*

That much was true; Byron had learned arts of Shadow magic from Tanarak's apprentice, and had in exchange shown him how to use a sword. Both had withheld something from the other, but given each other enough to suffice. One such art was wrapping shadows around his head and upper chest, to conceal from others his fleshless face and the Crest of Sidius emblazoned his chest plate. Both would give him away and he would be on the run again.

Yet he could only sustain the illusion for so long in any given day. As a result, he did most of his traveling at night, when the magic required much less focus and energy. Still, he would not return to the path of Sidius, the path of destruction and desecration. "I am no longer a servant of chaos," he whispered to the sword. "I am my own creature."

And what does that change, that statement, the weapon teased. *Nothing! It changes nothing, o wretched one! You can never be redeemed! Jump into the flames of the Hells head first, and you may at least become a General of Diablo's armies!*

At this, Byron opened the window, grabbed the sword and hurled it with all of the might he could muster into the distance. After a few moments, he saw the glint of the metal coming down from an incredible arc just outside the city. It mattered little; he had other weapons at his disposal.

"Was that really necessary," a tiny voice squeaked near the windowsill. Byron looked down to gaze upon Alex, his only companion since gaining his freedom. Like most Ki Fairy males Alex stood two inches in height, radiated a black aura of shadows, possessed an Elvish countenance, and had barbed spikes shooting out of his back. Ki Fairies possessed dark magics and the power of illusion, and were for the most part very nastily predisposed. Alex, while possessed of all of these traits, did not share one particular and vital characteristic of other Ki Fairies—he did not revel in other peoples' misery. That is, not unless they really deserved it. Sure, he had played his fair share of tricks on people, but he never went out of his way to maim or injure them as others of his Race did.

"Yes, my little friend," grumbled Byron to his diminutive ally. He looked down at Alex as the Ki Fairy threw his long, dirty brown hair back over his shoulders. "Had I not gotten rid of it, that sword would surely have found its way into the body of yet another hapless victim. I'll have no more of it."

Byron thought back on how he had gained Alex as a companion, and attempted a smile. His face, though a skull, was animated, and he could convey some emotions and expressions. He felt the smile slowly form, a slight, rueful grin made by one side of his jaw hiking up his face. The effect was less than desirable, and he shuddered at his image in the mirror.

He'd found Alex in the first town where Byron had taken refuge, a little farming community due south of Mount Toane. The Ki Fairy had been making people trip when walking through the doorway to the only inn in the town, and had not figured on Byron entering. As the Ki Fairy triggered his magic, the Dread Knight (as fallen Paladins are known) lunged sideways and drew his weapon on the innkeeper. "Who dares attempt the use of such magic on me," he had growled.

Alex had been stunned; no normal man, regardless of age or skill with the sword, could detect Fairy magic. Either the man was a powerful spell user or a creature not quite of flesh and blood.

The innkeeper had been flustered, for he had witnessed his guests throughout the day, and had seen all but this one man fall flat on their faces. Unfortunately for Alex, the innkeeper was familiar with Fairies, especially tricky ones. "M-most likely a Fairy or Sprite, my good man," he said.

"I am *not* your good man," Byron had bellowed, his caution and trepidation rising. He had been chased by Paladins, harassed by Knights, and accosted by Clerics of several orders in his flight. He needed rest, cover, time to think things through and recover himself sufficiently to organize his thoughts. His Shadow magic was failing.

Alex saw the creature that searched for him was a Dread Knight. But it was no ordinary Dread Knight, he thought to himself as he hovered in the corner. The once-man-thing had come into a civilized, rural town, straight to an inn, and had not slain the Human who tended the counter.

And it concealed itself. On this point, and this point alone, Alex had decided that he would risk his fate. No ordinary Dread Knight would conceal its identity, particularly in a small rural town such as this. His translucent wings flapping, Alex descended until he hovered a scant few inches from the creature's shining, white lights. "Greetings, creature," he whispered. "Can you see me?"

"Of course I see you, Ki Fairy," Byron growled in response, sheathing his sword. "You would be wise to not trifle with me. I shall forgive you your trespass, for you are a Fairy of the clan Ki, and are prone to such trickery. But in exchange for sparing you your meager existence, I require a service."

Alex fluttered slightly back, sensing a preparation of magical power in the Dread Knight before him. The creature could kill him on a whim, if it so chose.

"Certainly," Alex squeaked. "Whatever you require, good sir, um, what is your name?"

"My name is of no concern, little one. And what I require, is for you to accompany me to my room, and keep me company this evening." Alex had no words for his simultaneous relief and distrust. That the creature chose to spare him was surprise enough; that it wished to keep company with him was suspect. With no better choice available, Alex agreed, and that night Byron had related to him the events of his life. Alex had felt fear when Byron invoked his title as Byron Aixler, and greater fear at learning that the very same man was now this creature before him, Byron of Sidius.

And now the little Fairy was asking him, most seriously, if discarding the wretched weapon that Tanarak had given him was necessary. Byron continued his previous response. "Ridding myself of that blade has eased my troubled mind. More so, it has eased my heavy heart." Dust and smoke plumed from the Dread Knight's mouth as he spoke.

Alex waved his hands back and forth before him, to clear the air around his face.

"No matter my lord," he said through gouts of coughing. "I have a suitable weapon for you in my Fairyspace. Allow me to retrieve it."

Byron had long known of Fairyspace: pockets of magical space that Fairies could stash any number of items in, opening and closing on the whim of the Fairy. Alex summoned a rather standard broadsword from the pocket, and used his magic to float the weapon to Byron's hands.

The undead warrior hefted the weapon, measured its balance. The sword, though it looked like a standard soldier's weapon, felt feather light.

"Beg pardon, Alex, but is this weapon in some way bewitched or possibly Enchanted?"

A knowing smile spread across the Ki Fairy's face, though it bore a strong resemblance to the sort of smile that torturers possess when they are aware that their subject truly knows nothing.

"I am not certain, my lord. You tell me." He sniggered, fluttering up to sit atop the dresser in the far left hand corner of the room.

"Well, Enchanted or not, it is a good enough weapon. I thank you."

The two strange companions were silent a while, but finally, the Ki Fairy broke the silence.

"By the way, my lord. What exactly drew you to this city? I mean, why Koreindar? It is full of life and people, and people tend to talk and talking tends to lead to trouble, doesn't it?"

Byron had wrestled with this very question. Why had he been so drawn to the city of Koreindar? What could possibly be so important that he pay for a room for a fortnight? What could happen in this city in the next two weeks that wouldn't occur anywhere else? He could not answer.

And so he said simply, "I am not certain why, but I felt, compelled to be here."

Byron's explanation was sufficient for the Ki Fairy, who stretched out atop the dresser, and quickly fell into a deep, untroubled sleep. Byron wished he could do the same.

* * * *

Richard Vandross could not feel the sting of the cold, hard-hitting rain as it fell from the clouds over the area around the city of Koreindar. The storm neared its end, but even its final fury could not touch him. He could not feel it, for all he could feel was the desire to attain the full power of the warlock Tanarak of Sidius.

He knew *how* to attain that power. It was common knowledge, throughout the networks of creatures whose goals are what most men call wicked, that when Tanarak died, the five artifacts he had taken into his being had scattered. These were the Orbs of Eden's Serpent.

Richard Vandross was not an unhandsome man. He possessed a rugged, battle-worn look that had made more than a few women of the Human Race he belonged to ache for the feel of his loins. But his attractiveness came, for the most part, from the appeal that famous pirates and gladiators are known for: in short, he was bad news. Girls who liked that sort of thing loved him. The only blemish on his features that he did not care for, and tried hard not to think about, was the patch that rested over his left eye.

His recent group of servants had inquired about the state of the injury, and how it had occurred. One particularly curious Lizardman had asked after it so often that Vandross had stretched his palm flat forward, and summoned a Cone of Flame spell so potent it had reduced even the bones to dust. Thenceforth, none of Vandross' minions inquired about the eye.

Said minions marched behind their leader, watching as he strode towards the city like a juggernaut. His blue full-plate armor gleamed as bright lightning crashed into the ground. A leather belt held several vials of strange and assorted liquids at his hip, as well as a scabbard with his favorite sword. He brushed his long, black hair out of his vision, and stopped at the top of a hill overlooking the city. The first of the Orbs was here, buried under the Church of Oun. The priests therein knew of its presence and would attempt to guard the artifact. Not that they stood a chance against Vandross; he could snuff the whole of the city, he thought.

But as with all things in his life, his ego-tripped a trigger to balance his karma. At the moment he stared at the city, a wicked-looking, curved blade came shooting from the sky and plunged itself into the face of one of his lieutenants.

The Lizardman went down, and the assorted members of his Race and the Orcs and Trolls that also accompanied them fell silent and still. While Lizardmen lived a tribal and simple life, they contained enough brain matter to be reasonable, rational warriors. They might inwardly panic and tell themselves that such things were bad omens, but they never said such things aloud.

Greenskins, on the other hand, were big, dumb and superstitious. As the Lizardman hit the ground, Vandross inwardly growled. He would have to convince an entire half of his current group that this sort of thing happened all the time and shouldn't cause any uproar among seasoned veterans. *Ah*, he chided himself, *there's another problem*. Greenskins, meaning Orcs and Trolls and Goblins and Ogres, didn't *have* veterans, mainly because they didn't believe in the subtle art of combat known as 'defending oneself while making an attack'. In their own way, Greenskins made the most fearsome frontline attackers of any army. They didn't care who or what they hit, as long as it died. And the Orcs had a saying in their tongue that translated into the Common tongue as 'I will die this day. But though I die, I take at least two of mine enemies with me, *faroom*!' While a good quote, it lacked many survivors to keep it alive for any length of time.

As the Greenskins began chanting for protection from the angry gods who chose to rain swords upon their heads, Vandross turned his attention on the felled Lizardman. The blade appeared to have entered from a slight angle, as if coming down off of a tremendous arc. With his one good eye, he stared hard into the city. Who or what therein could hurl a weapon that weighed as much as his own two-handed blade? Surely only a Jaft or a Minotaur could make such a throw, but neither Race inhabited Koreindar. The Jafts always lived near the waterways, and the Minotaurs preferred the mountains they shared with the Dwarven peoples of Tamalaria.

"Right then," he said aloud to no one in particular. "Bael," he snapped, and a Lizardman in dark brown leather tunics and plate mail responded at once by coming before his master and dropping to one knee.

"What isssss your charge, ssssire," the General known as Bael asked.

"Inform the Greenskin Elder that his men may remain here if they like. I think our Lizardmen are enough for the task."

A brief look of doubt crossed Bael's face.

"Sssire, we number only twenty at pressssent. And three are old, too old to have agreed to sssswear fealty to you, ssssire. I believe their old memories of the halcyon dayssss when our people were feared and made powerful through allegiance to Tanarak have blinded them to their limitations. I beg that you let me kill them now, that they shall not be a liability later."

Vandross nodded his agreement. The Lizardmen struck him as an archaic society at times, but their devotion to efficiency on the battlefield made him smile broadly. As he watched, Bael approached the elder Lizardmen, and with a single motion, he beheaded two of them.

The third old creature put up a pleading hand, and hissed something in his Race's tongue. Bael handed the old one his sword, and the elder Lizardman thrust the weapon through his own heart. Withdrawing the weapon, Bael wiped the blade with a cloth and approached Vandross. "Now we are prepared, ssssire," he hissed.

"Very well. Speak with the Greenskin Elder, and inform me when you are done. Our time is nigh." As Bael left him alone, Vandross eyed the weapon that had stricken his second lieutenant. He reached down a hairy, muscular arm to grasp the hilt of the weapon. When he made contact, his entire arm recoiled as though struck by the venomous fangs of some viper. The trace signature of the weapon's former owner felt as anathema to Vandross. Somewhere within the distant city, someone had the power to defy him.

Whoever it was, he would crush them as flat as shale.

* * * *

"We are leaving, my lord?" Alex asked as the undead warrior packed his few belongings.

"Yes, Alex. Whatever reason I had in coming here, I can no longer bear to be ignorant to. We shall leave with as much haste as can be mustered," When he felt prepared, Byron wove his Shadow magic about his head and upper body. To complement the effect, he put on his black hooded travel cloak.

Moving as softly as he could, Byron retrieved the key to his room from the table, and walked down the hall to the check in desk. The same old fellow who had been there when he checked in stood there, but he paid Byron no attention. Instead, the old Human seemed to be watching something through the window facing the eastern entrance of the city. Byron gazed into his eyes, and saw flames reflected in them.

Whirling about, Byron saw through the window that a wicked-looking Human led a pack of about fifteen or sixteen torch-carrying Lizardmen up onto the steps of a church. At first, Byron considered simply leaving, not getting involved. Yet something assured him that he would be dragged into things anyhow.

"My lord," Alex squeaked beside him, breaking his focus.

"Yes, Alex?"

"Well, it's nothing really, but I think we would be best served by making away from this place post-haste."

Byron agreed inwardly; he did not want any trouble if he could avoid it, and this man and his Lizardmen were trouble. Swiftly, he dropped the key on the counter, and moved for the door.

Once outside, he saw that the Lizardmen had set fire to the church. The Human who commanded them seemed to leer with glee at their handiwork.

Byron had done such things in his service to Tanarak; of course, he had also done much worse things. Shaking his head to clear it of the memories that haunted his soul, Byron stalked to the middle of the road. He was prepared to turn and leave the city, but he felt compelled to watch this grim spectacle for a short time, if only to assure himself that evil still existed in the world. Evil that was not necessarily related to him.

* * * *

Meanwhile, only thirty yards away, Richard Vandross felt eyes upon him and his minions. Scanning the area, he saw a shadowy figure in the road a little way off. He could not discern any details of the man, but felt discomforted by his presence. Motioning to a pair of Lizardmen, he instructed them to "Take care of that witness."

The reptilian chuckles of his servants disturbed him, but Vandross knew they were dependable warriors; the job would be done quickly, and already he could see their victim scurrying off into the distance. It seemed he was no different than any other low-class fighter in the face of two experienced Lizardmen.

Vandross entered the burning church, stalking like Death incarnate up to the pulpit, where the last living priest knelt in prayer.

Gracefully, elegantly, Vandross put his left hand under the priest's chin, lifting the becalmed face to meet his gaze. The priest had longish ears, emerald colored eyes, and skin that was fair and soft; yet his face showed some signs of age, such as wrinkles and a smattering of facial hair. Half-Elf, thought Vandross with mild disgust. He had never cared much for Elves. For a Human to mate with one and produce offspring, well, he didn't hold with the idea. The mating, sure, he could understand that. Elven women were mostly quite beautiful. Still, he held the man's head in his hand gently, pondering his next move.

"The Orb," he whispered soothingly, releasing small amounts of Illusion magic into the priest via his touch. "Can you tell me where it is?"

In the priest's mind, he saw his former pastor pleading with him this question, and knowing only love and admiration for his mentor, the priest nodded and smiled.

"It is where we have kept it for years, Father Tora," the priest whispered back, seeing the flames growing larger on the edges of his vision. "But we must leave it, Father. The fire shall soon consume the church and everything in it."

"No no, silly boy," Vandross cooed, stroking the Half-Elf's left cheek tenderly. "We are protected by our faith in Oun. Remember, the great god shall not let harm come to us here in our home of worship."

The Half-Elf smiled, and tears streamed down his face.

Vandross felt a worm writhing in his guts at uttering the god's name. His father had been a believer in Oun, and what good had it done him? None, he thought bitterly, pushing the memory aside.

"This is true, Father. Come, I shall show you." The priest sprang to his feet and led Vandross towards the back door that led to his own chambers by the hand. The Half-Elf opened a wardrobe, and reached behind a priest's habit, pulling down a small lever. A section of his bedroom wall began to slide open, and Vandross looked behind him at it in triumph. There, on a pedestal, sat the first of the Orbs of Eden's Serpent he sought.

"You have done well, my son." Vandross reached back absent-mindedly and touching the priest's face. "It is safe and intact. I am going to take it away to a safer place than this. You have served Oun well." Vandross relished the hopeful and blissful look in the Half-Elf's eyes. "Now, go join him." Vandross reached out with his other hand, and with a deft twist, snapped the priest's neck. The Half-Elf's limp body crumpled to the floor, with the look of bliss still on his face.

Slowly, ritually, Vandross extended his left hand, placing his palm on the Orb. A deep, rumbling voice spoke to his mind from the artifact itself. *Doth thou seek the power?*

"Yes," he rasped in a sharp hiss.

Doth thou seek to behold the might of the glorious Mother of Destruction?

"Yes," Vandross said, louder than before. Warmth spread through his arm, up to his shoulder and down to his groin.

And to what end doth thou seek to use this might?

"To destroy, rend, and conquer! To be as a god on the Earth," Vandross shouted, lifting the Orb over his head. "To take for mine own a kingdom, nay, an empire, that shall be eternal!" He thought once more of his father, his mother, defending their little village from the bandits that had roamed the southeastern plains years before. They had been powerless, and had died for nothing. Richard had vowed, while watching them die as he was dragged to safety by his uncle Robert, that he would never be so powerless as an adult. Never.

Then so be it. Rippling waves of black and purple energy pulsated through the room, and the smell of brimstone permeated the air. A vortex of wind swirled and slashed about the room, sending up howls like a dying animal. Furniture whirled about, crashing into the walls and splintering into pieces, but still Vandross held on to the Orb of Eden's Serpent as if his life depended on this one moment. The dark glow of the Orb pulsed through all of his body now, working through his every blood vessel, and deeper, into his very soul.

His long, black hair whipped about his head in the Orb's maelstrom, and his robe flapped like a vulture's wings in the strange dark light. He felt his

31

muscles bulging outward. His magic pulsed in his mind and heart, warping, becoming something more. The smell of brimstone filled the air so thickly he felt he might gag on it, but his will to have the Orb's powers filled him with immunities.

After another minute, the mad purple waves of light pulsed more rapidly, as though racing against time. *Say the words, now, o seeker of the power! Speak, and the first bit of that power is yours!*

Throwing his head back in a baleful laugh, Vandross spread his feet apart to gain balance. "I, Richard Vandross, do claim that the power of this Orb of Eden's Serpent, is mine to command! The power over life and death is mine!"

The vortex kicked, and the wind became so wild that it extinguished the flames that had reached the back room. As one last shriek of unnatural delight escaped the Orb, a sound like a demon screaming in glee, the Orb flashed and disappeared, leaving only a small purple glow. This ball of baleful light entered Vandross' chest, and he fell upon his back.

Instantly he was back on his feet. Such power and strength he had never known, never felt. *So*, he thought, *this is what it feels like to attain greater power. I must have the other Orbs!* For a moment, he wondered after what strange new powers he might have available to him. But it didn't matter, he decided. He would find out soon enough. Out of curiosity, he attempted to punch through the wall to the outside. The result, he discovered, was merely a hurting hand.

"Well," he said as he stalked through the flames of the main church toward the exit. "It was worth checking on."

* * * *

Byron had only scant yards to go before he reached the safety of the open plains, when he felt vibrations in the ground from behind him. With a graceful twirl, he untied his cloak and threw it over the first would-be attacker, confusing the reptilian warrior long enough for a solid, metal-gloved punch to the skull.

The Lizardman went down in a heap, unconscious. The second creature gave pause a moment, drawing his long sword and circling his would-be prey. *Strange*, it thought. *I cannot see his face or chest, yet I know they are there.*

Byron drew his new weapon, the broadsword Alex had stored in his Fairyspace. Gripping the handle one handed, he took a fighter's stance, aggressive but withholding. Slowly he and the Lizardman danced around each other, the Lizardman sizing him up, and he inwardly yawning. Such creatures as Lizardmen offered him no challenge. His suspicion became truth as the reptilian warrior made a lunging stab that Byron could read a full second before it struck.

Whirling his blade against the Lizardman's weapon like a stirring stick, Byron parried the stab and let his motion spin him fully around, bringing the heft of the broadsword's blade crashing down through the Lizardman's skull. The weapon buried itself halfway through the creature's chest, and remained stuck there a moment as the warrior shuddered one last death throe.

Byron planted his right boot against the reptile's chest and pulled his weapon free, kicking the corpse to the ground in the same movement.

Crimson life fluid spattered Byron's legs, and in a few seconds he stood in a spreading pool of the Lizardman's blood. The Dread Knight held his dripping blade over his bare skull, allowing his fallen enemy's blood to splash down over the bone. A hissing arose from the spot it landed, and the crimson stain soon vanished, its energy absorbed to fuel his life force. Byron pulled his cloak off of the other creature and wiped his sword clean on the cloak's inner lining. With a satisfied grunt he looked over at the fallen warrior; he had dispatched the creature in about four seconds total. Roughly he slapped the unconscious warrior until it awoke.

The first thing it could see as its eyes came into dizzy focus, were the twin crimson lights of Byron's eyes as they flashed with bloodlust. Before the creature could cry for help, Byron clamped its snout shut with one powerful hand. The metal of his gauntlet chilled the Lizardman to the core, for the reek of untold horrors befouled it. He could now see that he had fought a Dread Knight, and on its chest plate, it bore the Crest of Sidius.

"Listen to me, little man, and answer my questions. If you do this well, I shall spare you your miserable existence," Byron growled in a low voice, his words barely audible, dust rolling out of his bone mouth. "I am going to release your mouth now. If you so much as squeak, I shall tear your head off with my hands alone, and drink deeply of the marrow of your spine. Do you understand? Nod your head for yes, shake it for death's sweet release."

The Lizardman nodded violently, nearly breaking its own neck. If there could be escape from Byron of Sidius, the reptilian warrior would accept it gladly. Slowly, cautiously, Byron removed his vise grip on the warrior's face.

The Lizardman rubbed its snout softly, trying to regain feeling in it.

"Ask your questions, Byron of Sidius," it hissed in a whisper. "I shall anssssswer." Byron twitched a little, because the creature did not whisper, but rather, spoke in a moderate volume that might attract unwanted attention. *I'll deal with that if the need arises*, he thought.

"Very good. Nice to see you've decided to be amiable. Now, first off, who is that Human that you work for?" Byron kept one hand on the hilt of his sword as he spoke, lest any more interlopers should come along. The fire in the church, he noticed, was spreading.

"Hisss name isss Richard Vandross," the reptile whispered. His tone had decreased at the mention of his master's name, as if the words were poison that could choke his soul.

Byron recognized the name vaguely, though he could not think of where he had heard it.

"What purpose does he have in destroying a church of Oun?" A sense of dread tightened into a knot in his stomach. In life, he had himself been a Paladin in service to the Church of Oun. Something big was going on in that church, of that he felt suddenly certain.

The Lizardman hesitated, looking back toward his brethren. Catching the look, Byron twisted the Lizardman's head towards him, clamped one hand over its snout, and with the other twisted and broke the creature's wrist.

In agony it writhed, its eyes watering over and its feet stamping the cobblestones of the road. "I told you to answer my questions well, reptile," Byron hissed dangerously. "The next thing to break shall be your neck! Now, what purpose does he have?"

As Byron removed his left hand, the Lizardman said through choked sobs of pain that wracked his body, "Go, fuck yourself." The creature spat blood into Byron's eye socket.

"Bravely said, whelp, but a poor move on your part. I shall leave you to think over what you've done. And I'll even leave your boss a little message, by way of maiming you, not to screw with me." Byron raised his right palm toward the Lizardman, and a stream of dark blue energy wrapped around the reptilian assailant.

His body floated into the air, as though he bore no more weight than a common house cat. The energy clamped his mouth shut, but Byron could make out the screams it attempted to let out. A sadistic streak in the undead warrior, one he had developed in his service to Tanarak, savored the creature's dismay. But that part of him that remained Byron Aixler, his very soul, cringed.

Abruptly, Byron changed the nature of his spell, a last second decision that spared the Lizardman further pain. Rather than torture him, the magic simply held him, and would continue to do so until long after Byron had left.

Turning his back with a satisfied nod at his handiwork, Byron whistled through his teeth for Alex, who had been hiding in his chest plate the entire time.

"Are we off now, my lord," Alex asked, sounding exasperated.

"Indeed, my tiny friend. Let us went." And so the odd companions left Koreindar, but not their troubles, behind.

Chapter Three
Realizations

Richard Vandross walked out of the flaming church, the blaze casting him in a silhouette. With each step he took, small ringlets of black energy radiated from his feet across the ground.

The onlookers of his horde, formidable warriors though they were, felt compelled to stop what they were doing, and bow deeply at the waist in reverence to him. Their eyes appeared to Vandross to have gained a sort of glossy sheen. Was this an effect of the Orb of Eden's Serpent, he wondered? Yet, he noticed, Bael did not appear to have been similarly affected.

"Hear me my minions," he shouted over the din of the burning and collapsing church. The screams of escaping townsfolk seemed drowned out by his voice; his words echoed in the air like a Giant's.

A large section of the church's roof collapsed into the main vestibule behind him, the sound of cracked and burning timber crashing against the pews music to his ears. The scent of smoke filled the air, and he breathed it deeply. "I have gained possession of the Orb, and have absorbed it. I have more power now than most any Human, or any man for that matter, regardless of Race! Stay with me, and you shall all know the glory of waging war on the whole of the land! You shall taste the sweet tang of conquering and conquest! I shall be as a god, and you shall be my chosen army!"

Bael, his right-hand man and leader of his Lizardmen, raised his fist high into the air and shouted, "Hail! Hail Lord Vandross!"

In response to their leader, the whole of the horde, joined by the Greenskins attracted to the fire, shouted like a pack of zealots, "HAIL!" Vandross noticed that even the Greenskins, though easily set to the uses of clever men, seemed strangely compelled to show allegiance. The only creature in his command who seemed to retain some bit of himself was Bael; but this was no surprise. After all, he was his tribe's leader. Perhaps when he attained more Orbs, Richard would have power over even him in this fashion.

"Not that I'm complaining," Vandross whispered to himself. "My minions," he proclaimed more loudly, "I am in possession already of the knowledge of where the next Orb resides. But I shall need more men for the task. Go you now to your clans, your tribes, and tell them that I command a legion, and they are to join it! If they do not wish to join, then show them the error of their ways!"

The assembled horde raised their fists and shouted as one, "HAIL!" Then, they split into packs and hurried out of the city.

Only Bael and a pair of his best warriors remained with Vandross. To him, Vandross whispered, "Remain here. I wish to check on the two warriors who I assigned the task of eliminating our shrouded witness."

Bael gave a stiff salute, and posted his two warriors to guard.

Before Vandross had made half the distance, however, a pair of grizzled veteran warriors returned, chanting low in their throats in the tongue of the

Lizardmen. Between them, floating in the air and wrapped in some sort of magical cocoon, lay prone one of the two scouts he had come to check on.

Misery hung off of the creature, a pain not at all associated with failure, but with physical suffering.

For a moment, Vandross could think of nothing to ask, to say, to do. After a moment's hesitation, he shook his head, clearing his thoughts. "Forgawr," he said, addressing the magically wrapped creature. Forgawr was one Bael's three cousins of Bael, though none of the talent had apparently rubbed off on this one. "What happened? Can you speak?"

Almost immediately, the stunned creature began ranting in his native tongue.

The veterans waved their staff-like weapons over their kinsman and chanted the same mantra that allowed them to bear him. Slowly, they began making arcane gestures in the air, allowing their own power to move the young Forgawr until he stood on bound feet before their leader.

Vandross straightened, said once more, "Can you speak? The plain and Common tongue?"

Forgawr shook his head negative.

"Would something in the magic crush you if you spoke any words other than your native language?"

Nod, nod.

"Did the man I sent you after do this to you?"

Nod, nod.

As Vandross looked at the weaving of the dark purple energy, he became gradually disconcerted by the familiarity of it.

"What happened to the other one I sent with you?" Forgawr stuck out his forked tongue, letting it flop on his lip like a dead thing, and crossed his eyes.

"Dead?"

Nod, nod.

"My lord," said one of the veteran Lizardmen. "We found the other's body not far off. He appears to have been slain with little effort."

Here was another affirmation for Vandross, whose newfound power suddenly seemed insufficient.

"Whoever did this," the Lizardman said, "is a skilled swordsman and wielder of magic. Before you proceed, lord Vandross, allow my brother and I to attempt an undoing to this magic that binds Forgawr."

Vandross acquiesced with a nod and turned to look back at the city of Koreindar. His forces had made short work of the little city, even without the Orb of Eden's Serpent. With the power the artifact gave him, he should be able to crush any opponent.

For a few minutes, he watched in numb anticipation as the veteran brothers undid the binding magic that ensnared Forgawr.

When the magic tore free, the young Lizardman gasped for air as though he had been drowning. "My lord," he sputtered, coughing and wheezing. "The creature who did this to me, I recognized him! We must flee at once, and go nowhere near him!"

"Pah! That's ridiculous! None is powerful enough to stand against me. And I already know where the second Orb is, though it is some way off. Tell me then, who was this creature, that you are so afraid

"My lord, it was Byron of Sidius!"

Somewhere in the pit of Vandross's blackened soul, a volcano of doubts and screams erupted. Byron of Sidius! How could that be? Byron belonged to Tanarak. With Tanarak's death, the Dread Knight should have crumbled into dust and ashes! How—

He would deal with that later, he thought. "Forgawr, you have done well to tell me this. You two, take him back to Bael, and have everyone meet back at our camp when extra forces have been gathered. I shall be there shortly. First," he cracked his metal-gloved knuckles in their gauntlets, "I must take care of some business."

With a burst of wind that kicked up around him like a small tornado, Vandross pelted out of the city. The Orb, it appeared, had not just given him knowledge and abilities, it increased his speed and endurance.

Oh, how wonderful it will be, he thought, *when I have all five in my possession.*

He ran out of the city heading south, following a set of tracks made by an unmistakably large pair of iron boots.

Byron of Sidius, he mused. *How wonderful shall it be to take you out of this world?*

Abruptly, he stopped dead in his tracks, because suddenly there were no more to follow. "What the he-" he started, but was cut off by a large, heavy body crashing into him from the side. In his pursuit, Vandross had not realized he had come into high grasslands, where trees were plentiful and bushes provided plenty of cover for an ambush.

Landing heavily on his back, a metallic thud going up into the air from the impact, he braced himself and heaved to his feet in a low crouch, his blazing scimitar unsheathed and held in both hands. In the darkening evening, he could make out a heavily armored and cloaked man a small distance away, hidden in the shadows.

Why was the man so far away, Vandross wondered; surely he could not have run that far back after colliding with the one-eyed warlock. Then Vandross suddenly, chillingly, knew how his opponent stood so far back; *he* had been tossed nearly ten yards off the path by the bulldozing attacker!

"Come out of hiding, you cur," Vandross spat. "I haven't got time for this nonsense, and I've lost a very important trail."

"I bet you have," the creature rasped from the shadows, stepping forward and drawing a broadsword. *Byron of Sidius,* Vandross screamed mentally at himself. *It's him.*

"Byron of Sidius," Vandross cooed, fully prepared to taunt the undead warrior. "I know a lot about you, you know."

"Most men with wicked hearts do." Byron circled Vandross, the two of them playing a game of cat and mouse, each deciding to try to goad the other into making a move out of anger, impulse.

"Byron, Byron, Byron. I am not a wicked man," Vandross said innocently, putting his free hand over his heart. "I am simply better educated in the ways of the world. For example, I know that those who have power, are the only people who are really free."

"What were you after in that church, vile one," Byron rasped, irritation slipping into his tone, dust slipping out of his teeth. "Why did you attack that city?"

"The Orb of Eden's Serpent, Byron." Vandross took a step closer, tightening their circular dance. "I wanted the artifact of power for myself, now that the warlock Tanarak is dead. I mean, he isn't going to be using it anytime soon, is he?" Vandross chuckled mirthlessly behind gritted teeth.

Byron made strange motions with his left hand, and Vandross hoped inwardly that perhaps the Dread Knight had suffered an injury while fighting his scouts. But soon he felt something stirring in the night around him—magic! Before Byron completed his spell, Vandross would have to strike the Dread Knight!

But as Vandross made a vicious overhead hack, Byron easily brought up his broadsword one-handed and let the blade slide harmlessly down his weapon.

Raising his voice, Byron finished his mantra and executed his spell. "HAGATAAAAA!"

A small, swirling ball of yellow force pounded Vandross' chest plate, beating him back and slamming him finally into the dirt. With another brief gesture, Byron made the energy pound on Vandross' wrist, holding his weapon hand still. Byron planted a heavy, metal-clad foot squarely on Vandross' throat, applying a slight amount of pressure. Vandross knew the weight of the armor alone would be enough to crush his larynx, but he still had a chance. If he could just free his wrist...

The tip of the broadsword came down two inches above his good eye. "Who are you, cretin? Who is your master," Byron growled. His voice sounded like a decaying crypt come to life.

"I am, Richard, Vandross," the one-eyed warrior managed as a small pressure pushed at his neck. "And I, serve no one, but myself."

"How do you know me, cretin," Byron demanded, the red pinpoints flaring dangerously in their sockets. "How is it you know me?"

"Well," began Vandross, deciding to take a chance on his natural sarcasm. "There's the skull, the eyeless sockets, and the big metal Crest of Sidius on your chest plate. That and you've acknowledged yourself."

Byron seemed to muse on this point a moment, grinning. Not that he had much choice in his facial expressions.

"Your lackeys seemed to know me. I know the Lizardmen served once under the thumb of Tanarak of Sidius. Were you one of his mindless slaves," Byron growled again, rage suffusing him. Slowly, agonizingly, he pressed down harder on the one known as Vandross' throat. The Human warlock coughed and sputtered under the strain, kicking and thrashing his legs wildly.

"N, n, no," Vandross finally managed as the pain subsided. How had he been so easily bested by the Dread Knight? He possessed an Orb of Eden's Serpent, and had his own arsenal of spells and sword techniques! How had he come so suddenly to this?

Be still, a voice from somewhere in his mind said to him. *Taunt him, but do not attack him. Let him think you weak and defenseless. He will let you live.*

And if I strike at him, then what, Vandross thought loudly in defiance.

Then he will crush you now. He will do it. Do not test him. Play on his mercy.

All right, Vandross thought to himself. He didn't like being forced to do such things, but it only added, he realized, to the long list of cunning things he had accomplished. Put on a show, sure, he thought.

"I should kill you right now," Byron said, almost to himself. More dust plumed out from his exposed neck bone, but a small amount of rotted flesh also rolled up over the edge of his armor, and dropped onto Vandross' face.

Nauseated, Vandross felt suddenly that half of what he was about to say were true.

"No, p-please," he whined, putting on slight waterworks. Just a little, he thought. Make like you're trying to hide it. "I just, I wanted to be powerful, like the Lizardmen, like Tanarak. Why should I always be a victim? Please, just, let me go. I'll forget about my vengeance, I swear! I'll never even go near the bandits," he said, pulling Byron along, trying to play on his mercies. Yet there was just enough truth to his words that he knew he could get away with an incomplete story; his childhood home had indeed been raided by bandits. The thing was, he thought to himself, he had hunted down and slaughtered the lot of them three years after their raid on his village. And he had taken his time with the last of them, their leader. Oh, how he had reveled in torturing that man to death.

But the plea had done its work. Byron let his foot off, and offered a hand to Vandross. Tenuously, Vandross accepted, and the Dread Knight hauled him to his feet with no effort.

Byron brushed him off, something Vandross hadn't expected. Mercy, sure, but not nicety. "Vengeance is a very attractive thing, young warrior," Byron rattled through his teeth. "But you must not let it control you. I understand your lust for revenge, as I have had lust for revenge in my time. But all things balance out, I think you'll find. They did for me, when Tanarak died. I am free willed once again, as you can plainly see," the undead warrior said, sheathing his sword. He placed his hands on Vandross' shoulders, the weight of his black iron gauntlets stressing Vandross' pain threshold. "You have absorbed the Orb of Eden's Serpent, this is true. But if you meditate on your acceptance of reality, and pray to, well, whatever god you worship, I am certain he or she can help you expel the Orb. For the time being, you are a hazard to yourself," Byron rasped, pulling Vandross into a tight embrace. There was something in the Dread Knight's tone, something like compassion, empathy. Could Byron of Sidius feel these things? Perhaps, but the last statement he had made carried another tone with it; regret.

With a deft snap of his elbow, Byron brought the ridge of his hand down into the back of Vandross' neck, and the one-eyed devil's vision went black from the impact. He floated downward, sinking through the various stages of consciousness with great alacrity.

As he strained to keep his eye open, he saw Byron pick up his scimitar and taking it away with him. *Great,* Vandross thought as he passed out. *Now I'm weaponless, and unconscious. Well, it could be worse,* he thought. *It could have been the Byron of old.* He could easily have been killed on the spot. But his mind wandered now, the soft, dark blanket of sleep wrapping him tightly in a cocoon of warmth.

* * * *

Byron stalked away from the unconscious form on the ground. Though he regretted harming the man, there would have been little other choice. Something still bothered him, though. In the back of his mind, Byron could feel something primal, instinctive and ingrained into his very soul screaming at him to kill the man. *Mercy is for the weak,* it bellowed at him. *The goal of combat is to destroy your opponent.*

"No," he mumbled to himself aloud. "I am not like that anymore. I am not that creature."

After that, he marched silently southward, Alex fluttered alongside him as a constant companion. But the little voice in him hadn't just been speaking from his former perspective as a creature of darkness. Something had been very familiar about the one-eyed man, something that made his right arm itch to go back and hack him in half.

Shadows loomed about him in the brightly moonlit night, and some of these he wrapped about his upper body, effectively erasing his countenance from sight. There was little or no sign of life around for some time as he stalked, until he came upon an emaciated pack of wolves. The pathetic pack predators eyed him, hunger making mad requests of them.

The Dread Knight allowed his eyes to smoke and glow red a moment, and all four of the lupine hunters swiftly turned and ran, the voice of their hunger cut short by the bellow of reason.

Still he plunged ahead into the night, taking shelter as the first rays of golden light shoot out over the land. The sun rose majestically, a single circular oriflamme, with its heat radiating through the air and the land it touched. "Time to rest Alex," Byron rumbled as he leaned himself in a seated posture against a large, thick oak.

The Ki Fairy fluttered up into the higher reaches of the tree, disappearing from Byron's line of sight. A few yards away, hidden and cowering in a jumble of brush, a trio of squirrels watched as the soft yellow lights in the undead warrior's eye sockets dimmed to nothingness. Sleep swiftly claimed Byron, and he went unresisting into that darkness.

The Dread Knight had not known a peaceful slumber in a considerable time. Often his dreams were the stuff of horrors, the sort of nocturnal imagery that drove men to their basements with a sword in hand, eyes wide with terror. Perhaps they came to him because of his bodily nature. Perhaps they came because he slept during the daylight hours. Whatever the reason, the former Paladin of glory could not find peace in his sleep. But stretched periods of sleeplessness often taxed his endurance, and so he resigned himself to rest periods every two or three days.

A soft gray fog rolled around Byron as he walked in darkness. This struck him as unusual, as his dreams rarely began so uneventfully. But something else was amiss. He could smell things in the dark and fog, and could actually appear to control himself. He slowed his shambling gait to a complete halt, looking around, attempting to pierce the veil of featureless smoke with his vision.

Slowly, his surroundings shimmered into focus like a mirage.

A village formed out of the mist around him. The inhabitants were tribal Cuyotai, were-coyotes. Byron attempted to summon the shadow magic that concealed his features, but found that he could not. Vexed at his inability to hide himself, he uttered a curse under his breath, and quickly darted behind a small thatch hut to keep from being seen.

As he rounded the back of the domicile, a stout Cuyotai Hunter passed within inches of his back, but the young warrior said nothing. A voice called out somewhere nearer to the center of the village, and the Hunter turned and ran toward the voice, through Byron. It dawned on Byron that he was insubstantial here, and so he moved to follow the youth.

As he stalked after the young Hunter, Byron overheard the trilling laughter and calling of the pups, the crackle of cooking fires, and the odd but melodic sound of adults carrying on in their native tongue. All in all, this appeared to be a quaint little village. Yet as he walked into the middle of the village, an ominous light shone from within one of the larger huts. Byron could only describe it as a glowing darkness, and it radiated in a rather circular fashion.

The smell of deer meat roasting on the fire distracted Byron, but only momentarily. The image of the village began to shimmer and distort itself, becoming wavy and vague. The sky overhead swiftly darkened, and thunderclouds rolled in with the speed of hawks. Flames erupted from all around him, and the image solidified once more. Lizardmen and Orcs, slavering and screaming, raged through the village, tearing apart the defenders like so much dried firewood. Only a small handful of the Cuyotai warriors held their ground, but they darted towards a wood line in the distance, attempting to flee the carnage in their home.

The scent of roasting meat rapidly shifted to the stench of blood and burning fur and flesh. The aroma made Byron heave and gag violently, doubling him over and forcing him to his armored knees. Why would Lizardmen and Orcs band together to attack a seemingly harmless village of tribal Cuyotai? Byron lifted his head and focused his vision on the hut where he had seen the dark glow; there, coming out of the hut and holding an orb over his head, stood the one-eyed man whom Byron had spared.

He screamed in rage as he watched Richard Vandross absorb the second Orb of Eden's Serpent.

* * * *

"Byron! Byron," a high, tinny voice shrieked at the Dread Knight's head. He could make out someone screaming as well, and as the red lights blazed in his sockets, he clamped his jaw shut and realized it had been him.

"I am awake, Alex," Byron muttered, smoke spilling out of his throat. He raised himself slowly to his feet, looking out of the small woodland he rested in. Dusk still approached, an hour or two away. Yet in the fading daylight, Byron could see a hamlet in the distance, just atop the next set of hills. "When night falls, we go into that town, Alex," Byron said as Alex flew up in front of his face.

"Oh yes, I'm certain the folks there will be more than happy to welcome the man who just sounded like a demon from the fifth or sixth ring of Hell." Alex mustered all of his formidable powers of sarcasm.

"This is no time for witty repartee, Alex. I have had a vision."

Alex's face scrunched up, and he harrumphed. "There's always time for my wit. Though, given the sounds you were making in your sleep, I'm willing to listen to an explanation."

Byron relayed briefly to Alex his dream.

Throughout his description, Alex remained quiet and seemingly thoughtful. "Well, I can think of two explanations, me lord. Would you hear them?" Byron nodded lightly, looking at the surrounding woods. A chill raced up his spine, starting from his thick steel boots. Eyes were upon him, he felt sure of it.

"The first explanation, me lord, is that you have indeed had a premonition, and the man you scuffled briefly with deceived you rather well. I did detect an intense amount of dishonesty in the man, but your old Paladin habits seemed to take over for you, so I saw little gain in telling you my thoughts on the matter."

"And the second explanation, my minute vassal," Byron inquired, looking as hard as he could into the Ki Fairy's eyes. Those blackened orbs held years of experience with the darker side of things, but they also held an unrepentant streak of mischief.

"The second explanation, me lord, is you're losing your mind and you have a penchant for seeing the worst in people." The little man flew around Byron's head at dizzying speed and laughed.

With a sudden snap of his hand, Byron caught Alex around the body, chuckling softly as the Ki Fairy spat curses at him and struggled futilely in his grasp. As he released Alex, Byron swung his broadsword up over his shoulder and into its scabbard. The black-armored warrior turned and walked out of the wood line, the sun fading behind his back.

"Come, Alex. We have much to do this evening. And we need information."

"Information," asked Alex, dusting himself off as he hovered where Byron had been standing. "About what? And who are we going to ask?"

Byron half turned to look at him.

"We need to find out about a Cuyotai village. And we are going to ask the most common, and often most reliable source of information any town can offer."

Alex cocked his head to one side inquisitively. "The mayor," he ventured.

"No," Byron said with whatever he could muster for a smirk. "The village drunk."

* * * *

Getting into the town presented no problem. Like many small hamlets in the eastern regions of Tamalaria, the town of Melarky had no guards. It had no watchmen. It had no real way of policing or protecting its citizens, but there was little threat of such a small place being attacked. The townsfolk probably thought that picking up and moving would be easier than defending their little township. It would be safe from bandits because there wouldn't appear to be much to gain from raiding it.

Wrapped in shadows and his great cloak, Byron slipped into the town. The businesses of the hamlet had obvious marking posts; the smithy had an anvil-shaped sign over his door, the inn a bed, the sundry goods store a satchel, and the tavern a mug of ale. "Rather cliché, isn't it," Alex whispered from inside of Byron's cloak.

"Yes, but it's quaint as well."

"That's just a polite word for boring," mused the Ki Fairy from his hiding place.

"Actually, Alex, it means charmingly odd."

"Oh yes?"

"Yes, especially in an old-fashioned way."

"Are we here to argue Common skills, or get information," Alex snapped.

"Yes, of course, you're right," Byron agreed grudgingly. He trod to the entrance to the tavern, its saloon-style swing doors adding to the flavor of the town.

As Byron opened the doors, he scanned the inside of the tavern for points of exit. It was the first of many things he did automatically when entering any enclosed space. In his years of service, he had learned that for a warrior to be an effective fighter, he must first be of a strategic mind. He must find and exploit all weaknesses of an enemy's defense, including terrain and available fighting room. In the event the warrior became disadvantaged, he must have a pre-determined escape route.

Seven men, he thought, *four at the bar, three together in the corner. Humans at the counter, most likely the smithy among them*, he thought. This he surmised by the smithy's blackened apron. His analysis continued: *a Human, an Elf, and a Cuyotai in the corner, most likely tradesmen, judging from their apparel. Three windows, one door behind the counter, most likely for a kitchen.* Byron had seen no eatery or restaurant in the rest of the hamlet, and so assumed this would be the only away-from-home-at-home cooking anyone could get in the town. A sign hung above that door saying quite clearly, *kitchen closes at nine*. The barkeep, Byron noted, was a burly Dwarven man, and a tall one at that. The Dwarf stood about four and a half feet, and Byron could see the glint of an axe head from his vantage point. All of this he absorbed in a matter of seconds, stepping in and letting the doors behind him shut.

One of the men at the bar seemed to be distancing himself from the others, he noticed, and so he chose to sit next to this man.

The barkeep approached, cleaning a glass in that most ceremonial way the barkeeps are apt to do. "What'll it be, stranger," he asked, his eyes darting about Byron's facial region, trying to get a look at this dark traveler.

"Scotch," Byron replied out of habit. "And get this gentleman another of whatever he's having."

The barkeep eyed him suspiciously. But when Byron placed seven gold pieces on the countertop, the businessman inside the Dwarf shoved his cautious side out of the way with a quick heave.

"I'd be careful about getting Clem here much more to drink," said the Dwarf in his thick tenor. "He's already half in the bag. I wouldn't want him here tomorrow complaining about another round with his missus."

"Aw, lay off Porum," slurred the downtrodden fellow. "Just keep 'em comin'. Thanksh pal." He clapped Byron amiably on the back.

The drunk called Clem shook his hand a moment, pain slightly registering that he had hit something quite solid and quite metallic. "Where you fum', stranger," he asked, looking not at Byron, but at his already emptied shot glass.

"Alexis, originally." Byron poured a little of the scotch down his throat, having to bypass the fleshless mouth. The shadows kept his actions well hidden, however. It tingled warmly in his stomach for a moment, and then settled just like everything else he put down his gullet.

"Wow, that's waaay out wesht buddy," the drunk replied. "What bringsh you to thesh partsh?"

"I have some business with a tribe of Cuyotai around here. I'm not exactly certain where it is though, so I'm at a bit of a loss." He raised the glass to his hood, but a tiny head poked out of his chest plate and consumed what little alcohol was left in the glass.

Growling inwardly, Byron motioned to the barkeep for another round for himself and his new 'friend'. With the money on the counter, Byron could have easily bought the bottle of scotch and the brandy Clem was drinking, and maybe the rest of the bar as well, but he found it best to get his information as quickly as possible.

After drowning his troubles a little more, the drunk turned to Byron and placed a friendly arm over his massive shoulders.

"Well, dat's not too hard, buddy, hic. You headsh to the easht shide of town, shee? You'll go about five milesh that way, and there'll be a good sizhed woodsh. In the middle of thosh woodsh ish the village you're lookin' fer. Might be a bit dangeroush goin, though." Byron raised his eyebrow, or what he could of it.

"Why's that?"

"Cause the Cuyotai and Lizardmen of this region have been fighting over that land for years," replied the barkeep as he cleaned another glass. "You'd best be armed, though I can see already that you are. And from the looks of your gauntlets, you're well armored too."

Byron nodded in agreement. He got to his feet slowly, trying to act as though the scotch were mildly affecting him.

"Thank you both. I'll be leaving now. And barkeep?"

"Yes," the Dwarf replied as Byron was already halfway to the door.

"Cut him off after that glass. Keep the change." Without another sound, Byron of Sidius left the town.

After walking to the edge of the town, a ragged old man approached him with a walking stick. The old man moved the stick about the ground in an odd fashion, and Byron recognized him as being blind. Yet without error the old man stopped a couple of feet away from him. After a moment of awkward silence, Byron asked quietly, "Is there something you need, aged one?"

"The evil you seek, lies at your destination," the old man rasped in a cryptic tone. "But the other who seeks it, is nearer. You will be too late." Stunned, Byron took a defensive step back.

"Who are you, strange one?"

"I am but a humble oracle, dead one. The one known as Richard Vandross approaches the second Orb of Eden's Serpent as we speak. You will be too late to stop him. But you must go there. There is a person there who you must save and protect. He shall aid you in your quest." Without waiting for a response, the old beggar shuffled off into the town, as silently and suddenly as he had shown up.

"What are we waiting for," asked Alex. "Let's go after him!"

Byron ran down the alley the old man had shuffled through, but when he arrived on the other side, the beggar was nowhere to be seen.

Another encounter with the one-eyed man, Byron thought, might not turn out as well as the first. He had used his entire physical force to bulldoze the man to the ground, and he'd cast his Hagata spell full power. Yet the man, Vandross, had not broken or suffered major wounds from it.

In the distance to the east, he saw smoke rising out of the woods. His vision, he thought, was about to come to pass.

Chapter Four
Tearfang

For Shoryu (Show-ree-you) Tearfang, routine was life. The village's way of life had been based on it, and had thrived for many generations. The Cuyotai people had survived their struggles against the Lizardmen of the east by adhering to the rules and routines of their daily life. Nothing had changed with his generation. Sure, the occasional scuffle broke out, but the Hunters and Knights of the tribe dealt with them swiftly and with deadly force.

On this morning, Shoryu awoke from his sleep and put on his Hunter raiment. The old leather creaked in a satisfying way to his pointed ears, and he already could smell the inviting scents of the morning meal his caretaker prepared. The village Chieftain, his caretaker since his father's death, possessed many amazing skills, one of which was being an exceptional chef.

Shoryu reached under his bed and extracted his yew bow and his quiver of arrows, slinging both over his shoulder with practiced grace.

Shoryu was a pup by Cuyotai standards, only thirty-four years of age. In another year he would undergo the Rite of Adulthood, a grueling test of his mettle in his chosen path, but he was already praised by the tribesmen as their finest archer and scout. He could run for days without rest, and could hit a moving enemy from a half-mile away. He brought home the largest kills for meals, and could move through woods and open plains as stealthily as any Ninja. Unfortunately, this got him the attention of his tribe's enemies as well. Many Lizardmen attacked the village hoping to find and dispose of the young Hunter. But all who attempted the task found themselves riddled with arrows before they could reach the outermost homes of the tribe.

The Senior Hunters allowed no error when it came to defense. Often as the Lizardmen cried for his blood, none cried for more than a minute or so.

One of the Seniors, Moksha Milak, a wiry and energetic woman, approached Shoryu, her face painted for the morning hunt. Along her lupine snout, three red dashes brushed through her fur, both sides of her mouth marked so. Her hair she braided on one side into a series of strands, each twisted in a different fashion, and the overall effect gave her an exotic and alluring look. Though forty years his senior, Shoryu couldn't help but feel protective of her, as if she were the sister he never had. His own kindred had died years ago, but to him, his best friends and comrades took the mantle of family just as well. "Good morning young Shoryu. How are your spirits this day?"

"I am in fine spirits Senior Moksha," Shoryu replied, the light, boyish quality of his voice belying his battle-ready countenance. "What beast do we hunt this day?" His grip on his bow appeared natural, as though the weapon itself drew life from his hand.

"We track a morenian, Shoryu," Moksha said, crossing her arms in front of her chest. "They are the tri-horned beasts with a hide like leather armor. You have hunted one before, have you not?"

46

Shoryu smiled, but felt a pang of regret. Morenians were not a difficult kill, and with no challenge, he felt somewhat disappointed.

"Yes, I have Senior Moksha. Perhaps you won't need me then?"

"Oh, we will Shoryu," Moksha began, walking away from him. Shoryu followed obediently, knowing that routine was life, and life was routine. One needed the other, and vice versa. "You see, this is the morenian mating season. The morenians become ferocious creatures indeed during this season. They shall not be so easily slain."

Shoryu's heart lifted a bit. If the creatures had indeed become menacing during the mating season, perhaps he would have an actual challenge ahead of him.

"All right Senior Moksha. I shall be ready in a moment. I would like to ask the Chief something before we depart."

"Be swift about it, young Shoryu. The others are already awaiting us on the western front."

Darting back through the village, the young Cuyotai Hunter made good time returning to his hut. The Chieftain stood in the central chamber, lost in meditation, until Shoryu came stumbling through the front door.

"Hail Chieftain, mighty and wise." Shoryu bent low at the waist in the traditional manner used when addressing any Cuyotai Chieftain. "My apologies for interrupting, but I have come with a heavy request."

The Chieftain stood perfectly still, his bulky, muscular frame silhouetted by the light coming from the windows of the hut. His hands clasped each other before his long, proud snout in prayer, and his furry forehead beaded with sweat from concentration. He was an impressively built figure for a Cuyotai, whose race generally could be described as wiry or lithe. But not this Chieftain. His brawn was matched by his wisdom, for his mind held many secrets and knowledge. The Chieftain knew bits and pieces of magic lore, a fact or two about the sciences, and he'd gained the ability to speak in nearly half a dozen tongues, quite a feat for a small tribe Chieftain.

Slowly, purposefully, the large Cuyotai unknotted his hands and turned his head to gaze at the young Shoryu. "Your apologies are accepted, *pup*," he said, adding this last word with a hint of irritation. "What is this request of yours, my son?"

"Mighty Chieftain, I request that you grant me access to my father's enchanted bow and quiver."

The Chieftain's head snapped around to look at Shoryu with darkened, clouded eyes. His lips pulled taut over his fangs, and for a brief moment, Shoryu hoped to his deity (Artemis, Goddess of the Hunt) that his caretaker was smiling. A low, menacing growl rasped through the Chieftain's teeth however, and the big Cuyotai took a heavy step towards him.

"You know that I cannot allow that yet. You have not yet completed the Rite of Adulthood. I cannot afford to show you favor just because you are like my own son. Now," he said, stepping away and turning his back to his charge. "Is there anything else you require?"

Shoryu hung his head, his snout touching his deflated chest. The smell of candle wax wafted into his nostrils, and for a moment he resisted the relaxing effect the aroma had on him. But he refused to be overly emotional, and so he took a deep breath of the sweet scent, straightening himself to his full height.

"No, wise Chieftain. I must make haste, for the Senior Hunters are awaiting me for the daily hunt."

"Go well, child," the Chieftain muttered, leaving the main chamber and going into his personal bedroom.

"Stay well," Shoryu said loudly and clearly. He pivoted on his heel and fled the hut, knowing that he couldn't argue the point with his caretaker. Instead, he focused on the hard pounding of his feet on the ground as he ran past dozens of villagers. He heard the sounds of a people who took life as seriously as they had to, and no more. Cuyotai were all fairly carefree in nature, making them great companions with Elven folk, who were of a similar mindset. Shoryu had only himself met four Elves, but they all seemed amiable enough people. One of the females had even caught his eye, and he found himself instantly attracted to her.

Shoryu thought himself strange for this. Cuyotai rarely mated outside of their race, but he felt that when the time came, he would like to be mated with an Elven woman. Even as he approached the line of Senior Hunters, he couldn't help but feel that no woman of his tribe would possess the qualities he sought in a companion. But as he stood pole-straight at attention, these thoughts escaped the forefront of his mind, burrowing deep into his inner mental chambers like refugees of a war. As Senior Hunter Moksha called off the names of the assembled Hunters, Shoryu focused his attention on the wood line. The village had always existed in harmony with the woods that surrounded the large clearing, harboring only the occasional threat of attack from Lizardmen and the rare beast that had no place in those woods. But something inside of Shoryu's heart warned him, called out to him in anticipation of horror.

Like any good soldier, though, he had learned to keep these thoughts and ideas in his own heart. *Eyes and ears open, mouth shut,* he had heard a Senior Knight once say. *Wise words,* he thought to himself.

Senior Moksha ran ahead of the pack, using hand signals to give out her orders. Shoryu immediately took up a position near the left flank of the group, running ahead with his bow in one hand, his other hand fixed to the quiver on his back. He was prepared to strike first, as always.

Within scant seconds, the pack of Hunters had entered the woods themselves. This territory opened to Shoryu like a mother's embracing arms, for he knew every tree trunk, every shrub, and spot on the ground where the fallen twigs and branches tended to collect. The scent of mighty pine trees permeated the air softly, lifting his spirits.

Leaping up into a nearby tree, Shoryu turned his ears up, increasing his chances of hearing any sudden movements in the woods.

For a while, he heard nothing but the trilling of wild birds and the squeaking of ground animals. As he stood poised to strike, he felt a sudden, scurrying movement on his arm. Turning his head slowly to his left, he came nose to nose with a squirrel, whose home he had apparently trespassed on.

The critter seemed to smile at him, and he gave the little nuisance a half-hearted grin.

As one might expect, a lycanthrope's smile always appeared suspect, if not outright threatening. The squirrel interpreted the gesture in the blink of an eye, and swiftly scurried up the tree trunk.

Shaking his head, Shoryu returned his attention to the floor of the woods below.

And none too soon. As he swept the landscape with his hawk-like gaze, he spotted a pair of morenians sizing each other up. A third beast stood a few yards away, and from the vantage point of the tree, Shoryu could tell that the two beasts circling each other were males about to engage in a fight to determine who would have this female for mating.

Shoryu shimmied silently down the trunk of the aged pine, all the while keeping an eye on his prey. All movements around him shaded in a gray smoke as he focused all of his attention on the two circling morenian males.

The beasts were indeed of good size, but they seemed to pulse strangely under their flesh. Senior Moksha had mentioned that the morenians became fearsome creatures during their mating season, and Shoryu no longer had any doubts of this.

The smaller male reared up, screaming primal rage and fury as a jagged row of bone spikes exploded from beneath its flesh. Blood rained down in droplets as fat as a small house cat over the woodland floor, splashing obscenely off of everything they touched.

Shoryu watched, transfixed by the suddenly war-like beast, as it reared up in the air and claws of ivory bone sprang from its feet. The hooked claws appeared to be serrated, and looked long enough to plough through five feet of solid tissue. In a moment, the larger male imitated this frenzy, only its own hidden weapons appeared to be considerably smaller and less formidable. The claws had no serrated edge, and the spikes only measured a few feet from Shoryu's perspective. In most matters of the forest, the larger you were, the better your odds. Apparently, that formula didn't apply to morenians.

Then, to his horror, Shoryu heard a loud snap of twigs and brush a little to his right. Head darting around to see the source, he caught a glimpse of several of the Senior Hunters preparing to fire on the beasts. Both male morenians looked at one another for a moment, and nodded in unison. The female darted off through the woods as quickly as her stout, reptilian legs could carry her.

The males, Shoryu realized, had made a temporary pact and put aside their battle in order to deal with the intruding parties. As the beasts moved towards the Senior Hunters, the sharp twang of nearly a dozen bows filled the air.

The beasts shrugged this volley of arrows aside with their now armed forepaws.

Shoryu watched with mounting trepidation as the Senior Hunters fell back a short distance, the enraged morenians now stampeding towards them, mouths opened to expose several rows of razor-sharp teeth.

In all of his years as a Hunter for the village, Shoryu had never seen a morenian behave in such a battle-ready fashion. They anticipated the arrows' speed and trajectory, and had reacted accordingly. These morenians must have survived previous hunts, or they would surely be slain by now.

Moving through the woods, riding the rails of adrenaline, Shoryu darted in and out of tree cover and brush, keeping himself alongside the Senior Hunters. Senior Moksha spotted him as she let loose another of her arrows, and she shouted at him, "Shoryu! The beasts' hides have hardened! Our arrows will not pierce them! You must flee to the village! We will handle things here!"

But Shoryu had had enough of following those sorts of orders. He had come out here on this hunt believing he would have little challenge. Now that a suitable one had come up, he would not relinquish or shirk his duties because of an order.

Shoryu dropped off the pace a bit, running parallel to the rampaging beasts. They had not spotted him, or if they had, they had determined that he posed little or no threat. This would be their fatal mistake. The world around him seemed to go into a slow-motion, as though time had ceased to retain its strangle hold on him. With pain-staking care, he notched a single red-wood arrow, his favorite due to its incredible strength.

He ran along, keeping his target in his sight: the larger morenian's right eye. Morenians' eyes were situated on the sides of the skull, in order to allow them a larger field of peripheral vision, and thus survive in the wild. But this would also pose as their largest weakness, Shoryu figured. A big, soft target on either side of the head, he thought.

Still he waited, restraining himself until the smaller morenian had lined itself up with the larger one. As the Senior Hunters ran rag-tag through the wood line, Shoryu spotted his opportunity, and let fly his redwood arrow.

Like a single bolt of lightning it spun through the air, a single, deadly shaft of wood. Guided by his instinct and skill, the arrow split the air around it with a high-pitched whine, complements of the customization the young Cuyotai Hunter had done to his weapons.

In a second, there came a wet, slick splashing noise as the arrow tore through the large morenian's skull, exiting the left eye and flying straight through the smaller morenian's head. With a death wail, both beasts fell to the ground, flailing and lashing out with their claws as the last grains of sand in the timer of their lives slipped silently into the bottom.

With one last heave, the beasts fell silent, their bodies slumping beneath them on the soft clearing grass. The stench of their last expulsion of urine and feces filled the air, stinging the eyes and noses of the Senior Hunters and Shoryu. Yet all wore broad smiles on their snouts as they pelted toward the young Hunter, hoisting him up on their shoulders and shouting praise at Shoryu.

The Senior Hunters carried him thusly all the way to the village center, parading down the rows of the huts. At last they set him down, and all gave the traditional salute to the Chieftain as he approached their pack.

"Hail Chieftain, mighty and wise," cried Moksha to the large Cuyotai. "We are returned from our hunt, which nearly became our last!"

The Chieftain raised an eyebrow at this, his unspoken question evident.

"This is the morenian mating season, mighty Chieftain, and we came upon two males preparing to do battle for the right to mate with a female."

"Indeed?" The Chieftain raised his eyebrow another notch. "Even though I have voiced my dislike and disapproval of hunting them in this season, you went anyway, Senior Moksha?"

His question lashed the proud Cuyotai woman like a whip, but he held her with his gaze. "Continue."

Moksha related the tale of the hunt to the Chieftain and the gathered villagers, all of whom whooped and cheered for Shoryu as Moksha ended her tale.

"It was a shot that legends alone can live up to, wise Chieftain," Moksha said, a slight gleam in her eyes. Shoryu had become suddenly suspicious of Moksha's intentions. The Senior Hunter had always seemed unusually friendly towards him, and he knew that after he completed the Rite of Adulthood, she would probably present herself to him as his first mate. Or rather, she would present herself to his caretaker, and the seniors would make the decision, according to tribe custom. His suspicion grew only further when Moksha said loudly, "Should this not earn him his place in Adulthood?"

The Chieftain stared wide-eyed at her for a moment, and then noticed her eager, but subtle, gaze at his adopted son. An impish grin spread across his face as he recognized Moksha's intention, as his son already had.

"Hmm. Perhaps, Senior Hunter Moksha. Though it is not yet his time, he has done a great deed, and should be commended accordingly. I shall consider this. Now, Seniors, bring the kills here, that they may be prepared for a great feast. As for you, my boy," he said, stooping close to Shoryu's ear. "I think we need to have a little man-to-man talk."

Hanging his head in newfound dismay at the situation, Shoryu followed his caretaker to their hut. He was in for a long day.

* * * *

In the woods to the north, a wicked creature looked into the village with the aid of a spyglass. He used the only eye he had available, for that creature was the one-eyed devil Richard Vandross. Several dozen local Lizardmen had joined his cause willingly, eagerly, for they so badly wanted the Cuyotai's land that they would follow anyone who could deliver it to them. Bael stood at his side, masked from enemy view by Vandross' illusions. "My lord, what do you seek to gain from this reconnaissance? There are enough of my troops and your Orcs and Ogres to easily crush these Cuyotai right now! We should strike with the advantage of numbers."

"Perhaps you didn't just witness the same activity as I," hissed Vandross at his second-in-command. He watched through the spyglass as a Cuyotai larger than the rest walked off with the talented Hunter, one fatherly arm draped over the shorter Cuyotai's shoulders with ease. "Which is to say nothing of the power in their apparent Chieftain. The local Lizardmen have told me much about these particular Cuyotai. They will fight tooth and nail to defend what is theirs. We have the advantage of numbers, but not of strength and skill. As such," he said, taking the spyglass away from his eye and facing his General. "We shall have to use the elements of surprise and superior tactics. That's why I have you, Bael. You have experience with military tactics. My own experience has been mostly limited to magic," he said, kicking the ground with a metal boot. "What sort of specialists do we have on hand?"

"A few Shaman, lord, and a single Beastmaster from the local Lizardmen. We also have a couple of Orcs with limited Pyromancy knowledge. Perhaps we can find a way to utilize their unique talents?"

"Yes," Vandross said, a wicked smile curling his lips. "Bring them all to me. I have some homework for them to complete."

Bael saluted smartly, and sprinted off into the woods to locate the specialists.

Vandross paced impatiently for a time, trying to cycle through his options. That young Hunter ground through his thoughts most, as the pup would obviously present a clear danger to his minions. He felt certain he had no archers in his troupe that could rival the youth. But if that bow were to go up in flames...

Moments later, Bael addressed him by clearing his throat. "Lord Vandross, these are the men you requested."

Vandross looked at the assembled creatures, and inwardly cringed. They might not be enough after all. But he would be damned if he was going to let this opportunity pass him by, and he could not send for the additional forces he had left behind at his temporary camp outside of Koreindar. Since regaining consciousness after his encounter with Byron, he had been hell-bent on getting the second Orb. Just one more should give him the power he needed, but he would wait to challenge Byron until he had all of the Orbs. The Dread Knight was on the top of his list of people to destroy now. But the truly vexing question was how the undead Paladin had managed to survive the death of Tanarak. How could he still be alive, and what's more, under his own free will again? Had Vandross forgotten something?

No matter, he concluded. *I'll figure it out later.* For now, he had to concentrate on forming a plan of attack. How would these creatures best serve him? Looking at the ancient Lizardman who appeared to be the Beastmaster, he had an idea. "You there, Beastmaster. What is your name?"

"I am Lornya," the old reptile rasped. "In the tongue of my people, it is Ra-pa-manamokshun. Lornya is a Human translation for easssse. What do you require of me, oh posssssessssser of might?"

The ancient reptile bowed reverently to show respect to Vandross, and he teemed with pride. He could now control any creature with the sort of wicked soul and heart that most of these creatures possessed. How easily he could amass an army with this power of the Orb alone. But he felt compelled now by a sort of hunger, a lust for more of that glorious, tainted power. He had to have it, and nothing would stand in his path. Nothing.

His goals, his purpose, had started simply enough. Attain enough power to carve a kingdom of his own out of the lands of Tamalaria. Yet the moment he had absorbed the first Orb, that goal seemed somehow beneath his full potential. His General, Bael, too had noticed Vandross's change in plans, but thus far he had remained silent on the matter.

"You have control over certain types of beasts and animals, yes," he asked, pacing back and forth, his plan taking shape slowly.

"Indeed, my lord."

"Those creatures that the Cuyotai hunted today, what were they?"

"Thosssse, Lord Vandrosssss, were morenians. They are currently in their mating sssseassson, and they can become quite fierccce during thisss time cccycle. But they alssso become more difficult to control. You may not have ssssseen them before, asss they are indiginoussss to the region."

"Good, then there will be at least a handful at your command within, what, five, maybe six hours?" The ancient Lizardman took a step back, flummoxed.

"I shall need the aid of at leassst one of these Shaman, in that casssse."

"Done," Vandross said, nodding to Bael. The General pointed to one of the four Shaman and indicated that he accompany the Beastmaster. "You two, Orcs, you are adept at some form of Pyromancy?"

The dumb, sloth-like creatures gave a slow, simultaneous nod.

"Good. From what range can you hurl your flames into the village?"

"We could do it from here, lord Vandross," said the smaller of the two.

"Excellent. Get yourselves up on the ridge there when dusk comes. You will launch your attack when the morenians our friend retrieves begin their charge. Bael," he said, turning to his General. "You will take a battalion of thirty Lizardmen into the village after the morenians make their first assault. Minimize casualties to our forces. A smaller force of ten of your best troops will wait just outside of the village in order to pursue anyone trying to escape."

"Begging your pardon, lord, but why not let them escape," asked Bael. "When you establish your new seat of power as a legitimate king, their territory will fall under your ownership."

"Because I am here not just to take the Orb of Eden's Serpent, but to send a message. This is not going to be a battle, General. This is going to be my next magnum opus! This is going to be a slaughter!"

* * * *

Shoryu sat complacently as his father almost merrily taunted him with Senior Moksha's suggestion.

"You know," his father added, grinning almost madly. "She's had an eye on you for some time. Perhaps, in light of your accomplishments, I should grant you the title of Adult. Then, you may be granted access to your father's bow."

Shoryu knew this was a bait tactic, and he wasn't about to bite.

"I am not yet of proper age, wise caretaker," he said, playing the very card he'd struggled against for so long. "I should wait just as all the others have."

The Chieftain smiled broadly at him. *Such a great young man,* he thought with pride in his heart. Before he could speak further, he caught the slightest whiff of something strange in the air.

"What is it, caretaker," Shoryu asked, standing to his feet.

"Hmm. I am not certain. I feel however, that something is amiss." The Chieftain led Shoryu into the village center. Night was swiftly approaching, and something had changed, some quality of the air. He immediately approached Senior Hunter Toremiam, the strongest of his Hunters, and inquired as to the location of their scout guards.

"I know not where they are, sir," Toremiam said, his gruff, low voice modified by worry. "They should have returned an hour ago. Night will soon be upon us. If they are not back by then, I fear something foul has occurred." He blinked rapidly, running through the possibilities. "They reported earlier that there had been some suspicious looking Lizardmen milling about in the woods. Perhaps they have been engaged in combat."

"That is a possibility," admitted the Chieftain. "How many did they spot?"

"A small force, sir, eight or nine of them. Large numbers for a foraging or spying party."

"So you think they're preparing to attack the village again," interrupted Shoryu, his voice cracking slightly.

The Senior nodded curtly. "It seems possible."

"Make ready the packs, then," growled the Chieftain. "Conceal one group in the southern tents. Stand one pack here in the center of the village. Shoryu, you shall stay here with the center pack. There is something I must see to," he said, his words distant, distracted.

Senior Toremiam began barking orders, organizing packs and placing them where he felt they would be most effective. Toremiam possessed the keenest tactical mind among all the Seniors, and had been placed in charge of defenses for some time. Shoryu looked at the posted assignments, and made note of the clever use of spacing. In the event an ambush charge came, there would be at least two packs of four men and women to defend any entrance to the village, with the open center of the village itself defended by Toremiam's own pack, which included him, Toremiam, Moksha, and Senior Knight Balgresh. In the event they were needed elsewhere, they would travel swiftly over the same distance to whatever side weakened.

But they could not be ready for what was to come.

* * * *

The Beastmaster returned with not two, but three of the brute creatures under his guidance. One of the Lizardmen was unaccounted for, however, and Vandross raised an eyebrow at the ancient Beastmaster.

"An unfortunate but necessary ssssacrifice, my lord," he said with a bow. "They are hungry, after all."

Vandross smiled broadly, toothily.

"No matter. Everyone has to eat, ancient one. And you have exceeded my expectations I see. You will be justly rewarded, I assure you." He laid it on as thick as he had to. When he had control of the second Orb, he would dispose of the old man. Though useful, such a creature would remember when Vandross was weaker and might easily turn on him—he would not have any of that. "Get them into position."

The old Lizardman tottered off with the creatures in tow.

Vandross nodded at the Pyromancy-wielding Orcs, and they placed themselves on the ridge. All was prepared.

"My lord," hissed Bael, approaching at speed and saluting.

"What is it?"

"My lord, they have smelled something, I am certain. They have arranged defenses." Bael smiled cruelly, though his heart was not in the gesture. Still, it would keep Vandross happy. "Not that they'll be ready for our assault, but my scout was worried."

"Really," asked Vandross, his expression puzzled. "Worried? Bring him to me." Bael returned shortly with the youngest Lizardman of his troops. Vandross patted the scout on the shoulder, feeling the muscles contract and shake under the scaled skin. "Are you afraid, young scout?"

"Yesss, massster," slithered the creature. He looked about hurriedly, as if afraid of specters in the night. "I have lived in these woods for all my life, and have fought often these Cuyotai. They are fierce warriors, massster, and I fear I shall not sssurvive thisss encounter!" Vandross tightened his gloved hand on the youth's shoulder, feeling the bone begin to give. The scout writhed and gibbered under the force of his grip, thrashing to get his shoulder free.

"You have sworn fealty to me, yes," he asked, lightening his grasp slightly. The creature nodded mutely. "You have seen what sort of things I can do to a man, yes," he asked, and once more the creature nodded. "Then you know there are much more dreadful things to fear than death at the hands of a Cuyotai, yes?" He beamed at the scout, his pearly whites flashing menacingly in the moonlight at the youth.

Finally, the scout seemed to calm down, and nodded.

"I shall fight for your cause, massster," he murmured.

"There's a good lad," Vandross said, patting him in an amicable fashion. "Now, go get ready for the battle." As the scout scampered off, Vandross motioned Bael toward him. "I've seen that boy fire a bow. He's quite good. Try to boost his morale, and make sure he isn't killed."

"I shall try, sire," Bael said, saluting.

"Don't *try* anything, Bael. Just *do* it."

His General looked at the ground for a second, then nodded.

Night had finally come in full force, as the sun set beyond the horizon. Vandross stalked from the tree line, up on the ridge next to his fire-wielders. He raised a single iron-gloved fist in the air, waiting as he watched the Cuyotai below. With the power of the Orb, he could see them perfectly in the night, gauging their movements. They were waiting for an attack. What he would bring them was an onslaught.

With a single snap of his arm, his eye fixed on the second Orb's dark glow, he signaled the beginning of the attack.

"Go now, and crush them my children," whispered the Beastmaster to the morenians, who stampeded down the slope toward the northern defenders.

Wild battle cries ripped through the air as the beasts crashed into the first Cuyotai pack, arrows flying and swords gashing along the beasts' sides.

"Morenians," one of the defenders shouted. "We are beset by beasts." His words were cut short as a huge set of claws ripped three holes in his stomach and chest. The damage was too severe to be regenerated by the lycanthrope, and he fell to the ground, the first to die.

In the village center, Shoryu used his piercing gaze to look to the north, where the first assault had taken place. Beyond that, however, up atop the slope in the distance, he could barely make out more shapes, more bodies. Lizardmen! And something else, some sort of Greenskin race. Before he could tell Toremiam, the Senior was leading his pack north, to the already faltering defenders.

"It is not just beasts," he shouted over the din of the battle they approached. "There are Lizardmen and Orcs or something up there!"

"Their Beastmaster," growled Senior Toremiam as he launched an arrow into one morenian's throat, killing it where it stood. The other two, larger beasts had clawed and maimed three of the eight northern defenders, but the tide of the battle had shifted to the defenders' advantage. "But why are there Greenskins?"

"I don't know," Shoryu shouted, looking back to see that other packs had begun to approach at speed. "It is surely an alliance to oust us from the village!" Before he could further speculate, he looked up in time to see three fiery red orbs floating at the village. "Fire magic! These beasts are a ruse! They intend to burn us where we stand!"

His cry and movement likely saved the defenders' lives, for they all retreated in time to avoid the engulfing ring of flames as the fireballs erupted on the backs of the morenians, reducing them to ash along with the nearby huts.

A swarm of Lizardmen approached from the western slope, and the Cuyotai warriors charged the force of thirty or more reptiles.

Shoryu took careful aim back up to the north, and let fly two arrows in rapid succession. They struck the fire-wielders, but not before two lines of fire ripped through the village, setting most of the homes ablaze.

The magic-users dealt with, he joined the defenders to meet the attacking reptiles. The first ranks of reptilian warriors crashed into the oncoming defenders with an earth-shattering impact, the force of which threw several combatants on both sides to the ground, leaving them open for swift strikes and killing blows. Shoryu, Moksha, and Toremiam kept a safe distance, rapidly firing into the Lizardman ranks. But their opponents wore heavy plated armor, and few of the shots penetrated their defenses.

The Cuyotai Knights made up for this by engaging the Lizardmen from their flank.

Shoryu turned his head about swiftly, looking for some sign of his caretaker, finally spotting the mighty Chieftain on the southernmost tip of the flaming village. He was rampaging through a force of some fifteen Orcs and four Ogres single-handedly, the rest of his warriors distracted by their hated natural foes.

Shoryu had to help, and quickly. He ignored his impulse to simply join the Chieftain, making his way through the burning streets to his home. There, kneeling next to his caretaker's bed, he grasped the enchanted bow and strapped its quiver over his shoulders. *Adulthood and rituals be damned,* he thought. *I'll not lose two fathers.*

But as he exited the hut, he saw that the Greenskins all lay dead, and the Chieftain was now battling both a strange, one-eyed Human and a huge and ferocious Lizardman, who wore the heaviest-looking armor he'd ever seen.

Shoryu stood frozen with dread, as the Human unleashed blow after devastating blow at his caretaker, who could only just keep up with the Human's enormous and swift-swinging sword.

The Lizardman's weapon of choice, a green-tinted axe, was heavy and ungainly, obviously not suited for prolonged combat. He was tiring rapidly. The one-eyed man took one hand off of his sword, and black strands of force lashed out at the Chieftain, knocking him back into the flames of a hut.

"Father," Shoryu shouted, leaping into action. But he was not swift enough. The single eye of the wicked Human caught him fully in its gaze, and for a moment, he faltered.

"Bael, deal with him," the Human said.

Before Shoryu could react, the huge reptile shoulder-tackled him, sending the young Cuyotai sprawling.

The human smiled smugly, only to be blasted in the chest by the wounded Chieftain's huge war hammer.

Through the air he flew, landing on the burnt-out remains of a home. He kick-flipped to his feet, smiling menacingly at the large Cuyotai. "Not bad, old one. But you'll have to do better than that." Once more he lashed out with his magic, this time using a lightning-fork to strike the old Chieftain to the ground, holding the energy flow as the Cuyotai writhed and shrieked in agony.

Vandross let up a little, kneeling next to him. "The Orb. Give it to me, and I may spare you." The Chieftain, filled with the pride of generations of leaders, spat blood into Vandross's good eye.

"An unwise decision," he growled, wiping his eye and standing to his feet. He unleashed then the full power of his magic, turning the Chieftain into a glowing thunderhead of force. But the Chieftain had gone beyond pain, and simply writhed, his body failing him, his fur smoking on his body.

Satisfied, Vandross released his body to the ground, and knelt by him once more.

The one-eyed devil rifled through the Chieftain's pouches, finally producing the coveted artifact. With a triumphant and maniacal glee he chortled, pulling the Orb into himself, letting the new power course through his veins. When at last the final purple streak of energy shot from his eye into the night, he shouted at Bael, whose skill had been stalemated by Shoryu's speed and agility.

"Bael, we are through here. I have the Orb," he said, looking north to see that the last of the Cuyotai had fallen under the weight of five Lizardmen. "Leave the others and my Orcs behind to deal with the runt. We have no further business here."

Bael saluted, baring his teeth at Shoryu one final time. He noticed that something had weakened in the youth, however, in the last minute or so. He followed Shoryu's line of sight to the Chieftain's corpse, and realized that the boy's spirit must surely be broken. For a moment, he almost felt pity for the boy. The Chieftain must have been the boy's father.

Bael sprinted to his master's side, leaving the boy to his fate. Secretly, he hoped the young Hunter would survive.

"And the elites, my lord?"

"Leave them here," Vandross said, an impish grin distorting his face as he looked to the north. "I do believe they'll be receiving a visitor soon."

"And the Beastmaster? Do you still wish him, disposed of?"

Vandross mulled over his earlier decision. He felt such raw power and magic within him now, that he felt almost foolish for thinking the ancient Lizardman posed any threat.

"No, Bael. Bring him with us. I shall have uses for him down the road after all." Vandross turned his back on the burning village, and accompanied by Bael, left the barren waste behind. It would be a message to Byron of Sidius when he found it. That message was simple: pursue me and die.

* * * *

Ashes. Ruins. Corpses. These were the only things Shoryu could see, or think about.

Defeat.

A word his mind could decipher, but could not feel or know. His lips had never truly had to form those words. Yet here, now, in his own home, they were the only factors that mattered. But these words, though they danced in his mind like the macabre waltz of the dead risen from their graves, did not come from his mouth. Instead, a single thought, idea, need, came from his throat. In the din of rushing weapons and claws, thirsty for his blood, a single utterance could be heard.

"Survive," he said.

But the reptilian and Greenskin warriors did not advance quickly. He had time to try to see if his caretaker clung to life. Grasping his weapon in a death-grip, he flung himself to the Chieftain's side. The big man's chest rose and fell in rhythm.

"Sho, ryu," he sputtered, blood choking his singed and crisped neck. "I have had, a, vision. Perhaps, my last," he gurgled, his hand finding Shoryu's and clenching it feebly.

The once powerful Cuyotai had little more strength left than a newborn pup. The sight of his caretaker in such a sad state of affairs left Shoryu speechless.

"My, boy. I have, seen, a holy man, in the guise, of, a monster. He shall, be, coming, soon. He, shall aid, you, and you, he. Go, with him. My boy," he gurgled, coughing out gouts of brackish fluid. His hand lifted to Shoryu's cheek, bloodying the already sweat-matted fur. "Be, strong, and, and, proud." With his final words said, the old Chieftain laid his head to one side, and embraced the dark-robed countenance of Death.

Standing slowly, his rage fueled by his caretaker's end, Shoryu turned and took aim with a first arrow. With his first assailant in his sights, he growled low in his throat, carrying the sound onward into a war cry. His arrow flew, and the remainders of the assaulting force pressed forward.

* * * *

Byron pried the last of the ten Lizardmen off of his bloodied blade, planting his armored foot on the reptile's chest and heaving with all of his might. His breastplate shone in the glowing light of the blazing village below, crimson lifeblood dripping off of him at every movement. He had arrived too late, he knew; but if he was lucky, there would be some survivors in the village, and they might be able to point him in Vandross's direction. The wicked aura had faded from the village, this much he knew from just looking down at the wreck that was once a noble home. The area had a blasted appearance, and Cuyotai corpses could be seen strewn about everywhere.

Yet battle still took place within the burning remains of the village. Sword over shoulder, Alex in tow, the undead warrior charged into the streets of the Cuyotai home. As he entered the village proper, an enchanted arrow flew past his face, missing him by scant inches. He skidded to a halt, looking behind him as the arrow erupted as it connected with an Ogre that had been apparently waiting for him. He spun around, his red glowing eyes fixed on the young Cuyotai Hunter who had already turned to volley arrows at the last of his assailants.

Yet something seemed amiss. He looked around, and too late saw one of the Lizardmen leaping down from the last burning hut to club Shoryu smartly on the back of the head.

The youth fell to the ground, landing in an unconscious heap.

He would keep this one alive, if only to discover what Vandross's next move would be.

The reptilian warrior made to crush the young Hunter's skull with the wooden club it wielded, but it heard the movement of another target nearby, and turned to glare at Byron of Sidius.

He sheathed the sword, crouching in preparation for the Lizardman to strike. This one circled him in the flame-gouted street, showing no fear of him.

As he looked into the Lizardman's eyes, he saw that they were strangely clouded. Some magic had a hold of him, and he would run from nothing.

Byron cross-stepped to match the reptile's circling pace, first right in front, then left, keeping his balance on his heels. The reptilian warrior was not so sophisticated in combat; it shuffled like a grunt in an arena bout.

Byron smiled inwardly. If it lacked proper balance, he could easily get the creature on the ground and begin pummeling him to a state of blissful unconsciousness.

Finally, the reptile made his move, charging with a banshee wail at the Dread Knight. Byron crouched further down, lunging aside from the overhead club swing. He landed with his right leg back, bent for a pounce, and he slammed into the Lizardman from its front-right, knocking it to the ground. In the blink of an eye, he sat atop the reptile's shoulders, effectively pinning his arms by cutting off blood-flow. As the reptile screamed and thrashed its legs, Byron raised a single heavy fist, slamming it down hard on its snout. There was a crunch of jawbone, and its eyes rolled back into its head. Yet as Byron lifted himself off of the felled Lizardman, its chest heaved up and down. He turned his head about to look for more assailants, but spotted the few of enemies still alive making for a retreat.

Do not let them get away, instinct screamed at him. Frustrated at his late arrival, Byron decided to give in to his darker impulses.

The undead warrior raised his hands over his head, lowering his eyes to the ground and summoning the power of the earth. Murmuring under his breath in the tongue of mages, he thrust his head skyward and screamed the final words of power.

In the distance, the ground split ahead of the fleeing Lizardmen, and each in turn fell into the rift, landing about fifteen feet down in the ground, no hope of escape.

Reversing the words, hands still upraised, Byron closed the rift with his magic.

The ground rumbled, and the trapped reptiles cursed and raged against the closing earth, arms snapping like twigs as they tried to hold the ground itself at bay. With a final, air-rending crunch, the earth closed around them, their blood spraying like a volcanic eruption out of the ground.

"Quite nice, my lord," commented Alex, his face as white as a sheet. He had yet to see such an act of mercilessness on Byron's part. He didn't care much for the power Byron commanded, but he respected the undead warrior's usual restraint.

Byron slumped to the ground, the magical energy expended draining his reserves of strength. The warriors he had dealt with outside of the village had been quite skilled, and he had taken a few lumps at their hands. The magic of the rift had nearly caused him to black out. But he still had something to do. He got to his feet, slowly, agonizingly, and walked over to where the now-conscious Shoryu sat, hugging his knees, his bow in hand. The flames around them, with nothing much left to feed upon, began to die down.

"Do what you must, creature," Shoryu whispered, no hint of emotion in his tone.

Byron took a step back, his hands out at his sides in a show of peace.

"I am not here to harm you, young Hunter. I seek a man. The one who probably perpetrated this atrocity. Did you see him?"

Shoryu looked dismally up at Byron, and a small sparkle lit his eyes for a moment.

"The black-cloaked man with one eye? The devil who slew my father?"

Byron's jaw hung open a fraction, as he tried to think of what to say. "Yes, that is he. His name is Vandross. Did you see which way he went?" Byron asked softly, trying not to aggravate the boy any further. After all, from the looks of it, he alone survived the massacre of his people.

"Yes, creature, I did. He travels southwest with a large band of these cretins. And I," he began, walking away from Byron. "I shall go after him. I shall have revenge for what has happened this night!" Shoryu stalked boldly for a minute or so, finally breaking down and dropping to his knees, holding his face in his hands as he wept. Moksha, Tomremiam, the Chieftain, all of them slaughtered! And for what? The artifact in his caretaker's charge? He sat and cried alone a while, until he felt a heavy, but comforting hand rest on his shoulder. He looked up into the undead warrior's lights, and slowly the sparkle returned to his wet eyes.

"Be still, young man. You have fought valiantly here, and have survived a great ordeal. Surely your god will reward you when your time on this earth is over, for the deeds you have done this day. Worry not for the souls of your kindred," Byron whispered, his voice becoming soft and almost human. "For they are already ascended to be with the heavenly host," he continued, looking and gesturing towards the stars. "The man you seek revenge upon is very powerful, and very dangerous. You must not go after him in blind rage, with your heart full of lust for his blood. You must find a new home, and make peace with what has happened here."

Shoryu shook his head fiercely, rejecting the notion of just moving on with his life without taking some sort of action.

"You insist on combating this devil, don't you?"

Shoryu nodded. "What is your name?"

"My name is Byron. This," he said, reaching into the air and grabbing Alex around the body, who gave a loud 'urk'. "This is Alex."

"My name is Shoryu Tearfang," said Shoryu, bowing stiffly. "You are the holy man, disguised as a monster, as my mentor has seen in his vision. I must accompany you, Byron. I beg of you to take me with you."

Byron stood flabbergasted for a moment. There was magic in the boy's bow, and his shot had indeed proven to be incredibly accurate. Yet, he felt that the youth was too young for a voyage such as his. He did not want to drag an otherwise innocent Hunter into his conflict. But somehow, the look of determination on Shoryu's face convinced him.

"You'll just follow me if I say no, won't you Shoryu?"

The boy nodded.

"And, being a Hunter, you know the lay of the lands very well, yes?"

Once again, Shoryu nodded.

"Very well then. Lead the way, young Shoryu. Alex, we have a new companion. And he shall guide us to our next destination."

"Which is where exactly, my lord," Alex inquired, wiggling free of Byron's grasp.

"Narfan," Byron said, pointing directly south. "I have an old acquaintance who should have some help to lend."

With a swift stride and a slight smile, Shoryu took point, and led the way to Ja-Wen protectorate town.

Chapter Five
Lee Toren and Bael

Byron looked over the sun-lit landscape, seeing the outskirts of the sprawling mass that was the suburb of Narfan. For three days he, Alex and Shoryu had marched southward, until at last they arrived at this point. Byron signaled for Shoryu to come back to him for a moment. "Before we enter, my boy, I must utilize my shadow magic to disguise myself."

"Why?" the Cuyotai youth asked.

"You're kidding, right," squeaked Alex from his mount on Byron's shoulder plate. "Lord Byron should not be seen for who he is in broad daylight, especially in a public place."

"But *I* see the good in him," responded Shoryu. "Is it not so for others?"

Byron shook his head. "I am afraid most people in the lands of Tamalaria do not possess your vision, dear Shoryu," he grumbled. "I am still known as Byron of Sidius in most parts."

Shoryu's eyes widened for a moment, and he took a defensive step back. "You, are Byron of Sidius? How is that possible? My caretaker told me you were a holy man in the guise of a monster! I know of the tales of Byron of Sidius. If you were him, surely you would have slain me already."

Byron wrapped his countenance in shadow magic, concealing his true appearance. "Things have, changed. I am returned to my living soul, Byron Aixler. But my body, and my powers, have not followed suit." Byron looked anxiously at the Hunter, who appeared ready to run for the nearest Paladin outpost for help. But he did not. Instead, the youth threw his head back and laughed gaily.

"You have made a mockery of me, good Byron! I would not think jokes to be in your capacity! It appears I am wrong!" Relaxing his body, Shoryu strode off lightly towards the residential outskirts of the city.

"Either he's in denial, or he's a card short of a full deck," rasped Alex, after which he found himself being flicked off of his lord's shoulder.

"He's neither, I think, Alex," said Byron, picking up his pace to catch up to Shoryu. "He's just young and a bit trusting is all."

All considerations aside, Shoryu let the undead warrior and the Ki Fairy catch up to him, slowing his pace to an easy walk as they passed into the entry streets of Narfan.

The living conditions of the people of the protectorate were survivable, it appeared, but not exactly comfortable. Five and six story apartment-style buildings filled the entire residential district, packing as much life and as many job-holders as the available space could afford, and some people had even fashioned crude extensions on the ground floors to allow for more breathing room. The low-pitch burble of local gossip flooded the air, as did the scents of ethnic dishes being prepared for meals. The people themselves dressed in simple tunics and robes, giving the local scene an almost uniform appearance of near-poverty.

But even poverty-stricken individuals know when to steer clear of someone's path, as these people did as the Cuyotai and his dark-clad companion walked through the streets. Heads swiveled as if on a glide-track to look at the passers-by, whispered suspicions and rumors already circulating through the crowds like the blood of a community entity. Already labels were being attached to the tall, dark menace that followed closely behind the Cuyotai.

Though he could hear their talk, Byron wasn't entirely surprised. He had seen no other lycanthropes in the city thus far, just Humans, Dwarves, and some Sidalis (mutants). His nostrils had even detected the foul odor that would surely come from a member of the blue-skinned Jaft race. Not that they could help it; it seemed to be their trade off with nature for their regenerative powers and brute physical strength.

He and Shoryu had almost passed into the business district when such a creature, a male of the Race, stepped out of an alley in front of him.

Shoryu took a step back from the tall bald man, readying his claws for a confrontation.

Byron placed a reassuring and calming hand on the youth's shoulder, and Shoryu stood still, retracting his claws.

"Yo, stranger," said the Jaft fellow, whose odor made Shoryu's sensitive nostrils flare and his eyes tear up. "Outsiders gots' ta pay a toll to go into da' bidness place." The Jaft extended one massive hand towards Byron.

The man equaled the Dread Knight in height and mass, but his linguistics left something to be desired. Byron shook his head slightly, appalled by the level of stupidity of some of these creatures.

"You don't want to do this," Byron rumbled deep in his chest. "You shall step aside and let us pass, Jaft."

The Jaft raised his eyebrows and crossed his arms in front of his chest.

"Oh, shall I? Yeah, since yous axed so nicely, sure t'ing." The Jaft snapped his fingers, and he was soon accompanied by three burly Human thugs. None of them appeared to be more than twenty years of age, and Byron rolled his lights in his sockets, sighing and shaking his head in disappointment.

"Now pay up, weirdo, you and da' wolf-boy."

"Actually, I'm a Cuyotai," interjected Shoryu with his finger up-pointed, trying to make a futile point.

"Uh, whatever," said the Jaft in his low timbre. "Just fork over the cash, lest me and da boys have to rough you up."

Byron began to chuckle, at first softly, then louder and more menacingly, throwing his arms back and laughing like a demon possessed.

The Jaft scowled at him, his fists clenched and his teeth set and bared. "You laughin' at me, buddy? I'll pound you into dust, you and your little pet here."

"By all means," Byron rasped, crouching into a battle-ready position. "You and your goons are welcome to try. Hehehehe, yes, by all means." He turned his eyes into smoking pits of crimson iridescence.

Shoryu brought out his claws once again, snarling and snapping in the air in front of him, letting his lips foam over.

The Jaft faltered a moment, backing away from the suddenly very real menace.

"Uh, you gets a free pass fer now, freak-job," he stuttered, backing away towards the building he and his faithful thugs had come from. "But I'll be seeing you around, you can count on it!" Turning tail and fleeing at maximum velocity, the Jaft ran headlong into the side wall of the neighboring apartment building, knocking himself unconscious.

Byron and Shoryu returned to their normal walking positions, Shoryu wiping the excess drool out of his fur. As soon as they were a hundred yards away, Shoryu and Alex both burst into gleeful laughter.

"Oh my gods, that was hilarious," choked Shoryu through a fit of laughter.

Byron smiled inwardly despite himself. He had been ready to pound the impudent little man into so much fleshy waste, but now upon hindsight, he realized that the situation had indeed been rather entertaining. But he had a purpose in Narfan, he had someone to see. An old Gnome acquaintance, and he didn't want any more delays.

"Come on you two, pull yourselves together. We have a tavern to visit."

* * * *

Elsewhere, near the Allenian Hills, a base camp had been prepared, with seven score warriors and two score magic users assembled under the banner of a single eye over a black field. Vandross's aura had assembled that small army, and his aura attracted more vile creatures to him every day, including some of the native Khan (tiger-men) from the Hills themselves. He sat at that moment on a comfortable throne-style chair, across a small table from his General, Bael. A chessboard sat between them, the match just started.

Vandross pored over the board, deciding his moves four or five turns in advance, then having to rethink because of Bael's movements. The Lizardman had already bested him twice, and Vandross had returned the favor three times in a row, but he had to admit that Bael would not easily let three victories turn into four. Still, the one-eyed devil knew neither man was fully focused on the game. Something gnawed at both of them.

"What's on your mind, General," Vandross finally asked, breaking the comfortable silence.

Bael looked at him from the board. "My elite warriors, sire. They have not yet returned. And my scouts tell me that some sort of magic weapon destroyed the force we left behind. My lord, I think the boy survived."

Vandross paused a moment, then shrugged before speaking.

"No matter. I doubt the boy will be in any hurry to come after us."

"No sire, I think he *will* come after us. You do not know the Cuyotai like I do. They take vengeance as a very serious part of their lives. And in all probability, the Dread Knight has slain my elite warriors."

"Necessary sacrifices General. War is funny like that," Vandross said, taking out Bael's bishop.

"My men have given much to you and your cause, lord Vandross. They are very loyal to me, and I to you." Bael paused, taking out Vandross's queen with a clever knight maneuver.

Vandross frowned at the board. "Is there some point to this, Bael?" Vandross paid little attention to his words, trying to figure out how Bael had cornered his most valuable piece.

"The men grow restless, sire. The new recruits want some action. Morale among the older fighters is slowly draining away. We lost many men in the assault on the Cuyotai village. I propose we give them a few days to do as they like in some of the townships near here."

Vandross looked away from the board, fixing his one eye on Bael's two. He respected the General's prowess, but something about his request seemed unnecessary, foolish even.

For Bael himself, the issue went beyond mere boredom in the ranks. He had promised the men of his tribes that they would be carving a new territory out of the lands for themselves, under the leadership of the powerful warlock Richard Vandross. He would be their king, and they would be the free and mighty inhabitants of a kingdom that knew no equal.

Once they took the surrounding villages, then Bael reasoned that he could talk to Lord Vandross about declaring the area his own, and the quest for these Orbs of his would come to an end. He would have power, territory, and from looting and enslaving the people, a temporary powerbase which could be turned into a government. That had been the plan, at least, at first. That had been what Vandross had promised to convince Bael to join him. As it was, his own men were falling more and more into Vandross's thrall, their original goals and dreams forgotten.

"Why bother, General? I know where the third Orb is, and we can begin a march on it tomorrow. We've got recruits coming in all day. We can burn and pillage anyplace on our way to the third Orb. Why let them waste this time?"

He moved his only remaining bishop into position, and was certain he would have checkmate in three moves.

"Because, sire, men who are fresh off of one battle will blindly and eagerly go into the next one. These forces will also suffer some losses, but at least we'll weed out the less effective members." He had already calculated Vandross's refusal. "Call it a selection process if you will. A training exercise."

Bael paused a moment, making a move. "The better to move out with a truly tested force than one with no experience. By the way, my lord, checkmate."

Vandross glared at the board, seeing he had no options left but to admit defeat. He smiled smugly, knowingly.

"Very well, General, inform the men they have four days to do as they will. But on the morning of that fifth day, we march west. Understood?"

Bael smiled slightly, still keeping his soldier's demeanor.

"Of course sire. Good game." He saluted and left Vandross's tent. Vandross peered over the board, identifying his mistakes.

"Good game indeed, General."

* * * *

Byron and Shoryu entered the seedy-looking tavern through a pair of broken saloon-style doors, looking over the inside of the establishment briefly. Shoryu had seen nicer places outside of the village, but this particular tavern didn't seem too bad. There were even some gentlemen reading the town paper in one corner. Byron moved toward the corner closest to the bar itself, and ordered a double shot of scotch for himself, and an ale for Shoryu. The Human barkeep looked at Byron suspiciously for a moment, until the Dread Knight plunked seven gold coins on the counter. Byron looked around at the customers for a moment, noting that only one man appeared to be any sort of threat, a burly Dwarven fellow who apparently worked hard at getting hammered before two in the afternoon.

Then, he spotted the man he'd been looking for, a simply clad Gnome with frizzled gray hair, and a belt covered with utility pouches.

He rapped three times on the table, looking at the Gnome at the bar.

The Gnome glanced in his direction, and rapped on the bar twice, very shortly.

Byron responded with one hard knock, then four short knocks.

The Gnome took his drink and climbed down from his stool, coming over and sitting at the last seat at Byron's table. "Do I know you, stranger," he asked, his voice thick with a northland accent.

"Indeed you do, Lee Toren, Pickpocket and ladies' man," Byron rumbled beneath his concealing shadows.

Lee beamed proudly at him and Shoryu.

"So you does. Who are you fella? And who's the boy?" He jerked a stubby thumb at Shoryu.

A Pickpocket. Shoryu checked his pockets to ensure his belongings still belonged to him.

"The Cuyotai is named Shoryu, Lee. I am Byron." Lee's eyes widened in shock, and he smiled broadly.

"Byron? But everyone thought you died!"

Byron leaned in close to Lee Toren, removing just a bit of his shadows to reveal his skull.

"I did."

Lee's smile turned into an appalled and horrified expression instantly. He almost leaped out of his seat as Byron replaced the missing veil, looking around sheepishly for a means of escape.

"Do not fear, Lee," Byron whispered. "I am in possession of my soul. The one you have known as Byron of Sidius is no more."

"Pardon me for being a slight bit skeptical," Lee sneered sarcastically. "It's not every day I sees a critter with bones for a face claimin' he ain't 'ere ta hurt me."

Shoryu leaned across the table a bit, a question in his eyes.

"Why are you guys whispering," he asked in a whisper. Lee looked at him perplexedly, shaking his head after a moment.

"Is 'e serious," he asked Byron, who simply shrugged his shoulders.

"I'm afraid so, old friend." Byron leaned back and took a sip of his scotch. The warm glow of it in his stomach eased his frayed nerves some, keeping him from dragging Lee outside and slapping him for nearly panicking.

Lee shook his head, looking at Shoryu intently.

"You don't get out in the world much, do you boy?"

Shoryu shook his head sheepishly, ducking his snout to his chest.

"By the way Byron, is this lad even grown enough for drinkin'? 'e adn't touched 'is ale yet , and I'm hankerin' fer another round."

"Oh, by all means, get yourself another drink, Lee. On me, of course," Byron rasped, plinking another gold piece on the counter, ten times the value of one of Lee's gin and tonics.

The bartender waited a moment, took the coin, and brought back change for it, as he had the previous seven. Once more Byron waved him off with a slight gesture of his hand.

My god, the barkeep thought, his face flushed with excitement. *I'll be able to pay this and next month's rent on time.*

"Well then, what is it you're after, friend," Lee asked as he took a swig of his drink.

Shoryu hesitantly lifted the mug of strange, amber-colored fluid to the light coming through a nearby window. The beverage, while it looked innocent enough, smelled of something foul, and not unlike the man who had fallen off of his stool at the bar. Mustering strength and courage, Shoryu lapped at the ale with speed. For a moment, his canine instincts told him that whatever this substance was, it held poisonous qualities, for both the body and mind. Shortly thereafter, a different, but related, instinct told him it was time to excuse himself and find a nice quiet corner to vomit into. He gave the two acquaintances the universal hand signal for 'one moment, if you'll excuse me', which roughly translated in Byron's mind to 'I have to rush off around the corner of this tavern so as to save myself the embarrassment of ruining someone's nice boots with the digested remains of this morning's meal'.

For a long moment after the young Cuyotai exited the tavern, Lee and Byron simply looked at each other, but it didn't take long for Lee's face to crack into a broad grin rife with laughter. "His first time, eh?"

"There's got to be first time for everything, Lee," Byron said. "Now give me back my money pouch or you shall be placed in a realm of pain so infinitely large and horrible that your eyes shall burst from simply realizing you're said realm's only resident."

Smiling widely, Lee Toren pushed the Dread Knight's money pouch across the table to him.

"Thank you."

Shoryu retook his seat, his mouth still hanging slightly open, his tongue lolling against his lower jaw.

"Now, what I'm after, dear friend," Byron continued, "is information."

"Ah, information," said Lee, looking at his drink with a look of concentration. "Some information's hard to come by, 'specially these days. Not too many folks still dealing in facts, so it can be a bit, er, what's the word?"

"Expensive," Byron sighed. "You shall be well compensated, my friend. I need to know the locations of the Orbs of Eden's Serpent. A man by the name of Richard Vandross seeks them."

At Vandross's name, apprehension swooped over Lee's face like a vulture.

"Is something the matter, Lee?"

The Gnome Pickpocket shook his head slightly, his mouth agape.

"You don't want any part of that man, Byron, I'm telling you now. What you really are going to want to know is how far it is to the nearest port off the continent of Tamalaria." Lee took a stiff swig of his drink, grabbing the barkeep's attention for another round.

"You fear this man?" Byron took a sip of his own drink.

"Fear's a word best suited to things you have a snowball's chance in the seven Hells of dealing with. That man is something else altogether. He's been at it for years, ever since the time of Tanarak. Even worked in league with the old warlock, though I don't know how extensively. You sure you want to deal with this man?"

Byron simply remained silent, waiting for his information.

"Fine, fine. The Orbs interested me a little after the old warlock died, big monetary gains available for a shrewd salesman, know what I mean?" He took a swig. "So I learned a few things about where I might, erm, find them, you know, maybe lying around."

"You intended to steal them," Byron said, a matter-of-fact tone, not a question.

"Well, that's what I does best chum." Lee winked at Byron and handing Shoryu his compass back.

The Cuyotai immediately checked his other belongings, satisfied that the Gnome was merely proving a point.

"Only thing is, each one is guarded by some person or group of people. Fer instance, one was in a church in Koreindar. Now I'm a thief, true, but that's sacrilege. I've some standards, mind you, so I was going to hire someone else to nick it."

"Does your moral bankruptcy know no bounds," squeaked Alex from Byron's shoulder, admiring Lee's unique 'code of ethics'.

"'ey, so long as it keeps me from financial bankruptcy, no. So anyway, another was guarded by this village of Cuyotai. I know when a group of people can kick my arse, or that of any of my associates, so I let that one go. I knows where two others are, one near Desanadron, and one in the Elven Kingdom capital of Whitewood. Now," he said, glad to be helpful for a price. "About payment?"

Byron took out four platinum coins, each worth ten gold pieces, and handed them to Lee. "Thank you, Lee. You've been most informative. Let us chat again some time." Byron stood up, and began to lurch out of the tavern.

"Sure thing, so long as you're buying," Lee called after Byron and Shoryu.

* * * *

In the town of Ashkemp, things were not so good. Bael's men had reduced the city watchmen and the occasional adventurer to heaps of bloodied flesh and meat, sometimes leaving not even that on the frayed and broken bones. The Lizardman General watched as the new Khan recruits tore men apart, splitting even heavy iron armor in half with their feral claws and giant swords. Of particular interest to him was the Khan called Bringel, a Berserker whose only clear measure of might lay in the cast off shreds of the town's elite guards. His axe crushed, maimed and rent everything he crossed asunder, and he apparently had little or no mercy for the young, sick, or elderly. He killed without prejudice, even destroying three of his own comrades.

But Bringel had only proved to Bael that his fury as a Berserker could not be controlled. Setting aside the consideration of a potentially lethal weapon at his command, he was preparing to send his own shock troops after the mighty Khan, when the ancient Beastmaster slid silently up to his side. "Such raw force, General," hissed the ancient one.

"Hmm. Indeed," said Bael, sighing as he summoned five men with a hand signal. "It is a shame he is so out of control once he gets going. We shall have to kill him. He is too great a risk to our own troops. Men, prepare a volley of arrows, and aim for the head."

"Wait, General," the ancient reptile said, holding his hand in front of the firing squad. "A Berserker is no different than a beast of the wild. I shall tame him. Observe."

The old Lizardman stepped forth in Bringel's direction, rapping his staff on the cobblestone street to gain the massive Berserker's attention.

As Bringel turned, his black and orange striped pelt soaked with blood, Bael feared for a moment that the monolith Khan would destroy them all.

"Nishimonji, Berserker! Nishimonji, Khan," shouted the old reptile, raising and lowering his staff, then twirling it in a circle before him. A faint blue light shimmered around the Beastmaster, and Bringel's eyes turned from black orbs back to the pale blue they had been when first Bael had met him. He approached the Beastmaster and knelt before him like a disciple.

Bael could hardly believe what he had just witnessed, but ordered the archers away.

"How, how did you do it?" Bael looked from the kneeling Khan to the wizened old Lizardman.

"All things in nature are beasts within. He is simply more in tune with that savage, animal insssstinct. And by the way, General, my true name, is Valk. I want you to remember that when you recommend that lord Vandrosssssss give me command of one of the platoons."

Bael smiled widely, his eyes turning into slits. Valk was old, but still possessed the cunning of a younger man. "Very well, Valk. Consider it done."

The Beastmaster stalked away, Bringel trailing behind like a lost puppy.

Bael felt suddenly certain that his grasp of things to come slipped further and further away from him all the time. He would have been satisfied with lording over a kingdom alongside Richard Vandross. But he had the sinking feeling that with such an army as was now amassed, Vandross would want more than a kingdom. He would want the entire continent.

Before any more doubts could creep through his mind, his soldier's instinct kicked in, and he knew what his duties were. *Serve Lord Vandross as General, carry out my orders, command the army, establish the kingdom and begin its groundwork. Nothing more, nothing less.* The General did an about-face, and began to check on the other recruits. He had an army to train. Besides, they would leave tomorrow for Narfan, near Ja-Wen for the final testing of their skills.

Chapter Six
Delayed Departure

As Bael reached the outermost reaches of the encampment, he noticed several creatures he had never seen in his whole life. They were garish black creatures, comprised entirely of morphing shadows and magic.

As one brushed past him, he knew from the sensation of guilt and fear what they were: Shadowbeasts. Here in the camp. And they appeared to be, packing up? He grabbed the nearest foul demon and hissed at it, "Where is Lord Vandross, lackey?"

The Shadowbeast's face was a barely discernable Human shape, and it pointed one warped finger towards Vandross's tent.

Bael tossed the Shadowbeast aside and stalked menacingly toward the one-eyed devil's tent, his own black cape flowing out behind him as he secured it against the cooling evening breeze. As he reached the tent, he thrust the flap aside and stormed in, coming to a halt in front of Vandross is a fighter's stance. "What is the meaning of this," he shouted, pointing out to the camp.

Vandross sat across from one of the minor demons, the only one Bael had seen sporting humanoid garb and chain mail armor. Its black head faced away from him, but he somehow knew it would not be a friendly face he saw. Two small horns budded from its forehead, and Bael wondered if that were a sign of rank among the demons.

Vandross stood and gestured towards the seated Shadowbeast. "This is one of my new powers, granted by the Orbs of Eden's Serpent. I summoned them here, with a great amount of effort I can tell you. This," he said, indicating the Shadowbeast as it stood and faced Bael. "Is Vilec Roak. He is the most intelligent and powerful of them all, and so has been named Shadowbeast Prime. He shall command their ranks, General."

"Under your command, of course," said the flat-faced Vilec Roak. His head had what seemed like hair, and a twin set of yellow glowing eyes, but no other facial features to speak of aside from the horns. He gave Bael a stiff salute, and Bael reluctantly returned the gesture.

"Of course," mused Bael, looking Vandross in the eye. "I also must commend Beastmaster Valk, and request he get his own command as well." Bael looked miserably at the floor at Vandross's feet, while the Human chuckled.

"Very well, then. We have the necessary numbers to do that, and I've decided that the recruits who enter from now until sunrise shall be a separate command as well. Assign one of your best men to lead them, General."

Vandross crossed the tent to Bael, and draped an arm over his shoulder, leading him out of the tent. "Something troubles you, my friend," he asked in a light lilt, which disturbed Bael.

The reptile General stepped away from Vandross and turned to face him, his eyes filled to the brim with anger.

"You bring demons to the earth to your command, undermine my authority, and propose that we divide these Shadowbeasts into their own platoon, YES! Something troubles me! What of your original goals, my lord," he asked, a hint of desperation in his voice. He clenched his fists before himself in an angry plea to his master. "What of the grand kingdom you said you would create for the misbegotten of the world? What has happened to those plans?"

Vandross's jaw dropped, and he looked at the ground as if searching for something to say.

Finally, dumbfounded but with a smug look of superiority, he answered, "Plans change to meet the times. This army has a new standing goal. The whole of Tamalaria, and no insignificant kingdom, shall be mine to command, Bael. And you will help me."

"I will *not*," Bael shouted so loudly that all eyes in the camp turned towards the two men. Vandross took a step back, his face fallen into ashes. He shook his head, and very slowly appeared to look almost pitiful to the large Lizardman.

"Those were not my intentions, they never have been. I cannot help you in this if you do not tell me all that you intend."

Vandross suddenly turned to face him, tears in his eyes.

"Perhaps you are right, my friend," Vandross said, picking his words carefully, but playing the part as well as he could. "Besides, I could not have accomplished any of this without you. You, who have always stood by me," he added, knowing that Bael had a weakness for his own fealty.

Bael felt a surge of guilt rush through him, a tidal wave against which he had no defense. He had been there for Vandross since he had met the Human, and despite this change of course, he decided he would be there for the man now that he truly seemed to need him.

"I am sorry, my lord," Bael said, bowing. "I was merely flustered about the rapidness of changes made to our forces and situation. I lashed out at you, my friend. It shall not happen again." He stepped forward and put a heavy but amicable hand on Vandross's shoulders. "Your vision is true, my lord. Let us rest now, and prepare for Narfan's attack. It shall be a fine final trial for the men, for the town's small army is formidable. You'll see, sire, that our army has no equal. They have you to lead them, after all."

Vandross nodded his head, faking a rub at his eyes. *Damn*, he thought, *tears are quite difficult to fake these days.*

"Shall we go have a game of chess then, Bael? Commander to General?"

"No, sire," Bael said amiably as they entered the now empty tent. "Let us have a game, friend-to-friend."

Vandross cackled in his heart at the Lizardman's sentimentality. If Bael wasn't careful, and again voiced any form of dissent, it would prove his undoing.

* * * *

Byron and Shoryu lay on their beds in the inn, Byron trying to decide what their next move should be. Desanadron, a massive metropolis defended by a Paladin Order of Oun outpost, seemed like a fool's errand for Vandross. The other possibility lay in Whitewood, which would also prove highly defensible. Vandross would need a force of hundreds if not thousands of Lizardmen, Greenskins and demons to breach even the outer defenses of the Elven capital. It would take the one-eyed devil time to amass such a force, which thankfully bought Byron some time in making a decision. Whichever city he went to, he was in danger if his identity became exposed to the defenders. But they would need his help, he knew, to combat Vandross.

Shoryu, meanwhile, lay on his bed, staring at the ceiling and thinking about his home, reduced to so much blasted land. The thought of bittersweet revenge kept him awake and alert. For a while, he paced, unable to get any rest, but Byron had asked him to knock it off as it was keeping him from getting any rest. Shoryu once more got out of his bed, exiting the room to the sound of Byron's unnatural grumbling. The young Cuyotai Hunter crept down the hallway, past other doors, into the lobby, and finally out into the streets of town. Even at this dead hour of the morning, the city teemed with life and activity, though much of it leaned toward the illegal side of things.

Something gnawed at his mind now, however, and he did not find any immediate relief in the crisp night air. The sky held nary a cloud, revealing the stars in all their shining glory. The moon shone full, but had a baleful red cast to it. Shoryu looked from it to the street, his nerves a jumble. Something dreadful waited to be set in motion. He sniffed the air, catching a hint of jasmine and rosemary from the fortuneteller's shop across the street, and heard the muffled talk of ne'er do wells in a nearby alley. Every shadow seemed to stretch to improbable dimensions on the ground, as if the light of the tainted moon and the torches on the street dabbled in dark magics. The youth took a deep breath to steady himself, and then set off into the city's busier areas. Perhaps with more life around him the dread would dissolve somewhat, he thought. He thought wrong.

As he rounded a corner onto Permission Street, a road in Narfan that held all of the municipal buildings such as a school, the library, the City Hall and the Mayor's home, his fears became reality.

He tucked himself back around the corner, back to the wall of the City Hall, poking his snout around and watching as four armed men accosted an old merchant on his way home with his wagon of goods.

"C'mon old man," one of the cloaked figures teased, a spiked mace in hand. "We wouldn't want to hurt ya! We just want some things and we'll be on our way!"

The older man appeared to be a Human, but Shoryu couldn't tell what the thugs were, due to their concealing cloaks. One thing was certain: the small, waifish one appeared to be their leader.

"Thinking about playing hero," a tiny voice whispered in Shoryu's ear.

Managing to keep his calm, Shoryu slowly swiveled his head and saw Alex fluttering about two inches from his snout.

"I wouldn't if I was you," Alex said, shaking his head. "I don't approve. Of course, the master probably would, but lord Byron seems to be more suited for physical confrontation than yourself or I."

"Well we can't just do nothing," Shoryu whispered at Alex as he poked his head around for a check-up.

The mace-wielding thug now had the old man up against the wall, holding him pinned with a single muscular arm.

The Ki Fairy hovered closer to Shoryu, landing on the Cuyotai's snout.

Shoryu looked cross-eyed at him and squinted his eyes in anger. "The elder one is defenseless," he whispered. "My mentor told me that it is the duty of the strong to protect the weak and infirm."

"Oh, yes," Alex said, crossing his arms and taking on a sarcastic tone. "And look at how much that helped him."

Incensed, Shoryu flicked Alex off of his snout and rounded the corner, drawing his bow and notching an arrow.

"Get away from the elder one," he shouted.

Each of the armed men looked at him, one another's darkened hoods, and finally at the short leader. On a barely perceptible nod from him, the mace-wielder, whose face Shoryu now saw had an Elvish look, approached.

Foul Illeck, dark Elf, Shoryu thought with disgust.

Before the Illeck took three paces, Shoryu let fly an arrow into the thug's leg.

The man cried out in shock and pain, falling to his knees and clutching at the wound.

Shoryu had been satisfied; not a crippling shot, nor fatal, but enough to take the Illeck out of commission.

The other thugs looked once again to their leader, who was already running from the scene. The other two took his cue and made a break for it.

Shoryu rushed toward the old man to check on him.

"Oh goodness, thank you my boy," creaked the old man as Shoryu helped him to his feet. "I was sure I was in for one dilly of a pickle," he creaked, dusting himself off. "What's your name, young man," he asked, turning his kind, wizened face up to Shoryu.

"Oh, my name's Shoryu sir. Shoryu Tearfang." He gave a small bow, and the old man's eyes squinted as he smiled, his face resembling a prune.

"Well, Shoryu, may I ask what sort of magic your bow possesses?" Shoryu looked at the old man for a moment, perplexed. He had not seen any magical effect of his arrow in the Illeck.

"Why do you ask, elder one?"

"Because," creaked the old merchant once more. "That man appears to be dying from a flesh wound." The merchant's hand was extended, pointing at the fallen thug. Shoryu spun on his heel to look at the Illeck, whose flesh was turning green, and whose veins showed through the skin with a thick purple cast. As the dark elf crawled towards Shoryu, his eyes rolled back in his head, and his outstretched hand turned to dust.

Shoryu gasped at the sight, nearly retching.

"Well, no matter my boy, you had to do it," said the old man from behind him. He held a pocket watch out to Shoryu, who took it delicately. "A token of my appreciation, my lad. Now if you'll excuse me," he said, getting in front of his cart once more and grabbing the leads. "I have some cats who are possibly miffed that I haven't been home to feed them." And without another word, the old merchant walked off, cart in tow.

Shoryu looked down with mounting horror at the Illeck's corpse dissolved into dust

"Handy work, I must admit," squeaked Alex from his perch on Shoryu's shoulder.

"I never meant to kill him," Shoryu growled.

The Ki Fairy became suddenly skittish about his position in relation to the Cuyotai's jaws.

"Of course you didn't," Alex said from a comfortable distance as he fluttered away. "But the fact of the matter is, you did. That's life. After all, you didn't seem to mind killing those Lizardmen who attacked your home."

"Those were completely different circumstances," Shoryu snapped, baring his teeth at the little imp. "Our home was under attack by beings who wanted to kill us all, without regret or thought. These men were common thieves, and did not deserve murder."

Alex smiled knowingly as he fluttered closer to the angry Cuyotai Hunter.

"Didn't they?" A serious look passed over his minute face. "They would have killed that old man, and if given half a chance, you too. No pun intended kid, but it's a dog-eat-dog world out there, and you're going to have to toughen up to that fact. Besides, you saved the old man, didn't you?"

Shoryu's anger fled, a fleeting jackrabbit gone into the high brush. He hung his head, realizing that Alex, while not a very nice Fairy, spoke hard, simple truths.

"Yes, you saved the old man. Now come back to the inn and get some rest. You've earned it."

Shoryu followed Alex back to the inn, into his room, and finally into bed. He slept the sleep of the dead, dreaming of nothing but darkness.

* * * *

Byron's sleep was not so peaceful. He found himself standing in a graveyard, covered with mist and fog. The air smelled of rotted flesh, a stench so foul it offended even his sense of smell. He peered around, realizing that once again he seemed to be in control of himself in this dream. Dead grass cracked and shuffled underfoot as he slowly wandered around the cloudy graveyard, hearing the rustlings of the wind in this dark place. The fences and gates appeared shrouded in mist, and were backed by walls of pure black nothingness, as though this small area were the entirety of existence. A crooked, warped maple tree stood in one corner of the area he stood in, its branches twisted and contorted beyond the designs nature had intended. The taste of blood seemed firmly entrenched in his mouth as he stalked from grave to grave, trying to make out the writing on the tombs.

"Byyyroooon," a wispy voice echoed through the air.

Byron spun full round, his pinpoint lights darting around to seek out the source of that ghostly voice.

"What do you want?" he shouted into the blank air, his voice echoing as if he were in a canyon and not a burial ground.

"They are coming, Byron," the bodiless voice reverberated off of the black walls of space. "You must be ready for them, Byron. They have seen the boy, and return to their master to tell him of it. You must be ready for battle."

The voice faded out like an imagined image, and Byron blinked his eyes against the sudden, violent gust of wind that blew at him from all directions.

"Who is coming? Who is their master?" The wind howled so loudly he was certain his question was lost in it. A burst of light from the eye of the storm smashed him with the force of a thousand Mystic Force spells. He was thrown back twenty or so yards. As he struggled back to his feet, he felt a warm glow in the middle of his chest.

"Take this gift from me. It was once yours, but over time, you lost it," the voice said as the wind died. "Use it as you did in the time before. Farewell, Byron." These words echoed for some time, and Byron felt the ground under him give way, and was suddenly being toppled into nothingness.

* * * *

As dawn drew near, Richard Vandross shaved his cheeks, carefully looking in his mirror as he held the razor to his face. As he made the first pass, his tent flap flew open, and one of the Shadowbeasts he had sent into Narfan to scout out the area for their forces' last training trip entered.

"My lord, I bring news of grave import."

Vandross made another sweep with the razor, looking at the demon as it brought down its hood.

"Go ahead," he said casually, continuing his shave.

"We found a source of information, my lord, a Gnome by the name of Lee Toren. We saw him creeping from a store with a bag filled with stolen goods. We bribed him for information, but he told us more than the city's defenses. He knew the location of the next Orb of Eden's Serpent."

Vandross nearly cut himself as he spun his head to smile wickedly at the Shadowbeast. He already knew the direction he had to go, but a specific location hadn't made itself known.

"Where?"

"Desanadron, my lord. But that city is defended heavily, both by guards and a Paladin Order of Oun outpost."

"No matter." Vandross returned his attention to the mirror and the razor. "We can deal with those easily enough. Is that all?"

"No, lord Vandross. We lost one of our Illeck while holding up a merchant. You should know, sire, that it was the Cuyotai boy with the magical bow. Taisha, one of the Lizardmen that was with me, recognized him."

This time Vandross did cut his cheek, scraping the razor suddenly against his flesh. If the boy had survived, surely Byron of Sidius would be with him. He got to his feet and immediately began to pack up his tent, one of the last to be

77

taken down.

"What is your desire, master?"

"Get me Bael, now," Vandross screamed, throwing his things into their boxes and bags.

A minute later, the Shadowbeast returned, with Bael alongside him. Vandross tossed a bolt of lightning into the Shadowbeast, leaving a smoking pile of ashes and salt where it had stood. "Bael, change of plans. Take the newest recruits, and Valk with his new plaything. Take them into Narfan, and slaughter everyone. Burn that shitsplat little town to the ground if you have to!"

"My lord, what is the matter? Why are we not all going with them," Bael asked.

"We now know the location of the next Orb, Bael. That scout also said one of the Illeck who went with him was slain by that accursed Cuyotai boy from the village. Byron shall surely be with him. I want those two dealt with, once and for all. Do you understand Bael?"

Bael saluted stiffly, coming to attention.

"If they somehow manage to survive, and you feel the heat coming down, get out of there. I won't lose my greatest tactician just because his troops prove to be unworthy, do you understand?"

Vandross was on the verge of ranting, and Bael felt a wave of apprehension slam him full-on in his heart. Why was lord Vandross so concerned with a Cuyotai pup and a walking dead man? He could not understand his master's obvious fear.

"You have your orders, Bael! Get moving," Vandross screamed at the top of his lungs.

The Lizardman General rushed outside, barking assembling orders and getting the newest batch of warriors ready. A sense of dread stole over him as he looked up at the descending moon. It had a blood-drenched appearance, and he suspected this did not bode well for him. A red moon meant certain death for those who battled before the sun rose.

But orders were orders, and he had sworn fealty. Even in the face of death or lunacy.

* * * *

Byron felt himself falling, and came awake as he crashed face-first into the floor next to his bed. He knelt quickly, looking at Shoryu and Alex as they giggled madly.

"Sorry, Byron, it was the only way to get you up," Shoryu said through a bout of laughter.

"Simply hilarious," he grumbled as he brushed himself off and wrapped shadows around his body. "He put you up to this, didn't he?" He pointed an accusatory finger at Alex, who was rolling on the dresser top. "I assume you woke me up for a reason, other than laughing at my expense?" Byron adjusted his chest plate, and strapped his sword to his back.

"Indeed, good Byron." Shoryu sobered up suddenly as he remembered his encounter and his sense of dread. "I had an encounter this night with some thugs. I wound up killing an Illeck while trying to defend an elderly merchant."

"A noble thing, young one," Byron commented as he tied his dark blue cloak over his shoulders. "What of it?"

"Well, I've got this bad feeling, sir," he said, addressing Byron as his elder. Byron had said such formality was not necessary, but it seemed to be ingrained in the Cuyotai youth's head.

Byron moved over to the window and peered up into the sky, seeing the bloody moon as it set in favor of the sun.

"I had a dream last night that I think may relate to your sense of impending disaster, young one."

Shoryu stared at him with a puzzled look as Byron turned to face him. He already knew the question. "Yes, Shoryu, I dream," he said, drawing the curtain shut. *And what a dream it had been*, he mused inwardly. "I shall have to tell you about it some time. But not now. Now, we have to leave. We have to make ready for battle. Alex," he added, looking over to the Ki Fairy, who was already preparing his prank-based magic. "Good. Shoryu," he said, who had his bow in hand. "Good. Let's get out into the streets. It won't be long now."

In a few minutes, they had left the innkeeper with their room key, and had chosen a spot in a wide market street to wait for the inevitable battle. The scents of perfumes and spices filled the air, clashing and vying for control of the group's nostrils.

Shoryu, having the sensitive nose of a lycanthrope, began to question Byron's choice of location, but the Dread Knight soon explained himself.

"I have the feeling you won't be the only lycanthrope in this fight, so the air here is perfect to mask our presence for a little while. Depending on the size of the group coming, it may take a while for them to locate us. In the meantime, they'll tire themselves out fighting the soldiers of Narfan."

Shoryu gave him a horrified look, much to Byron's surprise. "We're going to let the soldiers here die fighting a pack of creatures that most likely seeks us? We should go out and meet these marauders head-on, Byron. We needn't let innocent blood be spilled."

Byron stood stiffly, firmly in front of the youth, and gripped his shoulders hard.

"They're trained soldiers, Shoryu. It's their job to defend their city, for better or worse. Those who serve this city know the risks inherent in their job. More than likely, those who seek us will not be enough in number or skill to defeat them all." Byron tried to smile at the boy, but his bones just wouldn't obey him. Instead, he patted Shoryu on the shoulder and returned to observing the streets.

For a while, nothing seemed out of place. And then the screaming began.

Far on the northern side of the city, the roar of battle erupted, and Alex fluttered high over the street to get a look at the attackers' forces and numbers. What he saw was nearly a hundred and fifty assorted creatures, a massive and feral Khan among them.

The Khan moved with deadly speed through the ranks of the civilians and soldiers, and bursts of magic erupted from somewhere near the western side of the city.

Alex sped down to Byron and Shoryu, screaming at the top of his little voice, "It is a small army, my lord! One hundred plus creatures of many sorts are rampaging through the city already." He darted looks both ways, and continued. "It is only a matter of minutes before they get this far my lord. The city's elite soldiers hold the western streets, but not for long, for there are magic-users in their midst."

Byron stood stiff, shocked at how badly he had miscalculated the situation. The Dread Knight balled up his fist and shook it uselessly.

"Shoryu, we shall stand our ground here. Everyone," he shouted, addressing the distressed crowd with his hands over his head. He removed the magic that concealed his appearance. "Everyone, flee! Danger comes this way."

More than a few people ran out of fear of him rather than of imminent attack. In moments, the street lay barren.

Alex swept the street, placing magical traps on the ground and rooftops. He came back, swooping past Byron with a thumbs-up signal, and Byron drew his sword.

"Alex, take another fly-over and tell us who will attack first and when."

Alex fluttered high overhead, zooming his sights in on the huge Khan. An ancient Lizardman in a green, tattered robe followed behind the Khan, apparently controlling the battle-frenzied beast. Alex flew in closer, and identified the two as the closest and possibly most worrisome threat. Elsewhere, the city's soldiers were putting up one hell of a fight against the oncoming legions, thrusting them back and felling their weaker members.

Alex swooshed past Byron's head, coming to a stop just in front of Shoryu, who knelt with his back to the Dread Knight, defending the street from the west. "My lord, a Khan Berserker and a Lizardman mage approach from the east. They will be here in a minute if they continue on their course."

"Lead them this way. A Khan Berserker will be too much for any mere soldier to handle."

Alex flew off. Behind him, Byron heard Shoryu let the first of his arrows fly.

The young Cuyotai stared down the throat of a wedge filled with Orcs and Illecks, and he landed an arrow in the soft belly of a charging Orc. A bright orange light glowed from point of entry, and a massive wave of fire swept out from the arrow, engulfing the entire wedge in a circle of fiery death.

"Keep it up, Shoryu," Byron shouted over the din of approaching battle. Looking towards the east, he saw his minute friend flying toward him as swiftly as a Fairy could, the Khan and reptile close on his heels. The Berserker stopped in his tracks, seemingly waiting for his companion to give him his orders.

"Ah, Byron of Sidius," hissed Valk from beneath his hood. "Lord Vandross was right," he said.

Byron's heart skipped a beat. These were all Vandross's men? He had scarcely had more than a hundred men only four days earlier. Did the Orbs of

Eden's Serpent give him the power to command such numbers? Surely that, and an experienced commander or two at his disposal.

"I had hoped that I could have confronted you in the Cuyotai village with my morenians," the Lizardman continued, "but alas, it was not to be."

Shoryu stood, staring wide-eyed at the Beastmaster.

"You," he shouted, baring his teeth and growling at Valk. "You helped that devil destroy my people!"

"That'sssss right, young Hunter. And now that genoccccide shall be complete! Bringel, crush them!"

The massive Khan screamed in rage and beat his chest, rushing forward with his massive axe in hand.

Shoryu and Byron both leapt aside as the deadly Berserker brought his axe crashing down on the spot where they had stood moments before. Byron landed with his feet splayed to either side, preparing to dodge the next attack and counter-strike, but the Khan rushed Shoryu instead.

Before Shoryu could react, the Khan used his fist like a mace, smashing into Shoryu's side and throwing him through the air like a dead bird. Shoryu landed with considerable force in a horse-watering trough.

"It's me you're after." Byron desperately tried to get Bringel's attention. He positioned himself behind one of Alex's traps, goading the Khan on. "Come and get me, you oversized throw rug."

With an earth-shattering roar, the Berserker charged Byron.

The Dread Knight moved aside and the Khan stepped on Alex's trap, a thin blue sheet of ice appearing over the Khan's head. Being the simpleton he was, Bringel stared in fascination at the sheet.

The ice quickly turned into a single massive stalactite, and fell at speed into the Berserker, smashing him into the ground with Aquamancy power.

Byron rushed to check on Shoryu, finding the bowman notching an arrow and loosing it into yet another attack wedge approaching from the east.

Once more the pack erupted in deadly flames.

Byron breathed a sigh of relief just as the Berserker sank its axe head into his back.

Yelling in pain and falling forward, Byron hit the ground and rolled onto his side, thrusting a single iron boot into the Berserker's groin as it pulled the axe out of Byron.

In shock, the Khan held its privates, dropping his bloodied weapon to the ground and falling to its knees.

Byron drew back his sword and gave a single stroke, decapitating the mighty Berserker. He breathed heavily, feeling at the wound in his back. The axe had drawn blood, something he had thought was impossible due to his body's state. *But then again*, he thought, *I haven't been seriously attacked like that for a good long time. Shouldn't come as any surprise.* He felt lucky that his armor had stopped the weapon from hitting his spine, much less cutting him in half. He and Shoryu both turned on the Beastmaster Valk, who gibbered in panic. Shoryu wobbled slightly, still jarred from Bringel's punch.

"Can I," asked Shoryu, his face soaked and his eyes flashing dangerously.

Byron simply nodded his approval, and Shoryu fired an arrow into Valk's face.

The resulting explosion rendered the Beastmaster a pile of singed meat that not even the most desperate dog would eat. Throughout the rest of the city, the Narfan soldiers, aided by Alex's clever use of magic, had beaten back most of the living forces. Alex flew to Byron and assured him that victory was at hand.

"Good. How bad were the town's casualties?"

Alex's head dropped slightly at the question.

"Nearly three hundred men and women, Byron. Almost every soldier is dead. Only the elites and the high commander remain, though the reserves haven't been called up yet. But the people have shored up their own defenses. Even that stupid Jaft you bumped into yesterday is fighting the good fight with his band of merry morons. Not that there's much of anyone left to fight."

"Except me," said a familiar voice. The Lizardman who had fought the Chieftain alongside Richard Vandross stood twenty or so yards away from the group, axe in hand. "I have given the order of retreat, Byron of Sidius. You have defeated lord Vandross's newest recruits. But that means little in face of the odds you are ultimately up against." Bael looked at Shoryu, at the enflamed anger lying there. "I am still needed to command my master's armies. We shall do battle one day, dead one. But not today." He put his blood-encrusted axe on his broad back. "I plan to fight you man-to-man, Byron. No friends, no sneak attacks. We shall do honorable battle, I vow it. But today, I concede that the Narfan soldiers and you three have done well. Besides," he waved his hand revealing Alex's traps. "I wouldn't want to fight on such turf. Would you?" Without another word, but with a pained grimace, Bael turned and stalked away.

Shoryu brought his bow up to fire at his back, but Byron put his hand on the bow, lowering it.

"Another time, young one. You'll get your chance yet."

Chapter Seven
Fort Flag

Richard Vandross's army had marched for five solid days when Bael and the remaining force from the Ja-Wen protectorate returned to their main body. General Bael stormed immediately to Vandross's position near the front lines of the march, reporting the results of the battle with Byron and Shoryu.

"So they killed both Valk and the Berserker," Vandross mused, a storm cloud looming over his brow. "And this Ki Fairy. What is it exactly?"

"They are a form of Fairyfolk that rely on trickery and magic, lord Vandross."

"All Fairyfolk rely on those things, Bael," Vandross retorted shortly.

"Yes, lord, but most tricks of Fairyfolk do not involve magical ice shanks and blades of fire gouging one's eyes and tearing one's scrotum." Vandross paused a moment, shivering slightly at the thought of total blindness or losing his manhood.

"Well, at least you didn't do anything rash, General." Vandross's army had moved out during the night that Bael's detachment had made for Narfan. They numbered now in the thousands, having grown exponentially as the collected Orbs of Eden's Serpent drew creatures with wicked hearts.

Vandross calculated they had at least three or four days lead on the Dread Knight, Cuyotai Hunter and the Ki Fairy. But marching so many it would slow their progress. He had to make certain he did not confront the trio before he reached Desanadron's gates, at least not without the full force of his army at his back. Perhaps it was time to truly test the Shadowbeasts.

"General," he said, "bring me the Shadowbeast Prime, Vilec Roak. I must speak with him."

Bael gave a quick salute and marched off through the wading masses of troops and battalions.

Something about Bael's movements and manner disturbed him. The Lizardman had seemed almost distant in his report, as if his mind and body stood miles apart from one another. Perhaps it was the prospect of another five or six days' march the Lizardman didn't like, or the fact that he'd lost so many of his detachment to Narfan's soldiers and Byron. The man was a military sort, but casualties meant more than just numbers sometimes.

Vandross himself felt the lash of defeat at the news that Valk had perished. A potential platoon of wild beasts had been lost with the Beastmaster's death. Mayhap Vandross would find another, but not likely one so masterful as Valk. He had to admit that sending the old reptile was a mistake.

Before he could brood much further, Vilec Roak stood beside him.

"Roak."

"Yes, master." The Shadowbeast nodded his hooded head ceremonially.

"I need you to run some interference. Leave two groups of five Shadowbeasts behind the army, one set to ambush the Dread Knight and his friends, and another to come in for support if things start to fall to shit. Make

83

sure they're both skilled and clever." He thought a moment longer, trying to figure out how best to delay the trio further. "Better yet, fetch Bael. Get some ideas from him. He's better at military tactics than me," he concluded bitterly. He had chosen well in selecting Bael as his General. But he had to start learning from the man if he didn't want to have to depend totally on him. The power of the Orbs would mean nothing if he didn't learn how best to use his army.

Vilec Roak shifted through the ranks of troops, slithering here and there like a venomous serpent, taking Bael by surprise as he slinked up behind him. "General," Roak said suddenly, making the reptile start. "Lord Vandross has ordered me to leave two detachments of five of my kin behind to distract Byron of Sidius from pursuit. He says I should consult you for tactical advice."

Roak's innards squirmed; he didn't like the reptile, and he could tell Bael didn't care much for him. A mutual distrust kept the two from speaking much, though they shared a similar responsibility to their lord. But though Bael didn't like him, he was a professional soldier. He knew and did his duty to his utmost ability.

"Right," Bael began, eyes directed forward. "Lay the first group in an ambush point, over a ridge perpendicular to their path of travel. Attack only when Byron has his back to them. Make sure they strike and scatter. Have the second group attack from the opposite direction. Again, strike and scatter. Have the first group attack again, and when they are slain, as I assure you they will be, have the second group head for the hills in any direction other than ours. Byron will not be able to resist the urge to follow and destroy them. He may even try to interrogate them. Make sure that your men die first."

Roak nodded, impressed by the General's ability to take a situation, however limited his resources, and make it work out in the end. He may not have liked the General, but he now respected him. Perhaps he too could do something to wring respect out of the old reptile.

Returning to Vandross, Vilec Roak stalked alongside for a few minutes. He knew of some of Vandross's new powers, including a few the Human had not yet discovered. But Roak had been around in the days of Tanarak, serving as a scout and spy for the dead warlock. "My lord," he began hesitantly. "Before I send those men, I wonder, have you yet tried to teleport any of the army?"

Vandross came up short, looking at Roak with a puzzled look.

"It was one of Tanarak's powers, sire," the Shadowbeast said. "He could create a one-way door in the air to send troops through, twenty or thirty at a time. I just thought, since Fort Flag is so near to Desanadron, they are bound to see us coming. Perhaps a distraction or a preliminary attack will weaken them, make them less likely to defend the Orb in Desanadron."

Vandross mused over this information a while, chewing on his upper lip.

A minute later, he closed his eyes and stopped marching, concentrating on the Orbs within him. He could not see anything, he just felt himself scaling into the canyons of arcane power that flowed through his body. A warm glow stretched through his inner being, filling his consciousness with the presence of the Orbs. He felt nothing beyond this perception at that time, his whole being locking out all other input.

He fought to maintain his connection to the Orbs, and for a moment, in his mind's eye, he saw them, two twin spheres of dark power.

What doth thou seek, he heard them ask in his mind.

The power to move men a great distance in an instant, he thought in response.

Concentrate, and open the gateway then, Richard Vandross. Some shall not make it through, but most shall.

He mustered his mental defenses and powers, bringing his magic into fluctuation around him. The air cracked with power, and his entire body began to tremble. The army had stopped marching, and had circled around their great leader.

His eye turned purest black, and his left hand stretched out to his side, launching a single bolt of black energy wrapped in ribbons of purple power. When he came back to full awareness, he saw at a rippling pool of purple energy in the shape of a gate.

You can send one score of men through there, to near the Paladin fort, the voices said.

"All right, I need twenty volunteers to go through here," he shouted over the assembled masses. "This doorway will bring you out near Fort Flag, the Order of Oun outpost! Your job will be to attack that outpost, and reduce its numbers as much as possible. I do not lie to you, this is a suicide mission, but it is in the interest of our greater cause. Who will go?"

A handful of Greenskins, two or three Lizardmen, another handful of Illeck, and two Khan stepped forward to complete the group. Without another word or question, weapons at the ready, the Greenskins filed through the gate, followed by the Illeck, the reptiles, and the Khan.

When all were through, the gate disappeared, and Richard Vandross fainted.

Bael ordered over a stretcher, and he and another Khan bore Vandross for the rest of that day until nightfall. When Vandross awoke, he sensed his men in the distance, attacking the walls of Fort Flag.

* * * *

Earlier that day, over a hundred leagues away, a single stoic figure stood atop a battlement wall. He was a stocky man, of a little less than six feet in height. His dusky, tanned skin and rough hands showed signs of a man who worked arduously on a daily basis. His half-plate steel armor shone in the high afternoon sun like a calm lake in the noon light. Well-developed muscles twitched on scarred arms, ready at any moment to snatch at his weapons, to defend his life and the lives of others. Thick black hair covered his blocky head, cut short and close to keep it out of his eyes and avoid being grabbed by a desperate opponent. And gray eyes looked out east over the plains stretching away from Fort Flag, into the distance of other lands.

His name was James Hayes, a Human Paladin in the Order of Oun. Though he had the appearance of a very tall Dwarf, with a thick, braided beard and a battle-ready gait to his walk, he did not possess their single-mindedness in matters of warfare. Dwarves locked onto a single target and flailed at it until it or they were dead. James Hayes observed all nearby threats, defended himself, and looked for opportunities. Thus far, he had survived with this strategy. At the moment, he patrolled the eastern wall of Fort Flag, keeping watch for signs of attacking forces. Though he normally went about his duties with little expectation of conflict, reports had been steadily coming in from other cities via messenger bird and horsemen. An army of some sort had been assembling, far east near the Allenian Hills and the city-state of Ja-Wen.

One particular scout, a Knight who had arrived the day before, had said that the leader of this army was the one-eyed warlock Richard Vandross. Vandross had been known to the Order of Oun for a while now, and some members of the Order even knew of his purposes. They had learned that Vandross had stolen and absorbed one of the Orbs of Eden's Serpent.

Until that time, the Orb they guarded had been kept in the safekeeping of a church in the city of Desanadron. But after many talks with the leader of Fort Flag, a Paladin by the name of Roderick Mensia, it had been agreed that the Orb would be best off in the care of the outpost. Though the city had a larger standing army, they agreed that the Order outpost was better suited to protecting the ancient artifact.

Hayes tapped his fingers along the stone parapet of the high fort wall. Since the scout had returned, his right arm had been itching to draw his sword and take a platoon of men out to meet this attack. But he knew he had to be patient. Best to let the enemy tire themselves out marching.

A pair of young Paladins approached him from the southern wall, laughing and cajoling each other. As they reached Hayes, they stood erect and saluted, trying to look serious and grim.

Hayes smiled at the youths, returning their salute. "How goes it gentlemen? May I ask what's so amusing?"

The two Humans looked at each other mischievously, deciding silently that the skinnier man would speak. "We are well, Captain," the young man said. "We were just joking around about what things must be like outside of the Fort. We've both been training here for four years, so we've sort of lost touch with the rest of the world."

Hayes nodded, agreeing with them that sometimes life inside the Fort was like being in an isolated country. He couldn't bring himself to say it, as he often left the Fort on assignment with his own detachment. These boys were just getting ready to take their final tests to become full members of the Order, and so they would only start asking questions if he mentioned what he'd seen of the world outside the Fort.

As the two boys walked past him, he thought about his first mission after he'd passed that final test. He had been sent with Byron Aixler's army to Mount Toane, to do battle with the warlock Tanarak of Sidius. The attack had been well-designed, but it had failed. Byron Aixler had supposedly died in the mountain, along with hundreds of others who joined the assault. James had been fortunate enough to be under the command of Lieutenant Grey, Rimzan's son, whose troop had been posted at the entrance of Mount Toane. When the mountain had trembled and the survivors of the infiltrating units had come fleeing out of the mountain, they had brought behind them all manner of Shadowbeast and undead creatures. Hayes had been skilled for a new member of the Order, but even he had suffered several injuries. He held his wrist up to the sunlight, looking at the long scar along the wrist where a Healer had reattached his hand after he returned to Fort Flag. He had decided to never transfer to another Fort that day. Fort Flag was home, it was sanctuary. It was where he had learned that even in the darkest hours, hope could shine bright.

Hayes was brought sharply out of his memories when he saw a glowing circle of energy materialize in the distance. Purple and yellow energies swirled, and a sound like a banshee's wail split the sky. Winds tore out of that hole, swirling through the Fort, tossing those sentries who didn't have a good balance down off of the eastern wall into the courtyard below.

None were injured too badly, having broken their fall on hay bails placed at the bottom of the wall for just such an event.

Blinking and squinting his eyes into the unnatural gale, Hayes watched as creatures began to pour out of the hole, each more aggressive-looking than the last.

Strangely, they did not attack immediately. Instead, they formed ranks in a militant fashion. When at last the rift closed, twenty foul creatures stood in formation. At the front, two Khan wearing some sort of black leather uniform barked orders at the assembled creatures, until from one of their shadows stood a single Shadowbeast.

"Sergeant," he heard the Khan say as they saluted the Shadowbeast. The demon appeared in the form of a hulking Jaft, bald headed and slightly blue-skinned, though the color was off due to the demon's nature. It wore a black uniform much like the Khan, with three yellow stripes on the right arm. There was a muffled exchange between the Khan and their leader, who looked at the wall with his baleful yellow eyes.

Hayes saw two of the access doors on the east wall open and thirty young Paladins poured out onto the field between the dark platoon and the east wall of Fort Flag.

The Shadowbeast motioned to the Khan, and they took up their positions at the front of the three-man files. The Khan on the left, whose fur was slightly more red than orange, raised his left hand flat-palmed to the sky. The entire force raised iron shields off of the ground, locking them into place at their sides.

"What's the situation, Captain?" Commander Mensia asked Hayes, who hadn't noticed the Elven Paladin at his side.

"They're using a phalanx formation, Commander," he replied, not looking away from the field. No one had made a move yet, each side seeming to be weighing the situation. "It's an old military tactic, wherein the shields are locked together to form a defensible, mobile wedge. I haven't seen one of them carrying any sort of scaling hooks or ladders, so I don't see how they intend to get into the Fort itself, sir."

Both Captain and Commander looked on in confusion, each trying to figure out exactly what the next move would be. But neither man expected what came next.

The Shadowbeast, standing in front of the troop, raised his hands over his head, magic sparking between his fingers. He thrust his head back and chanted. "Thundering force, come to my call. Tear asunder mine enemies' wall. Haaaargh!"

Thunder cracked, and a single fork of lightning blasted down from the cloudless sky into the eastern wall, throwing the defenders down to the courtyard and tearing apart the men who had gone out to meet the threat.

Hayes and Mensia had been fortunate enough to land on a barracks roof, but many of the others fell to their deaths.

"By Oun our god, the demon is formidable," Mensia exclaimed as he got to his feet. He looked around for Hayes, but the stalwart Paladin was already barking orders left and right.

Archers rushed toward the hole in the eastern wall, bows in hand, as the dark troupe advancing on the artificial entrance.

Hayes had the archers line up, and went up the line, endowing holy magic on the arrow tips. He raised his sword, looking out at their enemies, timing the release. When the Shadowbeast was within thirty yards of the archer line, he lowered his sword, and the twang of high-strung bows ripped the air. Two or three of the arrows hit solid targets, felling them immediately, but the remaining nine struck armor and shield, stopping.

Arrogant, the Shadowbeast approached at higher speed, until he sensed the fluctuation of magic. Turning around, he looked at his detachment as white light began to glow and the arrows quivered in their place. Before any of them could even panic, a white ring of shock wave erupted from the center of their ranks, leaving little more than a blasted stain on the earth. It had been easy to do, thought Hayes, but they had not acted quickly enough.

"Well done, men," Commander Mensia said as he joined the line of archer Paladins. "You there, Corporal! Go to Desanadron on a horse and find a Gaiamancer who can work this stone back together. And hurry! I don't think this is the last we'll see of these forces." He ran a hand over the shattered stone wall. "Hayes, prepare yourself and as many of your detachment as possible. We'll be ready for the next group." The Elven Paladin stormed off towards his private quarters in the Officers' barracks. Hayes found his First Lieutenant and gave her the order to prepare the men. He had some private preparation to do in the Fort's rectory.

* * * *

Byron and Shoryu made good time across the open flatlands, the grass supporting their steps with a sort of springiness. But as the afternoon rolled around, Shoryu's nostrils flared, and he sniffed the air a moment, holding his hand back to stop Byron and Alex. "I smell something unusually good Byron. The scent of creatures that follow Vandross, but which I never smelled before Narfan. There are four or five of them, coming our way."

Byron smiled inwardly, knowing from his own experience the way Shadowbeasts made a person feel and look around in paranoia. More than likely this was another attempt to impede the group's progress. Warned by Shoryu, he could hear the faint shuffling of their black, shadowy feet skimming along the ground. They were indeed close, but they were more in number than four or five. It was more like nine or ten.

Byron jumped forward, tucking his skull into his chest and rolling from shoulder to hip to avoid a sword through the back. Springing to his feet, the undead warrior drew his blade and stood ready, backing up until his back met Shoryu's. Oddly, there were only five Shadowbeasts, which puzzled Byron slightly. He had felt more.

Shoryu left his bow strapped to his back, extending his claws for melee combat.

The five black magic demons circled the two travelers slowly, almost dancing like children playing a game. Each had the physical shape of a large Human, and each held a sword. One of the five, the only one wearing actual mortal garments, also carried an iron shield, and his arm had three yellow stripes on it.

A sergeant, Byron thought. Definitely members of Vandross's outfit, but why were they so far behind? Wouldn't they be best served with another detachment for support? Before he could answer his own question, metal weapons were twirling through the air at he and Shoryu, and both blocked and dodged as best they could.

"Sorexia," Byron muttered under his breath, standing to his full height. The sergeant charged at him, plunging his sword hard at his breastplate. The Shadowbeast's blade bent and snapped in two on the hardened steel, which Byron had strengthened with a dark spell. His jaw hinges slid slightly up his skull, creating a sadistic grin.

The sergeant trembled and backed away, calling in his demon tongue for aid, but two of his comrades had fled from sight, and the other two were busy trying to hack at Shoryu.

Byron advanced slowly on the creature, feeding on its fear, swimming in its refreshing panic. He punched the creature hard in the stomach, doubling it over before him. The stench of vomit rose up as the creature retched the contents of its damaged stomach on the ground, making a noise like a dying canine. Its whole body quaked with the knowledge that its existence, short as it was, had come crashing to an end.

Byron grabbed the sergeant's head in his left hand, and gave a quick, sharp twist. The creature's neck snapped like a dry twig under the force, and its body dropped to the ground, disappearing in a cloud of dust.

Shoryu, meanwhile, had his hands full with the two Shadowbeasts who remained. Blow after blow he nimbly dodged, backflipping away and rolling to the sides of his attackers' assaults. Even he, however, could not evade such fury forever. Finally, he managed to create an opening, rolling aside from the larger demon's downward swing. Crouched like an animal, he swung a sweeping kick at the back of the shorter demon's legs, dropping it to the ground. He leapt on top of it, and snarled in its face.

He glanced up to see the larger demon straightening its legs for a downward stab. As the blow came down, Shoryu leapt up, pushing the sword down into the smaller demon that lay prostrate, and now, dead, on the ground.

The survivor backfisted Shoryu, knocking several teeth out of the young Hunter's mouth. Before either Shoryu or Byron could give chase, the Shadowbeast fled.

The two companions stared at each other. "Are you all right, young one," Byron asked Shoryu, trying to get a good look at the Cuyotai's face.

"I'm fine, Byron. My teeth will be replaced shortly, no worries about that. I think—" he began, but his eyes widened and Byron turned at the last instant, snatching the oncoming arrow out of the air with two armored fingers.

Byron's eyes burned crimson in their sockets, and he saw a short distance away five more Shadowbeasts, three with bows at the ready and two preparing spells of some sort.

Streaks of fire ignited before them and rushed across the field towards Byron and Shoryu.

"Get down," Byron screamed, tackling Shoryu. "Shigen-Shen!"

A blue arc rippled in the air in front of Byron, and he drew his sword once again, stampeding toward the Shadowbeasts.

The archers disappeared before he had covered half of the distance, but the spell-casters had prepared another volley of deadly Pyromancy. Two cones of flames shot out at Byron.

As they neared, the blue arc reappeared, and the cones reversed direction, heading for the casters.

Neither could move swiftly enough to avoid their own flames, but they did not die right away. Burnt and in agony, the Shadowbeasts wailed as Byron brought his heavy iron boot down on one's skull, and his sword down through the other's neck. Byron looked down at himself, and saw that some of the magic had gotten through his reflective barrier, singing his metal gauntlets.

Shoryu had spotted and shot dead the archers who had tried to flee. Byron returned to the pup once more, keeping his sword at the ready this time. Shoryu pointed south, and Byron followed his line of sight to the surviving couple of Shadowbeasts from the first pack. "We should follow them Byron," snarled Shoryu, strapping his bow across his back. But Byron shook his head, sheathing his weapon. "Why not?"

"A dog returns to its master when it is kicked in the street, Shoryu. But a clever dog, when kicked, leads the way to a larger, fiercer pack, far from the master. They seek to goad us into giving chase. But they are going to be disappointed." And so he and Shoryu walked on, continuing to march west at their own pace. They hadn't been delayed long, but Shoryu, due to a kick to the head, had lost his bearings.

They would have to make camp early, Byron decided, and he would watch guard over Alex and Shoryu. It was going to be a long night.

* * * *

James Hayes, Captain at Fort Flag, Paladin of the Order of Oun for nearly twenty years, knelt on the floor, praying toward the altar. His hands had turned knuckle-white, clenched together so powerfully he could not bring them apart. The scent of slowly burning candles filled the vestibule, caressing his mind and easing the knot on his wrinkled brow. At forty years of age, he had seen and done much. Mount Toane had been the ultimate test of his faith. But the destruction of the eastern wall upset the fragile balance of his hopes. Hopefully, the scout that had gone to Desanadron would return soon with a Gaiamancer to repair the damage to the Fort, and all would be back to normal.

A cool breeze rushed through the chamber as the aged oak door swung inward on rusted hinges. The squeak of aged metal grinding caught Hayes's ear and tortured it slowly, like nails on a chalkboard. He looked over his shoulder a moment, long enough to see Commander Mensia walk to the altar and kneel beside him. The old veteran hadn't aged a day in twenty years, but such was the way of Elves. They lived long, enchanted lives, with little danger of aging into a deathbed. Hayes, at only one quarter of Mensia's age, already felt the icy grip of old age claw at him. He still held skill and power, still retained the abilities of a master Paladin, but he did not look forward to another encounter with creatures of chaos.

"There is more trouble brewing, brave Hayes," Mensia said softly. "Our scouts to the north have not returned. The time of their return draws near, but I cannot sense them. I am afraid, Captain." He dropped his eyes to the floor.

James looked over at his Commander, a man he had known for all of his years, and the man who had hand-selected James for the Order of Oun. Mensia showed signs of his true age: his hair was graying in spots, his shoulders sagged slightly under the weight of his full plate armor, and his eyes had dulled from their once brilliant blue shine, to a soft sky colored hue. The Vow no longer sustained the Elf as it once had. Hayes could not look at the proud Paladin in his state, and so he looked away, once more at the altar.

"We will be enough to meet the challenges, sir. Repairs to the wall will begin soon. We shall be prepared."

Mensia stood and headed for the door, looking back at the stout Human. "You say that all is now calm, James Hayes," he said, his voice echoing hollowly off of the church walls. "But every storm has an eye."

Hayes remained still, his innards quivering. *The worst has yet to come*, he thought. *The worst has yet to come.*

"I'm going to send you and your men to Desanadron, James," Mensia said quietly.

Hayes gaped at his Commander, his question stopped by the look in the Elven Paladin's eyes.

"We're looking at a massive assault force coming our way, James, I know it in my heart. These walls, and the outskirts of Desanadron will soon be set upon by thousands, perhaps tens of thousands of enemies. Your unit must go to Desanadron to shore up their defenses."

"That's not the only reason you're sending us, is it?" James asked.

Mensia shook his head. "No, James, it isn't. I'm sending you to ensure your survival from oncoming attack."

* * * *

Richard Vandross grinned from ear to ear. His General and the Shadowbeast Prime had proved that they could work together. The two had talked at great length the day before, shortly after Vandross had dispatched his detachment to Fort Flag. They had combined their knowledge of the land, their rationing strategies, and their collective magic. After an hour or two of deliberation, they had both approached the warlock and reported that they had determined a way to increase the movement rate of the entire army and had already devised a plan to weaken Fort Flag.

Vilec Roak had reported that the detachment had been slain, but not before he detected the aura of the Orb of Eden's Serpent within Fort Flag itself. Capturing Desanadron was not necessary, but it would help in their strategy.

Bael had explained that Fort Flag was obligated to help defend Desanadron, despite the city's formidable standing military. At least one platoon would be dispatched from Fort Flag to defend Desanadron if it came under attack. Bael's plan was to deploy a large force to Desanadron and attack with full force, to lure Fort Flag's defenders from that Fort. They would leave men behind to defend the Orb, but their numbers would be significantly reduced.

Bael himself, along with Vilec Roak and Richard Vandross would lead a second force into the Fort while it remained weakened, destroy their enemies, take the Orb, and meet with the deployment in Desanadron. They would then lay waste to the city and claim it as a permanent training, recruiting and staging ground.

This last part of their plan, alone, Vandross disagreed with. He had his own choice for his army's home—Mount Toane, where Tanarak Sidius had ruled. Though he didn't tell them of his past with that dark place, Richard silently wondered if perhaps he might have left something behind when last he'd been within the confines of the mountain.

Both General and Prime yielded to his wishes, but they wanted to take the city anyway, to keep a constant presence in the west.

"Very well, General," Vandross said. "You may choose whom to put in charge there if you'd like. I'm very glad to see the two of you working together, by the way. I had gotten the impression that you would try to kill each other." Vandross laughed mirthlessly, not knowing that Vilec Roak, respected Bael, but did indeed intend to kill him and take the mantle of General.

"Lord Vandross, I shall assume control of the city once we have command of it," Bael said, standing at attention. Vandross hadn't expected the Lizardman himself to take responsibility for the city. Besides, he would still need him around. *Or,* he thought, looking at Vilec Roak closely, *will I? The goodly General has been awful outspoken about my changes in plans, after all.* Yet another thought he would let stew a bit.

"No, Bael, I cannot allow that. I need both you and the Prime."

Bael had saluted and gone off to talk with his elite soldiers. Vilec Roak had disappeared too, but returned as Vandross mulled over the meaning of the previous day's accomplishments.

"My lord," Roak began, bowing ceremonially. "Our spells have more than tripled our travel rate. We shall approach Desanadron from north tomorrow. At least, our main force shall. We can make it to Fort Flag within hours from our chosen campsite. What shall we do until then?"

Vandross thought the question over for a moment, then shrugged his broad shoulders.

"Have everyone prepare. When the scout from Desanadron returns to our position after the Order dispatches defenses to the city's aid, we shall launch our assault on the Fort. Aside from that, we wait, and make ready. Has Bael chosen a commander for the city and Fort once they are taken? If they are taken? After all, Desanadron is a rather large city, Prime."

"Indeed, sire," Roak hissed, grinning broadly. He approved of the General's choice, as it didn't take any of Roak's own warriors. "Captain Sorm, a Black Fur tribe Werewolf. He is a powerful Knight with use of some Aeromancy spells, sire."

Vandross nodded his acquiescence. Bael's influence in the plan to take Desanadron laid thick atop it, like the upper layer of stew that most men skimmed off. If his own goals had not been so radically altered, Vandross may have been content to make the city-state of Desanadron his own and call it quits. But he wanted more, now. With just one more Orb of Eden's Serpent, he would have powers he had never dreamed of. With only two, he could command all of these creatures, could create portals of teleportation, and had increased the power of his own magic tenfold. He could rule the known world with three, but he still had Byron of Sidius to deal with. Delay tactics would not work on the Dread Knight forever, that much was certain. He would eventually have to send a worthy opponent at Byron and his companions.

If he only had a third Orb already in his possession, he might be able to repeat an experiment of much earlier days, days before he had even been known in the lands of Tamalaria. Quite by chance, the warlock had once summoned up a very powerful demon from the Seven Hells, and had been forced to entomb its essence in a safe place until he could release it into another mortal being, preferably one near death. The opportunity did eventually come along, and without exactly snapping his fingers, Vandross abruptly remembered what he had once left in Mount Toane—Molis.

But he could not control Molis, not completely. He could only ensure, back then, that the creature would never do him harm directly. Having done that, he ordered the creature to slumber, until one day he returned for it. *And oh*, he thought, *I shall return in the most grand of styles.*

But for now, his plans would continue on as they were. "Very good, Roak. You are dismissed."

The Shadowbeast went to join his kindred, leaving Vandross to plod along with his army alone. This didn't bother him; on the contrary, he needed time to be alone for now. Time to think without someone waiting for an order or response. Time to envision the chaos and destruction of Desanadron and Fort

Flag.

* * * *

Though the attack had seemed very structured, militant, and purposeful, James Hayes still could not figure out the attackers' intent. A Shadowbeast in a uniform with sergeant's stripes had led them. Yet they had only accomplished the temporary destruction of the east wall, currently being re-formed, and a few casualties among the Order.

Hayes found sleep difficult that night as he thought about what Mensia had said: 'Every storm has an eye'. If the attack had been the outer fringes of a storm, however, it wasn't a very big one. Hayes slept fitfully, waking up before the sound of reveille.

He dragged himself to his washroom, using the toilet and then looking long and hard into the mirror. Thin scars pulsed at him from years long gone, battles fought in the name of the Order, battles fought in the name of decency. He ran a stubby finger over the latest scar, a thick slash just in front of his left ear. He had gotten it five months ago, when he and his own unit had gone south to the Cave of Urduros to do away with the demon's son, who had taken over the Cave a few years earlier and had begun to summon other demons from the seven Hells. Urduros's son, Urbaro, had been a huge bat-demon, and had nearly split Hayes's skull in half. But Hayes had dodged enough of the weapon to launch a counterattack that killed the demon.

The Cave had been sealed by Paladin lore, and none but the Order could enter. It had been decided that as a last resort, the entire platoon of Fort Flag would retreat to the Cave to regroup. But an enemy would first have to take Fort Flag from the watchful and vengeful hand of Commander Mensia. Hayes smiled at himself in the mirror. Fat chance of that happening.

He continued to smile and look forward to the day as he donned his armor and weapons. He didn't yet know that what had occurred before with the fort wall was only the foretelling winds of an enormous storm, not the storm's eye.

* * * *

As Byron rose groggily, he shook his head and went down to the stream to get some water. He hadn't fed for several days now, since meeting Shoryu. He hadn't want to frighten the Cuyotai youth by revealing the extent of his twisted nature, but Byron had to absorb blood through his bones for sustenance in his current body. He had not done so since he had slain the Lizardmen outside of Shoryu's village and was growing weak as a result.

Kneeling by the stream, he cupped his gauntlets and scooped some water up to his exposed throat. His flesh began just under his collar plating, and he poured the liquid directly into his throat. He had done this with the scotch too, but water felt much more refreshing at the moment. No matter how satisfying the stream's water was, however, he needed blood for strength.

Shoryu came trundling up to Byron, a half-hearted smile on his face. "Well, while we didn't go for those Shadowbeasts' bait last night, I'd say they still did their job. I have smelled much magic in the air, though I could not discern the nature of the spells used. However, from the look of the tracks they've left behind, they used magic to accelerate their movement rates by at least three or four times normal running speed."

Byron passed a hand over his skull, trying to focus.

"So we've lost a good deal of time on them by resting," he mused under his breath, but he remembered Shoryu's sense of hearing. "Well, we'll just have to try to make up for that lost time. Get your things ready, Shoryu," he said, walking towards the camp. "I'm going to go get us some game for later. A small animal should do." Byron moved away swiftly, jogging out of Shoryu's sight. He continued jogging until he saw a large buffalo, probably straying from its herd.

Byron wasted no time, drawing his sword and rushing at the beast blade-first, hacking it into several dozen gory chunks. He grappled with the beast's heart, tearing it from protecting bones and organs, squeezing its life-giving blood onto his ivory-hued skull.

Dropping the crushed organ, he felt power racing back through his body, sensed a small, buried part of himself come alive. The lights in his eyes flashed crimson for a moment, and returned to their dull white shine.

He looked at the pathetic creature's remains, and chastised himself for his weakness. He had to absorb energy in this way, though, if he was going to go after Richard Vandross. It was a necessary evil, one he needed to stay alive. And he could not take small amounts of blood by simply wounding, for he did not just take the life essence of his feeding victims, but also a measure of their sanity and self-control

He looked at his gauntlets, and after a moment, removed the left one. Half of his hand was rotted away, revealing stringy muscles and bones. "This isn't quite being alive," he muttered to no one in particular. Replacing the gauntlet, he ran back to Shoryu, a slab of buffalo meat in hand. The Cuyotai seemed distracted, and didn't ask any questions, which was fine by Byron. After a meal shared in silence, the two men and Alex hurried off west, toward Desanadron and Fort Flag. They were a full two and a half days behind Vandross's army. But luck seemed to be on their side.

As the pair moved through the high grasslands, Shoryu brought Byron up short with a gesture of his hand, motioning the large undead warrior to lie down and hide in the grass. Despite his bullheaded nature, Byron did as he was told, in a manner of speaking, and waited.

There was a short conversation, Shoryu speaking in Elven to a pair of gentlemen. There was a gale of laughter, and then the clomping of hooves. Shoryu reappeared, a horse tether in each hand.

Byron stood to his full height, grinning like a madman, as much as his face would allow. "How did you, pay for these Shoryu?"

"'E didn't," said a familiar voice as Lee Toren hopped down from one of the horses. "I was escortin' these babies to a little place I keeps in the region. Me men was 'appy to lend 'em to ye, old friend," he said, limping over to Byron. The Dread Knight gaped in dismay at the sign of bruises and lacerations on Lee's face and chest. Lee looked up at him with one half-shut eye, swollen so by a large bruise. "Case you's wonderin', a couple a beasties did this ta me in

Narfan, night afore the attack." Lee looked at the ground in shame. "They caught me coming from a friend's house-"

"In the act of a robbery," added Byron.

"-an 'ey says, hey you there! Yeah you! You seem to know your way around here! Tell us 'ow many guards is in this city!"

"Except they used better grammar, I'm sure."

"Now's not the time fer semantics mate," Lee continued, scowling at the Dread Knight and snickering Cuyotai. "Anyways, I tells 'em, bugger off you lot! The mighty Byron of Sidius is 'ere, and he'll tear you and yer friends apart! So they gets all fidgety, start landin' blows down on me 'ead, as you can plainly see," he said, pointing to his swollen eye. "They wants to know how I know you, and they starts cuttin' me wiv a knife! I sort of told them what I tol' you in the tavern, mate. Just to get them to goes away, you know?"

Byron shook his head, putting one hand to his forehead in embarrassment for his little friend. He didn't hold it against Lee; he was a thief, it was what they did.

"So next day, me an' the boys is sittin' around in our hidey hole, waitin' fer me to heal up afore we leaves, and all hell breaks loose in the city. So we deals with it like real men, roight?"

"You ran and hid."

"Hey, I didn't say we did it like real bloody foolish men, just real men," Lee interjected on his own behalf. "Well, when everything quiets down, we goes to a chum's place and borrow a couple a horses, as I intended to get as far the hell away from all this business as I could."

"You went to the stables and stole them."

"Same difference mate, same difference. Only as we's traveling, we narrowly avoid being spotted by a large army of some sort. Looked a lot like the fellas we hid from in Narfan, so we decided to fall off the pace a bit. Then yesterday, we thought we spotted a couple of dead Shadowbeasts lying about, and I thinks to meself, well gee whiz, 'o coulda done somefin like this?" He smiled amiably up at the Dread Knight and Shoryu, revealing large gaps in his teeth.

"Did those men punch out your teeth too," asked Shoryu softly, truly concerned for the Gnome Pickpocket's health.

"Wha, these? No, I just need to bone up on me personal hygiene 'abits boyo," Lee said.

Shoryu visibly deflated as Lee tore the air with his gut laughter. "Well, we're very near to me local hidey hole, friends. These are yours, then," he said, patting one stallion on the leg. The three-foot nothing Gnome turned his back nonchalantly to the three travelers and made his way back to his own men. Before he went down off of the hill they stood atop, he turned back to face them, a sober look on his face. "Be careful, mates."

Byron thought long and hard about how lucky he had been with his choices of friends in life. And Lee was practically married to lady luck.

* * * *

Vandross's army had made camp, and the force that would march on

Desanadron had already departed. The entire day had passed by like a flash, the army moving rapidly across the plains despite having no steeds. Vandross himself sat in his tent in the smaller camp north of Fort Flag, whiling away the time with Bael and yet another tournament of chess.

The reptile General had trounced him three times out of the four games they had played, but the one-eyed devil kept his composure. No need to get angry at a silly game at this point, he thought. He was so confident and relaxed that he began playing recklessly, carelessly moving his pieces into position without even thinking. The last match he'd won entirely by chance, because Bael had been so focused on strategy that he hadn't even bothered to see that Vandross had made checkmate by simply moving a bishop into position. Bael had trapped his king while trying to defend him.

But the momentum had quickly turned back in Bael's favor. He took less time defending, more time attacking. In a matter of six more moves, he had declared checkmate. "You're not even trying, are you my lord," he asked as he rearranged the pieces.

"I've got bigger things on my mind, General," Vandross replied lazily. He had done away with his armor for the night, preferring to sit in his old tunics.

Bael made no comment, and began the next game. Halfway through, a Shadowbeast came panting into the tent.

"My lord, Byron of Sidius survived our attack," panted the surviving creature. "Myself and Rodan escaped, but only barely. My lord, you must prepare the entire camp to defend against him! Surely we will all be killed by him if we do not prepare!"

"My foolish little friend," Vandross said soothingly. "Vilec Roak and several Illusionists have disguised this whole area. The Dread Knight will never see us. Besides, you were but ten men. We here have hundreds against them."

"How then did I find you," jabbered the Shadowbeast, quivering with fear and doubt.

"Because you are one of my own men, demon," Vandross said, not looking up from the chessboard.

Bael had stood and faced the cowardly demon. He had his axe in hand at his hip, his legs braced. "Are you so afraid? Then you may leave." The Shadowbeast smiled broadly, pleased to be spared the trouble of dying at Byron of Sidus's hands.

"I can?"

"Of course. Bael, show him the way out." Vandross smiled toothily at the demon, whose eyes widened in panic just before his head came rolling off of his shoulders. Bael kicked the body of the creature he had just decapitated to the ground, and in a moment, it faded into ashes.

"Bael, why do only some of these creatures disappear like that when they die and not all of them?"

"The weaker ones dissipate, sire," Bael said as he returned to his seat. "Checkmate."

"Good. I don't want to bother leaving signs of weakness." Vandross moved from his seat to his cot. "Good night, General."

"Good night, sire," said Bael as he left the tent.

Tonight, Vandross thought, the attack would begin on Desanadron. Tomorrow, he would have the third Orb.

* * * *

James Hayes was in prayer beside his bead when Commander Mensia barged into his chambers, winded and wide-eyed. The reek of sweat came from the hallway, more specifically from a scout covered in wounds.

Hayes got to his feet immediately, absolute dread coursing through his veins like a cobra's venom.

"Hayes, get ready and get your men," Mensia rasped in a harsh rush. "Desanadron is under assault! Make ready your squadron and ride out now!"

Hayes hadn't bothered to salute, as such situations tended to favor expedient action over military formality. In moments he was armored and equipped, and he took his necklace with the Order's deity symbol adorning it. He would need all the heavenly aid he could get.

James Hayes and Commander Mensia stormed through the enlisted and officers' barracks, getting the captain's unit up and prepared. Horses had already been lined up outside of the fort. Although it was still the middle of the night, he could not hear the normal sounds of crickets as he walked through the west-facing gates of Fort Flag, nor could he smell the familiar and calming scent of the flower gardens. Instead, he heard the sounds of far off battle, smelled smoke and attar, and in the distance, four hours ride away, he saw flames shooting up from the great city of Desanadron like beacons that warned of doom. No doubt the creatures that had attacked the day before had come from that force. He would have to be swift, and he would have to charge the stallions that bore his men harder than he had ever done. More than a couple would likely pass out on the way from bearing a load of around three hundred pounds of fully armored and equipped Paladin at maximum run.

His unit numbered seventy-two men. Among them were fully trained and ordained Paladins, Knights who had not taken the Vow, and Clerics to perform healing and supportive spells. Surely, when combined with the might of the Desanadron army, they would prove enough. But if more of the Shadowbeasts like the one who had decimated their eastern wall stormed through the city, both his unit and the Desanadron people would suffer great amounts of casualties. Such was war.

As he took his unit of brave warriors out of Fort Flag at high speed, he felt suddenly vexed. He felt the glare of eyes upon him. Or more accurately, although he did not know it, he felt one eye.

* * * *

Richard Vandross had not been able to rest. He lay on his cot for hours, but as the night dragged on, his nerves began to jump and quiver. Finally, he swung his hairy legs over the side of the cot, clenching the side of it until his knuckles whitened and a soft groan from the wood told him it would soon break under his grip. Vandross stood and dressed and armored himself. He packed his belongings and then his tent, knowing that all the while, several of his minions watched with grins spreading over their faces.

The one-eyed devil almost jumped as Vilec Roak arose from the darkness on the ground.

"What stirs you from your slumber, sire," asked the Shadowbeast Prime.

Vandross looked into the distance, at Fort Flag. He watched as a large squadron of the fort's defenders left at break-neck speed for the city of Desanadron, which was already under siege.

"Nothing, Roak," Vandross said with a smug smile. "I haven't slept. Our opportunity to strike nears. Get Bael and wake everyone up. We attack in an hour."

The Prime saluted and slinked off into the night, first awakening Bael from his bedroll on the ground.

The General had seen little need to put up a tent if they would be attacking in the early morning, and seemed not bothered at all when awoken and told to get his men ready. Indeed, he seemed almost devoid of emotion.

Roak made a note of this, for he could sense that something had broken within the General. He and Bael roused the troops, forming them up into ranks to prepare for the charge on Fort Flag. The Shadowbeast returned to Vandross's side when all the preparations had been made, leaving Bael to give some sort of inspirational speech to the minions.

"Everyone is ready, sire." He saluted the one-eyed devil.

Vandross smiled broadly at Vilec Roak. Such a creature is fit for command, thought Vandross. Bael is good, but he's just a soldier. And the third Orb would give Vandross more knowledge and dark powers than any other warlock in the land. He wouldn't need the Lizardman General after the third Orb was his to command. Additionally, Vilec Roak would not question his orders or goals, regardless of how they might change. Roak had shown an ability for military tactics, something that Bael had as well. However, the Lizardman didn't have the powers of dark magic that the Prime held at his fingertips and he had been asking disturbing questions—questions that proved his loyalty was not absolute. If Bael survived the assault on the fort, Vandross decided, he would not survive for long.

"Good, Roak. Very good. By the way," he said, placing his hands on the Shadowbeast's shoulders. The feeling of arcane power flooded through his hands, and he knew now why Tanarak of Sidius had used these creatures. They were powerful, possessed of unearthly magics and lore. They were perfect soldiers. And they were very hard to kill, unlike the Lizardmen, who he had to constantly use Bael to control. "I have one more order for you when this is all said and done, Roak. You see that man," he asked, pointing at Bael, who was still pacing back and forth in front of the assembled ranks, most of whom were Orcs and Shadowbeasts. Most of Bael's faithful reptiles had gone to Desanadron.

"The General, yes sire. What of him?"

"When the third Orb is in my power, take him east of the fort and kill him," Vandross said, and Vilec Roak's yellow eyes widened, but not in shock. Razor-sharp teeth glinted in the moonlight. "It is time for a change of command."

"As you wish, master." Vilec Roak bowed deeply. *And to think,* he thought to himself, *I had so many plans of killing him on my own.* Pleased beyond belief, the Shadowbeast rejoined Bael as he finished his speech.

An hour having passed, Bael and Roak led the march on Fort Flag. Vandross walked behind his death-corps, his sword in hand, his magic prepared.

Within another hour's time, the outermost defenders atop the northern wall began shouting into the fort, and the great gates on the west wall were shut. Arrows whistled through the air, thin wooden harbingers of death, but none struck the troops under Vandross's command. Shadowbeasts had put up a mystic shield over the squadron, and as they got nearer to the wall, the entire unit broke ranks and charged the fort walls.

Dark and holy magic lanced back and forth in the air, lighting the sky like stars, and Vandross stalked through the battlefield as members of the Order were dispatched through hidden access doors in the outer wall. A pair of young Paladins approached him at speed, swords in hand. With a flick of his wrist, he sent a burst of force slamming into them, throwing them into the stone wall at fatal velocity. The crunch of armor and bones exploded in his ears, and the wet splurching noise of blood shooting out of the Paladins' mouths were music to his ears. The thick, musty smell of discharged magic flowed through his nostrils, and he breathed deeply of its vapor.

Vandross finally got to his destination, ten yards from the northern wall.

He sheathed his sword and called defenders to his side, each swinging their weapons wildly to keep him safe.

Vandross waved his hands in the air, muttering under his breath. Arcane shapes traced themselves where his fingers passed, and the ground rumbled with raw magical energy. Yellow glowing light flared from the sigils he drew, and his muttering became louder, more rapid. Soon all that could be heard over the clang of steel and the screams of the dying was his lone, tenuous voice. Finally, he threw his arms wide in the air and screamed. As he bellowed, the northern wall of Fort Flag exploded toward its own defenders.

Spurred by their master's display of power, Bael and Vilec Roak's men charged into the courtyard of the fort. Vandross, however, felt drained and weak. He crouched for a moment, breathing hard with his hands on his knees.

"My lord, are you all right," said a familiar voice. Vandross looked up to see the concerned face of his General staring intently at his face.

"Yes, I'm fine. These new powers of mine will be easier to control with the third Orb. Now let's get in there and get it."

Vandross stormed inside the courtyard, following the throbbing pulse of the Orb of Eden's Serpent to a small church. It called him to it, summoning him to take it for his own.

He marched through packs of combatants, avoiding direct contact with them and moving straight toward his destination.

With a heavy armored boot, he kicked in the twin oak doors, sending them flying off of their hinges. And there, on the lectern, sat the third Orb of Eden's Serpent. In front of it, blazing holy sword in hand, stood a tall Elven Paladin, his eyes squinted with righteous fury.

The fully armored Elf took two steps toward Vandross, who straightened up and smirked. "Trust me holy man," he mocked. "You don't want to get between me and that artifact."

The Elf said nothing, advancing another two steps. Only ten or eleven yards separated the two of them when a stray blast of Shadowbeast magic launched into the church, setting the inside ablaze. The crackle and smoke of fire filled the air of the small church, embers flying around the two men as they stared each other down.

The Paladin, Commander Mensia, had trained all his life for a battle like this. He had summoned up the power that lay dormant in his blade, which had been wielded by the great Rimzan of Grey before his death shortly after the defeat of Tanarak of Sidius. Though the warlock had used his last breath to curse Rimzan to his grave, the Morning Glory, his great and holy sword, had remained unscathed. And now Mensia possessed its might, as well as his own magic and swordsmanship. He would stop this one-eyed menace here and now.

Commander Mensia took an attacking stance, his eyes set on Vandross's face.

The warlock smiled broadly and spread his arms wide in a taunting gesture.

Mensia lunged forward, two hands on the handle of his heavy sword.

Vandross easily dodged the first downward strike, and even danced aside from a horizontal slash, but he hadn't foreseen that the Paladin was setting him up.

A bolt of white energy rocketed from Mensia's palm into his chest, shaking Vandross where he stood and tossing him through the air to the back of the church.

He landed in a heap on the floor, falling twenty feet from where the blast had knocked him. Growling, he spat a loose tooth out of his mouth, bringing his magic to bear. Purple waves of force encircled his hands, and his eye glowed crimson with dark power. He stood from behind the table he'd nearly fallen on, calling on the power of the Orbs.

The region trembled as he screamed incantations in a tongue long since dead, weaving shapes of magic in the air.

Mensia tried to move toward him, but gagged on the smoke from the fire and the stench of rotted flesh that suddenly permeated the air around him. Eyes filled with tears, he dropped to one knee, bracing himself with the Morning Glory. His skin felt hot and wet under his armor and clothes, and he had the sensation that something, many somethings, were crawling all over his flesh. The sound of Vandross's voice became alien both in words and in tone, and as Mensia looked, thousands of strange, winged insects poured through a hole in the floor of the church. He watched in horror as hundreds of them poured through the links and gaps in his armor.

He realized all too late that they were feeding on him, burrowing into his skin and sliding through his insides. Like small knives their mandibles ripped through his skin and muscle.

In agony he screamed and flailed on the ground, kicking and thrashing about like a madman.

Richard Vandross stood over him, chuckling. "Do you like them? They're called Hell Beetles. Shadowbeasts, who once served as torturers and now serve me, told me about them. Quite painful, isn't it," he asked in a tender, jeering voice. He threw his head back and roared with laughter as Commander Mensia spasmed with pain.

The end would come soon, Vandross thought. This Paladin will be dead within two minutes. Turning his back on Mensia, however, proved a nearly fatal mistake.

With the last vestiges of strength left to him, the Elven Paladin swung his weapon up, and Vandross barely dodged a blow to the back of the head. His dodge was not swift enough to save his right arm from the elbow down. With a wet smack, his limb fell to the ground, and the holy power of the Morning Glory burned him as nastily as the Hell Beetles burned Mensia.

Screaming like a wild beast, Vandross turned and aimed his left hand at Mensia, releasing a bolt of lightning magic into the Paladin and reducing him to smoking meat.

Come to me, Richard Vandross, called a voice nearby. *Come quickly, and be restored!*

Vandross walked to the Orb of Eden's Serpent, holding his severed arm at the elbow. He was losing blood at an alarming rate, and wondered if he even had the strength to absorb the third artifact.

Worry not, tainted one, said the voice to him. *You have my brethren, and so I shall willingly join you. I have searched your soul, and find you fit to command my power.*

Vandross held the Orb of Eden's Serpent over his head with his left hand, and the purple vortex engulfed him, as it had twice before. Wind howled through the church, dousing the flames around him from sheer velocity. The Orb disappeared, and fire ran through his right arm to the elbow. Doubling over on the floor and clutching at his arm, he watched as a new limb appeared, black scaled and clawed at the fingers. In wonder he flexed his new fingers, enjoying the strength he felt in his new arm. Forgetting his pain, forgetting his trouble, he listened with his eye closed as the Orb passed its wisdom and knowledge on to him. Enraptured by its voice, he knelt in the church for a long time.

Finally, he heard the sounds of battle dying down outside of the church in the fort proper. His forces had destroyed Fort Flag. Satisfied with his victory, Vandross prepared to leave, when something glinted to his left, catching his attention. The Morning Glory. A magnificent blade, surely, he thought. I think I'll take it. He stooped down to pick up the sword with his new arm, but the weapon pulsed, and a field of magic repelled his touch. The light burned just to look at, and Vandross hissed at it, spitting on the weapon and leaving the church.

Vilec Roak met him outside with a salute. Only three-dozen men had survived the bloodbath of the courtyard, and when he looked around, Vandross could not see Bael. "Vilec Roak, where is the General?"

"Sire," Roak said, a razor-toothed smile spreading across his lips. "He has been dealt with, as you requested."

Vandross smiled and nodded at his new General. The majority of the survivors from the battle were Vilec Roak's brethren, but a few Lizardmen who had come looked dejected and battered. One of them called to Vandross, asking where the General was.

"It is unfortunate, but he has been slain in combat, my minions." The Lizardmen looked even more depressed, despite their apparent victory. "Fear not, though, for I have established rules of ascension in the chain of command. As Prime, Vilec Roak will now be named General of this army. Out of respect for the late General and as thanks for your work for me, reptile warriors, I give you the chance to leave my army if you so choose. Bael was your leader in more than military affairs, I know! He was a father figure to many, and his defeat seemed impossible! But I shall not sully his good name or memory by keeping you against your will. You have fought bravely, and no one can take away from you what has been done here today! If you leave, go with pride, and the knowledge that when I rule this land, the Lizardmen nations shall be befriended and honored!"

The unit, including the Lizardmen, raised their weapons and cheered, Vilec Roak included. He knew how to play along.

After the celebrations and much talk over meals consisting mostly of fallen Paladins, the Lizardmen all formed ranks, saluted Richard Vandross, and left Fort Flag. None remained under his command save those that had gone ahead to Desanadron.

Vilec Roak sipped his brandy that Vandross had offered him, looking at the reptiles' backs as they left into the southern distance. "Shall I have them killed, sire?" Vandross smiled, but shook his head as he closed his eye and thought.

"No Roak. They served us well. But they are an inferior brand of warrior and I would have eventually ordered them to leave. Let them give their respect to a good leader."

Vilec Roak stared at Vandross a long moment before taking another sip of this foul mortal drink called brandy.

"Do you regret your decision to do away with the General," he asked.

Vandross didn't appear to have heard him as he lounged on the floor of the courtyard, thinking about the trip to Mount Toane they would all soon undertake.

"No, Roak, I don't. I only regret that I had to make the decision in the first place. He was a good General, a strong leader of his men. But he was becoming too sentimental, too emotional. His goals did not share the scope of my own, and he would have eventually started second-guessing me. Better to get rid of the problem before it starts, I say."

Roak smiled once again, and tipped his drink to Vandross. After a good meal of flesh, the Shadowbeasts formed ranks in front of Vandross as he addressed them. "I know many of you can move through the Shadow Plane, but I cannot. I don't want to slow you down, so I'm going to use my magic to teleport myself great distances at a time. We go now to Mount Toane, which shall serve as the new seat of my power! We shall amass more forces in the mountain from across the land! There shall be certain standards of acceptance into my army! And you shall all be among this great power! When our forces in Desanadron are finished, they will return to Mount Toane, for I have already told them of my intentions!"

"But sir," called one demon from the front row. "We know already where another Orb is! Why do we not go and take it?"

"Because, soldier," Vandross said, pacing up and down as Bael had before the attack on Fort Flag. "It lies in the city of Whitewood, in the Elven Kingdom. Whitewood is home to some of the most powerful magic wielders in the land of Tamalaria. And surely news of what happened here will reach them before we arrive at the city. They will have allies in great numbers and strength! So we must amass a more powerful force than we have now. Even if they don't have allies, surely our enemy who chases us will aid them. I speak of Byron of Sidius!"

A visible shudder ripped through the assembled masses, but Vandross held up his new hand to silence them. The scales on his new limb had become smoother, and it appeared to Vandross that it would become nearly human eventually. "Gentlemen, do not fear. Even if he shows up and defeats you by the dozen, I shall personally step in to stop him. He cannot harm me."

"And what makes you say that, my lord," asked Vilec Roak, intrigued by this statement.

Vandross smiled and laughed hoarsely at the night sky.

"If he harms me, he harms himself, General. After all, I helped create him!"

Chapter Eight
Ruin and Recollection

Byron and Shoryu had been riding hard for several days, and now the wind whipped at them like a gale force. Somehow, they had lost ever more ground on Vandross and his forces, likely a result of the magic users in his forces increasing their speed exponentially.

As the sun began to creep up above the horizon on yet another new day, they arrived at the top of a steep hill. At the bottom, smoldering and blasted, sat Fort Flag. The stench of burnt flesh and blood wafted up the hill at them, taunting them, mocking them for their failure to arrive in time to aid the Fort and its men.

Hanging his head in shame, Byron led Shoryu and Alex down to the ruins of Fort Flag. But they did not even get to the Fort when they came upon a tattered body they recognized.

The reptile General who had challenged Byron in Narfan lay prostrate, facedown in the grass. Stab wounds covered his back and sides, and Byron dismounted, knelt beside him, and rolled him over. Bael's eyes were closed, and his entire front had been scored by claws and blackened by magic. Byron shook his head slowly. Paladins hadn't done this, he knew. "What happened to him," Shoryu asked softly.

"From the looks of it, Vandross didn't have any use for him anymore. Poor fellow," Byron said, inspecting the wounds. "Doesn't look like he had much of a cha-" but he was interrupted when Bael's hand shot out and grabbed him by the arm. The reptilian eyes cracked open wide, his breath harsh and rasping.

"Po, tion," he rasped as blood spilled over his lower lip. "Back, pack," he said, pointing at his torn bag. Shoryu rummaged through it, his hand closing on the green vial of healing fluid. For a long moment, he thought about crushing it in his claw, denying the Lizardman the mercy his caretaker had deserved. But no, he thought, this man didn't kill him. The one-eyed one was to blame for that death. Shoryu pulled out the potion, and sped over to the Dread Knight with it in hand.

Byron poured the viscous liquid down Bael's throat, and green light emanated from his wounds, sealing them over and healing them. Even after that, Bael was still very weak, and Byron had to help him into a sitting position.

"Thank you," Bael finally said after a minute. "It's funny," he said morosely. "First I threaten you both, and then you turn out to be my saviors." He looked imploringly up at Shoryu, his lips moving but his heart not finding the words. "I am, sorry, young one, for your losses. I do not deserve your mercy." Bael lowered his head. "I have done many despicable things under the command of Richard Vandross, and should pay for my deeds. You should have let me die."

For a long moment, there was silence, only broken by early morning birdsong. Though he felt awkward, Shoryu put a gentle hand on Bael's shoulder as he stooped.

"Everyone deserves mercy, um—"

"Bael."

"Everyone deserves mercy, Bael." Shoryu patted the Lizardman's shoulder. "I'm a Cuyotai! I can forgive you if you can forgive yourself, Bael!"

The Lizardman was speechless. For so many years he had hated the Cuyotai out of instinct, out of upbringing. He had been raised by his father to hate their entire Race. Yet here was a young Cuyotai, barely an adult, and he had known the boy for all of five minutes and liked him. Perhaps he had been raised with the wrong ideals.

"What happened here, Bael," Byron asked, motioning Shoryu to take a seat. "What happened to you?"

Bael took a swig from his canteen, wiping his scaled and parched lips with his forearm. "Well, where to begin?"

* * * *

His axe had cleaved easily through the outer defenders' armor, hacking and chopping them into bleeding piles of meat. The metallic scent and taste of blood filled the air and his nostrils until Bael felt he would surely vomit from it. Bael had slain many an enemy before, but never a Paladin. And something about it felt very wrong indeed. But he hadn't had much time to think about it, as he barely rolled out of the way of Lord Vandross's spell, which had torn apart the north wall. A breach had been made in enemy defenses, and his militaristic nature and training took over. He pointed to the opening with his weapon and led his men inside.

But he had noticed that Vandross had not joined them. He briefly checked on his leader, and then stormed back into the courtyard. The number of defenders inside the walls was stupefying. How could so many men live in such a small base? His forces were easily outnumbered three to one, but the Shadowbeasts tore through the Paladins and Knights with ease.

Bael himself had moved easily through the ranks of defenders, until he felt a small weapon stab through his armor in his back. But it had not stopped with one stab. In the chaos of battle, he turned with his weapon in hand, but stopped short. Vilec Roak stood before him, a bloody dagger in hand and a grin plastered across his black face. "There are going to be some changes around here, lizard," he had hissed.

Bael had been teleported by Roak's magic outside of the battle, out of the fort altogether, where three more demons waited for him. He'd been shocked from displacement, so they had been able to tear into him quickly. But he had regained his senses long enough to fight back and destroy two of them. Then Roak reappeared, using the same magic to move himself to that point as he had Bael, and blasted him squarely in the chest with a ball of black force.

Bael lay on the ground, quivering and bleeding to death. Vilec Roak and the other Shadowbeast had returned to the fort to report to Vandross that the job was done. Bael had watched them go with hatred in his heart, for both Vilec Roak and himself. How had he not seen this coming? He should have known that Vandross would eventually do this to him, especially after their quarrel over their goals. But darkness had encroached upon his vision, pulling down over his sight like a curtain over a stage. The smell of his own blood and wicked magic curled into his nose, and the soft grass under him seemed to sing to him a soothing lullaby.

He could not remember his dreams in the hours that followed, except that they had been filled with delirium. Still, sleep was peaceful, and didn't expect anything from him.

* * * *

"And that was when I felt a great wave of negative energy coming from the fort. Surely Lord, I mean, surely Richard Vandross has taken the third Orb of Eden's Serpent." Bael tore through the stew that Shoryu had prepared for the trio, his body longing for more sustenance. He hadn't eaten such a good meal in a long time. Being a military man, Bael usually had to settle for cold, dried meat and hard bread. To him, Shoryu's 'simple meal' was fit for a king. "Is there any of that stuff left," he asked, looking at the pot.

"Well, sure, there's a little, but it's the stuff at the bottom of the pot and—"

Shoryu stepped back as Bael tipped the pot back, draining the last contents directly into his mouth and stomach. He set the pot down, and Byron and Shoryu exchanged a glance.

Byron shrugged his shoulders, not wanting to get between the former General and a hot bit of food.

Shoryu took the pot off a short way and began washing it with some of his canteen water.

"Thank you for the food, Shoryu," Bael called back, and Shoryu smiled and waved at him. It had been a long time since Bael had seen an honest and innocent smile, and didn't know what to make of it. "Is he always so cheerful," Bael asked Byron quietly.

"Most times," Byron replied, looking over at the young Hunter. "He never took the Rite of Adulthood in his village, so I'm guessing he's still very young. The Cuyotai live a very long time you know. Physically, he may be forty or fifty years old, maybe more. But according to their lifespan, he's just a teenager." Byron took a swig of Bael's whiskey, feeling the warm glow of it in his stomach.

Bael shuddered. *Teenagers, gugh.*

"What are you going to do now, Bael?"

The Lizardman hadn't given this much thought since Byron and his odd friends had shown up. He couldn't very well go and exact revenge on Vilec Roak, the Shadowbeast was too powerful, and would be surrounded by his army. But then his anger flared once again, and his thirst for revenge seemed suddenly unquenchable.

Shoryu rushed over to the two men, his face flushed and his eyes filled with fear. "Byron, a large pack of Lizardmen is coming this way!"

Bael and Byron got to their feet, weapons in hand. One of the reptile warriors, a scout from the looks of him, looked up from the ground and stood shocked, staring at Bael. He shrieked something in his native tongue, and the entire group of Lizardmen charged towards Byron's company. But they did not raise weapons, and were cheering and smiling from the looks of it.

Byron sheathed his weapon, but kept his magic at the ready, and Bael put his axe back on his hip.

"*Garag nishiiii, Bael,*" they roared in unison as the scout leaped upon the former General, embracing him like a father.

Bael, awkward and unaccustomed to such displays, patted the boy's back. Then he realized it was the boy Vandross had told him to protect in the Cuyotai village.

Bael and Byron looked over at Shoryu as the young Hunter growled and aimed his bow right at the foremost reptile. The pack backed away a short distance, but Byron lowered Shoryu's bow.

"Put your weapon away, Shoryu," Byron pleaded, seeing the look of confusion and loss in the young Cuyotai's eyes.

"Why," Shoryu spat, not taking his eyes off of the pack or his hands off of his weapon. "These bastards took my life from me! They burned and killed my home and people! Why should I grant them mercy?"

"Because you have granted Bael mercy. Like him, these men followed Lord —"

"No," Shoryu screamed in Byron's face. "I have seen them before! Many of them! They attacked us constantly, made war against us for generations. These are no strangers to me. They are enemies." But his rant lasted only as long as he could dam up the tears in his eyes, and he dropped to the ground and wept openly.

With the sound of Lizardman speech behind him, Byron stooped to the ground, and in a moment of uncertainty, wrapped his arms around the youth.

Shoryu responded immediately, nearly crushing Byron's armor with the force of his embrace. But somewhere inside of Byron, some restraint snapped, and he stroked Shoryu's head like a father would his child. He was feeling something he hadn't felt in the longest time: affection. Had this been the gift spoken of in his dreams? Had he regained some of his Human nature?

A moment later Shoryu pulled away, much to his spine's relief. "I'm sorry," he said, trying to smile. The Cuyotai stood and put his bow away. "I apologize to you all."

"You needn't apologize to usssss," hissed one of the larger reptiles. "We truly have been unfair and unkind to your kindred. We can perhapsssss make ressstitution now. Our leader sssays he wishes to aid you however he can. Though he issss no longer a military leader, he issss sssssstill our leader." A unified cheer went up from the pack, and Bael beamed with pride.

"How shall we assist you, Byron of Sidius," he asked as he turned to Byron, whose jaw had slid up on one side, giving him a grinning appearance.

"First off, Bael, it's just Byron. I no longer belong to the Sidius clan. Secondly, tell me what you can about Richard Vandross. And I want to know everything, down to what he wears when he sleeps."

Bael raised a scaled eyebrow at Byron, who still grinned.

"You're quite serious, aren't you?"

Byron nodded and sat down once more.

Bael asked him first for the use of a horse, so one of his men could check the situation in Desanadron.

Byron let the young scout who had embraced Bael take his own steed, and the scout took off at a high-speed gallop.

"Well, first off, he sucks at chess. Man can't think more than three moves ahead."

"Played him a lot, did you," asked Byron.

"Yes, almost every night. He and I were friends in the beginning. We shared a goal of making a nation where those held in contempt by the rest of the world could live in safety. But after Koreindar, when he took the first Orb, he changed. He became distant, distracted. He was fixated on having the other Orbs, and did nothing but talk and think about the power he would wield with them. I know much about him, so you may want to prompt me with some questions, Byron."

The undead warrior thought long and hard as Shoryu talked at length to the reptile warriors behind the two men, showing them how to better aim their arrows.

"Doesn't miss a beat, does he?" Bael asked.

"No, no he doesn't. He didn't have many friends in his village, I think. Sure, he cared about them all," Byron said, looking at Shoryu. "But I don't think anyone got too close to him. Maybe his foster father and a few of the Seniors as he called them. But beyond that, I think he's going to look for every opportunity he can get to be sociable. Amazing considering he was ready to kill them all a few minutes ago. But such is the way of most Cuyotai. They're fickle folk." He turned his attention back to Bael, who was taking a swig of his whiskey. "Not too much of that, Bael. I want you to remember what you can." Both men looked at each other a moment and laughed hoarsely. "Why did he send troops to Desanadron?"

"To lure as many Paladins from the fort as possible," Bael said, lowering his eyes to the ground. "It was my idea, actually. I just got into the role of General and lost my reason. I think in strategic terms all the time now, and it's hard to get out of the soldier mode, you know?"

Byron nodded, knowing full well what that was like.

"Well, Vandross also decided to take a foothold here in the west before he heads back east to his new home. Mount Toane." Byron trembled inwardly at the name of that cursed place. The place he had lost his humanity, his pride, his very body, and nearly his soul.

"Why does he seek to make Mount Toane his seat of power? Why not someplace nearer to the center of Tamalaria?"

"Because, there is deep and dark magic at play in that mountain and its catacombs," Bael said, not looking at Byron. "I know you have been there. Vandross spoke often of your former being after you trounced him outside of Koreindar. He ranted for days afterward about his revenge. I told him that you would slaughter him if you truly had returned to your Paladin self, but he said it didn't matter. He said that you could only annoy him, that you could never kill him." Bael edged away from Byron, as if he knew something that he didn't want Byron to know, for fear of the Dread Knight's reaction.

"And why would he say such a thing," Byron asked, too curious for his own good.

"Because, Byron," Bael said, staring into those pinpoints of light. "He helped create what you are today. He was the apprentice of Tanarak of Sidius."

* * * *

It was noon when the scout returned from Desanadron, and Byron's horse nearly fell dead on its side. Shoryu tended to it while the scout reported the condition of the great city to a still-stunned Byron. The army and the unit from Fort Flag had contained the attack and turned the blitzkrieg into a long siege. Denizens of the city had erected walls of magic fire and ice, and Vandross's army had been forced to camp outside of the city and wait until they could mount an effective assault.

The city itself had been badly torn apart in sections, and was slowly losing ground in the overall campaign, but it would hold for a few days more.

A few guards had accosted the scout himself, but he had informed them that a group of deserters from Vandross's army lay in wait near Fort Flag, ready to give aid to the city. The city's temporary leader, a woman by the name of Selena Bradford, had told him to return immediately with this group to aid the city. A squat Paladin had been with her, a man by the name of James Hayes.

Byron thought this name was also familiar, but in the same way that Vandross's name had been. It was a name from another life, his Human life. Many of those memories were lost on him, but day-by-day he recovered more of them. Byron thanked the scout and headed over to Bael, relaying the information.

"Well, that's simple then. We march for Desanadron!"

Byron shook his head at Bael.

"And why not?"

"Because, Bael, you have only twenty or thirty men here. And while you are healed by the potion, your strength is still not recovered. Take your men and go to the city of Whitewood, the Elven Kingdom capital. Tell them what you know and convince them that you want to help. Shoryu, Alex and I will meet you there in about a week. If you cannot convince them, find others of your brethren and camp with them."

"That is convenient," said Bael with a smile. "My home village is in the Elven Kingdom. Perhaps a side trip to see my father is in order."

Byron grinned at him, grasping his hand firmly and shaking it. "We shall be off then, sire." Bael saluted Byron, who returned the motion as Bael barked orders at his men to form ranks. Once a soldier, he thought, always a soldier. Bael and his company marched in step south, continuing until they were out of sight.

"What now?" squeaked Alex, who'd had surprisingly little to say throughout the day's events.

"You ask that an awful lot," said Shoryu as he packed up his rucksack and slung it on his back.

"Hey, I'm just looking for a little direction in my life, that's all," Alex said as he doused the Cuyotai with a bucket of water.

"Now we join the fight in Desanadron, my friends."

Alex rolled his eyes as he sat on Byron's shoulder.

"I was afraid you'd say that."

* * * *

A shimmering wall of fluid light flickered back and forth in the evening light, preventing Byron and Shoryu from gaining entrance to Desanadron. The scout had never told Byron exactly how he had gained entry into the smoldering city streets; he had merely told them that he had been 'clever'. Unfortunately, Byron hadn't thought to ask. He dismounted from his steed and gave it a firm slap on the hindquarters.

It had driven itself nearly to execution twice on his behalf, and as it whinnied and galloped gratefully away, he waved to the equine sprinter in thanks of all his service.

So he led Shoryu and his horse, along with Alex, who kept a safe distance back and above the group, south around the perimeter of the barrier. For hundreds of yards he slowly stepped over rubble and blasted earth, trying to discern with his eyes a visible sign of some weakness in the defense. But thus far, he could find none, and he had nearly gone clear to the southern side of the city. Shifting direction, he turned north, towards Vandross's force. Though they were about three miles away, there were hundreds, nearly a thousand of the creatures, spanning the range from Human to Shadowbeast. Scores of campfires were being lit to prepare meals of a sort and warmth for those of Vandross's followers who required such comfort. They had become thoroughly entrenched, and could wait out the inhabitants of the city. They could afford another week or more of sending their own men into the temporary openings in the walls of magic, letting Desanadron use up its supplies and its defenders weaken, both physically and mentally. Then they would make one final push to defeat the city's army and Hayes' unit.

Unless Byron figured out a way to get inside and assist the city with Shoryu and Alex. And they would be in danger of being seen by Vandross's troops if they went any further around the barrier. Vexed at his situation, Byron sat on the ground and contemplated his options. The stifling smell of magic wafted into his face as he leaned back against the barrier, arms crossed in front of his chest. He began to tap his skull with a finger, when he fell backward through a sudden opening in the barrier.

From where he'd fallen, Byron stared up at Shoryu and Alex, his mouth agape. "I, uh, knew I'd think of something," he sputtered, embarrassed that he had been taken off guard.

Shoryu and Alex looked at each other, and then behind them. "What?"

"I don't think it's coincidence, sire, you falling through the wall," Alex reported tight-lipped. "The defenders of Desanadron are weakened from strain and concentration, and there's a rather large number of people with pointy and sharp objects running this way, and I just thought we might—"

Byron cut Alex off by grabbing the Ki Fairy in one huge fist and sprinting through the streets into the city of Desanadron.

Shoryu followed immediately behind, his horse galloping past Byron in panic.

Armed guards charged out of alleys with weapons raised, screaming war-cries and advancing on the trio.

Byron tucked his arms into his sides and barreled through them with the force of a battering ram, splitting their wedge and forcing them aside. But he never once used his magic or his weapon. Together, he and Shoryu dodged and parried as many of the attacks as they could, watching as the crushing weight of at least a hundred of Vandross's creatures stormed the city behind them.

"Put up the wall and hold your weapons," cried a loud, commanding woman's voice above the din of metal weapons. The soldiers looked puzzled, and mages appeared on the tops of nearby buildings, closing the barrier and trapping half of the charging creatures inside the dome that currently served as Desanadron's doorway to battle. A regal, beautiful woman with long, auburn hair and a flowing red dress approached the trio. She was Human, and Byron could smell soot and smoke from her.

So this was the Pyromancer, he thought.

Behind her limped a beaten and bloodied Human Paladin.

Upon seeing his face, though sore and battered, Byron remembered him. James Hayes.

"You are the strange ones who the reptile said would come to aid us. Where are the others?" the woman asked, her tone commanding and firm.

Byron turned his gaze on her, but she did not flinch. Attractive and brave, he thought. Good qualities to have in a woman.

"I have sent them ahead to Whitewood, capital of the Elven Kingdom in the south, m'lady," Byron rumbled, smoke pluming out of his throat. His eyes glowed wide, and he tried to cough casually to one side, to make certain he didn't blow it in this woman's face. She was on to him, however, and she laughed lightly, musically. Byron tried to smile, but his skull wouldn't cooperate.

"You are a funny man, creature. What is your name?" But before he could answer for himself, James Hayes stepped forward.

"He is Byron of Sidius, formerly Byron Aixler," said Hayes in a subdued tone. The Paladin's eyes appeared hollowed out, devoid of hope or a soul. "But he has not come to kill us. He is here to do something, but our deaths are not on his agenda. Tell me, Byron, what news have you of Fort Flag?"

Byron lowered his eyes to the ground, trying to figure out how to break the news that all of his kinsmen, Paladins of Oun, had been slaughtered. Unfortunately, there was no easy way.

"There are no survivors. The fort was attacked after your unit departed for this city. It has all been a trap laid by Richard Vandross to attain the Orb of Eden's Serpent from your Order."

Hayes simply nodded and stared into the Dread Knight's chest, as if looking through him, not at him.

"It does not matter. We are all forsaken."

Byron stood in stunned silence as Hayes turned away from him and the others, limping as well as he could away.

Scowl upon his bony face, Byron spun Hayes around by the shoulders, gripped him, and shook him hard. Over Hayes's shoulder, Byron watched as the men and women who had trained weapons on him and Shoryu dispatched the last of the fresh batch of intruders. Six of those Desanadron warriors lay dead on the street in the aftermath.

"A true member of the Order would never say such a thing! Never! I know!" He shook Hayes once more, but the Human Paladin struck him hard in the side of the face, knocking him to the ground.

"How can you say how a Paladin should speak? Did not Oun and our Order forsake you? Look at you, Byron of Sidius. Look at what Tanarak made of you. Do you not think that Oun has forsaken you?"

Byron's temper flared, and his eyes glowed crimson for a moment. Dark thoughts and impulses ran through his mind and his heart, his mind's eye already shaping a vision of violence as he got to his feet. His left hand itched to release arcane power into the injured Hayes's face, a point-blank burst of power that would leave a spouting funnel of blood from his neck, where his head should be. Yet, he resisted these images. He understood the Paladin's mindset. He'd traveled that long, black road alone for a very long time.

"I did, once. But my soul was sealed away in this body. I had no choice in the acts I committed. But I'll tell you this, Paladin. Oun only forsakes those who forsake him. A man is measured by his whole life and choices of free will. Not one portion of it. You chose to come here, away from the fort, to do his will, and defend those who needed protection from evil. You cannot be forsaken yet."

Hayes seemed to think this over a minute, and his legs gave out under him. He still stared into space, but his eyes had a more focused look again. He was coming back around. "Now, proud Hayes, Paladin of the Order of Oun," Byron said, extending one armored hand to Hayes, helping him back to his feet. "Let us get somewhere inside, and tell me what has transpired here."

The assembled group shuffled away from the area, leaving the bodies and combatants behind. Smoking, smoldering buildings stood all around them, ruination claiming many of the residences and businesses. A few sections of walls fell into the streets around them, and they carefully navigated around the rubble and destruction, giving brief nods to the soldiers they passed here and there. Some moved to intercept them, but Selena Bradford held a hand up to stay them. They all got into an abandoned tavern, and everyone poured themselves a drink.

"All right, Byron," Hayes said. "I'll tell you now what happened."

* * * *

James Hayes led the charging battalion on into the night, the thunder of seventy-plus sets of hooves stomping the ground, sending tremors through the land. The smell of smoke filled his lungs as the battalion neared the city. In the middle of the night, Desanadron was lit like a bonfire, casting huge, garish shadows across the ground all around the unit.

As they rode closer, shapes began to take form in these shadows, and a second too late, Hayes gave the order to ready for combat.

The first rider had already been knocked from his mount by a tall, gangling Shadowbeast, its arms formed into spiked cudgels.

Blood oozed from several punctures in the fallen Knight's armor, but he got to his feet and cleaved the demon in twain with a timed slash from his sword. The Knight remounted, and Hayes smiled despite himself. Even ambushed, his man had survived. Or so he thought.

As the Knight mounted his horse, his skin turned as white as a sheet, and blood pumped out of his wounds in a sickly greenish hue. His eyes clouded over, and the Knight turned and with the same swing technique he'd used on the Shadowbeast, decapitated one of the Elven Paladins following behind him.

Chaos broke out in the ranks as dozens more of the minor demons surfaced from the shadows and darkness of night. A pack of four huge Khan stormed at the confused and flailing riders, knocking half a dozen men to the ground and snapping their spines over thickly muscled legs with a flat crunching noise.

Hayes dismounted, his horse becoming too frightened and skittish to be trusted in battle, and most of the rest of his unit followed suit, sending their mounts off at a high-speed escape. Two of the Khan knocked their way through the ranks of Knights and Paladins to reach him, but Hayes was prepared. He thrust his sword in one's chest all the way to the hilt, leaping up over the other's claws and kicking him squarely in the jaw with a metal-plated boot. The first beast fell dead, and the second had regained its feet, crouching in preparation of a killing leap. But Hayes held his ground, thrusting his fingers toward the Khan. "*Habnas, eturgai,*" he mumbled, and a streak of holy magic erupted from his fingertips, lancing through the Khan's body.

It shuddered and lay still on the ground. It would remain still forever.

He spun around, trying to get a quick head count on his men. Though the attack had come suddenly, his unit had dealt with it well. He had only lost ten men total, not bad considering the strength of their enemies and the severity of the assault.

Minutes later, Hayes's unit pushed its way into the city of Desanadron, where several of the city's officers met him with a salute.

"Captain Hayes," said a short Jaft man in uniform. The sounds of far-off battle reached his ears, drowning out most of what was said among the city officers. The Jaft man walked right up to Hayes's side, nauseating him with his natural odor. "Captain Hayes, sir, now that you're here, we're going to put up a magical barrier to protect the city and limit the number of enemies that can get through. One of our chief mages, Miss Bradford, thought of it a couple years ago, when the vampire Dolec van Geshul attacked us. We held him off and killed his minions a few at a time."

"I remember," shouted Hayes over the screaming and fires only a hundred yards away. "But this is a much larger and much livelier bunch than van Geshul's zombies and ghouls. Is Bradford here?"

The Jaft shook his head affirmatively in an exaggerated fashion.

"She's in charge now. The Commander fell in battle two hours ago."

Hayes drew his weapon, readying himself for the approaching battle. But he had no need. Desanadron's defenders made short work of the Lizardmen and Orcs that approached, but not without suffering about two-dozen casualties themselves. The din of battle died away as the last invader was struck down.

"Come with me," said the Jaft, lowering his voice. "I'll take you to her."

Hayes followed the Jaft, his weapon still in hand. He sensed that something else had come through the barrier, something that had not joined in the senseless charge against Desanadron's army.

Through several dank and putrid smelling alleys they walked, stepping over corpses here and there. Already two waves of marauders had come through, the first one breaking on the city unexpectedly. The casualties in that first assault had been many, and as Hayes looked at the bodies they walked around, he saw that there was no prejudice in death's domain. Women, children, the elderly and simple pets were slaughtered where they had stood. Even the drunk and homeless hadn't been spared.

Finally, the officer brought him up in front of one of the several libraries Desanadron was home to. "She's in there, sir," the Jaft said, saluting.

Hayes returned the motion, and the Jaft left him to return to the bulk of the defenders. He looked up at the beaten and burned building with trepidation rising in his throat. Something was wrong, something approached from the encroaching darkness, but he could see nothing as he looked around. He walked up the stone slab steps and entered the library, moving slowly, with caution. As he opened the door, a spear comprised entirely of flames whipped past his head and buried itself in the solid oak door. He rolled inside, his weapon raised, and saw the most beautiful Human woman he'd ever laid eyes upon.

Selena Bradford was an elegant woman, her skin darkly tanned and her auburn hair long and flowing. Her eyes sparkled with flickers of flames, and her crimson lips were full and perfectly pouted. Her hand, however, at that moment, was extended towards Hayes, which brought him quickly out of his reverie to look at the spear that dissipated now into smoke.

"Hold, Selena Bradford. I am James Hayes, Captain of Fort Flag and leader of the unit that has come to give aid."

Bradford put her hand on one hip, tilting slightly to the side. Her blazing red dress was figure hugging, and revealed the voluptuous curves of her body, but Hayes tried to steady his mind. *No impure thoughts*, he said to himself, *no impure thoughts*. But that was getting difficult as the woman approached him, her hips swaying suggestively.

"I'm terribly sorry about that," she said in her husky voice. She had an accent similar to those who lived in the city-state of Tarum [Russian], and though it was not unpleasant, it held a tone of aggression. That wasn't surprising, though. The woman was a Pyromancer, and they tended to be more war-like than other mages. She extended one slender, dainty hand towards Hayes. "Please, accept my apologies, da?"

Hayes shook her hand firmly, and her grip was anything but ladylike in his hand.

"I thought you might be with them."

Hayes looked at her, confused.

"Who?"

"Them," she said, pointing out of the still open door. On the street, advancing slowly, stealthily, were half a dozen winged Shadowbeasts. "Don't worry about them, though. I'll deal with it." Selena waved her hands in front of her, spinning to face the advancing beasts at the last motion, and they stopped dead in their tracks. "*Flaguel*, Burn to Death," she screamed, magic coursing through her arms and flowing out into the air above the creatures.

They looked about them, confused. There was magic at work, yes, but where would it strike from?

Hayes watched in awe as the magic hovered over them, forming into flaming stones and slamming down into their midst, exploding on contact with their bodies or the ground. Ten, twenty, thirty of the flaming spheres thundered into them, the concussion force knocking Hayes back to the floor. As Selena stood over him, the smell and taste of ashes and attar stole over him like an assassin, clouding his thoughts and muting his speech.

He sat up with her help, and looked out at the smoldering piles of black flesh and demonic meat. The sound of sizzling and cooking meat filled his ears, moans and final death throes shaking their ruined bodies. He smiled up at the Pyromancer. "Pretty handy work," he said, even more impressed than he had been before.

"Da, that it is. But now is not the time to have a friendly chat. Now is time to discuss strategy."

Hayes walked with her back to the main defending force, where assignments and shifts were being changed to give everyone a chance to rest.

"How are we on supplies," asked Hayes of the Jaft officer.

"We can hold out for a week, maybe a little more. After that, we will have no food, and only enough fresh water to last us another four days, at best. If we are under siege for too long, we will become weak and easily defeated."

"What about Aquamancers," Hayes asked.

A visible shudder came from Bradford. Pyromancers were especially vulnerable to water and ice magic.

"Couldn't they create water?"

"Possibly, yes," said the Jaft. "But we only have three, and they are taking turns two at a time holding the inner ice barrier around the city. The third takes rest, and they rotate. We will exhaust them if we ask the third to make water."

Hayes cycled through his options, trying to think through the situation.

"What about Gaiamancers? They can create food from fertile soil, maybe even create irrigation tunnels to the streams and rivers near the city."

The Jaft shook his head, lowering his eyes.

"We had five of them, sir, but they all were felled in the second assault. None survived. The majority of our local Gaiamancers' Guild are on a trip to the Elven Kingdom."

Damn and blast, thought Hayes. He looked at Bradford, seeking help or suggestions.

"We have a Q Mage," she said, her eyes moving to one of the soldiers in the nearby group. "She can use her magic to strengthen one of the Aquamancers enough to buy time for the other to make more water. But," she said, lowering her eyes.

"But what," asked Hayes, growing impatient with the situation.

"The effort of making water will tire the Aquamancer, and he will also have to rest. The Q Mage will have to exhaust her resources helping the barrier hold. The Aquamancers are old and mighty in their craft. But the Q Mage is young and not as experienced. The effort could render her unconscious for a long time."

"It's worth the risk," said Hayes firmly, coldly. Now was not the time to be emotional: it was time to be tactical. "Get her rested and ready. She'll support the next Aquamancer, the one resting now. That will minimize the effort on everyone's part. I'm aware that the strain will still be great, but it must be done if we're to have a fighting chance at surviving a long siege. My own men require rest as well. I'll send half to the library to rest, and keep half awake to aid the army. Agreed?"

Selena Bradford hesitated a moment, then nodded. The Jaft officer walked away, returning with a young female soldier, a short Werewolf woman with white fur.

"This is Corporal Natalie Bloodclaw, sir. She is the Q Mage, but her skills are best used in combat. Salute the man, Corporal, he's a Captain!"

The Werewolf gave a perfunctory salute, which Hayes returned.

"Have you been told what is expected of you, soldier," Hayes asked, raising an eyebrow at the fully armored lycanthrope. She was huge, he thought. How could any amount of magic tire her?

"Yes sir," she said, her voice deceptively child-like.

How old was this pup, Hayes suddenly thought.

"How long have you been using magic, Corporal?"

"Two years, sir," she responded, much to Hayes's dismay.

Only two years? She would only have a handful of magic energy to offer! How would she do what he demanded? He began to have second thoughts about his strategy, when another opening appeared in the city barrier, and several dozen creatures came rushing in, seven or eight gargantuan Khan among them.

Bloodclaw moved to join the fight, but Hayes stopped her with a mighty grip on her wrist.

"Sir!"

"No, Corporal. We need you right now for our plan! Go with my men to the library and rest. You will be fetched when the next Aquamancer takes his shift."

"Sir, that's in an hour," said the Jaft Lieutenant at his side. Hellfire, Hayes thought as he spat. Hell and blood.

"Well then, sit down Corporal! You're going to need your strength for your task. And don't even think about moving." Hayes stepped swiftly to his unit, deploying half to the battle, and the other half to the library for rest. The battle itself only lasted a few minutes, but the Khan slaughtered thirty of the city's men alone, and half a dozen of his own men.

"Lieutenant," Hayes bellowed, the Jaft officer coming over in a rush. "How many men are left to defend the city, Lieutenant?"

"We still number about five hundred throughout the city, sir. I'll be getting a report from other units soon, sir, via runner. Do you want to hear the numbers then as well?"

Hayes nodded, and the Jaft ran off again, barking orders at the top of his lungs. Five hundred was a good number, but if the other units were taking the same losses as this one, those numbers would dwindle quickly. Hayes lowered his rucksack to the ground, sitting on the steps of what was once a smithy's shop. He removed some dried meat and some bread, taking in a meager meal. He didn't want to use the city's supplies unless absolutely necessary. After he cleaned himself up, the Jaft returned, his eyes hollow and his mouth slack. Bad news was coming, he knew it. "What's the report, Lieutenant?"

The Jaft shook his head and dropped to the ground. Hayes rushed over to him, slapping the man's cheek, bringing him to and sitting him up. "What's the report?"

"The Eighth Battalion has been decimated by a pack of Black Fur Werewolves. They are coming this way, fast. They numbered fifty men. The other units haven't seen combat." *Fifty men*, Hayes thought. *By a pack of Black Furs? Inconceivable.*

"My son was in command of the Eighth," the Lieutenant muttered.

Hayes felt the impact of his words. The man had just lost probably his only son. The Jaft Race weren't very fertile, and their numbers reduced with almost every generation. The loss of his son probably meant the end of his bloodline, something that the Jafts held dear.

"Get up Lieutenant. You have even more reason to fight now. We must get revenge for your men, for your son. If you survive this, you can have another child. But you have to live now."

The Jaft stood, but shook his head and tears silently, slowly, ran down his cheeks, as clear and crystalline as water dripping from an icicle.

"My wife died in the first assault. She was a Sergeant in command of the Fourth Battalion, and they were the first to die."

Hayes stared in shock at the Jaft. His family was dead, and likely he no longer cared about his own fate. The man would be a danger to himself. Hayes led him by the arm to Bradford, who stood with the Jaft's unit, the Fifth

118

Battalion.

"Selena Bradford," Hayes called to the Pyromancer, who shuffled over to him.

She looked worriedly at the stiff Jaft, whose eyes had glazed over. "I am stripping this man of his command! He has lost his family and is no longer fit to command in his condition." Hayes stripped the single bar from each of the Jaft's shoulders. "Assign a suitable replacement for him. Lieutenant, can you hear me?"

The Jaft nodded.

"Your command will be returned to you when you are able to command again, but for now, you're in no state to do so. Do you understand?"

Again, a small nod.

"Good. Now for the love of Oun, go to the library and rest. If trouble comes, defend yourself, but by no means join a fight you don't have to. Understood?"

Nod nod. The Jaft wandered away like a dead man, his gait zombie-like. He was barely out of sight, when a scream went up from the Fifth.

Hayes saw a pack of eight Black Fur Werewolves storm towards them from around a corner.

With Hayes's men, the defenders numbered just shy of one hundred men, but numbers hadn't mattered for the Eighth Battalion. Hayes was in command here, and began to give the order to do battle, when battle began despite him.

The Werewolves wielded no weapons, using their claws and teeth to tear through handfuls of men at a time. They were swift, and from their movements, Hayes could tell they possessed Monk Class abilities. They used self-defense techniques, martial arts grapples and strikes, and moved effortlessly through the defenders of the Fifth.

Black Furs, he thought, stupefied. The only known tribe of Werewolves to ever be wholly considered wicked.

As Hayes's Paladins and Knights broke into them, they faltered, and two of the eight went down in a bloody heap, five or six swords in their chests and faces.

One of the Black Furs, the slimmest and fastest, worked his way directly towards Hayes.

The Paladin balled his left hand into a fist, and readied himself.

A moment later, the Black Fur tossed a Knight from Hayes's group aside with a sidekick to the chest. Teeth bared and growling, it came at Hayes in a whirl of claws, teeth, and timed kicks and jabs.

For a short bit, Hayes parried the blows with his sword, but a kick to his leg knocked him to his knees, and another claw swipe ripped through his armor and tore deep into his right arm. Thick, crimson blood sprayed up at the Black Fur's face, matting his snout and staining it red with Hayes's life fluid.

In pain Hayes screamed, the sound of his cry turning from agony into righteous fury. The Black Fur retreated a step, his eyes suddenly filled with fear and worry. The sound of Hayes's scream was terrifying, almost like that of a great Dragon enraged.

All of the Black Furs hesitated for that moment, bespelled by the Paladin's war cry.

Hayes had called upon one of his Paladin abilities, commonly referred to as the *Terrible Shout*.

Seeing that their enemies were stunned, the survivors of the Fifth stabbed and slashed, killing the Black Furs almost instantly.

Hayes himself grabbed the slender Werewolf by the lower jaw, pulling his mouth open. He shoved his now-glowing left fist into the Black Fur's mouth, and discharged an explosion of holy force that blasted the creature's body into gory pieces, leaving his head intact on Hayes's arm. The Paladin softly chuckled to himself, almost in reverie of his violent deed. But shame soon overtook him, and he pried the dead beast's head off of his arm, dropping it with a wet smack to the ground.

Midnight had fallen on the city, and it was time for the Q Mage Werewolf to give her support to the Aquamancer and the city barrier. The effect was immediate. As the Q Mage channeled her energy into the Aquamancer; the city barrier shimmered and became almost see-through. Hayes watched the other water mage prepared a large basin with liquid from thin air.

It would not be enough, he decided, his spirit drained. His own forces had suffered heavy losses, and there seemed to be no end to the siege in sight. A scout reported that more wicked creatures had arrived to support the force north of the city, and another troop had been deployed to the southern edge of the city, filled with magic users. Now the defenders would have to watch both ends of the city, stretching even thinner their forces.

Hayes peered up at the roof where the Aquamancer and Q Mage stood. He stared helplessly as the Q Mage's body shook and quivered. It was too much for her, he knew, and she would soon exhaust herself completely.

The dome barrier shimmered and pulsed rapidly, as if in tune with her heart. "There is enough water now," he screamed at the Aquamancer. "Go and help her!"

His order proved to be too little, too late. As the second Aquamancer took his post, the Q Mage Werewolf fell from the roof, landing on the ground three stories below in a heap. Hayes rushed to her with a Cleric from his unit at his side. But the Cleric shook his head, his eyes shut, and made a sign over her.

"Her heart failed, sir. I am sorry, but it was too much for her. However, her magic has been permanently fused to the barrier. She sacrificed herself for the city."

Hayes was already stalking away, however, his heart heavy with guilt. It had been his fault. The death of his men, the death of the girl, and the horror of those Black Furs as they were butchered without being able to move. He had brought death to the city, to those near him. He felt no better than the savages that had assaulted the city. Spiritually drained, he retired to the library to rest. He wished for death to befall him. But Selena Bradford had summoned him, interrupting his rest. There had been a strange fluctuation of magic in the barrier the next day, and she had returned to the Fifth with Hayes in tow.

Their numbers were even fewer now than they had been when he had left them late the night before.

And that was when he had seen Byron of Sidius with a Cuyotai and a Ki Fairy.

* * * *

"And that brings us to now, Byron. I am sorry I have despaired, but I have had little left to me but despair."

"No matter," Byron said, waving off Hayes's apology. The man had been through a lot, and Byron's news probably hadn't helped matters. "What of the Lieutenant? I assume he is better?"

"Much." Selena took a sip of water from her dirty glass. "He has returned to his duties with a fervor. He wants revenge badly, and it has made him fierce in the battles since we noticed you outside. We let you wait a few hours while we thought about what the Lizardman scout said. Do you have a plan, Byron?" She eyed the Dread Knight suspiciously, obviously not comfortable with his presence.

"Indeed, I do. I am quite versed in matters of magic, as is my friend Alex," he said, nodding to the Ki Fairy who was sitting on the table. "You see, Q magic is a sort of battle support magic. It amplifies other magic and can endow warriors with temporary enhancements. I intend to use the latent magic that girl left behind in the barrier to our advantage."

Alex grinned atop Byron's shoulder, already aware of what the Dread Knight intended to do.

"Vandross's men can only cross breaks in the barrier. They can't pass through the barrier itself, or even touch it, right?"

Selena Bradford and James Hayes nodded.

"But your own men and women *can* touch it. Doing so, they can absorb some of that Q magic. How many fighters remain in the city?"

"About three hundred," said Hayes, whose eyes slightly sparkled. He was beginning to understand Byron's plan. "And they will be prepared, Byron." Byron looked deep into the Paladin's eyes, and nodded, grinning as best he could.

"Would you care to tell me what you plan to do, since it seems everyone else already knows," snapped Selena Bradford testily.

"I plan to lead half of those three hundred men through the barrier, and out to do battle with those scum. Our men will be outnumbered, but they'll all be enhanced by the magic in the barrier." Byron put his fingertips together and leaned back, pleased with himself and his quick thinking. Vandross's forces wouldn't expect an outward attack, and couldn't know how the barrier's magic would affect the fighting men and women of Desanadron. "We will accompany them as well. We will benefit from the barrier as well, though I am not certain how much, or in what way. I am a Dread Knight, formerly a Paladin. Hayes is a Paladin. We both possess fighting prowess and magical powers, so I'm not sure which category will be buffed. We'll just have to pass through and see."

Selena Bradford laughed under her breath. Her own mighty Pyromancy would be amplified? Surely then this Vandross fellow would suffer greatly. Desanadron had been her home for her whole life, and these bastards had come and ruined it. She would taste the sweet flavor of revenge.

"Let's get going then," she said, standing up. Byron got up, putting his hand up to stop her.

"It will very dangerous, m'lady," he said, feeling a tad foolish. The woman was obviously powerful, he could sense it. She didn't need his concern.

"While I appreciate your intentions," she said, shouldering past him. "I don't need warnings. The only danger will be to our opponents. The only real danger," she said, her eyes smoking and rimmed with flames. "Is us."

The men in the room gathered themselves up, preparing to join the assault on Vandross's camp. Even though he felt sure the one-eyed devil wasn't there, Byron would take great pleasure in demolishing his forces.

Looking at one another, each of the three men, the Paladin, Dread Knight, and Hunter, nodded. Alex cackled like a madman as they left the building to join the assembled forces of Desanadron. As they arrived, the Jaft Lieutenant saluted them, and they each returned the gesture.

"Her ladyship has told me everything you intend," said the Jaft, his great warhammer in hand. "We have assembled one hundred and fifty-four men. We would have split the number evenly at one hundred and fifty-two, but a couple of civilians joined from the underground shelters. They are Monks, and could not sit by idly any longer."

Byron nodded and looked at the ranks of men and women. Many of them would die in this effort. But their success would preserve the lives of an entire half of the army, a number of Hayes's men, and the civilians who took shelter somewhere beneath the city. The sacrifice would be well worth it.

"We are ready to march on your command, sir," the Jaft concluded, speaking to Byron.

"I'm not in charge here, soldier," he said, looking at Hayes. "He is."

Hayes smiled grimly, walking out in front of the ranks of men and women.

"All right. We march straight north, until we reach the barrier. I will pass through first, to ensure that this plan of action is safe. If the magic of the Aquamancers' barrier is lethal to us, we'll know immediately, for I will perish. You will all have to resume your duties in that event. Now, on cadence, four step rhythm, march."

As one, the men and women from both Desanadron's failing army and Hayes's decimated unit moved forward. They marched in an organized pattern, all the way to the northern border of the barrier and the city. The march took the better part of half an hour, as they had to move over and around rubble and corpses piled in the street. How Vandross's own men moved so effortlessly through all of this waste when they attacked, Byron couldn't understand, but they were not organized or forced into ranks. They moved freely when they entered, so they didn't have to worry much about movement.

Fifteen feet away from the barrier, Hayes called the troops to a halt. He moved forward swiftly, determinedly. He stretched one hand out and touched the barrier, feeling the thrill of magic entering his body. Q magic raced through him for a brief second, but he did not feel the chill of the ice barrier. He pushed his body through, and came out the other side effortlessly. He felt stronger, faster, clearer.

He turned back to his men, and with a war cry they charged through, breaking ranks and rushing toward the camp of their enemy.

Byron, Shoryu, and Selena Bradford passed through last, each tingling with the sensation of Q magic running its course in them.

Hayes saw the first of Vandross's men look up from his campfire, dropping his bowl in shock. Several dozen Greenskins stood stunned as one and a half hundred angry, bloodthirsty soldiers and a few magic users charging at them, clearly bent on their total destruction.

Hayes tore through a dozen of the heavy-footed Orcs and Ogres before they could rise to defend themselves. Blood sprayed through the air and matted his armor in seconds, his blade flashing and dancing back and forth, a crimson-stained harbinger of doom.

Hundreds of Vandross's men fell in the first two minutes of the battle, torn apart by blades, crushed by maces, blasted by magic, shredded by the few Werewolves in the Desanadron army. Panic ripped through their numbers like an airborne plague, and scores of the wicked creatures fled for the hills.

Byron used his own dark magics to summon large raven-like demons to tear Shadowbeasts and Black Fur Werewolves into bloody lumps.

Shoryu's arrows flew into packs of Shadowbeasts and Greenskins, exploding on the ground and blasting them open, exposing ribs and organs and pools of blood.

Selena Bradford's Pyromancy reduced scores of creatures to flaming piles of meat and ashes.

In twenty minutes, Vandross's camp was reduced to a smoldering, broken, bloody pile of carcasses and scorched earth.

A victory cry broke out, initiated by James Hayes, who stood atop a huge Black Fur Werewolf, his sword sunk to the hilt in its chest. He joined Selena, Byron, Shoryu and Alex a few minutes later, after the remainder of the men and women of the attack joined together to drink and celebrate. Only a dozen of them had died, though many were wounded. Byron couldn't have hoped for better results.

"Well, now what do we do," asked Selena Bradford.

"Do you intend to join us," Byron asked, a smirk on his skull.

"You have proven yourself worthy of my trust and admiration, Byron," she said, sitting on one of the Greenskins' cots, her legs crossed over a water basin. She was trying to clean her hair of the blood it had accumulated, and she wrung it in frustration. "Where shall we go once we have rested up here?"

The Q magic was wearing off, and everyone was feeling worn and weary, but they celebrated nevertheless. The barrier around Desanadron lifted, and cries of triumph could be heard from the city itself as civilians were brought back to the surface.

"I will join you as well," said James Hayes.

Byron was not in the least surprised by the Paladin's statement. He had fully expected the man to want to join his group, now that he had renewed purpose.

Hayes had not come through this most recent battle unscathed. He had several gashes and lacerations, but nothing he couldn't heal with spells available to him. A stab wound in his leg might slow him, but otherwise, he would be whole again for the trip ahead.

"Very well," Byron said, taking a swig of scotch he had purloined from a Black Fur's tent. "As for your question, Miss Bradford, we go to Whitewood, in the Elven Kingdom in the south. The next Orb of Eden's Serpent that Vandross seeks is protected there. We will go there, and we will wait for him. When he shows up," he said, looking to the heavens. "We will be waiting. And we will stop him."

Chapter Nine
Dreams

A thin, waif-like woman knelt in front of the church of Gaia in the city of Whitewood, praying under her breath. Her deep brown traveling cloak hid her grass-green dress and its embroidered designs of flowers, as well as her long brown hair and emerald eyes. Her Elven skin was fine, almost porcelain, and her necklace pendant hung just below her lowered chin, dark in contrast to her pale flesh. She sought strength from mother Gaia, strength for her body, soul, and Gaiamancy. She would need them in the days ahead.

She had been to the city's seer earlier that day, for her dreams had confused her the night before. In them, she saw a great and fearsome creature, wearing a set of blue full plate armor, wielding a blazing sword through scores of faceless creatures. Strange magics flowed at its command, and all around it bodies fell. Others fought alongside the creature, but she could not see them clearly. Before she woke, the creature turned, almost as if to face her. She stared into the eye sockets of a skull, with red blaring lights burning brightly at her. A snarl escaped the creature's throat, along with a cloud of dust, and it lurched towards her. She awoke screaming in her bed, and knew she had to speak with the seer.

Through the busy and crowded streets of the Elven capital she had walked, taking in the smells of spices sold in the marketplace, the sounds of Elven children singing songs and speaking with the animals around them. From a very young age most Elves were able to commune with certain animals, and each Elf was different. Some spoke to only a few animals, but did so very well. Others were able to communicate very basically with almost all animals. The skill varied from person to person, and Ellen Daires herself enjoyed listening to the banter of animals she herself couldn't understand. She only spoke with canines herself, dogs, wolves and coyotes. Coyotes were her favorite animal, for their carefree spirit and wandering nature. She exchanged a few words with a pack of stray dogs as she passed, wishing them a good day and hoping they would find homes soon.

These things did much to lighten her mood as she walked to the seer's home. But the closer she got to her destination, the greater her sense of dread became, going above the level she had experienced the night before. Ellen stopped dead in her tracks; did she really want to know the meaning of her dream? Did she dare expect it could mean anything good? But there was only one way to know for certain, and it lay only ten or twenty feet away, on the other side of the seer's front door.

She approached slowly, smoothing out her dress and tucking her hair behind her pointed ears. She rapped twice on the door, and it swung slowly open, creaking as it did so. Surely not a good omen, she thought. But she screwed up her nerves, and walked inside.

The entry chamber of the seer's home was warm and inviting, with lavish landscape paintings on the walls. Two oak benches sat opposite each other, their dark wood almost seeming to call to her to sit and rest. Instead, she looked ahead at the beads that hung in the doorway to the next room, out of which furled smoke clouds and the sound of someone humming low in their throat.

"Come in, my child," said a withered voice. The seer.

The room beyond the bead curtain contained a single, low table covered with a multicolored cloth. Tapestries and paintings depicting different stages of life and death adorned the walls around the room itself, each slightly more grotesque and disturbing than the one before it. A large crystalline orb sat in the middle of the low table. Seated across from where Ellen stood was the seer herself.

The seer was an Elven woman of venerable age, her hair long and tattered, wild and unkempt about her face. Unlike others of her Race, the seer showed physical signs of aging, from graying hair to wrinkles on her face. The air around her smelled of old mothballs and musk, the different aroma oils burning in the room mixing with her odor instead of covering it up.

The old woman was murmuring, possibly to herself, but the ball on the table fluctuated with light of some sort, so it was possible that she communed with the spirits. After another moment of the murmuring, the seer looked up at Ellen, a slight smile cracking her lips. "Please, sit young one. There is something you wish to ask of me."

Ellen nodded mutely, and took a seat across from the seer.

"Yes, there is wise one," Ellen said in a low whisper. "I have had a terrible dream this night past, and need to know its significance." Ellen related the events of her dream, right down to the last moment, when the terrible creature approached her.

The seer snickered low in her throat, and waved her hands over the ball in the center of the table. Her eyes widened, and she stopped laughing to herself. A look of fear or revelation passed over her face. Looking away from the ball, she locked her eyes on Ellen's.

"Your dream is related to the things I have seen in the crystal these past three days, my child. A mighty devil, blind in one eye, will descend upon our city in the days to come. He will be preceded by those who seek to stop his devilry. One will frighten you terribly, for who and what he seems to be, but you must trust in him and his companions. Together, you can stop the one-eyed devil for a time." The seer arose from her seat, and slowly turned away, shuffling towards her personal rooms in back of her shop.

Ellen stood as well, reaching out for the seer.

"Wait! There surely must be something more!"

The seer stopped in her tracks, turning to look tiredly at Ellen.

"There is nothing more that I can say on this. Dreams are strange things. Some deceive," she said, opening the door to her bedroom. "And some reveal the way you must take. But do not mistake this, all dreams are powerful." The seer went into her bedchambers and closed the door, shutting herself off from the panic stricken Daires.

* * * *

Once again Byron stood on a small hillock overlooking the cemetery. All was the same as it had been in his previous dream, except that there were more headstones. The black emptiness just beyond the cemetery fences seemed to mock him, jeer him for his inability to see beyond into the void. Yet nothing living appeared in the rows and files of graves; he alone stood in the vast expanse of burial plots. Byron could not remember having fallen asleep, so his presence here puzzled him. Had he blacked out? What was going on in the waking world? He looked off to his right, and saw an open pair of gates leading out of the cemetery and into the void.

He moved toward the gates, and heard a loud, harsh grinding noise like metal scraping metal. Ever so slowly, the gates began to swing closed.

His heart hammering in his chest, Byron tried to sprint for the opening, only to find that his own movements matched exactly the pace of the gates as they swung shut.

Enraged at his inability to move any faster, he bellowed in frustration as he reached for the left gate, only to watch it slam shut so suddenly that the cracking sound of it knocked him from his feet.

"All right, what in the seven Hells is going on here?"

A sharp, shrill wind cut through the cemetery, knocking several headstones over and pushing Byron back through the dirt, his heels biting into the ground to hold him upright. "This routine again," he called aloud, looking to the blackened sky. "I am going to tire of these games very quickly!"

"Byron," called a soft voice on the dying wind. "Do not be angry. Anger leads to hate, and hate leads to poor judgment."

Great, thought Byron. *Now I'm getting advice from a bodiless voice.*

"All right, I'll play along," Byron said, reaching the height of frustration. "I'm grateful for what you did before, giving me back my empathy."

"And another thing, which you have yet to use again," the voice said.

Another thing, Byron wondered. An ability, a spell perhaps?

"Yes, it is a spell from your days as a Paladin?"

Hmm, Byron thought. *Perhaps this isn't a waste of time.*

"Perhaps there is a reason you have been coming to me in dreams like this. Do you have a name? A form you can take to make this all a tad bit easier to deal with when I wake up?"

A shimmering light flowed down from the blank sky, and before his eyes suddenly stood himself, in his former Human countenance.

"That isn't funny," Byron growled.

"It isn't meant to be," said the voice. "This is the form I felt you might be most comfortable with. Am I wrong?"

"You're goddamn straight you're wrong! Pick something else!"

The voice's body shimmered, and took on the form of Edgar Cesar, his former Knight ally. "Edgar, you're—" he began, but shook his head. "No, you aren't Edgar, are you?"

"No, I am not. But this form seems to have calmed you somewhat. Byron, what do you seek from this conflict? You know now that Richard Vandross helped create you. Do you remember what that means?"

Truthfully, Byron could not.

"When Tanarak was slain, you regained control of your body. Your soul was freed."

"Indeed, it was," Byron said, crossing his arms across his chest. He didn't like the direction this conversation was heading.

"If Richard Vandross is destroyed, your life force will be freed. You will die."

Byron stood still, unable to say or do anything. If the voice spoke truly, he could never defeat Vandross. His own defeat would come immediately after he delivered the final blow.

"Do not despair, Byron. It is what must be done. Although, there are other ways."

"What other way is there," Byron said, suddenly keen to find a different solution to the problem of Vandross.

"You can contain him, imprison him. It is one solution. The Orbs of Eden's Serpent were once imprisoned."

Byron thought back to his studies of the Orbs from his days planning the Final Push against Tanarak of Sidius. That option had been discussed amongst him and his peers, but his superiors had demanded Tanarak be slain once and for all.

"A shame they didn't see what that would do," he muttered to himself.

"What?"

"Oh, nothing." Byron waved a hand at the apparition. He searched through his mental library, until he remembered what he had suggested to his higher officers. "The Cask of Darkness," he cried out, his eyes lighting up and blazing white in his head. "An artifact long used to contain the power of the Orbs of Eden's Serpent. But where is it?"

"Of that, I am not certain. I know little outside of your heart's domain."

Byron kicked himself for even thinking that a subconscious manifestation in his own head would know something so vitally important. Of course it knew about the Cask—it knew what he knew. Its memories were his memories.

"The time is coming for you to awaken. Take this gift with you." The voice reached its hands toward Byron. "It is another power you must reawaken, but you cannot until you awaken the first power I returned to you."

"How will I awaken these powers if I don't know what they are," Byron growled in frustration.

"The moment will be right. Trust in me on these matters."

Byron sighed heavily, and left himself exposed to the eerie light that flowed from the voice's hands into his chest. Power thrummed through his body, and the terrible gusts of wind blew at him once again.

"We will meet again," called the voice as Byron began to black out. The light danced about his head, striking him about the face, left and right, left and right.

"Wake up good Byron," Shoryu was saying as he slapped Byron and splashed liberal amounts of water over his face.

Byron sat bolt-upright, flames blazing about his skull from under his breastplate. The heat quickly dried his skull, leaving a slight scent of ash wafting about his head. He shook himself, placing one hand against his forehead and shaking his head slowly.

"We have rested through the night, Byron," Shoryu said as he offered a hand to help Byron up.

Pulling himself to his feet with the young Cuyotai's help, Byron looked around the woods they camped in.

"James Hayes says that a group of Elven Hunters came through late last night, wanting to know what we were up to."

Byron looked at Hayes, who was busy preparing a light breakfast.

"James? Want to tell me about it," Byron asked.

Hayes looked up and shrugged. "Not much to tell, really. I told them we were headed to the capital, told them why, and made sure they didn't get too good a look at you. Best thing for us, mind you."

Byron wrapped his cloaks of shadow magic about his upper body, deciding that caution would be highly advisable.

"We're about half a day's travel from the Suesance River, and after that, another full day's travel from Bael's village. Alex scouted last night to tell Shoryu and I where it was, and Shoryu has a Hunter's knowledge of traversing the lands of Tamalaria, so I think he should lead."

"He always does," said Byron with a grin no one could see.

The group ate a small meal and packed up for the day ahead. Byron thought back on the dream once more before he followed Shoryu's lead through the woods. He had regained two of his Paladin spells, but he hadn't yet used either one. What were they, and how was he supposed to awaken them? He decided that he would know when the time came. Lucky for him, that time would be shortly.

* * * *

Vandross and his army had finally arrived at the base of Mount Toane. The extensive use of his teleportation magic had drained him beyond reason, and his vision clouded over.

He led the way inside, his loyal thousands of minions waiting for him to enter their new home first.

Immediately as he entered, he knew that he had chosen wisely.

He arrived in the throne room in less than an hour's time. The blackened bone-and-mortar throne still stood silently and threateningly in the center of the chamber, but now the throne was his. He dragged himself up to it, and flopped himself down into the chair.

Vilec Roak bowed deeply before the throne. "What is your will, master?"

"I'm going to rest for now, Roak. Get the rest of the men inside and get everyone familiar with the place."

Vilec Roak smiled mirthlessly, which set Vandross ill at ease.

"What's so funny?"

"Nothing, sire, it's just that, I'm already very familiar with Mount Toane. I served here under the great Tanarak of Sidius when this was his seat of power. Familiarizing everyone should be easy enough." Vilec Roak left the chamber and Vandross, who sat alone, thinking about his current situation and his next move. But his thoughts became sluggish, and he fell quickly into slumber. He wondered if the creature Molis had awakened upon his re-entrance into the mountain.

On most nights since his taking of the first Orb, he slept dreamlessly, seeing nothing but blackness and void all around him. But already a dream was taking shape around him, and he was fully aware of it.

Richard Vandross stood semi-crouched in a huge stone hallway, stained glass windows allowing squares of light into the expanse of the hall. Dust swirled around everything, and large red tapestries depicting the many tyrants of Tamalaria's history hung on the walls.

He walked slowly down the hall, approaching a set of silver doors at the hall's opposite end. Onward he walked, amazed at the fine details woven into the cloth hangings on the wall. His metal boots rapped harshly on the stone floor, echoing through the air like thunderclaps, and the scent of burning flesh permeated the hallway. He breathed deeply of the odor, basking in it. He remembered the scent quite well—it was burning Cuyotai flesh. At last he stood before the doors, but when last he had looked at them, they were barren and silver. Now they were black steel, and a gigantic suit of armor stood before them, peering down at him.

Two bloodshot, feline eyes blinked at him, each easily the size of his head. "Thou shan't pass," said the armor slowly, methodically in a booming voice. "Lest ye know why ye have been brought here."

Vandross blinked rapidly. This was a dream, right? If it were, then why could he see things so clearly, smell them, hear them, feel them? The cold of the air around him raised goose bumps on his flesh, and the guard's presence suddenly sent a chill racing up his spine.

A colossal axe hung loosely in the giant suit's left hand, poised as if to swing with a turn of the wrist.

"The Orbs. They wish to speak to me, yes?"

The suit grumbled, but nodded.

"That is not enough, but thou art correct. What doth thou seek?"

Vandross smiled from ear to ear at this question.

"The power of the glorious Mother of Destruction," he whispered up at the suit. The giant nodded and stepped aside, opening the path from Vandross to the doors. Still, he protested. "Do not enter, thou mortal one, lest thou knowest what ye toy with."

Vandross waved his hand in dismissal at the giant, and grabbed the handle of one of the doors.

"I think I can handle myself," Richard Vandross said with the utmost disdain in his voice. With a heave, he threw open the left hand door, and found himself looking into a great and vaulted chamber.

Just on the other side of the doors was a dais of a sort, which connected to a slender, two or three hundred yard stone walkway that suspended over a lake of lava. Shimmering purple sigils pulsed in the stone floor and walkway, and out in the center of the lake of fire, hovering over it like a holy ground, was an altar. At the altar stood a figure, bent over it and hidden in a cloak with a hood over its head.

Vandross took a step into the chamber, and as his foot touched the floor, the ground rumbled, and the lake spat fire in an arc towards the unseen ceiling.

A line of purple and red energy shot through the floor at his feet, racing up the stone bridge like a bull, each second passing causing the ground to stir ever more. Finally, at the altar, the energy escaped into the air, taking the shape of an enormous, dual-headed spider.

At first, Vandross cringed at the sight of the creature; he had seen few things so hideous in appearance. Yet one of its eight legs crooked toward him, motioning him to join it and the cloaked figure at the altar.

Screwing up his courage, Richard Vandross started across the bridge toward the central circle. As he did, a serpent made of the pit's flames slithered up onto the circle and took a place at the hooded figure's side.

After what seemed an eternity, Vandross stood ten paces away from the trio of creatures. "All right, I'm here. Now show yourself to me," he demanded in a cool, collected tone.

The figure in the center pulled down its hood and opened its cloak to reveal a woman who was the spitting image of his own mother.

Vandross gasped, taking a defensive step back. "Do you mock me? What devilry is this creature?" He brought his magic to bear.

The woman passed a hand in front of Vandross, and his magic subsided, much against his will.

"Be still, Richard Vandross. You have many questions, and we may have answers to some of these questions. Allow me to introduce us. This," she said, indicating the spider-thing with a waving gesture. "Is Vengeance. He is our latest addition. You took him in with the third Orb of Eden's Serpent. This," she said, using the same sweep towards the snake of flames. "Is Spite. He was the second to occupy this space in your soul."

"This is my soul," asked Vandross incredulously. "This is bad comedy."

The woman simply smiled at him, her gray-blue eyes flashing darkly, menacingly.

"This *is* your soul, Richard Vandross. This whole temple, from its corridors, to its guardians, to this very chamber. Only we three and the guardian of this chamber are not manifestations of your own heart and mind."

Vandross had to concede that point—he did like the decor. But these creatures filled him with something he hadn't really and honestly felt in a long time. Dread.

"But make no mistake, we are not intruders. You have brought us into your being. I have introduced Vengeance and Spite to you, and they are yours to command, summon, and learn from."

"And who are you, woman," Vandross asked, raising his blind eyebrow.

"What is your name?"

"My name," the woman asked, putting her hand to her bosom in a very 'oh my' fashion. "My name is Power. And you are the one who wields me."

Vandross grinned despite himself. Perhaps this wouldn't be such a bad arrangement after all.

"Now, you have questions, as I have said. You may ask them of us, and we shall answer."

Vandross thought through his options, but decided to start small and work his way up.

"You came from the first Orb of Eden's Serpent, correct?"

The woman nodded. "Would it have mattered what order I absorbed them in, or does that bear no consequence on the order in which you appear?"

"It bears no consequence," she said, sitting on the steps before the altar.

Vandross leaned to one side, and saw a coffin of some sort behind the altar itself. *What is in there?* he wondered. *Later. Other questions to ask.*

"You have all three granted me new strength, wisdom, powers. What other purposes can I set you to?" Vandross himself sat cross-legged on the floor of the suspended circle.

"We have, many purposes," answered Vengeance, whose voice was akin to someone trying to speak while they were drowning. "We can, be summoned, for a short, time, into physical, existence. We would, retain, our forms that, you see, before you here," it continued, venom dripping from its fangs. "I, can poison people's, souls. I can, taint them. Make them, petty, and weak."

"I can drive people to new levels of hatred," hissed Spite, arms of fire sprouting from his serpentine body of flame. "I can pit them against one another, feed off of their natural violence. I can open their minds to untold horrors, that they may inflict them upon others."

"And what of you, Power," asked Vandross, pulling on his beard. "What do you bring to the table?"

"I can create copies of you," she said, almost seductively. "They will have the same powers and abilities as you did before you took us in. They will have a short period of corporeal existence. But they can serve as good distractions. And they can be good shock troops, in a tight pinch. I gave you the gift of teleportation. And I can see and hear over great distances, to serve as your eyes and ears where you cannot know what goes on."

Very good, he thought. Very good. That almost covers all of my bases.

"All right. Who are the other two? Their names, at least."

Power looked at him with a confused expression for a moment, before Vengeance spoke once more.

"The two, that remain, are Deceit, and Despair. The last, two Orbs, will bring them, to you."

Power nodded, and regained her look of calm and control.

"Good. Look," Vandross stood. "I only have two more questions, and then I have to wake up. Things to do, you know."

All three creatures, Power, Spite and Vengeance, looked eager to hear his questions.

"Who is that guardian at the door," he asked, pointing in the direction of the doors leading in.

"Ah, that is Locke, a Keeper. One exists in all creatures who have a soul."

"Are they all that ominous? Or hideous," Vandross asked, a look of doubt crossing his face. "Or well armed," he added with a hint of disapproval. "If this is my soul, why did I have to get past a doorman?"

"It is thus for all beings," said Power. "The Keepers have their own agenda, and work directly for the Gods and the rulers of the Hells. They are neutral beings, and often simply do what they feel is best for the one they inhabit. In Locke's case, things are different."

"How?"

"We now, inhabit, your soul," said Vengeance. "Our, presence, has changed, him. He has, not always, been, as he, is," the spider beast finished.

"Well, all right. I think I know just about enough about laughing boy," Vandross said with a smirk. "My second question. What's in that coffin behind the altar?"

All three creatures stood and came together in a tight line before the altar. They all turned as one, and kneeled, bowing to the altar and the coffin behind it.

"When all five of us have been brought together, we can open it," said Power, her voice wrapped in awe. "Within lies what you seek. Within," she said, turning to face Vandross. Her eyes had become black, hollow sockets in her skull, and her mouth was filled with daggers. "Is the Glorious Mother of Destruction."

Vandross flinched as the coffin shook on the stone floor, rattling as if something inside wanted desperately to be free, set loose upon the world. He suddenly felt he would scream, and did the next best thing; he turned and ran for the door to the chamber. Rushing through, he stumbled, tripping over one of Locke's huge iron boots. He sprawled across the floor, knocking his head hard on the concrete floor of the grand hallway. The door slammed shut behind him, and a heavy sigh escaped the giant suit of armor.

Vandross rolled over, propping himself up on the palms of his hands. He gazed up at the Keeper and took in its every detail as best he could. Red, angular full plate armor and shadows. That was all there appeared to be to the monolithic creature, aside from its wide, bloodshot, feline eyes, which now glared at him as though they were the eyes of a priest seeing a heretic in his church. A furl of red feathers jutted out of the top of its helmet, giving it the appearance of a royal Knight of some sort.

"What the fuck are you staring at," Vandross screamed up at Locke, who didn't even appear to acknowledge the fact that such a small, squishy thing had spoken to him.

"I am no longer sure," the booming voice said in a slow, methodical manner. "I am certain the same can be said for thou. For thou hast gazed upon me once before, dark one."

Vandross tried to think of how that was possible, but he didn't want to go through the possibilities. What was he even doing here? He had just knocked off for a quiet nap, that was all. And now his vision was blurring again. Wait a minute, he thought, but his train of thought was interrupted by the snap of consciousness. He was totally alone when he came to and looked around the throne room. He did not see the feral feline eyes staring at him from the shadows.

* * * *

Ellen Daires finished her prayers and decided to take a nice long walk in the woods outside of the city. *Perhaps it will calm my nerves,* she thought. The woods had always had that effect on her, tuning her in completely with mother Gaia, her chosen Goddess. A hundred questions roiled through her mind, a mob of demanding inquiries that would break down her defenses and come rushing out of her mouth if she did not employ her self-control.

The twittering of the birds and the shuffling of dead leaves under foot made her own little reality soften to her. The ground was firm and slightly springy, adding bounce to her step. Her meditative state of mind beguiled her, however, for after a while, she realized the sun hung directly overhead. Already noon had come.

Ellen lowered herself to the forest floor with her back resting against a solid sycamore tree, pulling her small backpack in front of her. She took out some bread and a wedge of cheese, and ate a solitary meal. The occasional woodland denizen approached her, clicking or cooing or making whatever noise they made, all to Ellen's delight. The animals did not fear her; for one thing, she was an Elf, and nature tended to be kind to her Race. For another, she possessed the magic power of the Earth Mother herself, Gaiamancy. She had trained for years, decades, and now stood as the head authority on Gaiamancy in the whole of the kingdom. Her peers admired her, her family was proud of her, and her few friends adored her. She lived a good life.

Which, she reflected somberly, had been exactly why her dream had disturbed her so greatly. It had shown her things she feared, abhorred, distrusted. How would she deal with the seer's prophecy? And what link, if any, did it have with the crimson-eyed creature she had seen in her slumber?

She looked at her hand, watching as it trembled ever so slightly. She had to get up and move, she thought. Movement meant action of some sort, even if it were aimless.

Collecting her thoughts and foodstuffs, Ellen brushed off her dress and moved off again. She had wandered far from Whitewood, a couple of hours at least. The Suesance River flowed from west to east perhaps a mile north of her. Perhaps the clear, sparkling water of the river would ease her worried mind some. Ellen moved with the grace of an ethereal spirit through the great forest, unaware of her proximity to Byron and his group.

She nearly walked right into the furry chest of a Cuyotai man, and the sudden presence of other humanoid life caused her to react defensively, fearfully.

The Cuyotai appeared startled, as did the two Humans and the shrouded figure behind them. Ellen thrust her hands into the air, her magic singing in harmony with the movements of the forest. Huge tree limbs bent and extended down in front of her, forming a barrier of thick wood to protect her from these potentially hostile people. She could detect Pyromancy from the Human woman, a tall, regal woman with a blood red dress, auburn hair and flaring, flame-filled eyes. A Gaiamancer's worst fear was the earth-rending flames of a Pyromancer. Fire blasted earth, scorched stone, and consumed wood, the elements a Gaiamancer most loved. But the Cuyotai youth, a warrior of some sort from the look of him, and the Paladin man, whose face held a quality of innocence, made her think that perhaps these people were not so foul.

"Who are you people," Ellen Daires demanded, her voice frail and shaking. "What do you do here in the forest of the Elven Kingdom?"

The Cuyotai looked back at the dark cloaked figure, who used magic of some sort to conceal himself. Something suddenly sank in Ellen's stomach— these were the people she had seen in the haze of her dream.

"You there, strange one. Reveal yourself. Cast off your disguise. I will know who comes to my homeland."

The other three individuals looked at the shadowy creature, who seemed to shrug his shoulders.

"You aren't going to like what you see, miss," rumbled the cloaked man.

Ellen stood her ground, readying her defenses and preparing to strike if need be.

The figure's arm waved in a semi-circle, and like a cloud of flies darting into the darkness, his masking shadows dissipated. Beneath them stood a large man in blue full plate armor, his black travel cloak hanging loosely from his shoulders, atop which sat a skull. A skull with white lights in the eye sockets instead of eyes.

"Aaaauuuggggh!" Ellen screamed and released her magic into the forest around her.

Byron drew his weapon, but not in time. A huge oak tree limb slammed into him, tossing him thirty feet into another tree, breaking it in half and toppling to the ground with a thud and a groan. Selena Bradford began to weave her own magic, but stopped short as something slick and wet. She looked down to see a thick stream of moss covering her body, gagging her and choking off her incantations.

At the same time, Hayes and Shoryu were backing away from half a dozen wooden golems summoned from the trees themselves. Shoryu launched his mystic arrows at the wooden warriors, but they had no effect.

Ellen Daires watched from behind her barrier, terrified and yet satisfied.

Until a set of burning red lights appeared just on the other side of her barrier, inches away from her face. They were set in the eyeless sockets of the creature she had seen in her dreams.

Byron shouted at her from behind the interwoven branches. "Stop this at once, woman! We don't want to harm you, but if we must in order to preserve ourselves, rest assured we will!" Byron raised one metal-gloved hand, extending his fingers and lashing out with thunder magic at the branches.

To his and Ellen's surprise, the wood held. A shout of panic from Shoryu distracted him, turned him away from Ellen. Hayes had gone to help Bradford out of her moss imprisonment, and Shoryu was being backed into a group of trees that had somehow shuffled together to form a wall.

Byron sprinted in front of Shoryu, gripping the Cuyotai tightly and lowering him to the ground, leaving his own back exposed to the wooden golems. They rained heavy fists and clubs down on Byron's back, forcing groans of pain from the Dread Knight.

"Byron, let me go," cried Shoryu, trying his hardest to tear free of the undead warrior's grip. But he could not. He could feel the hammering blows vibrate through Byron's armor. "Let me help you! James, Selena," he shouted, reaching one hand out to the Humans. "Help him. They're going to kill him." But both Humans struggled fiercely with the moss.

Ellen, however, stood stock still in shock. The dark creature was risking his own life for the Cuyotai's sake. She had misjudged him.

"One will frighten you, for who and what he seems to be," she whispered to herself, repeating the seer's vision. With a snap, she halted her magic and the guardian magics she had employed vanished back into the ground and trees.

Byron fell to the ground, his chest heaving and coughing up smoke. He sat up, and a small, white light glowed in his left hand. In awe, he pressed the palm flat against his own chest, and felt an exhilarating rush as healing magic flowed through his body. He flopped back onto his back a moment later, a grin plastered on his skull. Both powers he had regained had come alive. The blows from the wooden warriors would surely have crushed Shoryu or even him, despite his armor, but the Paladin spell known to the Order as Human Shield had reduced the damage and he had used the Healing Hand upon himself. Despite the severity of the situation, he felt great as he lay on his back, the crest of Sidius on his breastplate rising and falling with his breathing.

"Well, everything seems to be in order," he said, sitting up. Shoryu was visibly shaken by the ordeal, but he was smiling nevertheless. James Hayes and Selena Bradford stared hard back at Ellen Daires, who approached the group.

Grouped together, Byron's company was small, but Ellen's magic had been running low near the end. They would have been able to hang on. Were they creatures aligned with the dark, she'd surely be dead by now. Thank the Gods for small favors.

"I have made an error in judgment," the Elven Gaiamancer whispered to the group as a whole. "I did not mean to bring harm to good people."

"No harm done, miss," said Byron with a dismissing wave of his hand. This was a bit of a lie, however. Despite his Paladin spells, he felt raw and bruised from the battering he'd taken. Selena Bradford held an aggressive, battle-ready stance, her arms out at her sides.

"If I didn't need to invoke my magic through words, Elf, you would be little more than a smoking wisp of bones," Bradford hissed.

Byron shot her a look, as if to stop her short, but Selena Bradford was a passionate woman, and hadn't finished having her say. "Your magic is indeed impressive, Gaiamancer, but it will mean little when the man we combat against sends his armies this way. I hope that whatever little village you're from, you're all as talented as you, and willing to die despite that fact. The one-eyed devil will crush you all for certain, for he has none of our mer—"

Ellen interrupted her however, by dropping suddenly to the ground. A haunted expression locked on her face, and she rocked herself back and forth. The seer's prophecy, again. These people sought to stop the devilry of a one-eyed man, just the old seer foretold.

"What's wrong?" Shoryu placed a hand on Ellen's shoulder.

She came suddenly to, looking up into his deep, dark Cuyotai eyes. Here was a handsome specimen, she thought, immediately chastising herself for her wandering thoughts.

"I must take you all back to my city, now," she said, getting off of the ground with a heave and moving silently and swiftly away towards the southeast. "I come from the capital, Whitewood. A wise seer told me that you would come soon, that you would precede a wicked force."

Intrigued and guided by instinct to follow her, Byron led the way behind her.

"Can you describe this wicked force," Hayes asked out of curiosity.

"A one-eyed devil moves on the capital as we speak. I know not how, or why, but he seeks to bring us to ruin. And though we are mighty, our city shall need the aid of someone who is experienced in dealing with him. Will you help?"

Byron took a step toward her.

"We were on our way to your city. We had planned on a short visit to a friend of ours, Bael, but that will have to wait. We wish to deal with Vandross as quickly and forcefully as possible. Lead the way."

And so Byron's company grew in numbers by one more, but Byron had a feeling that one more person was necessary. He would find that ally in Whitewood, though he did not yet know who. At the moment, all he wanted was another chance at the man-devil Richard Vandross.

Chapter Ten
Inside the Soul

Richard Vandross paced about the throne room, trying to come to terms with the implications of his dream. He had already decided what to do, and had set his plans into motion. He had summoned around two hundred Shadowbeasts from the Hells and a contingent of three hundred creatures of his army, placing Vilec Roak in command of, and ordered them to begin the long march to Whitewood. That much hadn't required too much effort. In addition, he had cast out his manna, and felt his first demon, his experiment as an apprentice, awakening. Grigory Molis would be under his control once more.

The next part of his plans took quite a bit out of him. He had called Vengeance into physical existence. As the cone of purple energy flowed from Vandross's good eye, he had felt as though his body and soul were being torn apart. After the howling winds and shrieks of what sounded like damned souls, the smell of foul bile and vomit had died, Vandross had looked up to see the monstrosity within his throne chamber. It had not changed from his dream.

"You, called me, master," it shlooped.

"Indeed," Vandross wheezed. "I have sent a platoon to Whitewood. You possess the teleportation magic, so in three days I want you to join their group and report back to me on their progress. Without myself and with the wide assortment of Races I dispatched, I doubt very much that any use of magic will speed their progress."

Vandross chided himself inwardly; it would take twenty full days of marching with little or no rest for the platoon to get to the city of Whitewood from Mount Toane. He hadn't thought about the needs and habits of the creatures he sent to Whitewood. He knew very well that the Shadowbeasts could travel for days without food, water or rest. But they had only been one third of the forces he sent. Greenskins, Khan, and several types of unnatural abomination had gone along as well, including a handful of Vandross's own Dread Knights.

"I have, heard, your worries," slurped Vengeance. "It is, not such, a bad, thing. You, will be given, time, to plan your attack, on, the city. Also, I have, some news, of, my own."

Vandross returned to his throne from his pacing, weary and worn out. He signaled with his hand for Vengeance to continue.

"It, concerns, Locke."

Vandross sat upright in his seat. The guardian, though fearsome, had intrigued Vandross, mainly because the Keeper had supposedly existed in his soul from birth.

"He has, become, irritable. He does not, allow, any of us, to roam your mind, freely, anymore. He, only allows, one of us, out, at a time. And, he, accompanies, whomever, leaves, the chamber. Earlier, he, locked us in."

"Can he do that," Vandross asked, amazed that he was carrying a conversation with this creature, who resided chiefly in his soul, about another creature who also lived within him. Madness seemed to crawl all around him. He hadn't ever considered that the soul could encompass its own reality.

"He, apparently, can. But Power, was able to, open the door. When she did, the Keeper, Locke, was not, there."

Vandross paused a moment, running his fingers through his stubbly beard. The implications disturbed as well as intrigued him. The Keeper roamed through his soul and his mind, but for what purpose? How, or better yet, why, had he locked Power, Vengeance and Spite in the central chamber? Vandross decided that he would speak to the Keeper when next he slept. He would get the creature to divulge whatever information Vandross needed or wanted, or he would pay for it.

"My lord, I, think, I know what, you plan, to do. I would, advise, against it." The spider-beast skittered a short way away, toward the entrance tunnel to the throne room.

"Why is that Vengeance?" Vandross heard a trace of fear in the watery-voiced manifestation, and it didn't sit well with him.

"Keepers are, inherently, neutral. But if, you confront him, his neutrality, may not rule over, his, rage. He was not, as, intimidating, or aggressive, as he, is now, until we, showed, up."

"He wouldn't dare harm me," Vandross growled, his ire rising, turning his blood to liquid fire. "I am his host. Besides, Power said that Keepers act in the best interests of their host." Vengeance's multiple eyes blinked rapidly, making a wet smacking noise like bloody hunks of meat slapped together.

"Usually, yes, they do. But," Vengeance said, raising one of his eight legs like an upward thrust finger. "Not always. Keepers act, as they do, in what they feel, is the best interests, of, the host. Their idea, of what's best, for the host, sometimes, is in, disagreement, with, the host's idea. Now then, let us, change, the subject."

Vandross was all for that. The topic of Locke had made him reach the high limit of his tolerance. But he was tired once again, and dismissed Vengeance in order to go to the old quarters where he had slept during his apprenticeship to Tanarak.

After the long walk to the dusty chamber, he felt even more fatigued. Richard Vandross stood over his bed a moment. Then he fell face first onto its soft, welcoming surface. He was asleep in seconds.

* * * *

Ellen Daires led Byron's company through the city streets of Whitewood, the Dread Knight following closely behind, wrapped in shadows and smoke. The scent of freshly baked pastries warmed everyone's noses, and each in turn smelled their own clothing. None were satisfied with the difference.

"Could we take baths at your home," asked Shoryu, who had shown a keen interest in the Elven Gaiamancer.

She smiled and nodded at him, a simple gesture, but one that filled the Cuyotai youth with a giddy fluttering in his stomach.

Byron held back a moment, drawing himself parallel to the young Hunter.

"Quite taken by her, aren't you," he whispered into Shoryu's ear, making the pup start and jump. But Shoryu grinned broadly and shoved Byron playfully.

"Well, I've always had a thing for Elves. And she's gorgeous."

Byron agreed with Shoryu's assessment. Ellen Daires truly was a fair Elven woman, fairer than most he had seen in the city.

"And she likes canines," added Alex from Byron's shoulder, also concealed by the shadow magic. "Gonna see if she wants to share your bone," teased Alex, which earned him a flick from Byron's finger.

"Get your mind out of the gutter, Alex," Byron growled at the Ki Fairy, glaring at him from under his hood. "He's just a boy."

"A young man as I recall," retorted Alex, hovering just in front of Byron. "And young men have to do certain things to become real men. Like, I don't know, having a little-"

Thwack. Once again he was struck, only this time by Shoryu.

Ellen, a good ten feet in front of the group, had been spared this little bit of banter, and Shoryu couldn't be happier about that. He didn't want her to think he was some sort of pig, or child. At last Ellen approached the front door of a small cottage on the outskirts of the south end of the city.

"I have an old friend over, so I'll pop in first and tell him I have company. I'm sure he'll be interested to meet you all." Ellen slipped inside, and Alex fluttered up to the keyhole.

"It's a Dwarf," he squeaked, stunned to see a single Dwarven man in a city full of Elves. "Burly fellow."

"Most Dwarves are," commented James Hayes, who until that moment had been wrapped up in his own thoughts. He was thinking back to Desanadron, and the short trip he had taken to Fort Flag. The place had lain in ruin, bodies already decomposing in the sun, flies raging with the sound of a thousand hornets. Something had drawn him back, leading him directly to the small church within the fort walls. His mentor, Commander Mensia, had been eaten alive by something, but his weapon still hummed with holy power in the middle of the floor. Hayes had retrieved the Morning Glory, sheathed it, and gone back to Byron in Desanadron before they departed.

"Thank you, oh master of the obvious," snapped Alex. He had been unusually grumpy, Byron noticed.

Perhaps the Ki Fairy felt left out. After all, with the company's assorted powers and abilities, the little trickster must have felt useless. Byron hoped inwardly he'd come around soon, but he would be patient with the Ki Fairy if he didn't. After all, Alex had been his first friend since Byron had regained his free will.

"Augh," Alex shouted as the door swung open on him.

A Dwarven man, tall for his Race, stood in the doorway, his features craggy and weathered with time and battle. He wore a dirty white tunic, and black flowing pants, very lightweight protection for a Dwarven warrior. But his face appeared to have been broken many times over the years, and his beard was better trimmed and shorter than most men of his Race. Open fingered gloves hung tied together from his belt, blades sticking out of the knuckles. He was a Boxer, Byron realized, and very, very familiar.

"Friends," Ellen said, "I'd like to introduce you to a good friend and companion of mine for about the last ten years. This is Morek Rockmight."

A rushing gale of static noise blared inside of Byron's head. Morek Rockmight! He had led a unit of his men in Mount Toane during the Final Push. He had survived the horrors of Tanarak's minions, and all the years since. Byron saw that he was not alone however, in remembering the Dwarf.

"Morek Rockmight," breathed James Hayes.

"James Hayes," rumbled the unusually light, tenor voice of the Dwarven Boxer. The two shook hands, stepping back afterwards. "I'll try to guess the rest of you. You must be Shoryu," he said, shaking the Hunter's paw. "Selena Bradford." Another handshake. "Alex, the Ki Fairy," he said, merely nodding at Alex, who was rubbing his head. "But you, stranger, Ellen did not name. Who are you?"

Byron hesitated a long moment, uncertain of how to proceed. Dwarves tended to react violently at the sight of things like Byron. Dread Knights weren't exactly on their list of teatime invitations.

"Let us go inside first, Morek," Byron said, looking up and down the busy street. "I don't want to reveal myself in public."

Morek raised an eyebrow at him, but went inside anyway. The front door led directly into a comfortable den, where everyone took a seat on a chair or the couch. Morek's belongings sat on the floor next to the day bed, where he had slept the last two nights.

"All right, we're inside," the Dwarf said, getting right to the point.

Typical Dwarven impatience, Byron grumbled to himself.

"Who are you?"

Byron waved his hand and dismissed the concealing magic.

Morek Rockmight immediately put his gloves on and took up a fighter's stance.

"You have known me, Morek Rockmight, son of Tumari Rockmight, son of Shugek Rockmight. I am Byron, formerly Byron of Sidius."

"Formerly nothing, beast," screamed Morek as he tensed himself. "The foul crest of Tanarak and his people stands on your chest!"

"Let me finish," Byron sighed patiently. "I am Byron, formerly of Sidius, formerly Aixler." Morek stopped his habitual bouncing, his hands slowly drooping to his sides.

"Byron," he asked quietly, looking the undead warrior up and down. "How was I so stupid? Byron Aixler disappears, and suddenly," he said, walking to the couch, flopping down beside James Hayes and Selena Bradford. "Suddenly this creature, Byron of Sidius, appears? I should have known." Morek Rockmight stood up like a bolt of lightning, a grin spreading maliciously across his face. "So you say you're Byron Aixler, eh," he asked.

"Formerly," Byron said with a nod and a frown. He added it in the same way he added bits to Lee Toren's stories.

"Well, I guess you won't mind answering a few questions then. Just to prove you're not still the beast that slaughtered the men and women in the end of the battle of Final Push. First question, creature. Who was the first man killed during that battle?"

Byron knew this one easily; it had been funny, in a macabre sort of way.

"It was Harold Dutchess, a Human Knight. He was seventy-four years old, we all wanted to let him get his dying wish, one more battle. He had a heart attack before we even entered Mount Toane."

Morek nodded his head slightly, impressed but not going for it yet.

"All right, next question. Who was your family?"

Byron's heart hammered in his chest, and his lungs felt suddenly tight and useless. His wife, his son, both dead. How, he could not remember, but he knew that they had died after his own ill-fated defeat at Mount Toane. He could remember the smell of his wife, Alexia, as she held him tight to her body, begging him not to join the Final Push. His son, Jonas, clinging to his leg, determined not to let his father go into battle. The dampness on his finger as he dried Jonas's streaming tears, lifting his chin and telling him to be brave for him. Byron realized he had been staring at that pointer finger for a minute or two, Rockmight still waiting for a response.

"My wife was Alexia Ashburn, daughter of Father Victor Ashburn, a Cleric in the Order of Oun. My son," he said, his voice breaking inexplicably, catching in his throat. Though he had no eyes, Byron could feel the hot sting of tears welling up inside his sockets, somewhere behind the twin pinpoints of light. "My son, was Jonas Aixler. He was my whole world," he said, his words and voice trailing off. A flush of embarrassment hit him, and he excused himself momentarily into Ellen Daires's kitchen. He waited until the door between the two rooms had swung shut, and proceeded to cradle his face in his armored hands. Jonas, he thought. My sweet, playful boy. His mind reeled with memories of his Human life, and he swayed where he stood, experience a bout of vertigo that would easily unbalance a normal man.

But his presence of mind kept him upright. He didn't want to wreck the Elven Gaiamancer's kitchen just because he couldn't control his emotions or his mind's eye. Another image flooded his mind, and Byron found himself looking at his son and wife over his shoulder as he rode off with the army that had failed to halt Tanarak of Sidius. In failing, he had been reduced to the creature he now was, and had lost his family. He had nothing left to live for, except to see Richard Vandross brought down. It would have to be enough.

"Are you all right," a soft, feminine voice spoke next to Byron, who still held his hands over his face. He expected to see Ellen Daires next to him, but it was the Human Pyromancer, Selena Bradford. A look of honest concern lay on her face, her eyes open and searching. Byron had not known the woman long yet, but he had formed the opinion that she was an impenetrable fortress when it came to emotions. Yet there she was, a hand touching gently on Byron's elbow.

"I was just, remembering," he offered weakly, his hands lowering to his sides, his chin touching his chest plate. "My wife and child are dead. I am not certain how I know this, but I do." He took a deep breath, his chest expanding, and slowly released it, smoke and dust misting out of his armor.

"If it's any consolation, I'm sorry," said Morek Rockmight in his guttural voice as he too entered the small kitchen.

Byron slowly turned to face the tall Dwarf, who had removed his gloves and had one thick hand extended. Byron took it in his own, easily holding the whole of it in his palm.

"All is forgiven," Byron said, a small grin pulling his jawbone up. The two men kept their hands locked a moment longer.

"It's good to have you back, Byron," Rockmight whispered, releasing Byron's hand and standing almost at attention. "The young lad, Shoryu his name is?"

Byron nodded.

"He's briefly told me the situation. Vandross is a name that does not carry well here in the Elven Kingdom, I'll tell you that. And not just because of recent transgressions either." Byron wanted the chance to know anything about Vandross that he could find out. Perhaps Rockmight could provide.

"Does he have a history here, Morek?" Byron moved to return to the den, but Morek stayed in his path. "Something wrong?"

"Well, er, the lad, Shoryu that is," Morek said, apparently embarrassed. "They seem to be hitting it off rather well. Thought we might give them a chance to chat, get to know each other." The normally taciturn Dwarf grinned like a fool. "The boy's quite taken with her."

Byron rolled his eyes and shook his head.

"We've noticed," squeaked Alex from his perch on Byron's shoulder. "One can only imagine the sort of horrible mental images I'd get if they started getting, you know, reeeeeal close."

"Back to business," Byron said with a tone of seriousness, though he was indeed interested in Shoryu's attraction to the Elven Gaiamancer. Sure, she was pretty, and sure, that sort of relationship had occurred a few times in the land of Tamalaria, but would Shoryu be so open about it if his father were around? If his people knew?

"What do you know about Vandross, Morek?"

Everyone took seats around the kitchen table, including Alex on top of the table itself.

Morek grabbed a pitcher of cold tea from Ellen's cold storage closet, poured himself a glass, and sat down, thinking about where to begin.

Byron waited patiently while the Dwarf ran his hand through his well-trimmed beard.

"Well, first off, he's well known here in the kingdom. About ten years ago, he came through, looking like something out of the seven Hells. Big armor, big weapons, bad attitude. But he kept himself within the boundaries of the kingdom's laws, at least he seemed to. People noticed his frequent visits to the Lizardman villages throughout the area, especially the one near the capital here.

143

It's only a half-day's walk away from the city. Anyway, people didn't like him. A lot of folks talked about connections between him and Tanarak. Of course, no one could prove anything, so he was kept watch on, but no one made any move against him. The Elven Kingdom has laws stating that no one can just be arrested or jailed just for being suspicious, except in times of war." Morek took a long pull on his tea, wiping his mouth with a burly forearm. His eyes had the hazy aspect of someone remembering something unpleasant, but he continued despite his thoughts.

"Well," Morek said, continuing his tale. "He sort of dropped off of everyone's map for a few weeks. Disappeared from his inn room one night, and no one saw him for a while. When they did see him, he had company. About a dozen Lizardmen were allowed into the capital with him, because the Elves try not to harbor any bad feelings with them. But these particular reptiles, they came from a tribe well known for their aggression. That night, there were screams from his room, and guards were sent to investigate. They broke down his door and found him pulling his armor on. He had an Elven woman," Morek said, having difficulty continuing his story. He didn't like to recall these sorts of things; he personally held Elven folk to be one of the kindest, wisest and noblest of all people. What had happened was a tragedy to him and to the city. "He had her strapped to the bed, spread eagle. He had raped her and beaten her, though not to death. The guards moved in to arrest him, probably throw in a few good punches and kicks on the way," he said, spitting the words with disgust. "They ought to have killed him," he snarled, slamming a meaty fist down on the table.

Silence hung in the air a moment, until he continued.

Morek shook his head, his eyes glued to the table. "But he was quick. He used some spell on them, and the guards killed each other. Vandross ordered his men to accompany him out of the city. They slaughtered eight more guards and constables on their way out. No one has seen him here in the capital since."

"What about the woman," Byron asked, his voice hushed. He could tell that Morek was not on comfortable ground here. The Dwarven Boxer was not a man of words, but of action, and these were not words easily spoken, even by a neutral party, which Morek was not.

Morek took another long swig of his drink, then stood up and walked to the sink, washing the dish in the pump water.

"She lives still here in the city. And," he said, looking Byron in the eyes. "She has a son. He is the bastard child of Richard Vandross."

Byron, James Hayes and Selena Bradford all stared at Morek in disbelief.

"I only use the word because of the nature of his birth. Timothy is a good lad, even with his father's last name."

"She gave him Vandross's last name," Hayes asked incredulously.

Morek nodded somberly. "The young woman hates what was done to her, but she loves the boy. She thinks he will do something good with the name. Vandross has a long family history of Fallen Knights and Necromancers. I guess he wanted to follow tradition as hard as he could." Sarcasm edged

Morek's tone. "The boy is a Half-Elf of nine years of age, and has already shown some talent with magic, though the nature of his talents is disliked. He is a Void Mage."

Byron cocked the bone where his eyebrow had been over his left eye. He had never heard of a Void Mage.

"Right, you've likely not heard of them Byron. Void Mages are extremely rare, and typically despised by other magic users. You see, they gain magic powers by simply being around them. Anyone with magic near him may have their powers absorbed into his arsenal."

Byron was intrigued; a form of magic wherein years of study were not necessary.

"I assume he has to stay around the magic user to use that spell?"

Morek shook his head. "Once a spell is taken, the Void Mage has permanent use of it, at the same level of power as the one who it was taken from. But it is difficult to get a spell just being around it. The best way for a Void Mage to learn a spell is to be struck by it themselves. But Void Mages also learn fighting techniques in the same way."

Byron raised his bone-brow once again in surprise.

"Warrior mages who can learn by observation and receiving punishment? Hell's bells, sign me up," he jested, getting a chuckle out of the group. "But seriously, the boy and his mother can be of no help to us. He's too young, she too personally connected to this all. I'll just take what you've told me into account. I hardly want to learn anything from those poor people. In any event, we'll need to make ready." Byron stood and walked into the den, where Shoryu and Ellen were whispering to each other.

Both looked up and slid a little bit apart as the big Dread Knight shouldered through the doorway. A sloppy grin formed on Byron's skull, and he folded his arms in front of his chest. "Getting along well, are we?"

Shoryu's cheeks burned bright crimson, as did the fairer skinned Ellen, whose color change lit up the room.

Byron gut-laughed for a moment, and clapped Shoryu on the knee. "Not to worry young one. But you should wrap things up shortly. We still have to go talk to Bael, so we need to head out soon."

"I'll come with you." Ellen stood up razor-straight. There was a look of hope, and a look of peace in her eyes. There was also a slight heaving in her bosom.

Just how long had Byron been in the kitchen talking with the others? He leaned over to look at Shoryu, who suddenly found intense fascination with the design of the front door. *Heheh*, Byron thought. Why not? He'll have a new 'friend', and we'll have a competent mage along who doesn't want to kill everything in her path.

"Very well. But," Byron said, pointing an accusatory finger at her. "Pack light, young lady. We're only going to a Lizardman village nearby, and we should be back by morning. No need to be heavy with belongings."

She nodded, quietly thanked Byron, then skated past him towards her bedroom.

In her absence, Byron sat down next to the young Cuyotai Hunter. "Soooooo," he said, drawing the word out like a schoolyard chum might if he were teasing his friend for having a girlfriend. "You know, we may be on a long journey yet, Shoryu."

"I know." The pup, clearly still embarrassed, didn't look at Byron.

"And there may be, well, times when someone will have to buddy up, to keep our number of tents low," Byron went on, not bothering to hide his innuendo.

"I know," said Shoryu, slightly more flustered. He was practically sweating a waterfall.

"And you know, she is a very pretty girl. About your age I suspect," Byron said. Finally he decided to abandon the whole playful teasing. "Look, Shoryu, I've come to really appreciate your presence. Your friendship means a lot to me."

Shoryu looked into those dark, eyeless sockets, and for a moment, he saw not the fierce and capable warrior Byron was. He didn't even see the regal Paladin he had once been. He saw, in those cavernous spaces, heard in the tone of his words, the father Byron had once been. Shoryu's thoughts turned to his own father, and his caretaker after his father's death, the village Chieftain. He was still young, it was true, and for a moment he resented Byron's seeming assumption of the role of caretaker. But how could he be angry about it? Byron had probably saved his life from the very woman he was falling quickly in love with. He would let whatever Byron said go, and take from it what he could.

"When this whole business with Vandross is over, we'll have a long talk about your future. I see great things ahead for you, Shoryu," Byron said, patting the boy on the back as he stood up from the couch. "I really do."

In the kitchen, with the door cracked open barely an inch, Alex made a gagging gesture at Selena, Hayes and Morek.

The Paladin thwacked him with one finger, causing the Ki Fairy to mutter more curses than James had imagined could exist in one language.

* * * *

The world shimmered into focus around Richard Vandross. He was staring straight up at a high, vaulted ceiling. He propped himself up on his palms, looking around at what appeared to be a display room for statues. Busts of men and women, some of whom he knew and others he didn't recognize stood atop white marble pedestals in the circular chamber. He had not been here before, but he knew he was within his own soul once again.

A blue marble floor stretched all the way to the walls, the room itself about fifty feet in diameter. Vandross tried to get to his feet, but found the going rough. It required much more effort than he would have thought necessary, his lack of strength most likely reflected his fatigued state in the waking world. At least, that was his rationale.

He looked around the chamber once more, making note of doors on either side of him, both equidistant to his position. He would have left, but the statues held his interest. Slowly, methodically, he stalked from artwork to artwork, taking in the detail and arrangement of each piece.

Most were small sculptures depicting battles Vandross and his minions had fought under the rule of Tanarak of Sidius, but a few were of more recent victories. A few, however, were of his own men being butchered by soldiers and mages. He stopped to look at one that infuriated him the most, that of Byron standing over his body after the Dread Knight had knocked him out, weeks ago outside of Koreindar.

There were also paintings hung upon the walls, and these he cared for not at all. They were family portraits, pictures he recognized from his younger days. One was of himself, his mother and his father. His father, Brian Vandross, had been a simple, hard working farmer, quite unlike Richard's grandfather, Simon. Simon Vandross had been a Fallen Knight who had carved a nice chunk of the northeast out for himself. He had ruled over the Port of Arcade for forty years, mocking his son Brian for his ethics and morals, and eventually casting him out of Arcade.

And there, upon the wall next to the door to his left, was a shifting vision in paint, a replay of the slaughter of Richard's hometown and its people. The perspective was very familiar; he watched the scene of the carnage as he himself remembered it, the bandits hacking and piercing his townsfolk with blades and arrows, showing no mercy as they rampaged, looted and burned.

"No," he whispered, watching the bandits morph and shift into the forms of hulking black monstrosities. "No. That is not how it happened," he cried, watching his father beg for his life before being cut down.

A piercing headache throbbed painfully behind his good eye, the pain shooting suddenly from somewhere in the back of his skull. He clutched his head with both hands, cupping his ears as the pain produced a high-pitched whining noise in his head. Slowly the pain receded as he drew in large, calming breaths. "He was weak," he hissed at himself, at the painting. "He deserved his end, and so did those bandit fools."

He turned back to the statue of his defeat at Byron's hand outside of Koreindar. With one iron-gloved hand he swatted the artwork to the floor, smashing apart on the marble floor. He smiled, but noticed that only his own visage had broken. He growled deep in his throat, and crushed the figure of Byron under his boot.

"Was that really necessary," said a familiar, booming voice from directly in front of him.

Vandross looked up and saw the Keeper, Locke, standing there in his huge red suit of armor. The armor itself had become more angular since last Vandross had seen him, giving it an almost bladed look. Those huge, feline, bloodshot eyes glared out of the darkness within the red-feathered helmet, bearing down on Vandross without quarter.

Blind rage pumped through Vandross at the sound of that voice, the sight of those eyes. "Bite me, blowhard," he screamed at Locke, picking up a chunk of the broken statue and hurling it at the huge Keeper. The very action itself satisfied him, but as the object sail through the air, there was a blur of red movement, and in the blink of an eye, the giant suit loomed over Vandross. He heard the chunk of statue break apart against the wall where the Keeper had been standing. "How? That isn't possible," he rasped.

"That was foolish of you, Richard Vandross," boomed Locke. The Keeper brought his hand back, and slapped Vandross hard across the face, sending him sprawling to his right, ten feet from one of the doors out of the room.

As he got to his knees, he looked up, saw the big red menace slowly marching toward him, and tried to backpedal to the door.

"Thou hast no need to fear now. Thou struck at me, and I have struck at thee. We are even." Locke ceased his approach.

Vandross rubbed his cheek where he had been backhanded; the blow had hurt more than anything he could remember.

"Stand up, and I shall speak unto thee about the nature of this chamber."

Vandross did as he was told, his stomach filled with bile that made him want to wretch. *No need to fear*, he thought.

"I am Richard Vandross. I have no fear," he said stoically, stalking boldly up to the huge Keeper.

Locke's eyes remained wide open, showing no inflection or change of mental state. But there was something there, something more menacing than anything Vandross had ever seen in his life. He spoke brave words, but in truth, he was quickly becoming reacquainted with an emotion he had long since thought dead in him; terror.

"Indeed, thou speaks unto me bravely, but this is your soul. The vibrations within thee tell me a different tale. Now," Locke said, looking about the room and spreading his enormous arms wide. "This is my Hall of Truth. It is one of the few chambers within your soul that is my own, and mine alone. How thou arrivest within, t'is a mystery to me. But I shall explain as best I may what thou see. When first I spake unto thee, I warned thou about the things thou wouldst see here. Alas, that thou hast broken one of my finest pieces in thine anger."

Richard looked down at the crushed figure of Byron.

"You made all these," he asked in a hushed tone.

The Keeper nodded. "Indeed. All of your greatest moments have I sculpted and forged in mine furnace, to keep here, that I may review them at my leisure. I have even painted a few pictures, as you see. At present, I have little time for them. I shall not have time to replace that particular piece. It took me the better part of a week to do. Thou art busy lately, and I have little time aside from mine duties to spare for this hobby." Locke sighed heavily, bending slightly in clear disappointment. "You have a question," he said, knowing that Vandross was about to grill him.

"How is it that you are able to strike me, Keeper," Vandross demanded angrily. His fists began to ball up and shake with rage. "How is it that you are changed from the last time I saw you? What are you doing here? I don't want you here!"

Locke stood once more to full height, turning fully to face Vandross. The enigmatic creature easily had two feet on Vandross, and was broad in the way that roads are long.

"I do what I must to keep the host's best interests protected. Thou struck at me, the very protector of thy soul. So I struck you."

"What, for my own good? I find that very hard to swallow." He crossed his arms in front of his chest.

"As to your second question," Locke continued, ignoring Vandross's outburst. "I change as you change. Thy actions affect the soul, and thusly, me. Thy plans are to prepare for war, and so, I too must prepare for war. And lastly," the Keeper boomed, bending down so that his helmet visor was eye level to Vandross, his faceplate brushing the man's nose. "I don't care if you want me here or not. I have a duty to perform, and may still complete sufficiently. Thou may live long enough to see thy son."

"You cannot fool me," Vandross said, pointing his finger at Locke, who half turned to face him once more. "I have no son! I shan't fall for such a ploy."

Locke shook his massive head slowly, and pointed to one of the artworks near the opposite side of the room from Richard Vandross. The one-eyed devil's heart jumped into his throat, and a sickening quake shook his gut. He stalked swiftly through the statues, and came upon one that sparked his memory. It showed an Elven woman, tied to a bed, weeping, as Vandross adjusted his upper armor across the room. He had forgotten those events. He had spent most of those days in a drunken stupor, given vacation time from his master's death. The entire time had been little more than a blur for him, but memory had a way of slamming into him lately.

"Your son resides in the city you plan to attack, Whitewood. He is a Half-Elf by the name of Timothy Vandross." Locke approached Vandross once more.

There was silence in the Hall of Truth for some time as Richard Vandross stared at the sculpture. The air around him had gone cold, raising gooseflesh on his arms. The scent of jasmine, one of his favorite odors, wafted through the air in a haze. It had been the odor of the perfume the Elven woman had worn when he ravished her. The room had been cold. Slowly, the Hall of Truth began to take on more aspects of that moment, and Vandross shook his head against the encroaching memory.

"I don't want to, I don't want to remember," he rasped, feeling the Keeper's hand rest gently on his shoulder.

"Locke," a female voice cried out from behind them. Power stood in the Hall of Truth with Spite, both of them glaring disapprovingly at the Keeper. "You have no authority to bring him here."

"He came of his own volition," barked Locke back at the incarnation.

Power flinched, clearly afraid of the creature. "But thou art correct," he said with a sigh of disappointment. The room returned to its original stale, clean smell and temperature. "I have overstepped my boundaries. But know this," Locke said, pulling the same dashing maneuver he had pulled on Vandross. Vandross could see that Power had tripped over her own feet in shock, trying to put distance between herself and the Keeper. "Those boundaries only apply to you so long as he wishes you to remain here. The moment he comes to his senses and banishes you fiends, I shall fall upon you like the wrath of a furious God. Make no mistakes about that." Locke turned and vanished, simply disappearing into thin air.

Vandross felt a lifting sensation, like a great weight had been removed from him. He smiled at Power.

"Thank you, Power," he said, shaking his head. "I was beginning to lose my conviction for a minute there."

"Keepers tend to have that effect on people," she said, brushing herself off. "I sensed that you were here. There is something you should know."

Vandross raised his good eyebrow for a moment, interested. He gave her a hand signal to indicate he was listening.

"Our brothers, Deceit and Despair. Both are not necessary to resurrect the Mother," she said, walking gracefully toward Vandross.

His vision was becoming hazy, blurred. He knew his own body was waking up in the real world. He didn't have much time.

"So it can be done with only four," he asked, his voice losing strength. "Why do you tell me this?"

"Because Byron of Sidius prepares to face you in Whitewood. He has many allies now, and together they are a formidable foe."

"Wait," Vandross said, putting up a finger and shaking off the blurring in his vision. "How do you know that, yet I don't?"

"My connection to Vengeance. He has gone ahead to check the situation. All does not bode well. We need to proceed with caution."

Vandross nodded, knowing himself how dangerous Byron could be. With allies, it could get very ugly. And the former paladin's dark powers might still be a match for Vandross's own magic. He would have to get Vengeance back soon, so he could find out what the spider-beast had learned. Then it would be a nice trip right back into his soul for the drowning-voiced critter. Vandross's head began to swim in noise, and he sat upright in his bed.

* * * *

The village's new leader, a man who had been gone a long time but was still loved and cherished among the elders, walked from hut to hut, tent to tent, meeting and greeting the individuals under his charge. Life had been very complicated for the poor man, and here he was being given a second chance. But although life in the village seemed simple, many of its denizens had been soldiers at one time, and understood his requests. Smithies were hard at work pounding out weapons and armor, fletchers busy making bows and arrows. There would be war in the coming weeks, and they did not want to be caught off-guard or out of position.

The middle-aged leader, Bael, saw to the arrangements himself. On his return to his hometown he had convinced the people of the village that he was their long-lost son, the great General Bael. He was General no more, but he still commanded, and the village knew him to be the young reptilian warrior who had set out all those years ago to prove his greatness to the world. They had heard of his exploits, and though he held no pride in what he had done, they did give him their respect for his capabilities and commanding presence. He had been named the new leader less than three days after his return.

Now he stood in front of a smithy tent, viewing the progress on the repairs to his armor. He had promised to aid Byron and his company in the battle against Vandross, and when then he would return here, to a new life. He would be finished with being a soldier. But he needed one more battle, one more war. He needed one more victory. And he would stop at nothing to get it.

He walked around the outskirts of the village after seeing that all was going well with his armor. He nearly walked right into a pale young Elf woman, and had to excuse himself. Before he could look away from the Elven woman's captivating smile, his eyesight blurred as he found himself looking cross-eyed into a huge crest on a suit of armor. He looked up and into the depthless wells of Byron's eyes. The undead warrior's jaw pulled up to the left, giving him a wicked looking smile.

"Greetings, Bael," he rumbled from deep in his throat. "I told you we'd come to chat."

Bael smiled and embraced the Dread Knight, clapping him hard on the back and laughing. Dust plumed out of Byron's mouth as he coughed at the harshness of the blow. Bael seemed to forget that he was especially strong for his Race.

"Of course my friend," Bael said cheerfully. He looked at Ellen Daires and Morek Rockmight, a question on the tip of his tongue. Selena Bradford and James Hayes appearance didn't surprise him. They were just Humans. But an Elf and a Dwarf, he thought. "I see you've made a couple of additions to your band. Who are these two?" He pointed at the Elf and Dwarf.

"This is Ellen Daires, a Gaiamancer and a formidable opponent," Byron explained. "We stumbled upon her on our way. And her friend is Morek Rockmight, one of the leaders of the city of Traithrock."

"In the Western Mountains? Well," he said, crossing his arms. "You are a long way from home master Morek."

The Dwarven Boxer nodded and looked around at the scores of working and chatting Lizardmen and women.

"And the Humans?"

"They are James Hayes, Paladin of the Order of Oun, and Selena Bradford, Pyromancer of Desanadron."

Bael gave them a small bow.

"Come with me." He led Byron's company to the village's center. The whole of the village sat in the forest in much the same arrangement as Shoryu's home.

The young Hunter thought about home, and how much he missed it. He walked arm-in-arm with Ellen, with whom he quickly developed a strange sort of relationship. There existed a natural attraction, but he couldn't figure out if Ellen wanted him to make the first real move, or if he should wait on her. They had spoken at her house of the ways in which they seemed similar and the ways they seemed different. As they'd talked, they had inched closer and closer to each other, until Byron had opened the door from the kitchen and teased him.

Bael motioned for the company to sit around the circle of a huge fire pit. When everyone had taken a seat, Bael called, in his gruff, guttural natural tongue, to someone working one of the smithy shops.

A burly, busty Lizardwoman sauntered over and handed him a folder.

Everyone kept questioning eyes on Bael, who looked about with an expression of 'what' on his face.

"Pretty handy, Bael," chided Byron in the same fashion as he had Shoryu. "Strong, skilled, and ample. A looker for you, maybe?"

Bael sat stunned for a moment and then erupted in laughter.

"A looker, eh, Byron? Well, I should think so," he said, giving Byron a playful shove that knocked the Dread Knight off the log he was seated on. "My mother takes good care of herself! Hahahahaha!"

Feeling like a bit of an ass, Byron got back to his seat, the rest of the company giggling at his expense. *Fair enough*, he thought, grinning despite himself.

"This," Bael said, "is a packet of information I received from my allies. I've been getting them via messenger bird for a few days now."

"Information on what," asked Hayes, coming out of another memory trance. He had been slipping in and out of memories the last few days. He had been questioning his faith despite Byron's help in Desanadron. He had so many questions that he could not help but think them over when not engaged in conversation.

Selena had known to let him alone while he remembered, respecting his distance. She had seen the Paladin at his most desperate, and though she didn't have feelings for him like Ellen and Shoryu had for one another, she was concerned nonetheless. He wouldn't be much good to the group if he froze up.

"Information concerning Vandross and his movements. There's a large and mixed bunch marching on Whitewood right now," Bael said, leafing through the letters. "At their current pace, they'll arrive at the city's gates in about thirteen days' time. Byron, Whitewood needs to be warned, and they need to make some friends very quickly. They take well to alarms being raised, but not so much so to the idea of making non-Elven friends. No offense meant, miss," he said, nodding to Ellen.

She smiled at him slightly and shook her head.

"I do not agree with all of the policies of the city, Mr. Bael," she said calmly. "The entire kingdom needs to be a bit less centrist and racist. Do you know there are dozens of Cuyotai villages in the kingdom, and his majesty won't even allow them to live in the cities? They can come in and stay at an inn, sure, but they are not allowed to own property within a city. It is folly." She spat on the fire pit.

"What do you suggest we do, Byron?" asked Hayes, his eyes locked on the undead warrior. He still couldn't understand how Byron subsisted. How did the man eat? Hayes had seen him toss back water and liquor, but he hadn't seen the Dread Knight eat anything. Not that Byron couldn't eat: indeed, he enjoyed the taste of food, but it was all devoid of sustenance for him. He hadn't shown the others, other than Shoryu and Alex, what it meant for him to feed.

"I suggest, James, that we head back to Whitewood. It is the Elven capital, and so their military leaders will be there. Right?"

Ellen nodded in agreement.

"Good. Then all we have to do is convince them that their city is at risk. You folks will deal with that," Byron said, looking up at the sky. "I don't think they'd want to speak with one such as I."

"And what will you be doing, Byron," asked Selena Bradford, who was playing with her magic, making shapes out of fire in the air.

"I'll be looking for the Orb of Eden's Serpent, and a way to keep it away from Vandross," Byron said heavily. He was spoiling for another encounter with the one-eyed devil. At every turn, Vandross seemed to just slip away, just out of grasp. He had perpetrated the slaughter of Fort Flag, the nigh-destruction of Desanadron, the genocide of Shoryu's people, and gods only knew what other tragedies. There were probably more transgressions on Vandross's soul than even the seven Hells could handle. He might find himself in a nice position to ask for a job from Diablo himself. But he had to pay for his evils, in this life, if not in the next.

"You know the hazards involved in coming so close to the Orb, don't you Byron?" James Hayes spoke slowly, gauging the danger in his own question. He didn't want to offend the powerful Dread Knight, but he had to put it out there so that Byron knew the risks he took. If his former persona, that of the ruthless slaughterer and madman, were to break free as a result of proximity to the Orb, their whole purpose as a group would be for naught. Sure, he and Selena were powerful, and Ellen had proven greatness. Even Shoryu could be deadly in a battle, but all together they wouldn't be enough. Each would hold something back, hoping to subdue, rather than kill, their undead companion. But that wasn't going to happen, for Byron had been a completely efficient killing machine in his day.

"I am aware of the risk involved, my friend." Byron gave a heavy sigh, slumping forward with his elbows resting on his knees. "But there is little other choice. I have my own magic to counteract the Orb."

Hayes scoffed openly at that notion. "Byron," he said, rising from his seat.

The Paladin walked around the circle to Byron.

The Dread Knight looked up into those eyes, which had seemed desolate and wasted not so long ago. There was instead a look of grim determination, as though, despite his inner failings, Hayes had found the conviction to continue.

"Draw your sword, good Byron."

The undead warrior raised an 'eyebrow' at him, wondering what direction this was all going to go in.

"Draw your sword." Hayes stood there, his own sword now in hand. The Morning Glory blazed with holy energy and magic, burning brighter than any fire might.

The Dread Knight recognized the weapon, and knew whom it had belonged to. Commander Mensia, a brave and brilliant Elven tactician. For the weapon to be in Hayes's hands meant that the noble Paladin had been felled at Fort Flag. Byron stood to his feet, towering over Hayes by nearly two feet. He drew his broadsword, holding it lightly at his side.

With his free hand, Hayes took the broadsword from Byron, hefting it and testing its weight. Without warning, he thrust the Morning Glory's handle into Byron's hand.

Byron expected it to burn, to hurt, to react in some negative and violent way. But it did not. The white flames surrounding the blade seemed, for an instant, to flicker out. But then, a sound like the sea crashing into a break wall swept over the village, and power roiled within Byron's body. His head threw back toward the sky. Clutching the sword in both hands and holding it high over his head, Byron let loose a wild scream of power. A single cone of light shot from the Morning Glory to the skies above.

Everyone in the village gathered around to watch this awesome display. The light of the blade coiled down in a silver stream around Byron's body, wrapping him in its magic.

Surely this should kill me, Byron thought as he continued to scream. Silver power erupted from his eye sockets, rocketing into the sky and blinding him.

Everyone took a safe distance from Byron and watched in awe as the Morning Glory continued to stream energy into the heavens above.

Finally, Byron stopped, slumping forward and dropping to the ground.

Shoryu and Ellen rushed forward to check on him, giving the thumbs up to the gathered villagers and their companions. "He sleeps, I think," said Shoryu. "We'll have to get him rolled over."

Together with James Hayes, the two companions managed to get the armored Dread Knight onto his back.

The twin white lights in his sockets flickered into being, and he sat himself up, shaking his head and grasping it with one hand.

"Wow, that's a headache of another nature," he mumbled. In truth, his head felt sore enough to have been pelted with stones for hours at a stretch. "Feels like that sword burned through my hand," he said, offering Hayes the Morning Glory back.

"No, good Byron." Hayes raised his hands in protest. "The sword has chosen its rightful wielder. I cannot have it now."

Pain still seared through Byron's metal glove to his hand, and he put the sword down and began to remove the gauntlet.

"Could you two turn around? Certain parts of my body are in a slightly rotted state, and I'd rather you not see or smell this thing. It's probably burned up to boot."

Hayes and Shoryu walked back over to the rest of the group, while Byron turned his back to them. He expected to see his rotted hand was thoroughly burnt. Instead, his hand was whole, intact, and showed no sign of decay or rot.

He marveled at the Human hand, turning it over and moving the fingers. The movement hurt a little, but that did not concern him. *How,* he wondered. *How is this possible?* He put the gauntlet back on, feeling for the first time in a long while the cool feel of the gauntlet's metal against his flesh.

"All right folks," he said. "We're going to Whitewood. We're going to speak with the council on the matters at hand. We have to help them defend against Vandross, and we haven't got much time to do it."

Everyone nodded in agreement.

"Let's go."

And so, empowered by a renewed sense of purpose, Byron led his company out of Bael's village with the promise of his support, and made for Whitewood once more.

Chapter Eleven
Council

The company, Byron leading, halted outside of the high walls of Whitewood. The gates were closed, and there was a larger contingent of guards at the front barrier. Byron noticed that all of them wore heavy battle armor, and brandishing scores of weapons. The sight of these obviously seasoned warriors dismayed him. What could have happened in the short day they had been gone?

Byron called quietly for Ellen to come to the front next to him. The shadow magic wrapped around him to conceal him and he leaned in and whispered what he wanted Ellen to ask the sentries.

Behind the group, the forest came alive with the rustle of bodies and weapons. Before he finished conferring with Ellen, twenty or thirty armed elves surrounded the company.

How had he not seen them, thought Byron. But it was simple Elven camouflage; none of the hidden warriors wore any armor other than green and brown tunics and robes. They had waited silently in the trees for anyone to approach. And a group with such a strange assortment of allies must have registered as just a little offbeat.

Ellen, fearless in the presence of her kinsmen, stamped up to the commander of the group, one of the men at the gate. She glared menacingly at him, her hands on her hips, her eyes hard as granite. "Before I ask any questions about this," she said, pointing to the men at the gate. "I'd like to ask some questions about this," she growled, pointing back at the surrounded group.

The commander, a veteran Elf who had served the capital for many years, didn't even blink at Ellen's obvious rebuke. He simply stood straighter and stared over her head at his men.

"Scouts have reported that an army marches west toward Elven territory, miss," the Elven commander said, his voice gruff and raw.

He must have been shouting orders all day, Byron thought. "And ahead of them, quite nearer, has been spotted a large spider-like beast, foreign to our lands. All precautions are being taken to make certain no one gets into the city without first being judged worthy of trust and entrance." The commander looked down now at Ellen, a smug smile on his face. "We'll have to ask some questions, miss."

"You needn't ask any questions of me, Major Svelk, and you damn well know it."

The warrior Elf, Svelk, towered five or six inches over her, and seemed utterly unimpressed by her display of temper.

"Oh, sorry Miss Daires," he said, grinning maliciously at her.

It appeared to Byron that the man didn't know any other expression. The man's eyes and tone of voice seemed to substitute for actual facial articulation. Militants in a high standing often managed this effect. It must have come with the territory, Byron thought.

Svelk leaned in close to Ellen's ear, whispering in an unfriendly tone. "I am a Knight, Miss Daires. I am going to question you and your companions, and I'll know if any of you is lying. You know Knights possess this power. If there's anything you'd like to tell me before I have to make any arrests, I suggest you do it."

Ellen's eyes went wide with shock; he spoke the truth. Knights of all Races had the ability to discern the truth from people's statements, and the Major would surely want to know who the tall figure wrapped in black cloaks and shadows was. There might be trouble.

"Major," she said, a hint of pleading in her voice. She didn't want a situation outside of the city the company had come to help protect. "I urge you to let your protocol go this once. You do not want to temper with these good people. They have been through much, and may not want to answer any questions right now."

Svelk simply continued to grin menacingly at her, then gave her a light shove on the shoulder to send her back to her companions.

Shoryu bared his teeth at the Elven Knight, and several weapons moved to his neck.

The Major put up a hand to ward his men off.

"All right," he said, sauntering first up to Shoryu. The grass under his feet crunched under his metal shod boots.

Shoryu bared his teeth once more and growled at Svelk.

"Oooh, bad puppy." He kicked Shoryu's legs out from the side.

Byron stared in disbelief at the Major. He had never seen an Elf, even a military man, act in such a degrading fashion. But he could do nothing to help his young ward; he did not want any more trouble than they already had coming.

Shoryu got to his feet, his eyes slipping into slits in his face. He had a feral look about him, his lycanthrope rage on the verge of bursting forth and taking control of him.

Svelk put his baton under Shoryu's snout and lifted his chin up. "What's your name?"

"Shoryu Tearfang," the young Hunter gurgled through saliva.

"Very good. Class?"

"Hunter," Shoryu replied, his face returning to a simple appearance of annoyance. He had mastered himself just in time, and Byron knew it. Trained or no, these Elves would have had a hard time contending with a skilled fighter like Shoryu in a lycanthrope rage.

"Very well. Why are you here?" Svelk kept looking back at the rest of the group as he questioned Shoryu, making sure no one made a move on him.

"I am here to aid the city of Whitewood from the threat that approaches. We—"

"Enough," Svelk said, satisfied. His smile fell away to a look of neutrality. He seemed to want to find something to attack or arrest someone for. "He may pass. Moving on," he said, sauntering over to Selena Bradford. "Name," he said.

"Selena Bradford. And you're a total asshole," she said, spitting on Svelk.

Shocked, the Major wiped his cheek clean and balled his hand up. He sent his gloved fist into Selena's face, sending her sprawling and bleeding to the ground.

Before he could think about what he was doing, Byron reached over and hoisted the Major up by the throat. To hell with it, he thought. He pulled the shadows away from his body, revealing who he was.

Gasps of horror escaped the throats of every guard, and the Major himself thrashed in the grip of Byron of Sidius. His eyes bulged, terror racing down through his brain to his heart.

"And you know who I am," Byron growled up at the suddenly frail-looking Major Svelk. "You are a Knight, yes? You sense the truth in what people say, right? Then let me speak clearly," Byron said, setting the Major down and letting go of his throat.

The Elven man retched weakly to one side, spilling the contents of his stomach as he doubled over in pain. Svelk cast about; no one was moving to help him, not even his own men. "We have come to give Whitewood aid against the evil that comes to assault it. You know that to be the truth," Byron said more evenly, calmly. He gave his words time to sink in with the Major, who finished retching and stood upright.

Shock registered now on Svelk's face as he processed the Dread Knight's statement.

"You speak the truth, don't you," he asked.

Byron simply nodded his head in response, waiting for the Major's move.

Svelk hesitated, seeming to run through his options in his mind. Then, he looked up to the guards on the battlements over the gate and gave a simple hand signal. The gates began to creak open. Svelk looked at Byron's pinpoint eyes, keeping his gaze surface deep. Behind the Dread Knight, Hayes and Ellen Daires helped Selena Bradford into a sitting position and then to her. "The Council of Elders convenes tomorrow evening at the library. Speak with them then," he said, and watched as Byron wrapped the shadows about his body once more.

He balled his right hand into a fist, ready to strike the Major in return for Selena, but the Pyromancer woman put her hand on his arm to stay him. "No," she said. "This one petty man is not worth the potential cost to us."

The gates swung shut behind his company, and the Major got groggily to his feet to resume his post and duties. He hadn't expected the creature he had been warned about to be the legendary Byron of Sidius. Just the thought of it chilled him to the bone. But he had survived the encounter nearly unscathed. True, he had been choked, growled at and kicked in the crotch, but none of these things threatened to undo him physically. And even though Byron possessed an intimidating presence and powers, he would never truly be a match for the mighty Richard Vandross.

Svelk spoke to one of the shift commanders, a Lieutenant at the gate, to keep watch and command while he made a brief sweep of the area just beyond the hidden Hunters' positions. The man saluted the Major smartly, then returned to talking with his first sergeant about the state of affairs on the other side of the wall.

Svelk walked swiftly into the woods without, his feet guiding directly northeast toward the pond where he was to meet his contact.

Richard Vandross had first approached the Major some months back, the one-eyed Human promising Svelk a great deal of power in the Elven Kingdom in exchange for his service. Vandross had wanted information regarding Whitewood's state of readiness in the event of an assault. Even then, Vandross had been scheming to collect the Orbs of Eden's Serpent, though Svelk himself did not know what the man was about. He knew only that the one-eyed devil meant to have the Kingdom for himself, and that was fine by him. He would bide his time, and usurp the position of power from Vandross at his leisure.

He had been relaxing near the pond when Vandross had appeared to him that first time, and twice more had arranged to meet with him there. Earlier, the day before, Svelk had received a message via carrier pigeon, a small piece of parchment that read simply, 'meet at the pond as soon as possible'. There had been no signature or seal, as was Vandross's method. In the event someone discovered the letters, Svelk would arrange to meet his wife at the pond for a little romantic interlude. Anyone following would swiftly excuse themselves and leave the Major and his wife to their business. That back-up plan as yet hadn't needed to be tested.

He expected that Vandross would talk to him one last time and then be done with the Elf. When Vandross had what he wanted, he would attempt to do away with the Major. Of course, by the time Vandross got what he was after, Svelk would have taken his stash of bribe money and gone far away, perhaps to the eastern shore of the continent of Tamalaria. He had planned his escape meticulously after his last meeting with the one-eyed tyrant, sensing that the other man viewed him as disposable. He had packed a few saddlebags and bought a horse from the stables in Whitewood, a good charger by the name of Tonari. As soon as this meeting was over, he would take his packed bags from his basement to the stables, hitch up on Tonari, and ride out of the Elven Kingdom. He would never be seen again.

Brushing a few stray branches aside, he made his way to the pond's edge, taking his customary seat on a wooden stump some five feet from the water. Svelk's ears twitched at the sound of something or someone approaching through the woods off to his left, his hand instinctively reaching for his sword's pommel. Something about the air smelled different, a pungent, rotted aroma wafting from the direction of whoever approached. Svelk almost leaped out of his skin as Vengeance came scuttling out of the tree line. He bounded off of the stump to his feet, broadsword in hand, facing the menacing spider-beast with a scowl.

But the creature made no move on him. Instead, it held up one of its many appendages, as if to wave off his weapon. "Sit, Major, Svelk," Vengeance slurped.

Svelk raised an eyebrow at him.

"Did Vandross send you," he asked in a whisper, not wanting to be heard beyond the pond.

"Indeed, good major," Vengeance said, scuttling forward a few feet. "Please, sit."

Major Svelk hesitated, but eventually gave in to the monster's request.

"My, name, is Vengeance, Major. You needn't, worry, for your, safety. I, cannot, act, without my, master's, direct, orders," the vile creature shlooped in an almost amiable tone.

His words reassured Svelk—he sensed the truth in the other's words.

"What is it you need? What does your master want?" Svelk tried to sound annoyed, but his voice cracked like a teenage Human boy's would during puberty.

"My, master, wishes me, to obtain, information," Vengeance shlooped, lowering himself to the ground. His legs continued twitching, but otherwise he lay prone on the ground, seemingly comfortable. "He needs, to know, where, the Orb of Eden's Serpent, is, in, Whitewood." The creature's voice grated on Svelk's nerves. The wet, watery sound of it made him think the creature was in a constant state of drowning. But this creature had to be respected, he felt; it was abominable, but it was also powerful. And also, he felt it was not a natural part of this world. He decided to tell the creature what it wanted to know.

"It is kept in a vault deep within the earth, below the library. It is there that the Council of Elders gathers each week to discuss the state of the city. His majesty no longer resides in the capital, however. His whereabouts since news of Vandross's forces has been known only to a few. His eldest son holds the seat of power in the city itself until his father returns."

"Is the vault, guarded, against, intruders," asked the creature, seemingly uninterested with the news of the king.

"Yes," Svelk said, deciding to be truthful in this matter. It would do him no good to try to hide anything from Vandross. Just give the man what he wanted, and be done with the whole business. "The Elders keep a few of their most powerful magic-users down there to protect the Orb. They will not be easily dispatched, as I understand it. They have also laid a number of traps, so that only those who are allowed down there can know how to get to the Orb. I don't think Vandross will find them a problem, however. They are traps meant for lesser men, bandits and the like."

Vengeance waited patiently for Svelk to stop speaking, then remained silent for a while.

"Will that do," Svelk asked, getting to his feet.

"Yes, that will, do, just, fine, Major," Vengeance said, gaining his own feet. "Lord, Vandross, wants to know, where, you'll be, until, the matter, is all, settled. And also, where, your wife, will, be."

Svelk turned his back and began walking away from the beast, smiling to himself.

"I'll be staying with my mistress in Llandonen, to the south," he said merrily over his shoulder. "As for my wife," he said, chuckling at Vengeance from where he stood. "I may have the good fortune to find her dead when I return." Laughing to himself, Svelk trotted back to Whitewood, gathered his things, and took his horse. He left the city of Whitewood, not once looking back, in the guise of a trader.

Vengeance watched all the while, satisfied that the man rode south through the woods to where he claimed. The man would be tracked and killed later, at Vandross's whim. Vengeance secretly hoped that his master would allow him the personal pleasure. As Vengeance thought this last bit to himself, Vandross appeared next to him, glimmering into being after his teleportation. He looked haggard and worn.

"My, lord, are you, all right," asked the spider-beast.

"I am only one of the master's copies," said the one-eyed devil. "The use of the teleportation magic is a great taxation on my being, however temporary it is." His skin had taken on a pale cast, and he looked like a man on the doorstep of death. "What news have you, Vengeance," he asked, rubbing his temple.

"It is, under, the library. It, is in, a guarded, vault, sire. The Major seems, to think, that, it will, be difficult, to acquire," Vengeance shlurped.

Vandross nodded, thinking about how he would go about this business. There were Lizardman villages around that would probably like nothing better than to sit back and watch as Whitewood burned to the ground. But there were also many packs of Cuyotai. Perhaps he could find a way to turn those Cuyotai against the city. Unfortunately, his forward forces had been waylaid by Paladins in the northernmost edges of the kingdom; Vandross had not known that another Order of Oun fort had been cleverly disguised in the forestland of the Elves there. Instead of retreating and going around the Paladins, Vandross had given the order to lay siege to the fort. He would reanimate the dead Paladins as Dread Knights in his own army, and throw them against the city of Whitewood. The effort required would be great, but he was willing to stretch out his plans a bit. He had all the time in the world.

After all, Byron and his doomed little band of heroes wouldn't stand a chance against him and his armies now. They were but a small handful, and their power had limits. "Doesn't it," he asked himself in a whisper of doubt, fading as he returned to the real Vandross's body.

* * * *

Whitewood had become a maze of people cramming together in the streets to gather emergency supplies and weapons. The city's garrison was housed near the royal mansion where the Prince saw to the city's needs, and they were thankfully a large contingent. Fifteen hundred men and women, some of them employed as city watchmen during times of peace, like Major Svelk.

Of course, no one had seen or heard from the Major since morning, and no one much cared. The city would be under siege when Vandross's forces finished its business with the Paladin fort. Soon after that, perhaps only eight or nine days later, the main body of Vandross's assaulting army would follow behind.

Byron heard about the situation as the company passed through the busied streets toward Ellen Daires's home.

The slim Elven girl produced a key for her cottage from the front of her blouse, giving Shoryu an impish grin as she flourished it from its hiding place.

Bold, Byron thought. The girl must really be egging him on. Despite the seemingly impending doom the city thought it was about to face, and knowing the situation would indeed be grave, Byron gave thanks for the smile Ellen managed to get out of Shoryu at every turn.

The company poured through the small doorway into her den, each member taking seats on the couch or in chairs.

The room seemed perfectly undisturbed since their absence, but the attitude of the company was still fairly sore after dealing with Major Svelk. No one spoke for a while, Ellen fixing everyone warming tea to sooth their nerves. The silence among them was almost comfortable, each member of the company lost in their own thoughts.

Finally, James Hayes broke the silence. Byron had been letting the feel of the tea's warmth spread through him, savoring the sensation it gave him. The Gaiamancer had put some sort of special herb in it, he knew, and its effect was immediate. He hadn't felt so relaxed in a good long while. Hayes's voice brought him from the edge of his reverie.

"So Vandross's forces are currently destroying another Order outpost," he said, looking down into his empty cup. He cast about the room at the faces of the others, seeing reflected there the same sentiment; there was little to be done right now, with Vandross occupied, but the Council would convene the next evening, and they needed to speak with the Elders as soon as possible. After the outpost in the north fell, it would only be a matter of four or five days until the one-eyed devil's minions arrived at the walls of Whitewood, screaming and raging for blood. And they would have support shortly thereafter.

Morek Rockmight cleared his throat, shifting his weight uncomfortably in his chair. "The city's army regiment is young for the most part," he said. "They are inexperienced in the sort of warfare that this Vandross fellow will bring with him. From your account of what happened at Fort Flag, James, Vandross's forces sound as though they fight much like the old armies of Tanarak of Sidius." He looked to Byron for confirmation.

The Dread Knight nodded his head in agreement.

"Indeed," Byron grumbled. "But there is a streak of cruelty in Vandross that even the warlock did not possess. And there is a lesser sense of control and tactics in this man. He does not have the same motivations as Tanarak; that warlock already possessed the Orbs of Eden's Serpent when he began his wave of tyranny. He used subterfuge and cunning to attain them through. Vandross does not have the same knack for manipulation, though his methods appear to be yielding the same results."

"How many of these artifacts does he now possess," asked Selena Bradford, who had been rubbing her sore foot. The Major had worn some sort of protection against her kick, though in the end it had proven useless. Still, the Pyromancer woman's foot had swollen in the short time it had taken them to arrive at Ellen's home.

"Three," muttered Shoryu from his place next to Ellen.

Byron looked at Shoryu carefully; the boy had been momentarily lost in thoughts of his home, Byron thought. His eyes had taken on the sheen they had before when he talked about the attack on his home. An entire village of Cuyotai slaughtered just so Vandross could have what he wanted. It had been the same in Fort Flag and Desanadron, though that particular venture had been far more organized than the assault on Shoryu's home. With each Orb, the number of lives at stake had dramatically increased, as had the number of casualties. Only a handful had died in Koreindar some three months earlier. About a hundred Cuyotai after that. And then the massacre of hundreds, perhaps even thousands in Fort Flag and Desanadron combined. Each time Byron had failed to stop him because he simply didn't have the manpower and resources that his one-eyed counterpart did. He still possessed magics of darkness that could overwhelm his enemies, but he had refrained from using them almost the entire time he had control of his body once again.

Byron thought back to Shoryu's village again. It needn't have happened; if Byron had only killed the man when he attacked the undead warrior, the company would not be in this position. But then again, Byron's life would have been snuffed as well, a result of the bond of magic that he shared with Vandross. He had spared the man's life, and now it had returned to bite him. "The next one he seeks to take is here, in Whitewood," the Dread Knight muttered from under the veil of his inner thoughts. "This city will not withstand a siege. When the fort in the northern region of the kingdom falls, Vandross will turn his full attention on Whitewood. We must warn the Council of Elders and his majesty the Prince of the evils that Vandross and his minions are capable of. And we must do so swiftly."

"The Elders likely won't listen well to you, Byron," said Morek Rockmight.

The taciturn Dwarf was right; most of the people in Tamalaria remembered the tales of Byron of Sidius, and none of them were pretty. The cities of Ja-Wen and Desanadron knew what Byron was about now, but the Elven Kingdom had nearly been burnt to the ground at Byron's command. He had personally slain thousands of the kingdom's defenders. The Council would likely remember his countenance. But wouldn't they already know of his presence? Would not the guards outside the gates have sent a report to them?

"They'll remember what you've done to their people, not what you intend to do." As if on cue, there came a hard, rapid knocking on the front door to Ellen's home, and she glided gracefully over to the door. She opened it, and standing in the portal was Philip Masaton, High Elder of the Council. He smiled warmly at her, and Ellen turned a shade paler.

But the High Elder did not bother with introductions, or even an invitation. Instead, he slipped right past Ellen, into the center of her den, peering around at the group with a wizened grin on his face. His rotation stopped at last at Byron, his eyes filled with wisdom and laughter. His hair was a bright white, almost silver in sheen. As further evidence of his age, he had developed a small beard; Elves did not develop facial hair until very late in their lives.

Byron sat on his chair, humbled by the aura of knowledge the man radiated. He bowed his head, unable to meet the penetrating, smiling glare of the Elder any further.

"Do not hang your head, Byron of Sidius," the elf said in a gentle, wispy voice. "The past is the past, unchangeable and immutable. What matters now is the present, and what you do to change the future. Don't you agree?" His eyes squinted and revealed old, worn laugh lines. Smiling seemed to be the High Elder's natural state of expression.

Relieved, Byron stood, towering over the old Elf with his hands clasped behind his back. He tried to think of something to say, some way to begin apologizing for past transgressions. But the old man's calm demeanor disarmed him. He could say nothing.

"I have spoken with the spirits," continued High Elder Masaton, claiming Byron's seat for himself. "And I have spoken with my Keeper. All signs point to the city's assault. The enemy will be on us in ten days, but this is more time than we had before. Many had completely forgotten about the Order of Oun outpost in the northern region of the kingdom, but thank the gods for their efforts. We may save the city and protect the Orb of Eden's Serpent yet."

"How do you know about his intentions," barked Morek from his seat, a vein in his forehead threatening to burst.

"As I said, good master Rockmight, I have spoken with the spirits and my Keeper." Masaton's smile faded for a moment as he continued. "And they have told me of Richard Vandross. And of Byron of Sidius, and his quest," he added, smiling once more. "There is a great deal of work to be done in a short time to prepare the city. As High Elder, I need only seek the approval of his majesty the Prince for any plans you may have."

"I have a few ideas," offered Hayes from his seat. He looked around at the group, and they collectively held silent for him. "There are Cuyotai tribes living in this kingdom, correct?"

The High Elder nodded. "Indeed, there are, though many of them do not think highly of us. The King has decreed that they may not live in our cities, but may only enter for business." Masaton's smile faded once more. "I doubt they would come to our aid."

"Not necessarily," continued Hayes, a small grin creeping across his lips. "The Prince is in charge right now, correct?"

The old Elf nodded, an eyebrow raised in question.

"And any edicts he enacts right now are as good as any his father might make if he were present. That's how things go in any kingdom. Is that so here as well?"

Once again Masaton nodded, his eyebrow still raised.

Hayes made a gesture with his hands, trying to get someone else to say what was on his mind.

"So the Prince can call an edict into motion allowing the Cuyotai to live within the Elven cities, in exchange for their aid," said Selena from her place next to the Paladin.

"Bingo," Hayes exclaimed, pointing his finger rapidly at her. "Do you think it'll work?" he asked the old Elf.

Masaton rubbed his hand through his small silver beard, mulling the matter over.

"Someone will have to bring the idea not only to the Prince, but to the Cuyotai." All eyes turned on Shoryu, who stared back in alarm.

"What? Me? I'm no diplomat," the Cuyotai lad said, waving his hands to dismiss the idea.

Everyone smiled that rather fierce and sardonic smile that suggests that the one smiled at has no choice in the matter.

Finally, himself smiling like an idiot, Shoryu shrugged his shoulders. "All right, I'll do it."

"And I shall go with you," said Ellen, gripping one of the Cuyotai Hunter's hands in her own. Their eyes met for a moment before they returned their gaze to High Elder Masaton.

He merely nodded his approval.

"Very good. You two should depart soon, and while you are gone, I shall speak with his majesty." The High Elder, rose and patted Byron on the shoulder. "Thanks for the seat young man." He put a hand on his hip. "These old bones, you know, heh heh. Well, let's not dilly-dally. There is much to be done. Master Rockmight," he said, swooping in low to come face to face with the scarred visage of the Dwarven Boxer. "You are well known and well liked in this city. Do what you can to get additional help from the able-bodied citizens of the city. Anyone who you think has something special or unique to offer this effort, get them to help out any way they can. All right?"

The stoic Dwarf nodded.

"Miss Bradford," he said, standing erect and facing the young Pyromancer woman. "Study the forests just outside of the city. Take time and care to make certain that your raging flames do not threaten the whole of our forest. If you deem it necessary, have woodcutters go with you to clear out a perimeter so that only a small portion of our sacred woodland is burned, should the need for a wall of flames arise."

Selena said nothing, but rose from her seat and left the cottage, intent on doing something useful with her exceptional powers.

Finally the old man turned to Byron. "For you, good Byron, I leave the most arduous task. Come walk with me and we shall discuss it."

With the old man's arm hauled up and across his back, almost touching his opposing shoulder, Byron left the cottage into the streets, cloaking himself in shadows as he and the High Elder walked slowly through the streets.

For a good while, they simply walked, the elderly Elf saying nothing, and Byron not wanting to risk the comfortable silence between them. Finally, Masaton broke the silence. "Look around, Byron," he said, gesturing about them at various buildings, including a school where the young boys and girls of the city ran about on their recess hour.

The sight brought a smile to Byron within his shadows, the smoke curling to shape a haphazard and lopsided grin.

"These men and women and children have known little strife or war in many years," Masaton said. "Even in the time when you served Tanarak of Sidius, this city held its ground against the minions of darkness. Hope is the most precious commodity the people of the Elven Kingdom have, and they will fight to the bitter end to keep it." A trace of sadness lingered in his voice. "But I fear that even with the greatest of efforts from you and your companions, something may very well go wrong, and that commodity will decrease in presence. Do you know Major Svelk?"

The question took Byron off-guard. "Yes," he said in a low tone. "We met him at the gates. Miserable little prick, he is," Byron grumbled under his breath. "Why?"

"Because *he* has already lost hope," replied the old man. "He left a short while after you and your company entered Ellen's home. I sensed deception and a dark secret in him at the last Council meeting. He left orders with a Lieutenant to watch the gates, and left for a short while. When he returned, I witnessed him going into the stables in uniform, and coming out leading a horse with several saddlebags. He had changed into civilian garb, good Byron, and left the city south. He has sensed what is to be, and has fled."

"I don't understand," said Byron. "How is that important? So one man left, big deal. Why is he different from anyone else who chooses to escape?"

The High Elder came around in front of Byron, stopping the big Dread Knight in his tracks.

"He fought with the defenders of this city when you besieged it under Tanarak's banner," whispered High Elder Masaton. "He is a brave man, fearless despite any situation. He would not be afraid of this attack on the city that comes. He is motivated by something other than fear."

Byron cocked his head at the old man. "I still don't get it," he said, his voice muffled by his smoke and shadows.

The old Elf pressed in close against him, looking up at Byron with a look of fear, something Byron had not expected from such an obviously wise and capable man.

"Good Byron," he said, his voice trembling. "He has betrayed us!"

* * * *

Selena Bradford wasted no time, bringing Alex along with her to the outside of the city. "In case you haven't noticed," complained the Ki Fairy from his seat on her shoulder. "I'm not a woodcutter, lady. Never held an axe in my life. It's mostly because I'm, you know, two freakin' inches tall."

Selena smiled a toothy grin at him, causing him to retake his seat. "I know that, little man," she said, sauntering eastward away from the city. "But you possess magics of your own, and a few things I think may come in most handy during this whole campaign."

She walked for nearly an hour through the winding trails of the forest, not once turning from her path. Finally she stopped in the middle of the path. "This is good," she said to no one in particular. She sat on the ground then, leaning back against the trunk of a strong oak tree. She pulled her small rucksack from her back and rummaged through it for some of the dried meat and a small portion of cheese she had brought with her. "Would you like some," she asked, offering a bit of cheese to the Ki Fairy, who greedily snatched it from her fingers.

"Certainly, I'm famished," he squeaked, devouring the small portions of cheese and meat Selena offered him.

She pulled an aleskin from her pack and took a long, hard pull of it. Its warmth spread through her, mixing with the small summoning of her magic.

"So, what is it exactly that you think I can do to help you?" Alex asked, not forgetting that she had brought him for some purpose or other.

"You can move objects with your magic, right," she asked him, taking another strip of meat before she packed her food away.

"Yes," Alex garbled around a mouthful of cheese. "What of it?" Selena smiled gently at him and rose to her feet, facing north.

"Good. What I need you to do is no small task. Do you think you're up to it, little man?" She knew that insults and taunting would probably be the only way to get the Ki Fairy to do anything, and she knew better than most how to rile someone.

"Of course I am," Alex responded, puffing out his chest in a display of machismo. "Just name it, lady!"

"Great," she exclaimed. "I need you to part these trees, roughly twenty yards or so, a straight line. I need them parted for the next, oh, half a mile." Alex's eyes bulged out of his head, his jaw dropping as he took in the weight of what she was asking.

"Are you insane? I haven't even done anything mildly close to that scale of magical expenditure. I haven't done anything for the last few chapters. What makes you think I can do this? " The Ki Fairy ranted at her in his native tongue.

"Are you saying you can't do it? It's all right, I'll just go back and get some big, strong woodcutters to do what you obviously can't."

Alex hovered in the air behind her.

"Oh yeah," he screamed at her back. "I'll bet your stupid woodcutters can't do this. Hah!" Alex called forth a series of incantations, and Selena watched as a large floating orb of black and yellow energy pulsed and formed in front of the diminutive Fairy, his hands weaving strange, archaic symbols in the air. With a final movement and a scream of rage, Alex sent the orb of energy hurtling through the woods. As it raced past, the trees in front of it and to either side for thirty yards disappeared without a sound or trace, as if they had never been. Alex remained hovering in place, his hands together and his head lowered, chanting in the tongue of magic. Finally, after a little more than half a mile, he separated his hands, and the orb of magic disappeared. Alex dropped to the ground from the effort, panting and wheezing.

Selena ran over and stooped down, scooping his limp form off of the ground.

He opened his eyes a moment to smile at her, a full mouth of razor-like teeth gleaming in the patch of light filtering down through the tree canopy. "Can, your woodcutters, do that," he asked between gasps for breath.

"What was that," Selena asked, stroking the Ki Fairy's head. She had pushed him too far, she knew, and Alex had nearly used the whole of his life energy in turn. But he had indeed accomplished something no mere team of woodcutters could. He had cleared a straight path of trees—enough that no flames would reach from one side of the path to the other.

"Simple, really," Alex said, trying to sit up. With a finger Selena gently pushed him back down on her palm. "I sent them to the Shadowrealm. They, can be brought back, whenever, I choose." He hacked and wheezed for a moment after that. "I, need to rest, a while. How many more, or these lines, do you need," he asked, his eyes full of laughter.

"Three more," she whispered, seeing his eyes begin to droop. He would be asleep soon, and she didn't blame him. He had used more magic in one moment than many strong mages could in a lifetime.

"Well," he said, his voice beginning to slur. "We've got, ten days, like the old man said. I can get it, done. But right now, I think I'll, just—" and like that, he was asleep.

Selena carried him back to Ellen's home. In the back guestroom, she opened a dresser drawer, one with several soft sweaters in it, and laid him atop the soft fabric. She hoped he would be up to another of these sessions the next day. He had proven quite useful to the group, and she had taken a liking to him. His attitude meshed well with her own. Perhaps when the whole business with Vandross was over, she would ask Byron if she could take Alex with her. She hadn't had a friend like him in a long time.

* * * *

Evening had drawn close, the sun setting in the distance over the horizon, when Shoryu and Ellen came to the first of the Cuyotai villages. They had walked hand-in-hand the whole while, enjoying one another's company in silence, sharing the occasional kiss on their trail. But for the most part, they kept their attention on the surrounding woodlands. The Elven Kingdom was host not only to Elves, Humans, Cuyotai and Lizardmen, but to some of the stranger and more dangerous beasts of the lands of Tamalaria. They didn't want to be caught off guard this far away from the company.

Thankfully, the first sign of trouble they came across was a trap that Shoryu had brought them just short of. The trip line that had been carefully covered by leaves and foliage, however, one end of the line had become exposed from lack of maintenance. Shoryu followed the path of the cord to its termination, after a series of tightly drawn cords in a wall assembled entirely of wooden spikes, which would have swung down on them from the trees above.

He picked Ellen up, watching as she blushed and gasped, nearly crying out. He leaped smartly over the trip line, set her down, and took her hand again. They walked fifteen more feet when a pair of Cuyotai guards, these two lighter brown in color than Shoryu, came bounding out of the surrounding trees. Each brandished a short spear, the tips glistening in a patch of sunlight that broke in a shaft through the treetop canopy.

Shoryu and Ellen stood stock still, offering no defense or show of insult.

The pair of guards circled them, their snouts twitching as they sniffed the pair. Satisfied, the taller of the two nodded at his companion, who stood his ground, his weapon in hand, while the other went to fetch someone. In moments, he returned with a broad-shouldered, black furred Cuyotai of great height and muscle.

The black Cuyotai wore the open leather vest of a Hunter, along with a feathered headdress, clearly marking him as the village Chieftain. He glared at the pair from Whitewood, his big arms crossed in front of his barrel chest. There was distrust and a clear disdain in his eyes as his gaze swept over Ellen, but his eyes went wide with shock as he looked down to see that they were holding hands. After what felt like an eternity, the big man smiled a broad smile, and threw his head back in laughter. "Hahahahahaaa! Well met, young one. Come with me, and we shall speak. The nights around here are dangerous." His voice was tropical and jovial in accent, as if he came from an off-coast island.

He led the couple through dirt streets in a well-organized village. It had semi-permanent structures of a small town, the buildings low and squat, but made well enough to survive harsh weather. The majority of the Cuyotai had the light brown fur of the guards, but a few were black-furred and huge like the Chieftain. "Dis is my village, as you may have surmised," said the big man over his shoulder. "My name is Tandaba," he said, turning and bowing to Shoryu and Ellen. "Tandaba Bloodclaw, Chieftain of Inusama Village. And what are your names, good sir and madam?" He smiled at Shoryu and Ellen in turn, his eyes seeming to search them for their intentions.

"I am Shoryu Tearfang, formerly of Tanawabe Village. My home and people have been destroyed by the one-eyed devil, Richard Vandross."

There was a flicker of recognition in the large Chieftain's eyes, and for a moment, his face dropped into a look of stony silence.

"You mean, the village near Hamalot?"

Shoryu nodded his head.

The big Chieftain found a crate nearby and slumped down on it. He slowly removed his headdress, hanging his head near his knees. With a look of great pain, he raised his head to look up at Shoryu and Ellen. "My friend, many of our own villagers lived there a few years ago. I myself knew Chieftain Silek Stareye. Are you the only survivor?"

Shoryu looked away, off at a pair of Cuyotai cubs sparring. He nodded.

"Oh, good gods in da heavens above," muttered the Chieftain. He spent a few minutes in studied silence. Then he looked up at Ellen, his headdress in his hand. "I apologize, miss. I did not yet ask your name."

"I am Ellen Daires, of Whitewood. We need your help."

The Chieftain looked up at her, puzzled by her statement.

"Surely, miss," he said, his hands on his knees. "What is it you require of me and my people?"

"The one-eyed man that destroyed Shoryu's village. He brings an army to attack Whitewood."

The big Chieftain remained silent a moment, lost in his own thoughts. His eyes had the glazed look of one about to cry, yet he did not. Instead, he nodded to no one in particular. Standing to his full height, he let out a roar to gather the people of his village. Every man, woman, and child came to circle the three who had just met one another.

"Listen well, my people! There is ill news from afar! Behold, dis young man is da last survivor of an attack on our brethren in Tanawabe Village!"

One milky-eyed woman, a light brown furred Cuyotai of considerable age from the way she carried herself, stood. "What of my granddaughter," she asked in a hoary whisper. "What of Moksha?"

Shoryu turned to face her squarely, and a faint trace of a smile creased the old woman's face.

"Shoryu," she said, more a question than a statement. "As I live and breathe, Shoryu Tearfang!" She came forward in a rush, pressing hard against him, her sobs wracking her entire frame. "Oh, Shoryu, dear boy! She's dead, isn't she," she asked, looking up into Shoryu's eyes.

He could see that she was blind in one eye, and going so in the other. Kira Conata, he remembered. Granny Kira, who had left in search for a cure to an illness that was stealing her sight.

"I am sorry, Granny Kira." He cradled the old woman in his arms.

She cried against his chest, a strange yellow pus mixing with her tears.

He held her a moment longer, before she broke away from him to seek condolences from her husband, Goram Conata. He had once been a proud and noble Hunter for the village, gone with her in the hope that they could together cure her. It appeared they had failed.

Shoryu hung his head; so much had happened in recent years, so little of it good for his people.

"Some good can come of dis, yah," shouted the Chieftain over his people. "Da rat bastard dat done dis ting, he's marchin' on Whitewood as we speak. I say we go get us some good ol' fashioned justice, what say ya?"

No one responded however, and a youthful warrior stepped forward from the crowd.

"So what," exclaimed the youth. "The Elves have done little to make us welcome in their kingdom. If this foul man attacks Whitewood, we shall be well far away and left alone. Let the Elves fend for themselves."

A few of the young warriors of the village shouted their agreement.

Tandaba let them shout for a minute before raising his hand to silence them.

"No, Tokap. The Elves have been more gracious dan you tink. They do not encroach upon us, they let us alone, and they do not expect taxes from us. Not dat we could pay dem at any rate. No, do not protest," he said, holding a hand up swiftly to silence the youth from speaking further. "You know dat I am Chieftain here, and my word is law. But you know as well that I am a fair man. Anyone wishing to help da city of Whitewood will come with me to speak wit dem. Dose who want noting to do with da whole business, can remain behind. Agreed?"

There was a murmur of general consensus among the people of the village, and several older armored Knights and lightly dressed Hunters came forward.

The village divided into two groups; those who would go, and those who would stay behind. Most of those who agreed to come with appeared to be seasoned veterans, many of them originally from Shoryu's village.

He related what had happened to him since the attack, down to his coming to them, over a group meal around a fire in the center of the village. Ellen held his hand through the telling, and more than once he caught Tandaba glancing at their hands and giving him a kind smile and wink. As he wrapped up his tale, he noticed a very young boy, a boy with much the look of Tandaba in his face, peeking through the crowd. Shoryu gave a barely perceptible nod at the boy with his snout, looking into Tandaba's eyes, and the big Chieftain looked over to see his boy crouched in hiding among the crowd.

He smiled and nonchalantly stood and stretched. "Oh, goodness, dese old bones are tired. I tink I need a-HA," he cried, snatching the boy up from his hiding spot near him. The boy struggled in earnest as the Chieftain shook him playfully.

The boy swung the wooden play sword from his hip at the Chieftain's chest, finally giving up and being lowered to the ground. Tandaba ruffled the boy's hair and sat him on his lap across the fire from Shoryu. "Please excuse my son. He is anxious to be a warrior, big and strong like his pa, right boy?"

The pup's eyes lit up as he smiled and nodded at Tandaba.

"He doesn't speak much, Shoryu, so I'll have to apologize for him."

Shoryu looked at the crudely fashioned play sword for a moment, still gripped in the pup's hand. It had dirt and grime on it, and a slew of weed stains. He himself had done much the same thing when he was that young, but he had always managed to break his toys. His father had to constantly make new ones for him, and after a while, showed Shoryu how to do it himself. His first attempts had come out looking much like this boy's.

"How old are you, little one," Ellen asked softly.

The boy's eyes opened wide, and his jaw hung open a moment. Finally, he showed her eight of his little fingers. "Oh, you're eight? My, you're already very big for your age!"

The boy jumped off of his father's lap and scooted around the fire to Ellen's side. He looked up at her with a question twinkling in his eyes.

"Yes? Do you want something?"

The boy looked down at her hand in Shoryu's, then up at Shoryu.

"Is she your girlfriend," he asked suddenly, and everyone went silent before bursting into raucous laughter. The sound of it warmed Shoryu's heart, but also made him acutely embarrassed.

"Well, um, I don't think either of us knows yet," he said, getting a kiss on his cheek from Ellen. He blushed brightly under the thin fur on his muzzle.

"Yes I am little boy," Ellen said to the pup, who giggled. But immediately he looked up again at her.

"You have magic," he said, and once more a hush fell over those gathered. Ellen looked deep into the boy's eyes, seeing something she had not sensed before.

"Yes, yes I do," she said, as much to him as to the crowd. "Mine is an earthen born magic, known as Gaiamancy. Do you know what that is?"

The boy nodded his head rapidly, getting excited.

"Why do you ask?"

The boy said nothing more, but ran back in front of his father, who was now perplexed. The boy put his play sword in his belt, and turned to face the fire. He closed his eyes and pressed his hands together, as if in prayer. A soft green light pulsed from his palms, the light dulled by his hands. The entire village was on its feet, staring in wonder at the boy. He opened his hands, and a small sphere of green light hovered over the heads of those assembled, expanding swiftly into an image. It was an image of Shoryu as he entered the village with Ellen, though the shapes were slightly distorted in proportion and color. They had a slightly misty film over them, something Shoryu hadn't ever seen in an Illusionist image. Yet he was certain that this was what the boy had produced.

"How did you do dis, boy," Tandaba asked as he picked the pup into his arms. "How," he asked, his voice filled with awe and wonder.

"I saw it in my head, about an hour before they got here," said the boy aloud, and everyone looked from the moving image to the boy. "It happens sometimes," he added, his voice suddenly small and frightened. "I can't help it."

Tandaba hugged the boy hard to him. Tears streamed into the matted fur of his snout as he cradled the boy.

"It's all right boy," he whispered. "How often does dis happen?"

"Once or twice a day," said the boy. "Oh, I'm sorry miss," he said, bowing his head slightly. "I never told you my name. I'm Straig." He extended his small paw, and Ellen and Shoryu both shook it in turn.

That night, sleeping in the Chieftain's guest room, the couple from Byron's company lay close to one another, cradled in each other's arms. All the while, Shoryu thought about pups of his own.

* * * *

Byron stalked through the darkened tunnels beneath the library, making his way carefully past the traps and pitfalls set by the defenders of Whitewood. The traps in the tunnels were old and worn, many of them having ceased to function after a while. And the magic users who defended the chamber of the Orb of Eden's Serpent hadn't been heard from in many days. Had they died? Byron wondered. Had Vandross already sent someone into the city without his knowledge? *Impossible*, he decided, casting off his doubts. He would have known if one of Vandross's men had entered the city. He would have sensed and destroyed them.

Still, he couldn't shake the feeling that events were coming to a head. He had thwarted Vandross in minor ways; he had destroyed his Berserker, Shoryu had killed his Beastmaster, and they had together slain hundreds in Desanadron. Vandross had seemed bent on occupying the city, the better to get a stranglehold on the lands of Tamalaria. He had cast off his General, believing him dead and gone, something that Byron hoped would come back to haunt the one-eyed devil. But otherwise, Byron's company hadn't done much to foil him. Whitewood would be different, Byron vowed in the silence of the tunnels underground.

Thankfully, the High Elder had secured the Prince's cooperation in the effort. The Cuyotai would be allowed into the cities, to trade and live if they wished. When the King returned, the High Elder had jested before sending Byron to check on the Orb, there would be hell for his son to pay.

Byron turned his attention back to his current whereabouts, the shadows and darkness of the tunnels mixing with his own, making him appear to be a wraith, an inky black spot lurking through the depths of the earth. Not a bad analogy when he thought about it. The sounds of rats burrowing through the ground and bats stirring filled the air, echoing hollowly off of the circular walls.

Byron came around a turn in the tunnel, and found himself at a crossroads in the paths. He had been told to go left here, and moved to do so. But he had also been warned about a trap. *What had it been?*

His sense of hearing was on edge, his movements frugal; he did not want to alarm the guards of the Orb.

As alert as he was, Byron did not hear the trigger in the floor under his foot until it lifted up.

Stopping dead in his tracks he looked down between his extended foot and the one behind. He had stepped on a slightly raised portion of the floor.

"Ah, shit," he muttered as a dozen holes opened in the wall opposite him. Spears flew out, and he brought up a shield of purple energy to deflect them. He bent his knees to stoop next to one of them. The weapons were rusted and falling apart. He probably could have broken them on his armor. Still, the trap had been ingeniously hidden, and there had been little delay between triggering the trap and its execution.

He glanced about the chamber, then continued down the left hand tunnel where he saw a flickering pattern of torchlight.

Pressing himself against a wall, further into the shadows as he could go, he crept along the walkway, a silent predator stalking prey he had no intention of killing.

He stopped moving altogether as a single man, an older Elven fellow, stepped into the turn of the tunnel. He was dressed in the simple blue robes of a Thunder Mage, his tunics loose fitting and ragged underneath. The torch in his hand was barely there, casting shadows everywhere.

"Hello," the mage called. There was tension in his voice. "If someone's there, please help me. Derin has taken ill. Hello," he called, desperation in his voice. "I don't remember the way out. " He dropped to his knees, sobbing.

Byron moved from the shadows and placed his hand firmly on the Elf's shoulder.

The defender looked up suddenly, fear in his eyes. Immediately he threw a bolt of magic past Byron's face, showering the tunnel with rubble as the bolt tore into the earth. "Shadowbeast, begone," he cried, gaining his feet.

"Hold, good Elf," Byron exclaimed, putting his hands out to show he was unarmed.

The Thunder Mage hesitated, calling forth more magic to his hand, ready for release.

"I have been sent by High Elder Masaton to discover why no word has been sent from you. Take me to your friend. You say he is ill?"

The Thunder Mage, suspicion in his eyes, moved away from the large Dread Knight, still unaware of who exactly he was.

"Indeed, he is. He has taken a fever, and he raves as a madman. Come, I shall take you to him."

Through the darkened tunnels they stalked, two dark clad forms moving amid the earth's innards. , Byron tracing the mage's steps very carefully. He didn't want to unintentionally disarm any more traps than he had already. The spears brought that count to three.

Finally, they came to a steel door, which opened on a series of rooms. The mage led Byron to another steel door, this one reinforced. A single slat was at eye level to the mage, with bars in it.

Byron looked into the room beyond, and saw the other defender huddled in the corner of the room. Feces was smeared all over the floor and walls, crude, archaic symbols drawn in fecal matter and blood. The Elf had the look of a starved beggar, his white robes torn and frayed.

Byron shook his head: he knew what was wrong with the man. He would have to be killed.

"What is it," asked the mage, seeing Byron's head hang in the shadows he used to cloak himself. "Do you know what's wrong with him?" The Thunder Mage gripped Byron's cloak and pulling him close.

"I know what is wrong with him, good Elf. I am sorry. He is possessed by a Shadowbeast. He is fighting back, of course," Byron said, looking through the slats to see the madman pressed against the bars, his left eye pulsing yellow while the right one held the look of a trapped animal. "But it is a losing battle. He will be in the full grip of the demon by sunup. He must be killed."

The Thunder Mage did not scream; indeed, he didn't weep, cry, or even beg for an alternative. He simply turned his back to the undead warrior.

"Do it," he whispered, his voice cracking. He had clearly been a good friend with the possessed man, but that mattered little.

"Understand, good sir, that it is what is best for him and for your people," Byron said, trying to offer some measure of comfort. But the mage said nothing to him, and Byron turned to face the steel door.

The maddened Elf had returned to his corner, and Byron undid the latch and entered, closing the door behind him. The mad Elf growled at him, cowering in the corner from him. Byron undid his shadow covering, and both the Elf's eyes gleamed with fear and loathing.

"Yes," Byron whispered, his voice barely audible. "I have come to destroy you. Vandross will not be coming through any back door this time. He'll have to come through me. If you leave this man now," Byron growled, advancing on the skittering demon. "I may spare you your miserable life, Shadowbeast. The choice," he said, unsheathing the Morning Glory, its light filling the room. "Is yours."

The demon within seemed to be considering its options, then it flung a handful of feces from the floor to splatter against Byron's chest.

"Wrong choice." With a single deft motion, Byron beheaded the once-Elf, retaining his stance until the body fell forward against his leg. He took the sheet off of the bed and cleaned his armor, then sheathed the Morning Glory, extinguishing its light. In the darkness, he held the head over his skull, feeding off of the Elven blood; he had gone a long time without as he needed to, subsisting on normal food and drink. The blood left him feeling renewed, replenished, but he agonized over the decision he had been forced to make.

Thinking to spare the Thunder Mage outside any more grief, he summoned a vortex of wind, using it to clean the room and place the body of the Elf on the bed. He quickly used his dark magic to secure the man's head back onto his body. Then he pulled a clean sheet out of the dresser, and laid it over the body. It was the least he could do.

Silently, cat-like, he opened the door and exited the chamber, locking it behind him.

The Thunder Mage, wept openly on a crate he used to store foodstuffs.

"Come," Byron said, hoisting the man up. "We are leaving. The High Elder shall send replacements. You have done your part as well as could be expected."

The Thunder Mage nodded humbly, walking ahead of Byron. Together, they left the darkness of the tunnels beneath the library, out into the fading light of evening. The High Elder was there to greet them, and was taken off guard when the Thunder Mage embraced him and began to sob, unable to feel any shame.

Masaton patted the man gently, consoled him, and offered the man a tonic that would help him relax. When Byron explained what had happened to the High Elder. The old Elf shook his head in dismay.

"We shall have to place a pair of Clerics with the next defenders. They will detect evil much better than any mage. It is good that you have discovered this, Byron. Already you have done well. But it grows late. Go and get some rest, good Byron. We shall speak further tomorrow."

Byron took a long look at the now groggy Thunder Mage. The look in his eyes was unmistakable—*there is no hope for us.*

Byron, stalking the darkening streets of Whitewood, swore that hope would stay alive under his care.

* * * *

Two nights later, outside of the Paladin outpost, Richard Vandross fumed at the stupidity of his own men. They had lost nearly a hundred of their numbers, Greenskins and Shadowbeasts for the most part. These defenders had proven much more capable than those of Fort Flag. He had attempted the same trick as before, and it had nearly cost him his life. As he had stood before the towering stone wall, summoning the magic that would blast the wall apart, a hidden slot in the stone had opened and a hail of arrows had flown at him at high speed. Two or three of the bolts had embedded themselves in his shoulders and his hip, tossing him to the ground. The impact alone had saved him; one arrow had grazed his cheek as a result of the fall. It easily could have gone through his face. He had ordered a dozen Greenskins to stand in front of him, to defend him from such an occurrence. They had stood at his back, instead of his front. "Bumbling, blasted morons," he muttered from his field chair under the medical tent. He was fine now; the power of the Orbs within him had regenerated his wounds swiftly, but he needed to rest.

A skittering of legs clacking along the ground brought him to a sitting position, a long knife in hand. Vengeance stood at the door of his tent. "What do you want, Vengeance," he growled, angry enough to scowl even at the spider-beast.

"There, is something, that, can, be done, sire. But, you, must be, the one, to do it. I cannot, do, it, on my, own."

Vandross shrugged and beckoned the creature inside.

He swung his legs over the side of the litter. "As, I have, said, I, can poison, the hearts, of men. But, you, must be, the one, to, wield, the power. I, shall, return, to your, body." The creature shimmered into a cloud of purple smoke, and entered Vandross through his nose.

Power welled up within him. He felt alive again, in a way he hadn't since the spider-beast had separated from his body. Vengeance, it seemed, was the most physically powerful of the three he possessed. He heard the beast's voice in his mind.

"Summon, the power, from me," it whispered.

Vandross moved out of the medical tent, stalking through the ranks of his sleeping men. He stayed well out of arrow range from the fort, and placed his hands upon the ground. He traced signs of arcane power in the dirt, and the symbols pulsed with a sickening green and black glow.

Veins of the power began to show through the earth's surface, the lines slowly moving toward the fort.

Vandross smiled to himself—he knew instinctively what the magic would do to the defenders of the fort. It was not the swift solution he had wanted, but it would work better than any physical attack by his forces.

In a few days, infected by the power of Vengeance's magic, the defenders of the fort would turn on each other. Their fears would cripple their minds, playing tricks on them as no con man could. They would destroy themselves. And Vandross would be there to sweep up the remains into his forces as the walking dead.

"And with, another, of our, brethren," Vengeance informed him, "you, will attain, the knowledge, of making, Dreadnaughts."

Dreadnaughts, Vandross thought. The large, mindless undead creatures that were in fact amalgamated collections of the body parts of many various warriors and mages. A few of those, he thought, sure would be useful.

* * * *

Morek Rockmight did not like trolling taverns, but he had turned up a few good soldiers in this exact fashion. The taciturn Dwarf wasn't keen on socializing, but he kept his conversations brief and to the point. On a few occasions, he had been told to bugger off, which had earned a few men broken noses and black eyes.

Morek didn't think of himself as a man with a short temper; nor did he think himself deserving of being told to have sex with himself. A few people had been sent packing, so what? Byron would want the best of the best, and few of those he had convinced came close. Brave? Yes, they had been brave. Dead meat? Yes, most of them would be. But he would soon find a man they could depend on.

Morek sat nursing his ale, when a simply clad Human fellow had walked in. He wore the uniform of some sort of Monk, and Morek raised an eyebrow. "Pardon me, sir," he said in his booming tenor. "Are you passing through town?"

The Human looked directly at him, and Morek saw that the man was rather handsome for someone dressed as a martial artist. Most Monks had the same battered countenance as him. He also noticed that the man only had one arm. Perhaps he had misjudged.

"Me?" answered the Monk in a lilting tone. "No, I live here."

Morek raised his eyebrow once again.

"I've been out of town, training some new students. The name's David Spore. You are?" He extended his hand.

Morek took it in his own, immediately taken off guard by the power in the man's grip.

"Morek Rockmight. Pardon the intrusion, but I've visited here often, and I've never seen you."

"It's a big city," was the Monk's reply.

"Look mister, I'll get to the point." Morek put down his mug. "This city is going to come under attack in a few days, and we need some more able bodies to help defend it. Think you're up to it?"

The Monk smiled and got down off of his stool.

"I can do with one arm what you can't with both." A wolfish grin spread across his face.

Morek wouldn't take that kind of guff, especially from a one armed man. He hopped down off the stool and swung at the Human, who sidestepped and brought his foot around in a barreling hook kick. The impact of the blow sent Morek tumbling head over heels into a table, whose present residents decided to vacate.

Morek held his ribs, sore from the blow, and came at the Monk more focused. The man seemed to be dancing, anticipating his attack. But Morek proved the better this time. He parried a few of the Monk's jabbing kicks, finally grabbing his foot and spinning him around, full steam into Morek's uppercut.

The Monk flew back, crashing through another table. He was immediately back on his feet, charging Morek and leaping into the air, a flying kick aimed at the Dwarven Boxer's face.

Morek lunged aside, only to discover that the kick had been a feint. His back was now to the Monk, who stooped and swept Morek's legs out from under him. Morek rolled around, dodging axe kicks aimed at his groin. Finally, he caught the Monk's leg and pulled him down.

The Monk locked his legs around Morek's ribs and began to squeeze, putting pressure on the little man's already sore body. But Morek didn't yield— he rained down hammering blows at the Monk's head, connecting a few times, and finally the Monk waved his hand in defeat. Morek, panting and exhausted, helped the Monk up.

"So," said David Spore to Morek. "Where do we meet tomorrow? You know, to arrange for my post?"

Morek smiled, bought the man a drink, and began to discuss the matter at length.

* * * *

A bead of sweat, a lone traveler on the man's forehead, traveled torturously down toward its demise. The smell of body odor permeated the air around Richard Vandross as he stayed crouched to the ground, his palms trembling uncontrollably against the ground. Through ridgelines in his forehead, born from concentration and effort, that single bead of sweat slithered, running like pus instead of a clear liquid. Down to the jut between his eyebrows, sliding down the hawk-like nose, and down to the ground. When it hit, steam hissed up into Vandross's face, forcing tears from his dried out eyes.

For an entire day and a half, he had remained in his prone position, hands pressed against the ground. Fissures spread from his hands all the way to the fort and to the other side of the walls. Though he didn't know it, inside the fort, the defenders had already begun turning on one another.

His first relief came when he saw a large, brutish Human Paladin toss an Elven Cleric off of the high north wall to his death. The sounds of battle flared from within the walls, and Vandross, looking up to see his handiwork grinned toothily, pressing the magic even harder.

His arms throbbed from the effort, his muscles twitching involuntarily at strange intervals. His whole body felt like a collection of injuries screaming for his attention, none being tended to.

Vilec Roak came up to him from his own ranks, bringing a wooden cup filled with water to his lips.

For the first time since he had begun this effort, Vandross took a quick swig, not moving his palms from the ground. Fire raced through his throat, the clean, cold liquid working through his system already. He felt renewed, and strangely grateful.

His plans came to fruition as several portions of his own force stole up to the walls of the fort, ropes and grappling hooks in hands. While the Paladins,

Clerics and Knights within the fort sought to destroy themselves, Vandross's men would help the effort.

Vandross had been very clear from the beginning—do just enough to kill them, but try to leave them as whole as possible. He didn't want shambling zombies or incapable Dread Knights. When he raised the dead from the fort, he wanted to be able to fashion High Zombies and Dread Knights out of the majority of them. Perhaps even collect parts for a Dreadnaught or two, though that would require a great deal of effort.

After the ritual that he had nearly brought to a close, Vandross felt assured that he could do almost nothing, Orbs of Eden's Serpent or not. This constant effort and expenditure of energy had surely brought him right to Death's doorstop, and the hooded shepherd of souls needed only open the door and usher him in.

With renewed virulence Vandross sent a shudder through the rifts in the ground, shaking the very earth itself under all of their feet.

Several Paladins fell from the walls, their bodies making sickening crunches as their bones shattered on impact.

Then, as swiftly as it began, the end drew near. Vandross's eye went wide as the front gate raised up, two huge Trolls working the winches and then tearing them from their rigging as the gate stood open. No one would be able to lower it again, even if the fort's defenders should come to their senses.

Battle raged inside, the fort's defenders cutting each other down instead of the creatures who assaulted them. In minutes, his army pouring through the gate, the siege was over.

Vandross withdrew his hands from the ground, looking at his hands. They had been seared almost to the bone. He didn't care; victory had its costs, and he was willing to suffer this one.

Richard Vandross stood, his eye reflecting the light of the rising sun. Sweat poured down his bare forearms and his face, his crew cut hair shimmering and slick from not bathing. He stalked toward the fort, a towering visage of doom and dirt, looking as though he had been engaged in fierce combat for days.

He just made through the gate before he collapsed, unconscious.

Dozens of hands grappled him, carrying him over the heads of several men. Afloat in his own void, he felt his body carried inside a building, lowered gently to a bed, and stripped of his armor and clothes. A cold, wet rag was placed on his forehead, and voices whispered in awe and concern.

He was a great leader, he heard someone say, their voice scratchy and deep. A Shadowbeast, one he recognized; Vilec Roak. Then, he was unaware of the world around him, falling through darkness, into rest.

Chapter Twelve
Confrontation

Tandaba, the black-furred Cuyotai Chieftain, waked Shoryu and Ellen. The sun had poked up over the horizon, a single shaft of light beaming down through the window on Ellen's slender form beneath the sheets. "I know it's early, yah, but I tink we should get everyone ready to head out. We sent a runner to the other villages nearby about two hours ago." The Chieftain sat on the edge of the bed next to Shoryu, who remained lying peacefully under the covers. "He's just about back by now, I wager. We have arranged breakfast in the village circle, as we did last night for our meeting. When you're ready," he said, looking over at Ellen, who was rubbing her eyes. "We'll be dere."

The Chieftain brought his snout in close to Shoryu's ear. "And if yah are goin' ta be havin' relations, boy, make sure she keeps the sheets all da way up to her neck."

Shoryu looked over at Ellen, noticing that her shoulders were bare and exposed. That, of course, was to say nothing about her dress being heaped on the floor with his clothes. He flushed instantly, forcing a smile at the big Chieftain, who ruffled his hair as he stood.

The pair from Byron's company washing in a water basin, and dressed between sharing occasional kisses and light touches.

He had been thinking about a family of his own the night before, when Ellen had rolled atop him, saying nothing, but staring deep into his eyes. They had made love then, wrapped in each other's arms, time seeming to stop altogether. Shoryu chided himself for not at least tucking their clothes under the bed, so that Tandaba wouldn't be immediately aware. He felt a little bad about doing what they had done in the Chieftain's home, though the big man seemed more amused than anything.

They shared a wordless embrace for a long moment before leaving the house hand-in-hand. Ellen leaned close against him, and whispered in his ear, "I love you."

"And I love you." He grinned like an idiot. His heart knew that there were hard times ahead, battles with forces they could only wonder about. Richard Vandross was a dangerous beast, and their own lives would be in great danger when they rejoined the company from Whitewood. But he swore that he would protect this wonderful Elven girl. He would protect and cherish her for the whole of his life, he promised himself.

At the village center, breakfast already being served on large porcelain plates. They were each handed a plate from the pup Straig, who smiled knowingly up at them.

Ellen thanked him, but noticed a strange sadness in his eyes. She would have to ask him about it before they left.

A cheer suddenly went up from the group, and Shoryu and Ellen looked in the direction they all faced, seeing the village runner return with a group of at least two hundred Cuyotai. They all appeared to be from separate tribes, but had their arms raised in the symbol of victory, each fur-covered limb fisted at the end.

From different homes, from separate walks of life, they had come to the aid of Tandaba and his village. They had all agreed to aid the Elves in their time of need. One older warrior shouted that the Elven Kingdom was their home as well, and no man would take their homes from them without a fight.

"I am sorry dat dere isn't enough food for you all," shouted the big Chieftain to the assembled warriors, but many simply brushed the matter aside.

Five other headdressed Cuyotai, Chieftains all, approached the circle.

Tandaba moved out to meet them, and together they talked quietly, conferring on the matter of strategy. Tandaba motioned Shoryu and Ellen over to the group, and they stood before the towering Chieftains.

"Greetings, oh wise and noble Chieftains," Shoryu said, bowing in the manner of his home.

Each of the aged leaders bowed in return, smiling at him and the Elf girl with him.

"What is it that you wish of this meager Hunter and talented Gaiamancer," he asked, keeping his tone formal and his eyes slightly lowered. His home was gone, but his ways were still ingrained in him; he would not meet their eyes as long as they were engaged in their duties. As he looked at the ground, he noticed Straig clinging to Tandaba's leg. The Chieftain said nothing to his son, letting him cling.

"The boy is modest," said one of the Chieftains, a white furred man. White Cuyotai, Shoryu knew, were the rarest of his kind, masters of magic like few other Cuyotai. "Your name is Shoryu, right?"

The young Hunter nodded wordlessly.

"Why do you not look us in the eye, boy?"

"Because such was custom where I come from, wise one," Shoryu replied after a moment's hesitation.

"Well," the white fur placed a hand gently on Shoryu's shoulder, "it is a silly custom. Look at me, boy." His deep, gravely voice scraped like nails on a chalkboard.

Shoryu looked up into the Chieftain's red eyes, then started, flinching back instinctively.

"Never seen a white fur Cuyotai before, eh?"

Shoryu nodded.

"I have." Ellen took Shoryu's hand in her own. She curtsied to the Chieftains. "I am Ellen Daires, of Whitewood. We two separated from our company for the purpose of gaining your aid against the devil Richard Vandross. You have a plan," she said, making it a statement of fact, not a question.

The Chieftains all nodded.

"What is it?"

"Well, dis Vandross fellah, he doesn't know us from Sam, right?" asked Tandaba, patting his son on the head.

Shoryu and Ellen nodded.

"But he surely knows enough to know dat we're here, and aren't allowed in da cities, yah? Well," he said, folding his massive arms across his chest. "We gonna make it look like we attackin' da city ourselves. Him and his men, dey'll let us alone. Well, we'll have you tell the city officials to let us scale the walls, and we'll make noise, like we battlin' inside. One half will go inside, while da other half stay outside. When Vandross's own men make a move, da half outside will attack him from da flank. He won't know what's coming."

The plan seemed logical enough to Shoryu and Ellen, though neither thought that Tandaba knew just what the risks were. Vandross had more than a thousand men coming; the Cuyotai numbered just over three hundred men and women. If only half of that number attacked Vandross, surprised or not, the one-eyed devil would crush them with little effort. "You seem hesitant, boy. What's wrong?"

"Vandross has many times more men than we." Shoryu's voice was a harsh whisper. He was angry with himself, thinking it foolish to bring so many of his own kind to such risk. He and Ellen should never have asked them for their help: they would surely all be killed. "We should all go inside the city walls, every last one of us. Fewer lives will be lost that way."

"Lives are lost in war," said the white fur Chieftain. "It is the nature of war. But we are warriors, all of us. We know the risks we take. If the Elven Kingdom is at risk, we gladly lay down our lives to defend the thousands who live within it. A couple hundred is a small sacrifice in the face of losing a whole nation."

A war cry went up from the Cuyotai nearby, a wild and jubilant cheer. Indeed, it seemed they knew and accepted what was expected of them.

How many of those veterans and young fighters would live beyond the struggle? Shoryu wondered.

Ellen's hand tightened on his, and she smiled at him as he looked at her. He smiled in return, his hope rekindled. There would be survivors, and from those survivors, a new generation. He embraced her, and he felt the shocked gazes of the Chieftains apart from Tandaba.

Shoryu opened his eyes, and saw Straig smiling up at him.

"Please excuse dese young lovers," Tandaba said as they pulled away from each other.

"Not a problem," said the shorter tan furred Chieftain, a crooked smile on his face as he met eyes with Shoryu. "My wife is also an Elven girl."

"Oh, we're not married," Shoryu blurted, waving his hands as the Chieftains laughed at him.

Ellen put her arm around his slender waist, and he across her shoulders. "We're just, you know, together. Seeing where things will take us," he said, feeling Ellen jab him in the ribs playfully. "Right, let's be serious, wise ones. When do we leave?"

The white fur Chieftain barked an order to the assembled fighters, and they rapidly formed marching ranks. "Right now," he said with a wicked smile.

The Chieftains, except for Tandaba moved away. He knelt before his son, giving him a fierce hug and stroking the boy's head in a fatherly fashion.

The boy would not let him go, and started to beat Tandaba on the arm.

"Don't go, father," he said, sobbing. "Don't go!"

Shoryu and Ellen stood glued to their spot.

Tandaba stood, pushing the boy away from him gently.

"You can't! You can't," the boy raged at his father.

"Straig, me boy, what has gotten into you? I must go, you know dis. It is my duty to my people. To my family." He waved his hand to encompass the whole village. "To you, my boy," he said softly. He patted the boy's head and walked away, calling to his own men.

Shoryu and Ellen knelt next to the crying boy, concern mirrored in their faces.

"Straig," said Ellen softly, rubbing his back. "What's wrong? Why can't your father go with us?"

Shoryu patted the boy's shoulder, trying to be supportive.

"Because," Straig looked them both in the eyes. He seemed to choke on his words, coughing violently. "Because I have seen it."

"Seen what," asked Shoryu.

"I have seen what is to be," Straig said, facing Shoryu square on. "I saw a one-eyed monster in my dream last night. He is going to kill my father." The boy buried his face in Shoryu's shoulder, his flowing tears matting Shoryu's fur.

Shoryu held the boy a moment, then released him.

"We will protect your father," Shoryu said with an awkward smile. "Don't worry. He'll be fine."

The boy nodded, and waved goodbye to them as they left.

Shoryu couldn't shake his feeling that no matter what they did, the boy's vision would come to pass.

* * * *

Richard Vandross opened his eye and gazed up, seeing the domed ceiling of some sort of cavern. He felt the heat of earthen flames under him. He sat, holding his head as it throbbed, looking up into the face of Power. For just a moment, she looked too much like his mother for comfort, but he shook his head and banished the thought. His mother had died like the weak cow she was. None such fate awaited Power.

He was within his soul again. "What am I doing here? I have work to do outside, in the real world." He was nude save a pair of tunic pants, just as he had been in the waking world.

Straightening, he stalked forward toward the altar that stood before the pitch-black coffin containing the Glorious Mother of Destruction. "There must be a reason for your bringing me here."

Vengeance crept out from wherever he had been hiding.

"Indeed, there is, a, reason," shlooped Vengeance. "I, wanted to, congratulate, you, on, your remarkable, use, of the, magic. But, that, is not, the main, reason, behind your, summons. Power, has, something, to show you."

Vandross stalked over to Power, gazing over his shoulder at the snake-man creature called Spite. He hadn't offered much in the times Vandross had been in this odd place that was supposed to be his soul. Did the little beast hide something from him, waiting for the right opportunity? Or did he simply have little to offer? Vandross decided he would find out later, in the waking world. For now, he was interested in what Power had to show him.

"What is it you wish me to see?" he asked, a placating smile on his lips.

Power withdrew part of her robes, pulling a small crystal from one of her inner pockets. She held it up to the rock light of the cavern, letting the crimson light spill through the object in her hand onto her exposed wrist.

The orb shimmered, and revealed the image of a Shadowbeast slipping through the ground somewhere deep in the forest. It tunneled through the earth without a trace, moving itself through the Shadowrealm into a room far beneath the earth's surface. Finally, it crept up upon an Elven man who laid prone on a bed within the chamber. In a flash, the demon merged with the Elf, possessing him, but the Elf appeared resilient. Time passed, and Vandross watched the man become a raving lunatic, smearing his own feces and blood across the walls in arcane symbols, unable to get free of the room. Then, the crystal flashed, and Byron of Sidius stood in the room. He swiftly and effortlessly put an end to the man's life.

It was then that Vandross realized the importance of what he was seeing; the Orb of Eden's Serpent lay somewhere near that room. What was one of his Shadowbeasts doing there, however? He had not ordered any reconnaissance.

As if reading his thoughts, which she probably could do anyway, Power answered his question.

"The Shadowbeasts are naturally drawn to the artifacts. This one was weak-willed enough to go after it himself. However, this offers us some insight into the location of the Orb of Eden's Serpent. We know it is underground. And that it is defended."

Vandross cursed under his breath. He knew already of the Orb's underground location, but the sight of Byron infuriated him. How long would the Dread Knight be a thorn in his side? He had to get rid of the undead warrior somehow. Byron posed the greatest direct threat to him and his cause, and could easily destroy hundreds of his men. He had to confront the Dread Knight himself. But would he be enough? He felt a viper of doubt slither up his spine. No, not yet. He needed one more Orb of Eden's Serpent, and then he would be powerful enough. And with the fifth, well, no one would stand a chance against him. But ah, a head-on battle was not what he was working toward, was it? *No,* he thought, grinning sheepishly, *it isn't.*

He paced the stone floor of the chamber, his bare feet warm on the volcanic rock as he shuffled back and forth. The smell of sulfur rose through the air, clouding his vision. *This is a siege on the Elven Kingdom capital,* he thought. Thousands of lives were at stake on Byron's side of this particular conflict. He would defend the city, his primary concern being the lives of the people within the city walls. He was a Paladin in life, and such were the laws that governed all Paladins.

Vandross decided he would use that against the hulking Dread Knight. His grin turned slowly into a manic, toothy smile. The sound of voices could be heard, whispering in his ears. He stopped pacing and looked at Power.

"They are trying to wake me. Thank you for this information, Power."

Richard Vandross awoke, Vilec Roak looming over him, shaking him roughly by the shoulders.

Without thinking, Vandross brought a swift left hook crashing into the Shadowbeast's face, sending him sprawling against a wall of the small bedchamber they had laid Vandross down in. The one-eyed Human stood and immediately began donning his clothes and armor, strapping his belts and buckles in place, securing his shoulder plates.

"Sorry about that, Roak," he said, chuckling under his breath as he offered the Shadowbeast Prime a hand.

Vilec Roak accepted the hand and pulled himself erect, holding his jaw area.

"Quite a mean left hook you've got there, sire. The bodies have been lined up in the courtyard. Are you ready to raise them?"

Vandross stalked to the doorway, looking back at his new General. He flashed a wicked smile, his brows bunching together.

"General, I'm ready for anything." He spread his arms wide and cackling like a madman as he stormed from his room to the courtyard. *This is what it is to be a Vandross*, he thought, calling forth the arcane power required to raise the dead. *This* is the destiny of my bloodline, father. Not to be some teetotaling dirt farmer, but a conqueror.

* * * *

In Whitewood, the denizens of the city were preparing for war. The Prince had declared a state of emergency, making it public knowledge that Richard Vandross and his army marched on the city.

Those who remained to defend the city stood with Morek Rockmight, his crack team of specialists, as he called them. The Monk David Spore had been made Morek's right hand man and together they had convinced nearly a hundred men and women, most of whom had only been passing through the city, to stand beside the Elves in their time of need. No word had been received from the King, and many of the city's residents panicked in the privacy of their homes. Had their great leader already fallen in combat? Was he engaged in negotiations with a neighboring state for aid against this threat? No one, with the exception of the Prince, knew the truth. And he was in dire spirits as a result of what he knew.

The eldest son of his father, Ahren Helestion, the Prince stood atop a balcony in the Royal Mansion, looking out over the mighty city of Whitewood. His name was Eldric Helestion, and he was now King of the Elven Kingdom. His father's personal aide had sent a letter via messenger bird to Eldric three days previously. Ahren Helestion had been slaughtered by a pack of demons on his return to the city. The aide had hidden from the battle, barely able to keep from running himself. But there had been no sign of him at the city gates, and Eldric feared the worst; no one lived who could confirm the death of his father.

Not that he wanted any confirmation. He did not want to rule in such times as these. His younger brother, Jaimie, also wanted nothing to do with rule and royalty; he was the Commandant of the elite warriors of the kingdom, the Dark Watch. At the moment, Jaimie stood in the city streets with his men, issuing orders and plotting strategies with the High Elder, Masaton, and the enigmatic Byron of Sidius.

Though he knew the old stories of the Dread Knight, Eldric trusted the High Elder's judgment above all others. He would let things pan out as they would. He wanted no hand in the planning of the city's defense. He was no warrior—he was a Prince who had wanted nothing more than to marry and have a family, away from the Royal Mansion, away from the kingdom. He did not want to rule.

The only child of Ahren Helestion, fallen King of the Elven Kingdom, who wanted the role of leader, was their youngest sister, Deardry. She had always voiced her desire to rule, even to her father, who had always smiled and patted her on the head. "Now dear," he would say, "the ruling of a people is a man's job."

That, of course, had only made Deardry more determined in her cause. She had studied the history of the royal family back as far as it could go, trained herself in courtly etiquette, and become well versed in politics. Eldric thought her the perfect choice for ruler, but so long as he and his brother Jaimie lived, she would not rule.

A manservant approached him on the balcony. "My lord Prince, would you like a drink of tincture, to calm your nerves?"

Eldric looked at the short Elven attendant. This was not the life he wanted, but there seemed to be no escape.

"No, Terrance, but thank you. Bring my sister to me."

For a short bit, Eldric thought about launching himself over the balcony, releasing himself from his duties. But he could not—his people needed him to be strong. He was anything but, yet he was an excellent actor and would put on the brave face until this whole conflict was settled. Then, he would tell the people of Whitewood that his father had died bravely on the front, in the guise of a soldier. Of course, he had heard of the terrors that this Richard Vandross brought with him. Many bodies would not be identifiable. It would be the perfect way to preserve his father's honor.

A small, soft hand brushed his cheek, bringing him out of his reverie. His sister, a beautiful Elven woman now, stood beside him.

"Deardry," he whispered, embracing her as tightly as he could without breaking her.

"My brother, what is wrong?" She held him at arm's length and released him.

Eldric reached into a pocket of his tunic, and without a word, handed her the parchment that the aide had written upon.

Deardry read the words in silence, and finally looked at Eldric in shock. "Eldric, this means that you are King," she said in a hushed whisper.

"Indeed," he said, putting his back to the balcony railing. "And I don't want to be. Sister," he said, dropping to his rear end against the railing. "I am not fit to be King. I have never wanted it, and neither has Jaimie. You are best suited to rule, and you know it." Eldric buried his face in his hands, sobbing softly.

Deardry lowered to his side, cradling his head against her shoulder.

"What can I do to escape this fate, sister," he asked between sobs.

"There is a way, you know," she whispered. "You can use the tunnels, as father did, to leave the city without anyone being the wiser. I can tell the High Elder that you left in search of aid against the oncoming forces of darkness. And with Jaimie in command of the Dark Watch, I will be left in charge in your absence. And then, when you are free of the city, you can live your life as you have always wanted, dear brother."

Though she was a cold and calculating woman at times, Eldric could sense the sincerity and sadness in her voice. She turned his face to hers, their foreheads touching. "Is this what you want," she asked, clearly distraught.

He could not deny the truth of it, and he nodded.

Tears sprang from Deardry's eyes now as well. "Very well, then. You know where the tunnels are hidden, brother. Go well, and be safe. And for the gods' sakes," she said, kissing him on the forehead. "Do not suffer our father's fate."

Within an hour's time, the Prince of the Elven Kingdom was gone, leaving his younger sister to rule the Elven people. A better Queen, though no one knew it, could not be found.

* * * *

"What do you mean the Prince has left," Byron growled as he stood at the entrance to the Royal Mansion, his hands on his hips. He no longer bothered with the Shadow magic to conceal himself, as the citizens of the city had gone to ground for the most part. Now he stood before one of the Dark Watch who guarded the seat of power.

"He has gone in search of aid for the battle, and to locate his father, the King," said the impassive voice of the Elven warrior.

The Dark Watch reminded Byron of the stoic Rock Warriors of the Dwarven Nation. No sign of expression ever passed their lips or could be read on their faces, except in battle. And *then* one didn't want to see their faces, for they became almost demonic in their battle lust. "The King's daughter, Deardry, is now in control of the city. Do you wish to speak with her?"

Byron threw his hands in the air. "Of course you fool," he screamed, his pinpoint lights flaring red in his eye sockets.

The Dark Watchman stalked inside, and Byron stood outside, feeling like an idiot. *Too much red tape*, he thought to himself. If he could have spoken with the leader of the Dark Watch, the one they said was the younger Prince, he would have, but the man had busied himself with planning for the city's defense. That was fine by Byron; a military man had to have his time, he knew. But he had been forced to make an appointment to speak to the Prince two days ago, and now the boy wasn't here. Preposterous!

Finally, the Watchman returned, with a radiant and quick-smiling Elven woman in tow.

So this was Princess Deardry, he thought. She was breathtakingly beautiful, he realized.

"I apologize, Sir Byron, for my brother's sudden departure. How he got out of the city without my being aware of it is beyond me. Please, come with me."

Byron passed by the Watchman, stopping for a moment to snap his fingers in front of the man's eyes. Not even a flinch.

He followed the Elf Princess through the Royal Mansion to a great sitting room, where he positioned himself on a comfortable couch.

Instead of sitting across from him, Deardry placed herself on the other end of the couch, making Byron shift uncomfortably away, putting as much distance between them as he could. "Whatever you sought to speak with my brother about, you may say to me. I am well versed in the matters of war and politics, and will give whatever advice or assistance I can render. Tell me, what is it you require of me." Her tone and words sounded as though they had been plucked from some tree of etiquette.

Byron was pleasantly surprised; not only had she not seemed bothered by his appearance or reputation, but she bore herself as a respectable leader.

"My lady," he responded, trying not to rush his words. He related, as best he could, the plans of Shoryu and the Cuyotai who waited outside of the city.

She nodded and listened, waiting until he was finished before she spoke.

"And the High Elder, and the militia? Have they been informed?"

"Yes, my lady, they wait only for your approval, as acting head of state."

Deardry stood and summoned her notary, a squat Gnome fellow with a set of glasses so thick they made his eyes appear bug-like.

The Princess whispered something to the Gnome, who quickly jotted what she was saying onto an official parchment. She signed it, and the notary stamped it, speeding off out of the Mansion at top speed, stumbling here and there.

"This plan is a good one," she said, a smile tracing slightly across her lips. "I have waited many years to see the Cuyotai allowed within the cities. My father was not a bad man, merely isolationistic. Keeping them out was a foolish law, for the Cuyotai are an honorable and noble people. One of your companions is a Cuyotai, is he not?"

"Yes, Shoryu my lady. He is a proud Hunter, and the last of his village. Vandross destroyed his village to attain an Orb of Eden's Serpent like the one kept here."

"And I am told he has the heart of one of our own, Miss Daires," said the Princess with a grin.

Byron smiled despite himself, his jaw shifting and contorting.

Deardry's eyes widened, and she shifted closer to him. "How do you do that," she asked, her eyes full not of horror, but of wonder. "You are able to mimic expression, despite having no flesh on your head or throat. What other secrets do you harbor, Byron of Sidius?"

Byron stood to his feet, and without a second thought, removed his left

188

gauntlet to reveal a whole hand underneath.

The Elven Princess stared in amazement at it as Byron snapped his fingers.

"But I was told you are a Dread Knight. This is incredible."

"I learn something new about myself every day," Byron said with a chuckle as he replaced the glove. "I was a Paladin in life. My name was Byron Aixler." He felt something in the air around him change and looked back to see the Princess staring at him in shock.

"You, were Byron Aixler? The man who led the battle of the Final Push?"

Byron said nothing, but nodded slightly.

The Princess walked up to him, pressing herself against him, and he felt a strange warmth spread through his body. "I have heard the tales of what happened to you inside of Mount Toane. I know of the atrocity committed against you by the warlock Tanarak. And there is something you must know in turn," she said, turning away from him. "My father was under the command of Christopher Gray in the Final Push. He survived only because of your orders keeping the young Paladin at the entrance of the mountain. So too, did my brother Jaimie. It was after that loss to Tanarak that Jaimie formed the Dark Watch and devoted his life to the warrior's path."

"Why are you telling me this?" Byron asked in a hushed whisper.

But Deardry held a hand up to still him. "I must, Byron Aixler," she said, using his former name. "My father trusted in you, and so shall I. My brother Eldric has fled the city," she said.

Byron's jaw dropped a fraction in shock. "He had abandoned his duties? Why?"

"He does not wish to rule."

"But he does not." Byron tried to choose his words carefully. He sensed that something was terribly amiss. "The King rules upon his return."

"No." She shook her head as tears sprang anew to her eyes. "He will not return. He is dead, Byron, and my brother has abandoned his seat. I am to be the Queen of the Elven people. And they do not even know it."

She rushed forth, and cried against Byron's broad chest plate.

He gently held her for a time, swaying slightly back and forth to comfort her. The Elven Kingdom had been deprived of its leader, and the next in line did not want the throne. The other Prince had revoked his title in exchange for military leadership, leaving only this small, frail bodied girl, barely a woman, to lead an entire nation. And it was all because of Richard Vandross. Byron held the Queen at arm's length, and attempted a smile. It came out a grimace, and he quickly erased the expression.

"Your highness," he said, dropping to one knee and releasing her. He bowed his head, as was custom. "I swear that your people shall be protected. And may I be the first to say," he said, looking up at her with his pinprick lights gleaming white. "Long live the Queen." He rose then, soundlessly, and stalked out of the Mansion and into the streets of Whitewood. He would stand against Vandross here, and defend the Elven people. His concern no longer fixed around the Orb of Eden's Serpent. He would protect the people first, for Orbs of Eden's Serpent or no, Richard Vandross could not be allowed to crush the hopes and dreams of an entire nation. Byron of Sidius would not allow it. No, he corrected himself. "Byron Aixler," he whispered, walking towards the home of Ellen Daires.

* * * *

Three nights later, Richard Vandross lead his army of Shadowbeasts, Greenskins, undead and assorted other creatures of darkness toward the Elven capital.

He felt exceptionally good about the upcoming siege. As he had broken the Paladin fort, so too would he crush the Elven Kingdom. However, there were a few wild cards he hadn't bargained for. The first had come to his attention two night earlier, when Vilec Roak informed him that Bael had been spotted leading a platoon of his warriors into the city of Whitewood to aid in their defense. Roak had apologized for his failure, but Vandross had reminded him that he hadn't personally seen to the former General's destruction. The Shadowbeasts that had left the man alive had been summoned to Vandross and summarily blasted into oblivion.

The second bump in the road had been the report from a scout that Major Svelk had not been located, and thus, not exterminated. *A minor problem*, Vandross thought, and one that he had been personally responsible for. He should have known that the Elf wouldn't really tell him where he was headed. But Svelk would not be a bother. So Vandross let the matter go, mentally kicking himself for not having Vengeance kill the man.

The third development, which he had learned of only a few hours earlier, had really cheered him up. Vilec Roak had scouted ahead and found that several tribes of Cuyotai were camped outside the city, with arrows had been launched back and forth from the city and the camps. Imagine, he thought, using the very people he had eradicated an entire village of for his own purposes. The irony of it made him laugh aloud.

Two more days of marching remained before the army that Vandross had brought with him from Mount Toane arrived at Whitewood's walls. He could hardly wait for it, his anticipation growing as he thought of the carnage that awaited him. Blood would stain the earth red, magic would render the forest dead, and his nemesis would kneel before him in defeat. He intended to challenge Byron to an outright duel, and would keep the Dread Knight busy while his minions reduced the city to rubble.

The day passed without event, and much of the next day as well. That was when he thought something was amiss.

Perhaps an hour away from his destination, Richard Vandross brought his forces to a halt. An alley had been cut in the woods, forming a sort of perimeter around the city. Vandross tested the air with his magic; another magic, also powerful, had been used to clear this patch of earth of the trees that surely had once grown here. But for what purpose, he wondered to himself. Surely it was a trap. He had warnings sent through the ranks to stay clear of the pathway. They would have to march around it.

Disgruntled at this obvious line of defense, he led his forces east, hoping to find a clearing in the perimeter, but he found that another alley had been cleared going south. Once again he changed direction. He was losing time because of this nonsense, and yet he didn't dare lose any men prematurely. If a trap lay in those alleys of treeless ground, he would find a way around them.

Three hours later, he was back where he had started. The alleys were connected, forming a perfect square around the city's perimeter. He would have to risk crossing.

He sent a Troll into the alley, a huge, lumbering beast of a creature, whose superstitious nature made him fear the command he had been given. However, he faced immediate death if he refused, he only faced the possibility of death if he walked into the alley.

Gingerly, his thick metal armor clanking as he stepped onto the cleared ground, the Troll passed to the other side. There was a brief flash of magic, and then nothing. The Troll yelled triumphantly, and Vandross signaled his forces to cross.

As each set of feet crossed the alley, Vandross noticed a small spark of magic. A warning system, he thought. Clever. And that explained why they had seen no scouts in the woods. The city of Whitewood thought themselves well prepared.

"Nothing will prepare them for me," Vandross into the rapidly fading daylight. "Nothing."

* * * *

Byron's company rested in Ellen's home when Alex screamed in Selena Bradford's ear. "They're coming. They've crossed the barrier!"

Immediately she sat up, splashing water from her half-emptied cup onto her face.

Alex fluttered about the cottage, awakening the company. Without another word, Byron's company set about their appointed tasks.

James rushed to meet with Jaimie Helestion, leader of the Dark Watch, to relay the news. Selena bolted for a set of steps that would take her to the battlements atop the city walls, shouting the news to the defenders, most of whom had already seen the movements off in the distance. The charade with the Cuyotai outside of the city commenced anew, each arrow fired way off target, and with little effort or strength. Morek and David Spore, whom he had taken a liking to, prepared their motley crew of defenders for the oncoming battle. Byron sent word to the High Elder, who shortly joined him with the other members of the Council.

Brief words were then exchanged, and the entirety of the Council disappeared into the library. They would defend the Orb of Eden's Serpent from Vandross's men, for Byron did not believe that the one-eyed devil would go after it personally this time. Already a Shadowbeast had been sent for it, and it was obvious that Vandross would command the attack on the city.

Ellen helped the city's healers prepare poultices and healing salves for the wounded, using her magic to infuse the power of mother earth into the medicines and antidotes.

The company was split up, but each member did their part. Alex darted out into the woods to check on Vandross's progress and immediately flew back to Byron, who stood in the city square, which sat in the center of the city. He would be ready to charge to wherever he was needed if he was beckoned.

"They're twenty minutes away, my lord," the Ki Fairy squeaked into Byron's 'ear'. "It doesn't look good!"

"How so," Byron asked, his voice booming through the din of the city's army preparing itself for battle.

"He's turned men and women of the fort to the north into undead members of his army. And Vandross himself looks rather bloodthirsty, sire. His numbers have swelled, and already he prepares some ill magic for use against us. If you ask me, you should let me do something a bit more useful than reconnaissance."

"In due time, my tiny friend. For now, go to Selena. She needs all the support she can get. Her task shall be grim if she is forced to take it up." Byron was referring to a desperation defense he and the Pyromancer had devised the night before. If the Cuyotai outside the city fell, Selena was to set the forest ablaze around Whitewood. The trees were all far enough away from the city walls that no harm would come to the stone barriers of the city themselves. But many miles of woodland would be destroyed in exchange for the time and casualties the tactic would give the city. The Queen had agreed reluctantly. Only Byron had referred to her as Queen, he realized. No one else in the city knew of the King's death and the Prince's abandonment of his duties. He would not disillusion the Elves now, not when they needed to be strong.

Outside the city, in the Cuyotai camp, Chieftain Tandaba thought over his son's words before he had left on this trip. Straig had begged him not to go. Perhaps he was afraid for him, and that was to be expected. Few sons relished their fathers going off to war. Especially when the plan for that war was so risky. But Tandaba had to be here. It was his duty to his people, and he felt he owed the Elves his alliance and help.

So his thoughts turned to the matter immediately at hand. He heard Vandross's forces approaching from the north and knew the time would be soon. The Chieftains gathered together one last time before the battle. They exchanged blessings and tidings of a good battle, the white fur Chieftain even saying that today he may die, but he would die with honor. Vandross's forces could now be seen, and they had slowed to a halt, watching the exchange between the city's defenders and the Cuyotai.

* * * *

Vandross stood back behind a tall elm, watching with delight as Cuyotai and defenders fell away, dropping like flies. This might prove easier than he had anticipated.

Still, something bothered him, a scratching at the back of his mind. Something was amiss. The tree line had clearly been a warning system for the defenders of the city. Yet they had not been tripped by these Cuyotai, or the magic would have been spent. With his good eye, Vandross looked closely at the Cuyotai as they fell. The arrows indeed were coming close, but they were not striking the fallen warriors.

Too late, he realized the danger his forces were in. It was a trap and he had been caught in it.

"Look out," he shouted.

The Cuyotai warriors were already tearing into his left flank of soldiers. "Ambush! We have been tricked!"

As he barked orders to the lieutenants around him, Cuyotai warriors raged through the side of his army. They soon were joined by hailstorms of arrows and short spears being tossed from the high city walls. "Fall back. Fall back out of range," he screamed, his officers relaying orders in their harsh, guttural tongues to the ranks.

Chaos surged at Richard Vandross from all directions. His thoughts became a scrambled mess, and the only emotion aside from confusion he could understand was the rage that coursed through him like molten lava, laying waste to his fears and doubts, to his caution.

With reckless abandon, Vandross threw himself into the fray against the Cuyotai assault. His long scimitar flashed as he ripped it free of its scabbard, spraying the battlefield with blood as he tore into the first of his enemies. First one, then three, and before he knew it, he lost count.

He heard a banshee wail, terrifying and forceful. For a moment, he thought it was the Berserkers he had brought with his army, but realized that the sound had its origin in his throat. Magic poured from his throat, a thin blue wave of energy paralyzing his foes a moment before he got to them.

Incensed and encouraged by this newfound power of the Orbs, he struck warrior after warrior to the ground, only pausing once to stab a fallen tribal Cuyotai in the throat as he attempted to crawl away.

Shadows smoked out from the corners of his eyes, giving him the feral look of a warlock madman. His teeth shone in the fading light as he grinned wickedly, his face covered in speckles of bright red blood.

His men rallied behind and around him, and the collective effort and concentration of the army of Richard Vandross turned on the Cuyotai.

Rapt with the power at his command, Vandross leaped through the trees and brush, sending bolts of thunder from his outstretched left hand, turning Cuyotai men and women into smoldering piles of bloody debris. But behind him, Vandross heard the huge gates of Whitewood creak open, and a hundred or so men, ragtag wanderers from the look of them, charged out of the city.

Before he could return his attention to the battle before him, he felt a powerful set of claws tear at his armor, making a small incision in his chest. The armor held, saving him from a nasty wound.

He spun and found himself looking into the enraged red eyes of a tall, black furred Cuyotai Chieftain, soaked and matted in the blood of Vandross's men. He searched for wounds, a weakness of some sort, and found none. This Chieftain had plowed through a line of Orcs and Trolls to get to the one-eyed

Human.

Chieftain Tandaba threw his head back and howled.

A responding howl rose up from the throats of the fifty or so Cuyotai who still stood. Their bodies seemed to undergo some change, their muscles bunching and expanding, their already tattered clothes tearing and shredding to pieces as they grew.

Lycanthrope rage, Vandross thought, his heart skipping a beat. Cuyotai were the least aggressive of the lycanthrope Races aside from Werebears, but were known to be highly deadly in their enraged state. Vandross had to act quickly if he was to salvage his advantage of numbers.

As Tandaba neared the end of his transformation, Vandross sheathed his scimitar and lunged at the hulking Cuyotai. The two toppled end over end, each trying to remain on top.

In the end, due to his sheer size, Tandaba landed atop Richard Vandross.

The one-eyed warlock was prepared for him, however. Before Tandaba could move to crush him, Vandross grabbed him by the sides of the skull, calling forth arcane power into his hands.

A surge of power erupted into his arms, coursing from his chest down into his fingertips. With a single thrust, Richard Vandross sent lightning magic blaring through the Cuyotai Chieftain's skull.

Tandaba's entire upper torso exploded into gory bits, showering the nearest combatants with his bone fragments and innards.

Vandross shoved the remaining lower body off of him, and the entire Cuyotai assault abruptly halted.

In that pause, Vandross gave a single signal, thrusting his iron gauntlet into the sky. Vandross's forces converged on the Cuyotai, slaughtering them where they stood, motionless at the loss of Chieftain Tandaba.

High atop the walls of the city, Shoryu fell to his knees. He had sent his kinsmen into a madness from which they would have had little chance of escape. One half of Morek's crew of defenders joined the battle, only to be summarily pounded into dust. Vandross had lost what the archers guessed was somewhere around two hundred and fifty men. Shoryu took little comfort in statistics, however.

Furious at his inability to help, Shoryu drew his bow and an arrow, notching it and taking aim at the form of Richard Vandross. He knew that he could never hit the one-eyed devil. Something would warn him, some perverse luck. Instead, he took aim at a small knot of Shadowbeasts, letting his arrow fly.

The arrow buried itself deep in the head of one of the demons, exploding in a mushroom of smoke and magic, destroying fifteen other Shadowbeasts who were near.

"Well done, my friend," said a familiar voice. Byron of Sidius stood directly behind him, his arms folded across his chest, his pinprick lights small and distant. Byron's mind was focused elsewhere, but he had come to comfort Shoryu in this time of need. He had known that the ruse would end in the utter destruction of all of the Cuyotai outside of the city. Shortly, those who remained inside the walls would climb the stairs to stand atop the walls. They would keep watch throughout the night, staving Vandross off with arrows and short spears.

Vandross's army settled in, some three hundred yards off in the woods. Camp was made with tents and watch fires prepared. Vandross had prepared for a siege.

Byron looked out over their huge encampment; Vandross's forces still numbered nearly two thousand men, some of them beasts that needed no camp, some of them undead, who needed no rest or food, save the flesh of the fallen.

Alex fluttered past, a nearly invisible speck against the nighttime darkness. He was gone only a short while, flying back to Byron on the wall. "My lord, there is a problem."

"Tell me something I don't know," Byron grumbled, leaning forward on the wall's lip.

"Byron, the undead have only been fed the bodies of Morek's men who went out. Vandross and several Shadowbeasts raise the dead Cuyotai as undead servants as we speak."

Byron stood bolt upright. Such tactics had been employed by Tanarak of Sidius. He would crush a small city-state, take the dead for his own servants, and loose them to feed on the remaining living who resisted Tanarak's rule. Vandross now used the same tactic, only with Cuyotai. They were freshly dead, and would retain much of their battle skill and prowess. Worse, if any of them became Lordly, or High, Zombies, they would retain intelligence and memories. Their nature would be twisted and vile, but their knowledge would be fully intact, and that meant that they would have a base knowledge of the city's defenses. He could not allow that to happen.

Immediately he dashed down from the wall, leaping and strafing past lines of defenders and concerned citizens.

Byron made a beeline for the Royal Mansion, where the Queen would meet with the High Elder and Jaimie Helestion to discuss the progress of the battle each night. The Dark Watch guard stood in his way with a hand upturned to halt him but Byron ducked low, ramming the heavily armored man in the stomach while carrying him through the open doorway on his shoulder.

The former Paladin stopped abruptly in the sitting room, where Deardry sat in a high-backed rocking chair across from High Elder Masaton and her brother, who alone stood in the middle of the room. All eyes fixed on the lumbering Dread Knight, who set the Dark Watchman down on his feet.

The Elf rubbed his sore ribs gingerly, then fixed his gaze on Deardry. "Princess," he said, addressing only her. "I tried to stop him, but he, well," he fumbled with the words. Such things likely didn't happen to the Elven elite warriors, and this man was clearly embarrassed.

"It is all right," said the Elven girl, bidding the guard return to his duties.

"There's few men can say they've ever done such a thing to one of my Watchmen." A grinning elf sauntered over to Byron, his movements slight and reserved.

He could be dangerous, Byron knew.

"Jaimie Helestion, Head Commander of the Dark Watch," he said, extending his hand to Byron.

Byron took it and shook the man's hand hard.

"Deardry has confided in us two, and yourself, what has happened regarding the throne. I must say, I am amazed that you are fighting alongside the Elves once again, Byron of Sidius."

"You should not be, Commander. Vandross and I have some history together, little of it pleasant. I have something that all of you should know. Richard Vandross raises the fallen Cuyotai from their battlefield graves. He turns them into undead soldiers as we speak."

"Impossible," cried High Elder Masaton from his seat, his body stiffening. "The best Necromancers in the land cannot raise the bodies of the Cuyotai. They are a spiritually mighty people, and as such, few have succeeded in raising their bodies from the dead. How can this Vandross fellow do what almost no one else can?"

The High Elder's face was taut with fear and shock, his leg shaking nervously, sending small tremors through the wooden floor. The smell of incense filled the air, obviously for the High Elder's benefit, for his nerves appeared on the brink of shattering. He had become nervous since Byron had informed him and the Council of what had happened with the Shadowbeast and the guards of the Orb of Eden's Serpent. This revelation, Byron knew, would come close to breaking the old Elven man.

"He has three Orbs of Eden's Serpent in his possession," Byron said, his voice low and his tone even. "But he can be stopped. If a small group, perhaps three or four men, went out into the night, they could infiltrate Vandross's camp, find the undead Cuyotai, and banish them."

"We would need a Cleric to do that," said Jaimie Helestion. He rubbed his chin for a moment, collecting his thoughts. "I think it can be done. One Cleric, of the High Elder's choosing, to be accompanied by three of my men, to protect the father. I will choose them myself. It is a gamble, of course, Byron." He looked dead into the pinprick lights of the Dread Knight.

The two men glared at each other a moment, until Helestion looked away at his sister the Queen. "I shall go now to the barracks. Elder Masaton," he said, helping the old man up. "We shall speak again later, my lady," he said, bowing gracefully to his sister.

Odd, Byron thought. The man speaks not as though to a family member, but to a superior. Cold, formal, calculated.

Byron would keep an eye on the man; something didn't feel right about him. Even military men allowed their feelings to be known in closed chambers, especially around family. It was as though the Elven Commander didn't want to think of Deardry as his sister, but rather, as a member of royalty he had sworn fealty to.

But Byron could not spare any more time lingering in the Royal Mansion, thinking of such things. Bowing to the Elven Queen, he made haste past the guard he had carried earlier, and out into the streets of Whitewood.

Torches had been lit in the street lamps, giving the entire city an almost ghost-like cast. Only the soldiers and militiamen could be seen walking the streets, the lights blazing in the homes of the citizenry. The wooden structures of homes, taverns, and shops all appeared to be shelters against some unknown darkness, every lamp and lantern in every building lit, save for those that were unoccupied. Elves were not normally a superstitious bunch, but they took comfort from light and warmth.

Byron could not blame them: these were dark times. But another, more practical application came to Byron's mind. Shadowbeasts were said to be able to travel through the Shadowplane, disappearing into the shade of a tree on one half of the continent, and appearing only hours later clear across the land. Had Vandross thought about that? Or was the one-eyed warlock still unaware of the huge strategic advantage at his disposal?

Byron supposed not; Vandross's army was said to consist mostly of beasts of unknown origin and the more wickedly disposed Races of the lands of Tamalaria.

The undead warrior made his ponderous way to Ellen Daires's home. Walking through the door, he saw Selena Bradford engaged in some whispered conversation with Alex. The two had become close since Alex's efforts in creating the perimeter around Whitewood. The Ki Fairy had expended a vast amount of magical energy in the effort, nearly falling ill in the end. But Ellen and Selena had nursed him back to health.

Byron nodded to each of them in turn, offering no words, but then heard a shout in the street.

Spinning about and charging back outside, Byron saw a pack of Shadowbeasts emerge from the darkness of an alley near a healer's shack.

They came in the form of huge wolves, yellow eyes gleaming in the moonlight. Vandross would offer no rest for the defenders of Whitewood, it seemed. But he had just committed his first error in this siege—he had only sent six of his demons, and they would not be enough. Elven soldiers converged on the demons from all directions.

Byron nearly went back inside when a blast of concussion force knocked all of the Elves clear. The wave of energy even knocked Byron flat to the ground, and one of the wolf-like demons was atop him instantly.

Byron reached up and, in a single twist, broke the Shadowbeast's neck cleanly. He tried to stand, but found that the body had not reduced to ash and dust. He took a second look at the creature as he rolled it off of him. It was not just a Shadowbeast, it had possessed the body of a timber wolf before attacking the city.

Why, thought Byron. *Why has Vandross done this?* His answer came a moment later.

"They are wolves. Do not kill them! They must be subdued." The shout came from one of the Elven magic-users in the militia guarding the east wall.

Of course, Byron thought. The Elves held all life sacred, especially animals of the forest. Vandross had known enough to let the Shadowbeasts inhabit such creatures. And they appeared to possess the magic of the demons still, despite their bodily hosts.

"Kill them," shouted another, more familiar voice. Commander Helestion had one of the creatures impaled on a long spear, pinned against the ground. The wolf-demon thrashed about wildly, cavorting and snapping and growling as its life ebbed away.

Byron looked hard at the miserable beast; its body had been scarred and broken, shaped to give the soul of the Shadowbeast room to exist within the confines of its flesh. But he saw something he had missed in the wolf he had slain. A sliver of darkness, like black blood, flowed between the cracks of the cobblestone street.

Byron rushed forward and thrust his sword into the ground ahead of the draining fluid-like substance.

It came up short in front of his sword, suddenly whirling and taking the natural, man-like appearance of a Shadowbeast.

Byron cleaved the demon in half, and it turned instantly into ash and smoke.

The Commander raised an eyebrow at Byron, who stood crouched in a fighter's stance, facing down the remaining three Shadowbeast-driven wolves.

"Magic or enchanted weapons are the only way to kill the demons and the hosts in one fell stroke," Byron growled at the Commander. "Have two of your mages prepare to strike on my command."

Helestion nodded his acknowledgement. He sprinted to the nearest militia mages, issuing orders as Byron instructed.

Elven standard soldiers penned in the Shadowbeasts, but this time the men did not move to strike.

Jaimie's mages moved into position, and Byron shouted to the armed regulars to get out of the way.

As they rushed aside, Byron signaled to the mages to release their magic. Byron sent a streak of lightning slamming into one, as both mages, Aeromancers, sent lashing winds into them, shredding wolf and demon apart. The air stank of expended magic, and the threat was gone.

Or was it? What had become of the Shadowbeast that had been in the wolf Byron had killed first? He had not realized the problem of demon-host separation until he had seen the one escaping from Helestion's spear. He had to find it and kill it before it possessed someone else.

Byron used his Paladin senses, powers of observation from another life. Senses he was certain wouldn't function anymore. But he found he was wrong. He could smell the evil of the creature as it fled from him.

He darted after it, his sword flashing in the moonlight, pushing soldiers out of his way, coming up short in front of a weapons shop. The front door was shattered into splinters of wood and steel, and in the entryway stood the last Shadowbeast, weapons sticking from its black surface like they had been permanently attached. The Shadowbeast spun its body, long knives, axe heads, and sword blades flashing in a glittering spiral of imminent disaster.

The end of a long mace flail struck Bryon hard in the chest, sending him sprawling into a crowd of soldiers, each brandishing his weapon and attacking the whirling demon.

Like so much kindling, the soldiers were hacked apart and scattered across the cobblestone street. Bloody chunks of Elven flesh struck Byron as he regained his footing, watching in horror as, with each victim, the whirling mass of demon flesh added more weapons and bits of armor to its body.

He had never known a Shadowbeast to behave in such a fashion, no doubt it something else conjured up by Richard Vandross.

Fury rose into Byron's heart, erupting in his throat as he screamed uncontrollably.

Something burned in his chest, a flaming pain that seared his insides. He could not identify its source: the Shadowbeast had not cast any spell upon him, and he did not feel harmed by the heat in his body. But the power had a familiar feeling to it. It was something he knew, or had once known, in another life.

In a flash of thought, Byron understood. He knew the power he held ready in his heart.

Sheathing the Morning Glory, Byron removed himself twenty paces from the demon, his eyes locked on it as it slowly, menacingly approached, slowing only enough to let Byron see its yellow, glowing eyes. Byron thrust his palms before him, weaving symbols in the air.

Each symbol took shape and glimmered. The Shadowbeast advanced only one step further, and as it did so, its eyes went wide with recognition. It knew what Byron was about to unleash upon it, and was terrified.

"By the power of the Great God Oun," Byron shouted, raising his hands once more, palms flat, facing toward the Shadowbeast. "I cast thee from the mortal coil. Holy Cross," he shouted, and the light of the symbols took the shape of the holy symbol of Oun, the deity served by the Order of Oun.

White, blaring holy power rushed forth in a column shaped like the symbol, crashing into the Shadowbeast. As the power flowed through it, the demon's skin frothed and bubbled, and an ear-splitting shriek of pain and horror escaped it as it quickly crumbled into dust.

The weapons clattered to the ground, bloodied and chipped and silence hung over the city. Byron made the holy symbol of Oun in the air before himself, dropping to his knees from the sudden expenditure of Paladin magic. His chest heaved, and he felt nauseated. The world blurred and he looked up to see the face of James Hayes.

The Human Paladin was trying to say something to Byron, but the Dread Knight only heard muffled blurbs of sound as he passed out. He did not hear the cries of praise shouted about him by the Elven people, or the soldiers. He did not feel Shoryu's hand on his as he was carried to Ellen's home. He did not hear the angry scream of Richard Vandross from the other side of the city walls as he was told his night strike had failed. He did not see the tears in the eyes of his Cuyotai friend, or the soft smile of Morek Rockmight as they covered him, fully armored, with a blanket in Ellen's home.

He did not hear the people outside, proclaiming him a hero.

* * * *

What Byron of Sidius did hear was the ragged sound of his own screaming as he fell through the black void of his mind, landing with a hard thump upon a hardened burial plot. *Here again*, he thought. *The cemetery.*

Byron rose, dusting himself off gingerly, probing with his nerves to see if anything was broken.

Satisfied that he was still in one piece, he turned and looked down at the headstone of the grave he had landed on. It was worn, and he could not make out the inscription.

"It does not matter," said the Voice from the darkness.

Byron's shoulders sagged as he turned. As in the first times he had come here, no one stood about.

"It does to me," he whispered hoarsely, hardly able to speak. "But that is not the point. Why am I here? Is it the spell I unleashed? I remembered the incantation and movements."

"You remembered something more. Rather, you recovered something more."

"What's that supposed to mean?" Byron asked wearily, sitting atop the headstone.

"It means you have recovered some of your humanity," said the Voice.

Byron mulled over this information, choosing to remain silent, to wait for something more from the Voice.

"Understand that the curse on your body can never be fully broken, Byron. But your soul can be fully awakened."

"Really?" Byron moved his hand to his bony chin. "Why must my body remain in this state? Is it the curse tied to Vandross?"

"Indeed," said the Voice out of the stillness. "The one known as Tanarak of Sidius had locked away your spirit. Vandross locks away your body. If you defeat him, you may well lose your life."

"There is no other choice," said Byron, standing straighter. "All things done in the name of the greater good require sacrifices. This matter is no different." There was silence for a minute or so, during which Byron searched the cemetery in the vain hope of seeing the Voice.

"Very well. You have noticed that as you continue to struggle against this Richard Vandross, you regain small pieces of yourself. Not just your hands, but powers of your former being. You must be confident in your abilities, Byron. You must trust in the faith you once had, you once lived by."

Around him, the darkness of the void outside of the cemetery encroached upon the ground.

"You shall soon awaken. Take heart in this, Byron. Those who have sworn to aid you, shall not leave your side. They shall fight to the end with you. You have friends, Byron. You must protect them as best you can."

"I will," Byron whispered as he came awake.

Damnation of the Realm

Richard Vandross seethed. A small group of warriors and a Cleric had stolen into his camp and cast down the undead Cuyotai he had worked so hard to raise from the dead. The effort that had gone into making them his servants had been enormous, and left him drained and weak.

Vilec Roak woke him to report that the damage had been done, and the intruders had furthermore evaded pursuit.

Not even a full day had gone by, and Vandross's tactics had been thwarted.

He took some small satisfaction from blasting the fools who had been lax in their monitoring of the Cuyotai undead into tiny chunks of blood and gore. But now, covered in blood and sweat, all he could think of was the one man who could possibly have arranged the destruction of his new minions and destroyed the Shadowbeast infected wolves: Byron of Sidius.

The Dread Knight haunted him at every turn. No matter where Vandross concentrated his efforts, Byron was either a step behind, or already ahead of him. How, he wondered. "Tell me something, Roak," he growled, his voice hoarse from screaming at his own men. "How is it that we have already received such high damages, and yet have done virtually *nothing* to this damned city? How?" he screamed, springing to his feet and pulling the Shadowbeast to him, their noses touching.

Vilec Roak's yellow eyes widened with fear; he had not expected Vandross to become so openly hostile.

"I tire of these cretins who defy me, the Dread Knight and his Cuyotai charge," he shouted, thrusting Vilec Roak from him. Vandross paced rapidly in front of his tent. He stopped before the Shadowbeast, sweeping his lanky, unwashed hair back from his face. He seemed to calm a little, closing his eyes and breathing deeply for a moment. "Tell me what you can about the Dread Knight's personal company."

Vandross took a seat on a nearby log, close to one of his officer's fires, as Vilec Roak told him about the members of Byron's company. The information was mostly second-hand from a letter left behind by Major Svelk, in a small satchel left near their meeting place.

Roak handed the letter to Vandross afterwards, and Vandross looked it over with careful scrutiny.

A Gaiamancer and a Pyromancer, he read on. *The Elf girl had probably created the perimeter in the forest*, he thought. Simple enough work for a Gaiamancer, if she had the time. But that seemed unlikely, he thought.

Richard Vandross suddenly stood bolt upright, his entire body tensing. Something throbbed in his chest. *The Orb of Eden's Serpent*, he thought in wonder. *It calls to me.*

He closed his eyes, and his vision became a whirling tunnel. Layers of dirt and rock flashed past him, until finally he stopped in a dark, moist chamber somewhere beneath the ground. The artifact he had come for flashed and pulsed with the familiar purple light of all of the Orbs. It was as though he were seeing through the eyes of a tunneling creature, and his field of vision changed and flashed upward through the chamber's ceiling. There was metal plating in the ground, to defend against anyone tunneling through to the Orb, a point that made him nearly growl and break the illusion. But he held his temper in check, riding this fantastic vision to its conclusion.

Suddenly, his view became that of someone who might be standing in a library. Books lined shelves on every wall, and one particular tome caught his attention. He dashed over to it, reading the title on the spine; Demons with Wings, and Other Terrible Things.

A lever, he decided. As suddenly as the vision came, it left him, and he opened his eyes to smile wickedly at his second-in-command.

"My lord," Roak asked, his voice light and tense.

"I know where it is, Roak," he said in a hushed tone. "It lies under a library in the city. It is guarded from above by metal plates, so that none can dig to it. But we need only get inside the city, and get to that library. Prepare the ladders," he said, stalking slowly off towards the city walls. "We strike at dawn."

Roak saluted and sprinted off to inform the officers of each battalion of their lord's orders.

"You cannot resist me forever, Byron of Sidius," Vandross whispered to himself, grinning. "The Orb shall be mine, as shall your life."

* * * *

Byron and his company stood in the courtyard just before the sun came over the horizon. He had exchanged few words with the others since awakening a few short hours ago, only telling them that they must all be ready for an attack. They had all been relatively well rested, with the exception of Shoryu and Ellen, who seemed to have enjoyed the privacy of her bedchambers for most of the evening.

Byron smiled knowingly to himself. The boy was all right.

As the sun spread its first shafts of light over the land, shouts went up from the sentries on the walls. "Full assault! Full assault! The enemy is planting ladders!"

Byron and Shoryu rushed to the north wall, Selena and Ellen to the east and west respectively.

Iron-wrought ladders were propped up against the walls on three sides of the city, and blasts of dark magic sent the defenders flying to the city streets below.

Byron and Shoryu peppered the Orcs and Trolls, who were setting the ladders and climbing them, with hails of arrows and magic.

Shoryu let one Greenskin begin his ascent, ducking low behind an abutment to avoid taking enemy arrows or magic. As the face of the Troll hovered over the wall, he wrapped a strap of leather to the man's wrist, tying him to the ladder.

The Troll, confused, looked down at his hand, as Shoryu launched a swift, hard kick into his face. The Troll flailed atop the ladder, and his weight threw the ladder back, sending him falling fifty or so feet on the ladder to his death.

On the east wall, Selena Bradford summoned forth tiny flames at the base of the ladders' tops, where the enemy would first set foot when they came off of the ladders. As the first of Vandross's men reached the top of the ladders, each, in turn, looked at the tiny flames and then at the red robed woman.

With a flicker of her magic and a weaving of her hands in the air, Selena turned the tiny flames into scorching pillars of flaming death.

The city's defenders used long, steel spears and bo staffs to push the burning creatures off of the walls, kicking the ladders down to the ground below. Several of the ladders fell apart, and dozens of Greenskins, Shadowbeasts and Khan moved forward to make quick repairs, hauling the ladders back up against the walls.

On the west wall, Ellen called up several stone guardians, made from the city wall itself.

The huge, disfigured creatures of magic gripped the ladders, lifting them parallel to themselves. Enemies clutching the iron rungs as they lay prostrate and level with the stone guardians. With a turn and shake, several dozen foes dropped to their deaths fifty feet below, and the ladders were then hurled with great force into the forest, hundreds of yards away.

Vandross's attempts to scale the walls were being beaten back.

Byron, meanwhile, sped back to the center of the city to take reports from several officers. The walls were holding. None of the creatures who gained the top stayed alive long enough to do any damage.

Morek Rockmight ran up to Byron then, sweat pouring down his weather worn face. "Byron, something fierce scales the south wall! These other attacks have been a distraction!"

Byron followed Morek, who ran as fast as he could on his short, stubby Dwarven legs. Fueled by adrenaline, the trip to the south wall took only a handful of minutes. The two ascended the stairs that led to the top of the south wall, and Byron looked down the side.

A creature that appeared to be a mix of giant crab and mountain lion, its fur short over thick red plating, slowly made its way up the south wall. Arrows ricocheted off of its shell, short spears snapped in its enormous claws, and its eyes seethed with hatred. It was a monster unlike any of the others that Vandross had brought with him. And it was gaining speed. The creature was easily the size of a small dragon. Although its approach was slowed by the constant barrage of attacks, Byron knew it would soon make its way to the top of the wall and into the city.

Byron saw that the archers atop the south side were running low on arrows and spears. There were no mages of any sort here, and for a moment, Byron wondered why. Mages, Hunters, Knights, and a single Cuyotai Shaman had been placed at wall. Where then were the mages and the Shaman, he wondered.

Before he could ponder the question further, a cry sounded from below the beast, on the ground outside the city. Byron focused his sight past the monstrosity, at the tiny figures below. Two mages and a Cuyotai stood directly below the creature, and lanced magic into its backside. Streaks of light blue power shined out from the mages and several dozen golden, gleaming magical arrows launching from the Shaman's palm.

The creature thrashed about wildly, screaming in pain, until it lost its grip on the wall. "Get out from underneath it," he screamed, but his warning had been unnecessary. As soon as the magic had struck, the mages and the Shaman had reentered the walls through a secret door.

The beast thrashed as it landed on its back, its soft underbelly exposed.

Wasting no time, the defenders shot the last of their arrows, blood shooting out of the wounds they opened in the creature's belly. It lay dead within moments.

"Morek," said a strangely garbed man with one arm, who had appeared out of nowhere next to Byron. David Spore, Byron remembered. The one-armed Monk. "Vandross's assault draws back to its camp. The sun is out in full, and his armies are apparently less effective now. He rests them, I believe."

Morek nodded curtly, and the Monk sprinted off, leaving a trail of dust in his passing.

Byron took an instant liking to the man. He was humble, but had a sense of humor along the lines of the Dwarven Boxer, and he was capable and competent.

"Well," said Byron, clapping the little warrior on his broad back. "I'd say this calls for a drink. I'll meet you at the tavern in twenty minutes"

"You're not heading straight over," asked Morek, raising an eyebrow.

"No," Byron said, looking about at the weary defenders. "I have to check on morale and casualties with Jaimie Helestion. I'll be there shortly." Morek and Byron went their separate ways, the Dwarf to the tavern, and the Dread Knight to the eastern residential district.

Commander Helestion reported that only twelve of their own had been stricken during the attack, all of them regular army. None of the Dark Watch had fallen.

"Good. But keep your men on their toes," Byron said, turning to go join Morek at the tavern. "I expect Vandross has a slew of tricks up his sleeve. I want to know right away if it looks like he's getting ready to use one."

* * * *

Richard Vandross smiled gleefully to himself, his trap had sprung. While the city had concentrated on the ladders and the Belehest, the beast he had formed to attack the south wall, he had sent Vilec Roak and a handful of Khan to weaken the north gates, tearing wood away and employing a magic that would buckle the wood at its reinforcements. When their work was done, he had ordered the rest of his men back, under the guise of a retreat. The sunlight had, however, played a small factor. His demons walked about like wraiths or zombies, their movements sluggish and their temporary solid forms sliding and oozing at the edges. They retreated to the shade of the forest, taking the opportunity to rest and wait until dusk.

He could have heeded Vengeance's advice and tried the same magic that had taken the Paladin fort by surprise, but Vandross did not think that such a tactic would work here. These were Elves, a magically strong people. On top of that, the bothersome Council of Elders would likely counter the magic. He would bide his time. The tactics he had chosen to use were his own, and he was pleased when Roak reported that only one more session against the gates would leave them as fragile as glass.

Vandross would continue his feints, regardless of the casualties they caused his forces. Only a few score had died in any case; the bulk of his army was still intact. And if they could keep this up, in two days time, he would rush into the city of Whitewood with the rest. The defenders and the city's precious Dark Watch would be overrun. He would make his way to the library, which, thanks to the wolves, he knew the location of. And he would make his way beneath the ground to the Orb, kill whoever guarded it, and absorb it.

He would be one step closer to perfection.

The afternoon passed slowly, with little or no activity from either side. Vandross kept men posted near the trapdoors that allowed small knots of defenders out of the city. The dinner hour came, and Vandross had his personal aides prepare him a grand meal, served on a quickly assembled dining table. He invited his head officers, Vilec Roak, a Major Tong, who was a black fur Werewolf, Captain Florin, a Khan Hunter, and lastly, Colonel Pentz, a corrupt Human Knight who seemed to possess some Psychic powers. All sat in silence for a few minutes as the meal was brought to them on large earthenware plates and bowls.

Vandross took a deep whiff of the stew and the roasted meat. It had a slightly sweet scent, and he tried to think of what sort of animal it had come from. He looked up with suspicion in his eyes at the Orcs and Goblins who had prepared the meal. One in particular looked rather amused and proud of himself.

"Excuse me, corporal," Vandross said, calling the big man over.

The Orc still wore his uniform under his chef's apron, two yellow stripes on his left arm to identify his rank, and nothing more. Vandross beckoned him to lean in close, whispering in his ear. "What is this meat from, corporal?"

The Orc smiled and cocked an eyebrow at the one-eyed devil.

"Elf, sir," he whispered back. "I've been eatin' dat stuff fer years. Mighty tasty stuff."

Vandross felt a pang of disgust, but shrugged his shoulders. A meal was a meal, and he needed food. He motioned for everyone to dig in, and took a small, tentative nibble from a hunk of the cooked Elven meat.

He stopped midway through chewing, savoring the tenderness and taste of the meat. It really was good. He devoured his meal without further hesitation, enjoying the unique spices used in the stew and bread that had been made to accompany the main course. He would have to have the good corporal made his personal chef.

"Gentlemen," he said, wiping his mouth at last with a napkin of cloth, and pushing his plate and bowl away. He had had his fill, and felt good and nourished. "Tell me what you're thinking. Starting with you, Captain Florin. What's going through your mind."

"Sire," said the massive Khan Hunter, standing straight and saluting. He took a parade rest stance, his hands behind his back in perfect position. "I believe we're wasting our time. We should still be engaged in our attack, I feel, sire. If you would just let the Berserkers get a crack at scaling the walls—"

"Out of the question, Captain," said the Colonel from his seat. He had his boots up on the table, leaning back in his chair. "They can't be sent alone, as you've requested twice now. I've foreseen the outcome. That Cuyotai with the magical bow would pick most of them off, and the bag of bones, Byron, would use his formidable magic to destroy the rest. The Berserkers must be held in check until we have a sure way in."

"Agreed," hissed Vilec Roak from his seat on Vandross's left. "We'll need them and our Ninjas to deal with the Dark Watch when we gain access to the city."

"Perhaps we need a single concentrated thrust at one wall," chimed in Major Tong, the Werewolf. "We could assign one half of our mages to the eastern wall, and attack the wall itself. The Pyromancer defending that wall seems to be more concerned with keeping them off the walls with the ladders than the wall itself." The Major produced a crudely drawn outline of the city and the army's positions. Several markings had been made in charcoal pencil, each explained in a key at the bottom of the map. He pointed to the eastern wall. "The Pyromancer and defenders have made no attempt to stop the men while they are on the ground. The majority of their archers are on the north wall facing us, and the west and south walls. Without safe access to more trees for fodder, the archers will not be able to make more arrows. They will run out in another day or two."

"By that time," hissed Roak. "We will have the north gates sufficiently weakened. We will be able to storm the city in our full force." He waved a hand dismissively at the Major, whose eyes narrowed in anger.

"Perhaps so, but as soon as those gates fail, the entire strength of the city will concentrate its efforts there. We will suffer an extremely high casualty count in that event."

Vandross, chin on hand, nodded in agreement. The Major had a good point.

"How long will you need, Major," he asked abruptly, putting an end to the debate at the table.

The black Werewolf looked up in surprise, cycling through his thoughts.

"Two, perhaps three days. Long enough to weaken the stone as you have weakened the gates."

Vandross mulled the matter over in his mind, trying to think about strategy for a moment. It did seem the better course of action; the defenses of the city would have to divide, weaken its positioning at the last moment. He liked the idea.

"You have your time Major. Take those you need with you, but none from the General's personal squads. When you're ready to make the final blow, wait for my signal. Understood?"

The Major nodded and saluted smartly, moving away from the table already.

As the table was cleared and the officers moved off, Vandross called Vilec Roak back to his side. "Roak," he said, standing from the table. "If the Major's plan helps us in this, and he survives, make certain he is promoted to Colonel. Colonel Clent was felled in the attack on the west wall earlier. He needs a replacement, and the Major is worthy."

Roak saluted and moved off into the deepening shadows, watching as the sun settled toward the horizon. Nightfall was coming soon, and another session of weakening the gates would commence. The magic employed was delicate, and had to be properly balanced. The concentration required was exhausting, and Roak had wanted to do all of his work in the night. But such tactics would be clearly seen through, he knew. Lord Vandross was wise in these matters, and he trusted the one-eyed warlock's judgment. He would resume his work when the sun set. For now, he had matters of another nature to attend to. Though Richard Vandross had been unconcerned about the perimeter they had crossed days ago, Vilec Roak had sensed something sinister about the barrier. Why had so much of the forest been cleared? What purpose did it serve other than a way to detect their crossing? He moved off to his personal tent to think it through. He would not find out on his own, however. He would have considerable assistance.

* * * *

Byron and Selena Bradford stood atop the north wall, looking off at Vandross's camp. Byron had just left the Queen and the Commander after a meeting to discuss their next move. They would no longer wait for Vandross, they would let Selena Bradford unleash fiery hell on the unsuspecting army.

A vanguard of Cuyotai, enchanted by a local Q Mage to be immune to the flames, would exit through the secret doors on the west wall, and attack the front lines of Vandross's forces. The surprise assault would distract them from Selena's efforts, and they would all be caught up in the flames before they knew what was going on.

Deardry, the new Queen of the Elves, had approved. She had regretted that so much forest had to be sacrificed, but the lives of her people were more important.

Byron looked down at the muffled activity of Vandross's camp. They were preparing to assail the city in the same manner as they had earlier. They would be in for quite a surprise tonight, Byron thought as he softly chuckled.

"You're enjoying this, aren't you?" Selena said.

Byron smiled broadly, stretching his cheekbones and teeth as wide as he could.

"Yes, quite a bit. It's about time we took a little initiative." In a few minutes, the Cuyotai would strike, and Selena would cast one of the most powerful Pyromancy spells in existence, the Meteor Strike.

She began moving her hands, weaving the basis of the spell in the air. Red, thin flames sparked in the air, forming symbols of the art of Pyromancy, flashing in and out of sight.

A shout rose from below, and Byron looked down to see the first of thirty Cuyotai volunteers charging Vandross's front lines.

Vandross rose from his cot as he heard the battle cry of the lycanthropes, barking orders to his men nearby to engage the ambush.

What were they thinking, he wondered. They had to know he wouldn't be caught off guard. Perhaps they had become too confident. But the shadows encroaching upon the camp warned him of something else; as he looked up, he saw the Pyromancer, Selena Bradford, with her hands upturned and her eyes rolled into the back of her head.

Vandross looked skyward, and saw huge, flaming meteors streak toward his enormous siege camp.

"The barrier," he whispered, and finally understood. The perimeter had been created for this, so that the whole forest of the Elven Kingdom wouldn't catch fire and burn to the ground. It was yet another trap, one from which he could not save all of his men.

Immediately he ordered the ladders to the walls.

Seeing that Roak and his men had already begun their work on the gates unseen. Vandross dashed toward him, heedless of the fact that he would expose their purpose. "Roak," he screamed. He only had a few minutes, at the best. "Bring these gates down now. Hurry!"

Vandross didn't bother to explain, but instead pointed to the sky, and Vilec Roak's yellow eyes went wide with horror. The Meteor Strike would easily wipe out a third of Vandross's present forces. "Hurry."

A runner was sent to Major Tong to give him the order to disregard caution and get his men inside the city immediately.

Chaos broke out in the camp as the first of three flaming meteors struck the camp, blasting nearly a hundred of Vandross's men skyward in flaming heaps of flesh. Soldiers of Vandross's cause scattered in all directions, frightened and confused. Atop the stone wall, Byron of Sidius could be heard howling with laughter, the sound oddly wraithlike and wrathful.

"Byron," Selena whispered, fainting and falling back into his arms. The effort required of the spell had cost her a great deal of strength, but it was not in vain. As Byron watched, the second and third objects struck, exploding on contact. The concussion wave from the impact rolled toward the city, and below, Byron heard the north gates shatter. He looked down, and saw hundreds of Vandross's men pouring through the opening.

The gates should have sustained the blow from the wave, he thought. Had something been done to the gates without his knowledge? He pressed his hands to the stone, and read traces of dark magic. The gates had been weakened previously, and he had not noticed.

Now, still nearly a thousand men strong, Vandross's men charged into the city.

A hole blew apart in the west wall, and more poured into the city, far away from the main force.

"The walls are breached," Jaimie Helestion shouted from somewhere nearby. "Defend the city. Defend the Princess."

Byron stood paralyzed, still holding Selena, whom Alex with an ornamental hand fan. Byron gently lowered her to the ground, and drew his sword. He could make out Vandross, stalking through the streets, cutting down Dark Watchmen and regular army soldiers with ease.

The one-eyed devil's style was good, his form familiar. Byron rushed to confront him, but was constantly attacked by Orcs, Ogres, and Trolls, as well as a pair of Shadowbeasts who backed him away, keeping him on the defensive. They seemed not to be attacking him, but keeping him from reaching Vandross specifically. They too had some skill, and he received a pair of stab wounds for his troubles, one to his leg, one to his stomach. He swept the Morning Glory in wide, arcing slashes and hacks, blocked or dodged.

Beyond the Shadowbeasts, he saw Jaimie Helestion charge at Vandross, long spear in hands.

The Commander made several feints, circling Vandross, who finally took a defensive stance.

The Commander only needed to distract him for a short bit, just until Byron could reach him to take over the fight.

Byron finally caught one demon a stab to the chest, its body dissolving into ashes before him. But he was knocked to the ground by a Khan Berserker a moment later, the huge, drooling beast advancing as he got to his knees. A huge set of claws tore at his armor, ripping the deadened flesh beneath the chest plate. Nothing before had penetrated the armor, and Byron actually felt a slight pain from the wound.

He had been knocked clear of the Berserker's axe from the slash, however, a lucky thing for the Dread Knight. He was on his feet, and hurled a sheet of ice at the Khan, the magic slamming into the Berserker's axe arm, severing it at the elbow.

But the beast was oblivious to its injury, and charged at him again, slashing and punching at him with the arm that remained intact.

Byron ducked and rolled, leading the Khan back toward the Shadowbeast. He leaped over a sideways slash, letting the Khan tear the demon in half. As he landed atop the Khan's shoulders, he plunged the Morning Glory down through the beast's skull, kicking off and flipping back to the ground in a crouch. He stood before the wide-eyed Berserker, and kicked him over to the ground, dead.

Byron removed the Morning Glory, and moved for Vandross, who was in a deadlock with Jaimie Helestion.

But Byron was too late. As he dashed through the melee all about him, Vandross grasped the end of Jaimie's spear, and sent a surge of garish, emerald energy through the metal shaft.

Jaimie Helestion convulsed, his eyes glowing a green light. Smoke poured out of his ears and mouth. He was dead before he collapsed.

Byron made to attack Vandross, but the warlock was ready for him. As Byron leaped, cat-like and silent, Vandross tossed a bolt of lightning at him, which hurled him several hundred yards away, back near the gates of the city.

He lay prone for a moment, but a strong hand helped him up. Shoryu stood over him, and the arm that had hauled him up belonged to David Spore. The one-armed Monk forced a smile at him, and Byron thanked him quickly.

"Morek is engaged with a group at the west wall," the monk said, "along with Ellen Daires. His troop needs help, for many of the Orcs and demons have begun raiding the civilians, killing them in their homes."

Byron looked off after Vandross, but remembered his promise. Regardless of what happened to the Orb, he had sworn to protect the Elves and the other citizens of Whitewood first. He nodded, and followed after the Monk and Shoryu.

* * * *

Richard Vandross let several of his sergeants move ahead of him. Traps triggered harmlessly through the Shadowbeasts.

He had guided them directly to the library, and down into the tunnels. One Goblin was stupid enough to trigger an obvious trap, his curiosity getting the better of him.

No big loss, Vandross thought. He would soon have what he had come for. Ahead, he saw lamplight, and heard low muttering. Guards, who would soon be dead, he thought.

But as the first three Shadowbeasts made the corner, they were blasted with powerful beams of magic, obliterated to nothing but smoke and dust.

Vandross stared wide-eyed at what remained, and his brow furrowed with hatred. He knew now where the Council had hidden: they were the guards of the Orb. This might prove more difficult than he had wagered.

He summoned a spark of yellow energy, tossing it with care around the corner, spotting for a moment eight older Elves. There was an explosion, but he still sensed their life force: they had defended themselves well.

Vilec Roak crept up next to him. "My lord, I have a suggestion," he said, motioning one of his own men to them. "This is Selc. He has volunteered to be our sacrifice."

"Sacrifice," Vandross asked, raising an eyebrow.

"Yes, my lord," growled the one called Selc, a lumbering Shadowbeast. "When touched by magic, I can absorb some of it. You should get far back through the tunnels, my lord. When I self-destruct, the blast will be powerful."

Vandross almost laughed at the genius of such a simple tactic. *Why not? What was one more dead demon to him?*

He and Vilec Roak took the remaining three sergeants, an Orc and two more demons, and scurried off a safe distance. One of the demons forgot about a trap trigger, died, and left two sergeants with Vandross and Vilec Roak. They barely made it behind a barrier when the ground around them shook with a *ka-boom* from where the Elders had been.

When they returned, the guard chamber was caked in blood and organs. But only seven robes were on the ground among the bones. One had escaped.

No matter, Vandross thought, opening the door to the chamber where the

Orb of Eden's Serpent waited for him. *I have what I came for.*

The Orb of Eden's Serpent shimmered with dark energies, and he crossed the chamber to the pedestal it stood upon. He grasped it between his hands, and invoked the power of the other Orbs, pulling the Orb close to his chest, screaming in dark pleasure as the Orb became one with him.

Bursts of power lashed out from his body, and he felt something inside growl, anxious to be awakened. Vandross looked down to see he hovered a foot off of the floor. He smiled anew, and turned to his General.

Vilec Roak backed guardedly away. Vandross's eye burned crimson, and a faint light shone from behind the patch where his left eye had been.

"Let us be away from here, General," Vandross growled, his voice sounding like a mix of his own voice, and the voice of a demon. "We are finished here."

Vilec Roak and Richard Vandross made their way up into the library, and out into the street, Vandross's feet never touching the floor of the tunnels.

Vandross's forces were being pushed out of the city. Casualties on both sides mounted higher and higher, but Vandross had nearly five thousand followers at Mount Toane; Whitewood had only so many men. The city would be in ruins when Vandross pulled out. But not just yet, he thought with a grin. He wanted to test his new limits. As he hovered over the streets, he wove symbols of ancient demon magic. Trails of thick, ashy fog filled the air, pulsing with a sick green light. The earth around the city trembled, and from the ground below him, knocking Vilec Roak to his back, came screeching and growling an enormous demon.

The demon brought all battle to a halt as every living thing in Whitewood, Byron included, turned to gaze upon it. It stretched its broad, muscular chest and arms, standing there for a minute, doing little more than breathing the air.

It stood approximately twenty feet in height, with rough, bark-like crimson flesh, man-like in shape and anatomy. But huge, whipping tentacles extended from its sides, four of them, two under each massive, clawed and spiked arm. Two huge horns curved up from its forehead, and its eyes were the thin, milky white color of bed sheets. As it reared its head back and roared, there could be no mistaking its fury—it had answered a summons, and intended to feed itself.

As it moved, combat resumed between the defenders of Whitewood and Vandross's army.

The one-eyed warlock hovered over the ground, his arms folded across his chest. Red, garish light glimmered in his eye and, Byron saw, from under his eye patch.

Byron detached himself from the melee, and charged at Vandross.

"Go," Vandross called up to his newest demon servant.

The demon stepped forward, ignoring the Dread Knight, aiming its attacks for the smaller, less threatening mortals below.

Its first concern would be to feed, and Vandross knew this. He welcomed Byron's attack.

Vandross tossed another bolt of lightning at Byron, but this time Byron was prepared. He had a shield of magical force up and ready, knocking Vandross's magic aside with ease, gaining ground on him.

As he got close, he made a lunging feint, forcing Vandross to the left. Byron's subtle diagonal movement resulted in a successful slash across Vandross's sternum, knocking him to the ground, bleeding.

The one-eyed warlock looked up with shock on his face. But Vilec Roak's wave of dark energy hit Byron from the side, sending him sprawling.

Vandross launched a volley of magic at Byron, backing him against the only stone structure in the entire city, a church of Oun.

Byron felt his ribs give way and crack under the pressure of the warlock's newly powered spells.

Vandross did not relent in the slightest, carelessly dashing aside every spell and sword swing Byron unleashed at him. He growled and smiled at Byron. "This time, Byron of Sidius, you will fall," His twin voice started a fire somewhere in Byron's chest.

The Dread Knight focused his thoughts, keeping just enough magic to shield himself from Vandross's assault. He wove a set of symbols in the blood on the ground with his boot, out of Vandross's eyesight, muttering to himself. His pinpoint lights shone brightly, and he screamed at Vandross.

"Holy Cross."

Vandross stopped his advance, looking down at the white light that burned up at him. The holy magic spell slammed into him with full force, blasting him skyward and back, twenty or thirty yards, on top of Vilec Roak.

He got to his feet, grabbed his General, and whispered something to him.

Byron felt anger and hope slide out from under him—Vandross didn't appear to be harmed in any way.

"This isn't over, Byron," Vandross growled in irritation. Then, in a puff of smoke, he disappeared, leaving Roak to shout for retreat. They had done what they came to do.

Barely two hundred of Vandross's men made it clear of the city and the burning forest, fleeing before defenders who would chase them to their deaths.

Byron's vision faded once more, his wounds and expenditure of energy getting the best of him. He was unconscious, leaning against the steps of the church when the other members of his company found him. His armor was damaged, and his limbs were arranged oddly, the group having to untangle his huge, armored legs before carrying him back to Ellen's home. A healer came to mend his wounds, going into the back guest room where he lay alone, while the others waited patiently, making small talk. Among them was David Spore, the one-armed Monk, who had become friends with the company, and had agreed to join them in their endeavors.

When the healer came out, his Elven features were both strained and confused.

James Hayes was the first to question him, being next in line for healing services.

"What is it," he asked of the healer as the Elf used his magic to close and cleanse his wounds. "What's wrong with Byron?"

The healer shook his head. Shoryu, his lycanthrope regenerative powers having taken care of him, leaned in close.

"Is there something wrong," he asked, almost parroting Hayes.

The Elven man shook his head slowly, his eyes focused on nothing.

"No," the healer said. "There is nothing wrong. Just something, odd. You should see for yourself."

Shoryu gave Ellen a kiss on the forehead, and moved back through the house with Hayes in tow. What they saw was a shock and a mystery to them both. The healer had ignored his instructions not to remove Byron's upper armor, and he lay still on the bed, his torso whole and clean, Human. He appeared to be in peak physical condition, save for the fleshless skull. When they looked at his armor, hanging on the wall next to the bed, Hayes muttered a prayer under his breath. The crest of Sidius no long rested on the chest plate. Instead, the holy symbol of Oun, a fine and artistic cross, boldly gleamed in white.

* * * *

Richard Vandross had teleported himself directly to Mount Toane, knowing that it would only be a little over two hundred that returned with Vilec Roak and his newest servant, the Render Demon he would name Brink. He smiled widely as he sat upon his throne of bones and skulls. The world was his plaything now. Even without the final Orb of Eden's Serpent, he was now without equal.

Byron had injured him, but most of the damage was to his pride. And that no longer mattered; the people of Tamalaria would tremble at the mention of his name now. There was no one outside of his grasp at this time. Never again would he be like the powerless, helpless little boy who had watched his parents butchered. Never again would the world ignore him and his sorrows. But he felt fatigued, and floated down off of his throne, off to his bedchamber. He removed his armor and tunics and lay on the bed. He needed a bath, and resolved to take one after he woke from a well-deserved nap.

He had barely been asleep five minutes when he slipped into the realm of his soul. Something had changed—again.

He stood in the grand hallway as he had that first time, but everything seemed darker, the color drained from the tapestries and sculptures. He stalked through the hall, stopping in front of a mirror to look at himself. He wore only simple trousers and his boots and admired the way his musculature seemed to have increased. Then he noticed the red glimmer behind his eyes, plural. For a moment he stared in disbelief. He took a step closer to the mirror, and lifted his eye patch. A pinprick light, crimson as blood, shone in his empty socket. He lowered the patch and took a step back.

Without warning, the mirror image of himself began posing like a fool, mocking him.

Vandross took another step back, as blood seeped down the mirror's surface in rivulets, and the mirror-Vandross cackled with glee. He hurled a bolt of lightning into the mirror, shattering it.

"I wish you wouldn't do that," boomed a familiar voice. Vandross looked down the hall, to see Locke, the Keeper, approaching. The monolithic creature stalked silently, his heavy steps making no sound. He had changed again, Vandross realized as Locke stopped ten paces from him. His armor was still all angles and the color of blood, but his manner was even bolder, more aggressive. He carried his huge, wicked sword in his right hand. His feral yellow cat's eyes pulsed once, the light shining at Vandross menacingly. "They are waiting for you, Richard," the Keeper said. He stepped out of Vandross's way, but the one-eyed devil had a question suddenly pop into his mind.

"You're leaving, aren't you? That's why you haven't struck me for the mirror. You're leaving." He stood stock still, waiting for some response from the enigmatic spirit creature.

Locke swung his head to look down at Vandross.

"I cannot leave entirely, Richard Vandross. Not until you are dead, or so far from yourself that I am compelled to leave. No, Richard Vandross, you will obviously not be needing me much longer, for you intend to take the last Orb of Eden's Serpent. I am merely preparing for departure. The path you follow will release me, and sooner than you may think. I regret that I did not do better for you,"

To Vandross's surprise, Locke's voice held what was clearly both disappointment and sympathy. One huge, armored hand rested lightly on Vandross's shoulder for a moment before Locke moved off, silent as a whisper on the wind.

Vandross watched after him as Locke disappeared through the doors at the opposite end of the hall. He felt a sudden sting of guilt and panic—why should he feel this way? He was achieving what he had set out to do.

He shrugged the feelings aside, dismissing them as foolish. Instead, he stalked into the chamber he had become so familiar with, seeing Power, Vengeance, Spite and a new entity, Deceit, talking together.

Deceit appeared to be a smoky version of Vandross himself, a mirror image made out of mist. Vandross crossed the stone bridge, coming right up to them.

They parted before him, lining up in a straight row to greet him with sweeping bows. He grinned despite himself.

"Greetings, lord Vandross," said Power, her voice still as majestic and arousing as ever. If only she were a real woman, Vandross thought.

"Meet Deceit. Deceit, you are now under the command of this new host," she said, and the misty form bowed once more.

Vandross inclined his head slightly, never taking his eye off of the new creature.

"There has been a new development, Richard," she said, drawing his attention once again. "It is a spot of bad news. We can no longer sense the final Orb of Eden's Serpent."

"How is that possible," Vandross asked, his tone relaxed and slightly nonchalant. At this juncture, he didn't care. He had all the time in the world to search for the final Orb. Who in the lands of Tamalaria would be foolish enough to oppose him?

"It has been sealed away in some sort of safe place, its power and trace lost. It has been moved, we believe, though where to, we cannot be certain. It may take a great deal of patience in your world to find it."

"I am not too concerned," he said, walking over to take a seat on a clump of rock outcropping. He made himself comfortable. "With the power now at my disposal, none can truly oppose me. Not even Byron of Sidius and his rag-tag band of friends. I'm certain at least a couple of them died in Whitewood anyway."

Power shook her head.

"They're all alive?" Vandross asked, and Power nodded.

"Hellfire, hell and blood." He spit over the drop into the base of this cavern. He heard something sizzle below, and smiled. "I have a network of spies in the lands. I shall simply have to wait for word from one of them. In the meantime, I fully intend to relax and launch some attacks across the lands. I have the manpower, and can now summon even greater demons from the Pit. Don't worry," he said, seeing the troubled looks on their faces. "We have time. I don't intend to stop until I can have the power of the Glorious Mother of Destruction." Feeling himself fading as he came awake, he said, "Until we talk again."

He was telling them the truth, he thought as he bathed. He would have the power, one way or the other.

Chapter Thirteen
Memory and Recovery

For two days, Byron slept, his dreams filled with images of his life before the perversion of his body and purpose. Memories came and went before his mind's eye, filling him with joy, sadness, confusion, bitterness, and other less easily identified states of mind. He did not resist the dreams; he welcomed them with arms wide open.

Presently, he was dreaming about his son's fifth birthday. He walked through the grand house he and his wife had purchased in Desanadron, not far from his post in Fort Flag. The fine oak walls and floors creaked under his feet, and he looked in a hallway mirror. A handsome, blond-haired young man looked back at him, his eyes bright and shining blue pools, his smile quick and gentle. In his hands he carried the present his son had been begging for for months: an orange and white tabby cat, which purred in his arms as he pet it. "Come on then, cat," he whispered, creeping up the stairs toward the bedchambers. "We'll give him quite the surprise."

Byron stalked like a thief to his son's doorway, pushing the door open slowly, having oiled the hinges the night before just for this occasion.

His son's room was in its natural state, which was, of course, a state of disarray. Clothes and children's toys lay everywhere. But he would not bother Jacob today about it; he was a boy, and boys were messy. Let the child enjoy his presents, particularly this one, without worry. He watched the soft rise and fall of Jacob's chest, a scrappy and wire-thin youth who had his father's features, the same high cheekbones, the same soft blue eyes. Even the same quick smile and laugh, though Byron liked to think he sounded less a boy and more a man. He slipped into the room, avoiding the toys like they were caltrops, moving to his son's bedside and sitting gently on the bed. Jacob's eyes fluttered open, and Byron held the cat to his face.

"Happy birthday, Jacob," he said, and the boy screamed with delight. He grabbed the cat, petting it, squeezing it until it thrashed to be free, and finally letting it go to explore its new home.

"Thank you father," the boy said, wrapping himself about Byron's barrel chest. He embraced the boy in return, feeling a strange pang of regret. "Father," the boy asked, his tone worried. "What's wrong with your eyes?" Byron remembered then that this was a memory, but it was also a dream. He stood and stalked over to the mirror inside of Jacob's closet. His eyes had disappeared in his Human face, and had been replaced with two pinpricks of white light. He hung his head in shame and anger—even in dreams he was haunted by what he had become.

"I'm sorry, son," His voice was that of Byron Aixler, filled with sadness and pain. "Go now and see your mother, she has something for you."

Jacob moved off down the hall, dressing swiftly before he departed.

Byron looked up, and his Human features were returned to normal. Why was this happening, he wondered. What was the point of this memory-dream?

He determined to find out, and so followed the course of his memory.

He stalked through the halls of the mansion, passing servants who smiled widely at his passing, wishing Jacob a happy birthday, and reminding Byron that the party guests would be arriving later that afternoon. "Thank you," he said to each, smiling warmly as he had that warm summer day.

He found Jacob in the main den, playing with the toy sword and shield his mother had bought for him from the market, from a nice old Cuyotai man. Alice was a wonderfully beautiful woman, even here in Byron's dreams, her shimmering honey-colored hair swept back over her shoulders, the curve of her hips and breasts ample and suggestive, and her dresses always hung loosely, though not enough so to hide her feminine assets. Her eyes were the color of emeralds, glinting with kindness and a hint of playfulness that Byron had fallen in love with as a young man.

"Byron, dear," she said, calling to him to join her with her sultry, husky voice. "Come, sit. You look troubled, husband," she said, as she had that day.

Tanarak's forces had been extending their influence by this point, taking small villages and city-states under his control. Byron had stood against the warlock's injustices and had already assembled the resistance's first major factions.

"You can only do so much, dear," Alice said to him.

"I know," he replied, not fully in control of his words. Jacob lunged and jabbed at imaginary opponents, almost knocking over a maid in the process.

"Young master Jacob," she chided jokingly. "You shall have to remember that a good soldier never attacks a lady!"

"Then by all means, son, attack her," Byron jested, giving everyone a good laugh. There was a sudden flash of light, and Byron found himself standing in the middle of a burning building, a huge, black sword in his hands. Dark power surged through his body, and he was no longer in control of himself. Soldiers and magic users hurled attacks at him, and he moved like liquid night among them, cutting their limbs free of their bodies, blasting them apart with streaks of magic, blood and body parts flying all about him. In minutes he stood atop their bodies, walking over them like a carpet.

No, he said in his mind. His voice was not his own, and only heard in his own mind. Shadowbeasts met him outside, asking for further orders from their great General.

"Sweep the homes and flush all of them out. The Soribeasts have not fed yet," he said, his words coming out involuntarily.

Another flash of light blinded him, and he was standing in another familiar place.

He was in a small village, everything wrapped in flames. Tanarak's apprentice stood next to him, hidden in layers of robes and a huge great cloak. The apprentice led Byron into a small, untouched cottage. They slaughtered a few ill-equipped people on their way to the back room, where Alice and Jacob huddled together in fear. *No,* Byron shrieked in his mind. *Why am I remembering this?*

"Do it," the apprentice ordered, but Byron hesitated.

That's right, he thought. *I couldn't do it.*

"I said do it, Byron of Sidius," the apprentice shouted at him. "The master and I own you. Kill them."

But Byron would not.

"Fine! I'll do it!" And with a single stroke with his long sword, the apprentice cleaved both mother and son in half.

Byron screamed in rage and attacked the apprentice, punching him over and over, tossing him about the small room like a rag doll.

The hood came down, and Byron saw the face of Richard Vandross as he had been, both eyes filled with pain and anger.

"How dare you," he screamed, flinging magic at Byron to back him away. But Byron shrugged the magic off and came at him anew, and would have killed him, had Tanarak not saved him.

The warlock stood in the doorway, and drew Byron away from Vandross with a vacuum of force. Byron thrashed against his constraints, but Tanarak was the master, and he, the slave. He could do nothing.

"Apprentice Vandross," Tanarak hissed, calling the fallen man over to him. "You have much to learn about handling a sword, apparently. Byron, you shall teach him. And you, Richard, shall in turn instruct Byron in the ways of your Shadow magic. You each have much to learn."

The images faded to Byron sparring with Vandross outside of Mount Toane, the Human apprentice using sloppy form. Something deep inside of Byron still raged against his controlled body, and in a moment of spiritual strength, Byron forced his puppet body to grasp Vandross by the head and plunge his thumb of bone deep into the man's eye, spraying puss and blood as he gouged the eye out of the Human's skull. Byron had been punished for that incident, though he could not remember how.

He was suddenly back in the field, training Vandross, but keeping a lot of his sword secrets to himself. He was able to do at least that much for himself, despite being shackled inside of his own body. And Vandross in turn taught him Shadow magic, but Byron sensed that he too held back secrets. Neither trusted or liked the other, and the patch over Vandross's right eye was proof positive of that.

Byron woke then, fully clothed and armored. Shoryu and James Hayes, without his knowing, had put his clothes and armor back on.

He swung his legs over the side of the bed, testing his strength by trying to stand. He found he had no problems. But something was different, he felt it instinctively.

He walked over to a full height mirror, and gasped in shock. His armor was whole, but had changed. The symbol of Oun sat where the crest of Sidius formerly had. He took the armor off, wanting to make certain it was the same armor. He saw then that he wore a long sleeved shirt under the armor. He'd never worn a shirt before, he thought.

He pulled it up to his chest, and stopped, looking in the mirror—he was whole.

He tested the theory, just to make sure he wasn't delirious, by poking himself in the stomach. It was barely there, but he could feel himself jabbing his stomach. *How could this be?* He pulled the shirt down, donned his armor, and left the back guest room.

Shoryu, James Hayes, Selena Bradford, Ellen Daires, Alex, Morek Rockmight, and David Spore, sat around a large round table, playing some sort of domino game.

"Let's not get too comfortable now," he said, watching as everyone whipped their heads around to look at him.

Shoryu leaped up from the couch, throwing himself at the Dread Knight. The two went down in a tangle of laughing limbs and fur and metal. Byron tossed Shoryu lightly off of him, hopping to his feet.

"It is good to see you are all well," he said, still chuckling lightly to himself.

"As it is good to see you up and about," chided Hayes, grinning like a fool. "You were asleep for quite some time. Two whole days have passed while you snoozed. We have all mostly recovered from our wounds, though the city itself has much more healing to do. So, what's our next move?" he asked, his face turning solemn.

Byron moved over to the arm of one of the couches, taking a seat gingerly. He hadn't thought much about what he would do if Vandross were successful in his attempt to take the Orb.

"One final Orb remains. We must find it before he does." Byron shifted uncomfortably on his narrow seat, looking at the table. He looked at Shoryu's tiles, and made his move for the Hunter. "We must keep him from attaining it. The important thing in all of this is that we were able to keep the city intact. What were the final fatality counts?"

"Five and a half hundred regular army, forty Dark Watch, and twelve civilians," said Morek from his wicker chair. He alone seemed dark and brooding among the company. "The King and both Princes were reported to have been killed in the melee, the King and his second son having taken the uniforms of soldiers to help their people," he said, obviously unaware of the truth of the situation. "Deardry has been named Queen of the Elven Kingdom. The people of the city are banged up, but they are in high spirits. The High Elder narrowly avoided death, they say. He knew when to pull out of danger's way."

Byron was pleased to hear this, despite Morek's silence about the other members of the Council.

A sharp rap on the door came, and Ellen answered it. Bael stood in the doorway, his heavy armor battered and damaged.

"What happened to you, Bael?" Shoryu asked the Lizardman as he took a heavy seat on the floor.

"We heard the hundreds of Vandross's men fleeing the area. We, along with a small contingent of Cuyotai, tried to nab as many as we could, but there was this huge demon with them, a thing of terrible might. It butchered many of my men, and a few of the Cuyotai, though they are much more agile than we Lizardmen. We gave them a run for their money, killed about half a hundred of them before the big thing lost interest in us. I had the misfortune of meeting up with a Khan Berserker among the stragglers, very angry chap. I would be too if I'd been in the midst of a killing frenzy and been ordered to retreat, I suppose. But now that Khan's head sits atop a spear in front of my home, in exchange for the injuries he gave me."

Ellen moved to help him up, but he waved her off. "My wounds have already been tended to. But my village's smith was killed in the attack, so I've come to town to see about repairs. In the meanwhile, I'd like to talk with you, big man," he said, pointing at Byron.

Byron stood and strolled outside with the husky Lizardman. The two of them watched in silence as the Elven people of the city of Whitewood continued repairs to the homes that had been damaged or destroyed during the siege. They worked with the determination of a community that refused to be defeated.

"Casualties were kept low," Byron remarked distractedly as he watched them work. "Unfortunately, his majesty and his sons were slain."

"Then, the Princess, Deardry?" Bael asked, leaving the question unfinished.

Byron nodded, and Bael made a discontent noise in his throat. "Hmmm. It shall be difficult for her, you know. There has been a King for as long as many of even these long living folk can remember. She will have to be strong for them. They are her people now, her charges. The position of leadership can be daunting," Bael continued, accepting a mug of coffee that Ellen brought out for him with a smile. "How's the boy," he asked after his first sip, referring to Shoryu.

"He is well," Byron replied, looking after Ellen as she closed the door to her cottage softly. "He and Ellen have quite a thing going."

Bael nearly choked on his coffee, sputtering for a moment.

"You're serious? An Elf and Cuyotai?"

Byron nodded, grinning.

"Well, can't say I never saw it before. There's this one Chieftain, a Cuyotai, has an Elven wife. I met him, actually, chasing those stragglers. He came chasing after them from the city, went back home afterwards. Guess he had to make some rounds, tell a number of villages of their dead. I understand Chieftain Tandaba fell in combat?"

Byron nodded his head slowly, sadly. The black furred man had been full of life and laughter, and now was little more than a stain on the earth. Shoryu had spoken highly of him. Of course, that mattered little now. The boy had his lover to keep his spirits up, and if need be, he had Byron himself. The Cuyotai reminded him of Jacob, now that he thought about it.

"Too bad," Bael said, bringing Byron out of his thoughts. "I'd met the man not long ago. Seemed a gentle sort, a kind man. Never expected he'd be much of a warrior."

"Oh no. He and his men did some heavy damage at the beginning of the battle," Byron said, running his fingers over the cross on his breastplate absent-mindedly.

"See you've got some new armor," Bael said after finishing his coffee. "The old stuff get too banged up?"

Byron nodded, not really thinking much about the armor, as much as the symbol it now bore.

"Ah well. It happens to the best of us, as I can tell you. I've had this armor for years, never really considering how much a part of me it is. But, we all have things that we keep around. Oh, thanks, another cup if you would," he said to Ellen, who had slipped outside to check on him. She returned shortly with a refill, and Bael blew on it, smiling at the Elven woman. "Well, your boy has good taste. Quite a looker, that one is," he commented, grinning like an idiot.

Byron chuckled softly, still watching the reconstruction going on all around him.

"Bael, I need you to do me a favor," Byron said, looking Bael in the eyes, seeing there a sense of calm and contentment. "It is a small thing, and I hope you might have the resources to get it done."

"Of course, my friend," said the big Lizardman. "Name it, I'll do what I can." He took another long pull of the coffee. "Lord, this is good. The stuff my mother makes is like tar."

Byron laughed mirthfully, finding he enjoyed Bael's company when the man was in a relaxed mood.

"I have a contact, an informant I have relied upon for years. He's a Gnome, a Pickpocket by the name of Lee Toren. I need to get in touch with him before we take any course of action. He supposedly has a hiding place south of Whitewood. I need you to find him, and have him come to us here. He is a reliable fellow, with a vast network of spies and fellow thieves. Take this to him," he said, handing a small money pouch to Bael, who hefted it in his free hand. "Tell him it's payment for services he'll be rendering."

"Wait, that's the fellow that gave you the horses, right," Bael asked.

Byron nodded.

"I owe him much. If you hadn't had the speed of good mounts, I might have bled to death on the hills near Fort Flag. I have to thank him yet. I'll have trackers look for him. They're some of the best man-hunters my Race has to offer. Well," he said, draining the last of his mug, handing it to Byron. "I'll be off then to take care of this, after I drop this armor off with a smith. Tell Ellen I said thanks for the coffee," he said, removing his armor. Underneath, his flesh was ragged and mottled with scar tissue. There didn't appear to be a single patch of flesh that hadn't seen combat damage.

Byron felt for him; he too had known little outside of the soldier's life. He hoped secretly that Bael would never again don his armor. He wished the man peace. But a man like Bael knew little outside of the battlefield, and would likely be needed again in the future.

"Stay well, good Byron," Bael said as he stalked off towards the local smithy.

"Go well, friend," Byron called after the big Lizardman. He turned and walked back inside, seeing that a new game had begun.

Ellen took the mug from him, walking to the kitchen with Shoryu right behind, his hands tucked into the rope belt at her waist.

Byron took a seat where they had been sitting and took Shoryu's turn again. Everyone else grumbled, for he had made a well calculated move that the boy would likely have missed, standing up afterward to let the couple take back their seats.

For the next two days, the time passed easily with the company exchanging stories about their pasts, jokes and jests, and serious discussion about what they would do in the near future. On the third morning, as Byron rose and stretched, moving into the kitchen to prepare a fresh cup of coffee, he noticed that someone had already brewed a pot.

Groggy, he yawned widely and stretched again, sitting at the kitchen table with a large cup of coffee.

"You're welcome," said the squat little Gnome thief he had known for years.

The suddenness of Lee's appearance and his words surprised Byron, and he shoved quickly away from the table, unbalancing his seat and falling back to the floor.

"You could try not startling me like that, you know," he said, settling himself back into his seat, pouring the coffee right down his throat. "So Bael got someone to you?"

"Oi," Lee replied, taking a swig of his own mug. "Couple of days ago, little fellah come runnin' straight up ta me, says somefin about the 'mighty Byron wishing to have my council', or some other somesuch. Point is, the guy looked loik someone 'ad lit a fire under his arse. I left that afternoon, got here this morning. Asked around a bit, pretty much everyone 'ere thinks you're a hero, pointed me right 'ere. I let meself in, but I's plumb tired. Didn't sleep much last night, the ground was a bit uncomfortable. Anywho, whatcha need of a fine gentleman loik me?" Lee grinned broadly, revealing a set of tobacco-yellowed teeth, what ones he had left in his head.

"I need to know where the fifth and final Orb of Eden's Serpent is, Lee," Byron said softly, trying not to wake the others who were sleeping still in the living room. "Vandross got away with the one that the Elves kept here, no thanks to me. I was more concerned with keeping the damages to a minimum for the city."

"Noffin wrong wi' that," Lee said, taking a long pull on his drink. "Funny you should mention the Orb, though. Last I'd heard, there was this brotherhood of Monks what kept it in their temple, but they've decided to move it. Where to, I've got no idea. But I can look into it fer ya. Thanks fer the up front payment, by the way," he said, smiling widely. "By the way, where's that Cuyotai boy you 'ad wif you, Shoryu wadn't it?"

Byron nodded, and pointed to the door to Ellen's bedroom. "Huh, so he gets a nice cozy bed and yer friends don't. What's up wif 'at?"

"Well, the owner of this humble home is a young Elven woman, a Gaiamancer by the name of Ellen Daires. She has a, erm," he sputtered, trying to find a way to say what was to be said without Lee getting mischievous. "Well, an interesting relationship with Shoryu."

Lee raised an eyebrow, and when Byron tried to look away, the Gnome Pickpocket smiled like a devil at play.

"Yer kiddin' me, right? Oh that's too much. Hahahaaa!" He laughed loudly, and Byron tried to quiet him, too late.

Morek Rockmight, his eyes bloodshot from a bit too much late night drinking at the tavern with David Spore, stalked into the kitchen to see the little Gnome cackling like a mad fool. He slunk on cat's feet right next to Lee, who was still unaware of the Dwarven Boxer's presence.

"Oi," Morek shouted right in Lee's ear, sending the shocked Gnome to the floor.

Lee looked up into the cavernous, violent eyes of a Dwarf who didn't like his hangover disturbed by a lot of noise. Not that any Dwarf enjoyed hangovers in any circumstances, but Morek wasn't any Dwarf. "Who is this little piss-ant what likes to make noise enough for a circus?" Morek grappled with Lee, hauling him up off of his feet. Morek had a good foot and change on the Pickpocket, who thrashed around in Morek's powerful grip.

"Easy, Morek," Byron said, taking another sip of his coffee. "He's Lee Toren, an old ally of mine." He watched Lee work his way free of Morek's grip by somehow pulling the Dwarf's belt free of his trousers.

The Dwarf's powerful frame shifted, and he looked down wide-eyed when Lee held up his belt tauntingly. He dropped the Gnome, and took his belt back gruffly.

Lee laughed at the stocky Dwarf, who gave him a withering glare, shutting him up quickly.

"Well, I've got my work cut out fer me," Lee said, putting his mug in the sink. "If you want to, you might want to head northeast, toward that monastery I told you about. I don't fink those Monks would take the Orb far. I'm sure they 'ave some way of masking its presence, keep it safe, you know, but they ain't gonna risk keepin' it around."

Byron nodded, and Lee waved to him and the disgruntled Boxer as he slipped silently out the front door.

"Wake the others, Morek," Byron said, putting his own cup in the sink and rinsing it out with the handle-pumped water. "We'll leave this afternoon, after we make some provisions ready. I only know vaguely where this monastery is, but it'll take us at least a week to get there. Do you know anything about it?" he asked Morek, who had just sat down with a fresh cup himself.

"I think I do," Morek grumbled around his unusually ratty beard. He hadn't trimmed it since arriving in Whitewood, and it was beginning to look a tad messy. "There's a Monk brotherhood due east of Traithrock, about two days travel away. I'm from Traithrock myself, so I can get us there. That the plan, then?"

Byron replied yes, and the company awoke one by one, each told to pack some things and make ready to leave. They had done what they could in Whitewood. The big Dread Knight pulled Shoryu aside so he could talk to the young Cuyotai privately.

"Shoryu, you have a good thing here with Ellen," he said, gripping him by the shoulders. "You needn't risk yourself or her in this anymore. Stay behind and lead a life together."

Shoryu shook his head immediately. "You were there for me whenever I needed you, Byron. You brought me back from the brink of death. Without you, Ellen and I would never have met." He clapped the big man on the back as he stood along side him. "You and I started this thing together, and we'll finish it that way. I promise."

Byron smiled inwardly; they had all come to expect a great deal from him, but there was more to it than leadership. They were his friends, the best he could ask for.

A little after noon, they departed Whitewood with the Queen's blessing and the thanks of all of the Elven and Cuyotai people of the kingdom. And while the Lizardmen didn't have a presence in Whitewood, a single warrior by the name of Bael had already undertaken the task of assembling forces that would aid the Dread Knight in the near future.

* * * *

Richard Vandross stalked through the tunnels of Mount Toane, passing his palm across the familiar stone. *So many memories*, he thought. *So much began here.* He remembered that his master, Tanarak, had roamed the mountain in much the same fashion as he did now. War had been waged from this place, and was so now. Vandross had dispatched a force of a thousand men north, towards the Port of Arcade, a huge, sprawling metropolis that ruled over the surrounding lands. A good-sized city-state, and it would be a perfect first trophy for his collection. What he wanted, however, was different than what Tanarak had wanted. He had discovered through meditation on the Orbs the powers he could access now, and what he would have when he took the final Orb.

Among the powers he now possessed was the Immortal Rest. It was a way for him to enter a dormant state that would preserve him perfectly as he was at the moment he slipped into sleep, and it would seal him away from the outside world, to awaken again whenever he wished. His dreams would tell him of the world beyond his seal, showing him the state of the lands of Tamalaria so that he would not reawaken uninformed. He did not wish simply to dominate the land as its iron-fisted ruler, as Tanarak had before him, as he had once wished for himself. He wanted something better than that. He could sense the hatred and fear that the lands held for him, for he was becoming vastly known, and vastly feared. Children trembled at the mention of his name, and he could feel their terror from anywhere in the land. It made him feel wonderful, knowing as he did how they loathed and abhorred him. No longer the weak child himself, but a conqueror. It was a sweet thing, and as the days passed, it became almost as good as food to him. He craved more of it, an endless supply.

He told Vilec Roak his plans at dinner on the evening before Lee Toren arrived to speak to Byron in Whitewood "I do not want this feeling to end, Roak," he growled in his double-voice as he tore into his mutton. "Not now, not ever. And I know how to keep it going, how to feel it over and over again."

"Um, how my lord," Roak asked. He sensed a change in the man that he did not care for in the least. When he had first been summoned by Richard Vandross, Vilec Roak imagined a new stretch of service to a ruler and tyrant as powerful and wise as Tanarak had been. That, however, didn't appear to be in store for him and his.

"I shall terrorize and raze the land, Roak," Vandross said, smiling like a madman, the thin red lights behind his eyes gleaming brightly. "I shall slaughter thousands by my own hands, by the hands of my armies, until all fear and abhor me. I shall feast upon their sweet, honey flavored fears," he said, giggling now. "And when there is no one left who does not fear me, I shall send myself into the Immortal Rest, and seal myself away for a thousand years. It'll be time enough for histories of me to turn into lessons, then into stories, then into myths and finally into legends. Only the well educated or wise will fear the tale of Richard Vandross, and I will know it. Then, when they are most vulnerable, I shall rise from the slumber, and begin my reign of blood all over again. I will have the fear of a whole new generation to feast upon. Hahahahahaahaaa!" Vandross laughed like a fool for nearly an hour, slamming his fist down on the stone table time and again, overly pleased with himself.

He had seemed almost out of control, he thought as he floated past the chamber. Looking back on it, he thought himself temporarily mad with power. Such madness would keep him from accomplishing his long-term goal. He would become a cancer that resurfaced every thousand years to feed upon the lives and mortal fears of Tamalaria's denizens. But something stood in his way, aside from not having the fifth Orb of Eden's Serpent. He didn't need that for the Immortal Rest, he had access to the power now. But so long as he lived, without directly killing Byron of Sidius, the Dread Knight abomination would always be there to stand against him. Sure, his allies would age and die, but Byron remained eternal. He would have to be slain in order for Vandross to accomplish anything.

As he passed further down into the depths of Mount Toane, a small pain centering around his chest began to throb and expand, stretching to his fingers and toes and becoming a throbbing litany.

He fell to his hands and knees. None of his followers were kept this far down in the earth, so no one could help him. What was this pain?

He threw his head back and screamed, and a surge of bright red and yellow energy flowed out from his gaping mouth and his eyes. At first, the energy had no form, no substance, but it quickly became something he recognized, one of the few things in this world he feared.

After a moment, he stopped, the energy gone from him and formed of a new body. Locke stood before him on the stone floor of a massive chamber used for storing the bodies of the dead.

The huge Keeper was just as he had been in the realm of Vandross's soul, all gleaming crimson armor, its angles sharp and wicked-looking. The glinting slab of metal that was his sword was strapped across his back, and the feral, yellow eyes glared down at the one-eyed warlock.

"Richard Vandross," his voice boomed, echoing through the whole of the mountain. "I am leaving thou presently. Thou clearly hast no intention of abandoning the path you have chosen, and I shall no longer suffer you. I have spoken with the Mighty Ones concerning this, and they have granted me mine leave. Know this; I am no longer a part of thee, no longer responsible for what happens to thee, though I must remain neutral in all things. If thou attack me, or have any of thy minions do so, death will come swiftly to mine enemies. And one thing more I shalt tell thee," the Keeper said, lifting Vandross from his knees to his feet with a heave of one arm. "Thy fate is sealed," Locke shouted, his helmeted face only inches from Vandross's.

Normally, Vandross would have been petrified, yet something had died within him. The Keeper's threats meant nothing to him.

"Go then," he rasped in his double-tone. "Get out of my domain, creature, go to rot in whatever hell the gods have designed for you."

"I have been in Hell once already," Locke murmured loud enough for Vandross to hear as he stalked away. "It is the inside of thy soul." Without another word or sound, the huge Keeper was gone from Richard Vandross's life.

That was fine by him. Yet where Locke had been, he now felt a void. For a while he wondered if he needed the Keeper after all. But the pain from Locke's expulsion faded in moments, and Vandross felt thankful for at least that mercy. He had to think hard about shoring up his forces after the massive losses at Whitewood. The Elven army and Dark Watch, and Byron's company in particular, had devastated the members of his assault on the city, leaving less than fifty to return with Vilec Roak and his new beast.

Vandross wove arcane symbols of heretical magic in the air, summoning a hundred Shadowbeasts out of the darkness of the vast chamber he stood in. Each was a slavering, growling beast, each taking the vaguely humanoid shapes of his own soldiers in a moment's time.

He ordered them all to their assigned posts, sensing the powers of each and giving them an appropriate rank. Ranks, he thought. The Major he had suggested for promotion had been slain in Whitewood, along with three Captains and two Lieutenants. Two of the Captains had been ambushed by Bael and his Lizardmen, along with a fresh contingent of Cuyotai, during the retreat. Vilec Roak had described Bael's fury in battle rather accurately, for he had almost fallen prey to the bitter reptile warrior himself, but Vandross's newest demon had saved him from the final blow, bashing Bael into a tree. Roak had ordered his men away from the battle, those that remained.

But at least one replacement had been made, by filling a post with the half-demon creature he had created as Tanarak's apprentice, the one known as Molis. Vandross had come upon this stalking, armored half-breed upon his return to Mount Toane, and it had been quite subservient and remembered its master quite well.

Vandross had awarded him the rank of Colonel, and given him little more thought than to tell him that he should take up the training of some of the less able warriors in his armies. He could sense the half-breed's hatred of him, but knew that its nature and purpose would prevent it from ever directly raising a hand against him.

Vandross left the chamber and his thoughts behind, focusing at the task at hand. He summoned Vilec Roak and ordered him to send a small unit to the nearest village and decimate it. He was to leave ten alive to relate the tale to another town, and Roak was to then send another, larger unit, to whatever village or town that was. After the process had been repeated three more times, Vandross himself would lead a charge at the city of Ja-Wen. Surely news should reach the larger metropolitan city by then. He would bring his new pet along, too. His new one, he thought.

Forsaking resting again so soon, though he desperately needed it after Locke's departure, Vandross moved in and out of tunnels and passageways until he stood in the light of the midday sun outside of the entrance to Mount Toane.

Vandross thrust his hands to the earth, unleashing a wave of magic into the ground, summoning three more monstrous demons from the Pit. Each one looked like the other, all three standing well over twenty feet in height. Vandross knew what they were, for he had read about them in one of his many tomes on the subject of demons. These were Renkas, towering, bear-like creatures with the power of Aquamancy. They were intelligent beasts, more articulate than the creature he had named Brink, the demon summoned at Whitewood.

One of the Renkas turned its massive head and body to square himself with Vandross. "Are you the one who has summoned us from our duties, mortal?" Its voice was thunderous and deep, causing minor tremors in the ground, visibly rippling the air about the one-eyed warlock.

"Indeed, I am, great and mighty Renka. I am Richard Vandross, a warlock in possession of four of the Orbs of Eden's Serpent, former apprentice to Tanarak of Sidius. Heed my words and commands, for I am your summoner, and by the laws of magic and power that bind, I am your new master."

The Renkas turned, all three of them growling and drooling, their huge paws poised as if to strike. But none did; instead, they each in turn bowed to him, lowering their chins to the ground before him.

"You who has spoken, what is your name?"

"My name," rumbled the one who spoke, "is Tamriel, a torture master of the sixth ring of Hell. These men are my lowly apprentices, Moran and Doran," he said, rising up once more.

As the other two made to stand, Tamriel bashed them each back to the ground, to keep their chins on the ground. "My apologies for their lack of manners, for they know not when superiors are finished talking."

Vandross took an instant liking to Tamriel. He was obviously a physical menace, and he could sense the great magical power of the demon as he spoke. He had found his new Major. He rummaged through his pouches for a Major's cluster pin, and, finding it, flicked it up at the Renka.

"Pin that to your cloak, Tamriel," Vandross said, conjuring three huge great cloaks, one for each of them. Sergeant's stripes shone on the cloaks of Moran and Doran, and Tamriel pinned the Major cluster to his collar.

"No, slightly down further," Vandross suggested, and Tamriel adjusted it so that the pin was not hidden by his fur.

"You are familiar with military ranks," he asked.

"For the most part, yes," Tamriel replied, bidding his men to rise and put on their cloaks. "You have made my apprentices Sergeants. That is well enough, though it may be beyond them. What is your first order, lord Vandross," the huge bear-demon asked.

Vandross rubbed his hands in anticipation; he hadn't expected such eagerness from his new charges, but liked their initiative.

"Go west, into the Allenian Hills. Give the free Khan and the Simpa, the were-lions, a stern lesson in what it means to defy Richard Vandross. I will send fifty Shadowbeasts with you."

"No," said Tamriel, holding a hand up to cut Vandross off. "We have no need for their pathetic kind, lest they be Primes all," he boomed, turning away sharply. "We can handle this ourselves. Moran, Doran, come."

Vandross sent a streamer of magic to summon Brink from his lair nearby, and called to Tamriel to stop.

"Take Brink for a walk, too, if you would," he said, and the huge Renka nodded. He produced a wicked iron whip of chain, and lashed it at Brink, who walked ahead of the three Renkas like a puppy at play.

What an odd bunch, Vandross thought, grinning like a fool. And how useful they shall be. Satisfied with the present arrangements, Vandross moved off into Mount Toane, to prepare his men for their attacks. The whole region would suffer at his hands, and he would have a feast of fear to feed upon. The loss of the enigmatic Keeper no longer bothered him.

* * * *

Byron and company marched on through the evening, silent and hopeful. They would need another two days to make their way clear of the kingdom, but were satisfied that they would be safe within the forest.

At sunset, Byron called the company to a halt, each of them still worn from the ordeal of Whitewood, Byron more than the others.

They cleared a small patch of ground and gathered firewood, Selena starting the blaze and continuing to feed it deadwood. The company made a meal of the provisions they had purchased, assembling their ingredients into a pot Ellen had brought from her home.

"These are the better times," Shoryu commented, all eyes fixing on him now. "A warm fire, open, clear sky above, and none of us fighting for our lives, you know," he finished awkwardly.

"True enough," said David Spore, taking his white bandana off of his head.

He rubbed his left shoulder, where it had once been attached to an arm. "Makes me think about the day I lost this. I was in the mountains way up north, training, when I was heard by a rather hungry pack of wolves. I fought for dear life, but they got on top of me. Tore my arm apart, but I managed to break their necks and a few ribs with my legs about their torsos. I managed to get up, hobble back towards the monastery. But I didn't get far when one of them caught up, one I thought I'd taken care of. He got me face down in the snow, tore into my shoulder, and just ripped the bones apart. I was bleeding like a stuck pig, I'll tell you that."

"How'd you survive," Selena asked, ladling stew into her earthenware bowl.

"Well, I used a sutra card to cast a spell on the wolf, kill its sense of smell and sight. On a humanoid, it's only temporary, but on an animal, it's permanent. I figured it was enough payback for my arm. I bound a tourniquet about my shoulder, to stop the bleeding, then used another sutra to seal the wound. I've been this way since then, four years now. I've adapted my fighting style to suit the change, well enough to still matter in a fight. My sutras are my secret weapons now," he finished, serving himself some of the stew. "What about you, Morek? Any stories?"

The taciturn Dwarf finished his first serving of stew and remained silent a moment, letting himself think it over a minute.

"I've got a few, but Dwarven tales are long in the telling. Some stories take days to tell, and only our shortest stories would be suitable. Besides, I've few of my own tales that would compare to all of yours," he said, getting more food.

"Come now, humble Morek," chided Byron, giving the Dwarf a small shove. "You've got to have something for us. This is a good evening for stories, and we've little else to tide us over until it is time to sleep! Think of anything, tell us a story, even if it isn't one of your own."

Morek chewed his food slowly, purposefully, before he set his bowl down at last.

"All right," he said, putting his hands on his knees, leaning close to the fire so as to illuminate his face. "This is a story I've told to my wife and sons many times."

"You're married," Byron asked in shock. "And have children?"

"Of course," Morek said, looking up at the large Dread Knight. "Why, you didn't know?"

"I'm just surprised anyone but your mother could love such a face," Byron said, pinching and stretching Morek's cheeks.

The Boxer swung at Byron, who held him at bay like an older brother would a child.

Morek calmed down, laughing along with everyone else.

"Good one, bonehead, but anyway, let me tell the tale. It was a bitter winter's night, the wind gusting and blowing like a blizzard set in motion. It was in the mountains near Traithrock, seven years ago. I walked through the passes and paths north of the city, heading toward Moonmight, a town my brother Cole lives in. I wanted to have a sit down with him for some time, and he had just written saying he'd very much like that. The snow blew at me from everywhere, and I couldn't see more than five yards in front of my face. 'Bout an hour after sunset, I had to look for shelter, as my hands were turning blue beneath my wool gloves. I found a little cave to poke into before too long, and hunkered down for the night. It wasn't long before I heard something like growling behind me, in the shadows of the cave. Then, these three black bear cubs come walking forward. Now mind you, I'm no Hunter, or Gaiamancer," he said, nodding at Shoryu and Ellen in turn. "But I'm smart enough to know that where there's cubs, momma isn't far behind.

"Cept, momma never showed. There they were, three bear cubs, growling at me, but they stopped soon's I lit a torch. The fire likely scared 'em. Well, I followed a bit, but at the back of the cave there was nothing to be found, save for some fish from a nearby riverbed. I figured they'd been there for a day or so, and momma bear was likely out getting more food, but she was out in a blizzard. Black bear or no, it didn't sit well with me. So I picked up my things, and set out into the storm again. I trudged through the wind and snow, nearly freezing my arse off. Well, I march till about midnight, when I see a set of tracks in the snow, and not animal tracks, but Khan tracks. They like bear meat, hunt 'em wherever they can, even where they shouldn't be. I follow them tracks, and afore long, I see one of the tiger men, up in a tree. Momma bear's down by the riverbed, her leg caught in a nasty trap. This Khan, he must not have seen it, but in that wind, it was hard to see much of anything. Well, this bear's growling and snarling like the damned at him, and he's taking arrow shots, missing by only a little, mostly because of the wind. I snuck up to the tree, climbed up, and wailed on that rat bastard for a good while. Finally knocked him out of the tree to the snow below, figured he was at least staying down for a while.

"I went down to the bear, and sure enough, she was bleedin' pretty bad," Morek said, his eyes glazing over with memories. "She swings at me a few times, but I back off, put my hands up to show I'm no threat. Now, I'm not an Elf, or a Beastmaster, I've little experience with wild animals, but she seems to get it, stops swinging. She looks down at her leg, which is pretty messed up, and I pry the trap open, break the trigger. She tried walking, but didn't get more than a few yards before she dropped. Now mind you, this is well more than I normally would've done, I shouldn't have gotten involved. But those cubs need someone to take care of them. So I encouraged her to get back up, and used some spare bandaging and splinted the leg. Then I helped her walk, holding her up under that front leg while she walked. Damn near killed me from the effort, and the cold, but we got back to that cave just before sun up. I collapsed when we got back, and fell asleep. But I felt warm while I slept, and it was noon before I woke up to find they'd all curled up to me, kept me warm. I wrote a letter that day to my brother, and gave it to a hunting party passing by the cave to take to Moonmight. I wrote telling Cole I had to stick around to help out a while longer. For two more weeks I helped gather food for them, keep momma's strength up, until she mended. Finally, one morning, momma wakes me up, tearing at her bandages. She was good enough, she was telling me in her way.

"Well, I help her off with it, and then suddenly, there's an arrow in my shoulder. That bastard Khan, he'd found us! Well, while I fell and he tried notching another arrow, all four bears, momma and cubs, bull-rushed him, bore him down and tore him apart! I got up, drew the arrow out, and wrapped it up. That bear, I think she smiled at me then, as I made my way out and started home. I looked back once, and she was sitting there with her cubs, all of them grinning. Not like people, mind you, but I could tell."

The company sat in silence, smiling to themselves.

"Imagine you being such a warm-hearted man under all that gruff exterior," jested David Spore. "A much better tale than mine. How about you, young Shoryu," he asked, rolling out his bedroll and climbing inside to settle in for the night. "Any stories of great hunts for us?"

Shoryu looked up at the moon, thinking back on his relatively short lifetime. Cuyotai were among the longest living Races, their lifespans reaching over six hundred years before age claimed them. And he was barely a man, still almost a boy it seemed. But he had experience, he had no doubts of that, and one thing that none among the group did; his lycanthrope rage. He had only experienced it once, and that had been plenty for him.

"As a matter of fact, I have a story to tell, though the hunt involved was not one I am proud of," he began, looking into the eyes of everyone of the company. He hesitated a moment after looking into Ellen's eyes, her deep emerald orbs gazing lovingly at him. Would his recounting of this particular tale make her see him in a different light? He hoped not, but he should tell the story to be certain she cared for him despite his flaws. Love without acceptance of someone's differences was not true love.

"I remember the night perfectly, back in my home village in the east, the rain pouring down like the tears of the gods above. It hammered into the ground and into the roofs of our homes, the wind howling at us with its banshee wail. The hunting parties returned from the woods empty handed, their sense of smell betrayed by the washing downpour. This was twenty years ago, and I was still just an adolescent, so I was not allowed to hunt with the others. I had been playing with some friends, in the fields between the village and the forest on the south. It was a game we called *Shin jik aba*, which in our tongue means 'no blood, no foul'. It is a game of fighting; you call it sparring. We do it as youths in packs, to better prepare ourselves for the lives of true warriors.

"The rain did not dismay us, for it only added an extra measure of challenge. We continued, the four of us punching, kicking and grappling in the slick grasses, the game become more about skill and agility than sheer strength. Being the most lithe and nimble of the four, I gained an advantage on my friends, and had each other boy flat on his back in minutes. It was quite a good time," he said, smiling at the memory of it. He had most enjoyed those days. There had been no worries for him, and he had begun to notice his level of skill with the different weapons he and the other older boys practiced with. Mostly, he knew he had a natural skill for the bow.

"And then, during the rain, with the Chieftain yelling to us to get inside, an arrow flew out of the woods, and struck down one of the others. It was a simple shaft of wood, with no feathers, and we all knew immediately that it was Lizardmen. They had struck down a child, one of my friends. He would have survived if the arrow had been a little to the left or right, but it had pierced him in the heart. Silver or not, that sort of shot is fatal to we Cuyotai.

"The others scattered, but I could not move. Something burned deep inside, some all-consuming flame, and as I turned my head to look west, behind and to one side of me, I saw a group of ten or eleven of the reptiles. One of them used a crossbow to fire on me, a single silver tipped bolt through my left arm. Though it seared my flesh, I barely felt it. Something inside of me broke apart, and I began to feel, different. Stronger, faster, out of control. I slavered and growled, hunching down like a common animal, then rearing my head back and howling at the sky. My claws came out, longer and sharper in the fading light than I had ever seen them. My single thought was to kill them all. I sprinted at them through the rain and mud, coming on the first of them in a flash. I remember the look of confusion turn to horror on his face as I buried my claws into his chest, wrenching my arms and splitting his upper body in two. The snap of his bones, the wet slapping noise of his bloodied body striking the saturated ground, these were sounds that would have normally made me afraid. But I reveled in it, frenzied and wild. The next three fell as I pounced on them, bearing them each to the ground and ripping out their throats with my jaws. Blood flew, spattering my simple clothes and face, and I let their scaled flesh slither down my gullet.

"As I sat on one of these victims, another Lizardman swung his sword at me. I rolled away from him, then spun back and launched a kick into his chest that sent him flying back among his remaining comrades, who had all halted their charge. They fled back for the woods, leaving him on the ground. As he stood up, I slammed into him, my shoulder barreling into his shattering ribs. I snatched up his sword and ran it through his stomach, pinning him to the ground and taking the last of his life. But, it didn't seem that it was enough. Something inside of me, something primal, had come to life, and it needed more. It needed to kill, to feed."

Shoryu's voice had grown hushed, his eyes glazing over with the shame and terror he felt at the rush of sensations his memory brought to him. "I pulled the sword out and hurled it at the fleeing reptiles, spiking one of them in the head. The others had escaped into the woods, but I had to find them, get them all. I gave chase, and slaughtered the remaining three. The worst of them, I remember tearing his arm off as he swung at me, and beating him with his own arm before I gripped his head and buried by thumbs into his eyes. It was, as though I had been possessed. I collapsed then, reawakening in my bed some many hours later. I couldn't fully remember what had happened, but I was reassured that I had done nothing wrong. Still, my heart was heavy, and over the course of the next week or so, I remembered every last detail I have related to you. I felt like nothing more than an animal, ready to destroy everything I came in contact with.

"Those of my friends who had survived grew distant after that. They were afraid of me then, and I could sense their discomfort. After a while, I stopped playing with them," he said, letting out a long sigh. "As time passed, the villagers came to talk to me again, and I was treated normally once more. But that feeling of being alone and isolated among my peers never went away, not completely. Even after they talked to me again, those who had been my friends, I realized it had been four or five years until they felt brave enough to be near me again. I couldn't blame them. And that's my story," he said, finishing his tale.

The others of the company sat in silence, thinking over all he had told them. Ellen's hand tightened on his, and she stroked his cheek with the back of her free hand. He held her close, wrapping one large arm around her waist and feeling the warmth of her body. She more than the others seemed to understand, and Byron seemed the only one totally unaffected by his story. Then again, the Dread Knight's past, he realized, was darker than anyone else's could possibly be. He felt foolish for a moment, then realized that everyone in the company had their own secrets and pasts to deal with. But he felt better too, for having told his story, and he was enjoying the bonding he felt with the others of the company from Whitewood.

"I've a story," said Selena Bradford then, staring into the fire, a grin playing across her lips. "It is not as good as Shoryu's or Morek's, but it's my story, and I'm going to tell it anyway." She sipped on her wineskin. "It dates back eight years, when I was a teenager, and first learning to use my powers. I was living in Desanadron, as I have for most of my life. My mother had sent me to the market to fetch some butter and bread for dinner, me and my brothers and sisters, along with mom and dad going through a lot of both. There were nine of us in the house, after all."

"Wow," said Morek, sipping at his own cup of ale. "Lots of kids in that family. Not sure I could handle it."

"Neither could my parents," Selena said, chuckling. "More often than not my dad had to yell at us as a group, just to make sure everyone was accounted for." She laughed again. "Well, I was running through the crowds, just minding my own business, when these three local bullies pushed me into an alley. They were big boys, Jaft youths, the stench of their blue skin making my eyes water. One of them, he says to me, 'fork over yer money and we'll pound you'. Of course, I had to chuckle a little, his grammar being horrible. I said to him, 'are you sure you don't mean or?' He says, 'what,' gets this dumb look on his face. He looks at his friends, who just shrug their shoulders. I said to him, 'well, I think what you mean to say is, hand over your money or we'll pound you.' He growls at me, says 'are you some kind of smartass? Yeah, hand it over *or* we'll pound you'! Well, by that point I'd pretty much readied my magic, and I lit a small flame on each of their rear ends. They stood there, their asses smoking, and they sniffed the air, looked at each other, and one of them asked what was cooking. I pointed at them and said, 'you are, stupid.' Well, sure enough, they each turned to look, and started running around yelling at each other.

233

"They ran out into the market, and accidentally started a merchant's cart on fire. The guards snatched them up and slapped their butts to put the fire out, then walked them home to talk to their parents about paying for the damages. I got my mother what she needed, and walked home with my head held high."

"Sounds like something I'd have done," said Alex, laughing at the Pyromancer's tale.

"It grows late," Byron said, making note of the position of the stars and the moon. "If tales are to be told, they should be short like Selena's."

"I have no tales to tell," squeaked Alex from his perch on Selena's shoulder. "How about you, James? Or Ellen perhaps?"

But the reserved Paladin had little to say, it seemed, or at least nothing he wanted to share just at the moment. And Ellen had fallen asleep with her head on Shoryu's shoulder, her hand still over top of his.

"I think we should all take the opportunity to get some rest," Byron said, scowling into the night's darkness. He rose and moved away from the company. "I'll keep the first watch. I shall awaken one of you for the second watch, so you should all get some sleep."

As the other members of the company made themselves comfortable, Byron moved out, stalking the edges of the firelight like a great cat waiting to spring. But he did not jump or start when Alex fluttered up beside him an hour later.

"Alex," he said to the Ki Fairy, who set down on his shoulder plate.

"Lord Byron," Alex started, feeling a bit awkward. "I have something I need to tell you." He spoke slowly, almost embarrassed.

"No need to say it, my tiny friend," Byron mused, holding up a hand to stop Alex from speaking. "I have sensed a kinship between you and Miss Bradford since Whitewood. And even before, for she fascinated you as few have. Such a young woman, yet so powerful in her chosen field of magic. Yes, Humans are rarely so young when they gain such mastery as she is. You would travel with her when all of this is over, yes?"

He felt a slight pang of loss when Alex nodded, yet he knew it was for the better. He wouldn't be around long if he killed Vandross anyhow. The magic that bound him to Tanarak's former apprentice was permanent and binding, and there would be no escape from it. Best that Alex have a friend when the time came.

"Now go and get some rest, troublesome imp," he said, smiling as best he could.

Alex fluttered away, saddened himself that he should have to say to his long time friend, one of the few he'd ever had, that he was essentially leaving him while still in his presence. But Byron would be fine, he thought as he lay near Selena. He was made of sterner stuff than most.

Byron looked over once more at the slumbering party. Seeing Shoryu and Ellen curled up together gave him a sense of peace, of happiness that he hadn't felt in some time. He would miss them all when the time came for fate to take him. Whether he was destined for the freedom of paradise in the afterlife, or the fire of eternal damnation for his sins, he did not know. For now, he would watch over his few close friends, and be content with their companionship.

After his watch, he woke Morek to take the watch. The Dwarf splashed water on his face to wake himself up. He did not see the Dread Knight wrap himself in his blankets. He did not see the gentle tear stream from one empty eye socket.

Chapter Fourteen
Stalkers

Two days after Byron and his company had their night of storytelling, Richard Vandross sat in his throne room. Through the magical bond that tied him together with Byron, he was now able to locate him within a one-mile margin of error. He could not tell what the undead warrior thought or did, or even what happened around him. But he could tell where the man was. That would be good enough for now.

Vandross had forgone join in his minions' fun, leaving much of the army to do as Roak found necessary. When the Renkas had returned earlier that morning, they had brought with them several hundred power-hungry Khan who were now willing to join Vandross's cause. The numbers could have been higher, but Brink hadn't been easily contained or kept under control, the Major informed him.

"Always good to be on the winning side of a war," the Khan Chieftain had said with a smile. That man's head now rested on a steel spear outside of Vandross's throne room, and the remaining Khan had been assigned ranks and duties.

None of the Simpa the Renkas had encountered showed any interest in joining forces. They had been summarily butchered by Brink and Tamriel. The Renka apprentices hadn't been able to accomplish nearly as much, as their powers were far less than those of their leader.

Vandross thought to perhaps send Tamriel and his two men to hunt and kill Byron and his company, but the Dread Knight's company would prove too much for even the hulking demons and his pet. His feet itched from the cross-shaped scar Byron had left him with. A Paladin spell, he thought as he rubbed his beard in the silence of the throne room. Byron Aixler's soul had resurfaced, he was certain, but some elements only of his powers. He remained Byron of Sidius at his core.

How was he to deal with such a seemingly invulnerable bunch? Puzzling it over, he decided to speak with Vilec Roak and Tamriel and get their opinions on the matter. He suddenly longed to have the military thinking of his former General, Bael, to fall back on. But he had decided, rather hastily in hindsight, that the Lizardman was no longer necessary. With only a handful of reptile warriors and Cuyotai Vandross's former general had harried Vandross's fleeing forces after their retreat from Whitewood.

"Hellfire," he spat into the darkness of the tunnels as he emerged into the daylight. "Hell and blood." He made a direct line for Tamriel, who had dispatched his cronies to check on the perimeter of Mount Toane.

"Tamriel," he called up the huge, bear-like demon, who turned to look down at him. "Roak," he shouted, and instantly the Shadowbeast was at his side. "I need some options."

"Concerning what, my lord?" asked Vilec Roak. The Shadowbeast hadn't seemed the same since Vandross's outburst at the dining table, a fact that had not escaped Vandross's notice.

"I wish to have Byron and his companions dealt with, but from a distance. There must be some way to separate them, divide their numbers, so that they may be taken down more easily," Vandross explained, shifting his weight as he paced. "Get them all alone if we can."

"There is no need," Tamriel said, crossing his massive arms in front of his barrel chest. "I shall take Moran and Doran to find them, and together we will crush them."

"I think not," Vandross said, looking up into the demon's eyes. "No offense, but his little band of would-be heroes are more than a match for you three alone. What you did in the Allenian Hills they could do a thousand times over, if properly motivated," he said, his anger rising in his tone. "They are a nuisance, but a dangerous one."

"Sire," hissed Roak, deciding to be helpful. "I am sorry to say this, but, it will be nearly impossible to get any one of them alone. Our spies have informed me that the Cuyotai and the Elf girl are romantically entwined, which would make them virtually impossible to split apart. The new member of their party, the one-armed Monk, has made a strong and quick friendship with the Dwarf. The Pyromancer and the Paladin have been joined in combat since Desanadron, which shall make them most difficult to divide, for they have an alliance forged from hardship. The only one of them without a true companion is Byron himself, and he might still have the Ki Fairy as his friend, though it is always hard to tell if the bothersome little pest is around."

"Which is to say nothing of how hard that bag of bones would fend for all of them," Vandross huffed, sitting on a nearby flat surfaced rock. "You are both demons, and may have some insight that I lack, despite the influence and power granted me by the Orbs of Eden's Serpent. Surely there is some solution to our dilemma. If we allow them to come at us freely, we may all be in deep shit," he said, admitting finally aloud that Byron and his little clan was a threat to him.

"Lord Vandross," said Tamriel, his booming voice level and calm. "We have the might of an entire army behind us. We number nearly ten thousand strong. We should simply rush this Byron with the whole. He could not stand against so many."

Vandross stood then, suddenly, swiftly, and floated up to face level with the bear demon. He slapped Tamriel as hard as he could, power flaring into his palm, sending the demon sprawling to the ground.

"Fool," he screamed, his voice becoming the twin harmony it had when first he had absorbed the fourth Orb, the voice of a demon and his own speaking the words together. "I was often with him when he was still under the command of Tanarak. I have witnessed this creature slaughter thousands of highly trained soldiers and creatures of the gods themselves with his own hands and powers." Vandross swooped in like a hawk, bringing himself eye to eye with the huge demon, who cringed at his closeness, genuine fear revealed in his eyes. "I have seen him wipe entire cities off of the world's maps with only a handful of allies. You would be but a plaything for him to bat around if he felt pressured enough. Small numbers, the element of surprise. These are the things we need. Raw power and brute strength will not serve our needs where he is concerned," he said, calming down, bringing his anger under control.

"I have a suggestion," Vilec Roak said quietly, seeking to avoid his master's wrath.

Vandross stalked over to him, eye wide and burning red-hot. "Have you heard of Dreamstalkers, my lord," he asked, and Vandross shook his head. His eye lost its crimson cast, and he sighed heavily.

"No, Roak. Explain."

"They are demons that stalk their prey in their dreams, my lord. They live and travel in the Dreamscape, the spirit world of slumber we all escape to when we rest. Their company can be sleeping right atop one another, and it wouldn't matter. The Dreamstalkers have total control of the Dreamscape, and can play on their weaknesses from the start."

Vandross nodded, thinking it through. It was a good idea, he thought. The demons were disposable, in the event they failed.

"How many will be needed," he asked Roak.

"Sire, there are but ten of them in all the rings of Hell. They have never failed, so their numbers need no shoring up," Roak said with a wicked grin.

Vandross smiled widely; here was the news, the solution, he required. He would summon five of them, half of their numbers. If they had never failed, then he needn't pull on all of them. Byron would finally meet his match. And he would never even be awake to fight his enemies off.

* * * *

The following day passed in a haze for Byron and his company, rain pouring down on them, drifting in with storm clouds from the north. Everything about them had a grayish, dead cast to it, the grassy fields empty of life, the wooded expanses of land providing only partial shelter as the wind tore at the trees, whipping them back and forth like rag dolls. Progress was slow, and the foothills in the central western plains gave treacherous footing a whole new meaning. Morek, James Hayes, and Selena Bradford each went down several times in the slick grassland, and more than once Byron's heavy metal boots sank nearly four inches in the mud. Alex had been forced to stay on Selena's shoulder, clinging to her loose red robes and dress to stay attached. Only Shoryu and Ellen had no troubles at all, and David Spore seemed as though he were accustomed to such traveling conditions.

At around mid-afternoon, the company found a small alcove in a wooded area to take shelter in, making a small meal of bread and cheese. Shoryu brought Byron a small flask of some sort, and guided the big Dread Knight a short way away from the company, opening the flask and letting Byron sniff at it.

"Blood," Byron whispered. Shoryu smiled and held up a scarred palm. "While I appreciate the gesture, there's a few things you should know about this," he began.

"I understand, good Byron," said the Cuyotai happily. "You need blood to survive, and I give it. I am a lycanthrope, and so the wound heals quickly. The blood recovery is swift."

"Actually, there's more to it than that," Byron said, holding the flask but still not releasing it over his skull. He cast his eye lights down into the flask, gazing longingly at the liquid therein. "Shoryu, have you ever wondered why I only drip the blood of my fallen enemies on my skull to feed from?"

"I always assumed it was a matter of preference."

"No, not at all, and yes, completely correct," Byron said with a sigh. "You see, when I take this into myself, your life force is given from the blood. But if my, er, benefactor in these matters lives, the process also steals a small amount of their willpower, their sanity." Shoryu blinked rapidly at him, wondering after what precisely he was getting at.

"Good Byron, I don't follow, not entirely," he said.

"You remember that story you told us a few nights ago, about losing yourself to your rage?" Shoryu nodded. "By taking the blood of a living person, I take as well a portion of that control. By giving me your blood, you weaken your control over your anger, your aggression. Are you willing to accept that risk?"

Shoryu appeared to think this over for a few minutes, and then nodded. "We live in some troubled times as it is, my friend. I will need my aggression."

Byron thanked him and poured the flask's contents over his skull, feeling the warmth of the Cuyotai's lifeblood seep into his body. Refreshed, Byron rejoined the company as they mulled over the poor travel conditions. Morek suggested that they move on swiftly, for a small mining community lay only an hour or so further north. He had come this way on his trip down out of the mountains to visit his friend Ellen of the Elves.

Hitching up their supplies, the group moved out, into the pounding rain. The gray wash of the day hampered their progress and their collective mood. Only nights before they had been tightly knit, focused, and buoyed by each other's tales of times gone by. Now no one spoke, not even to tell amusing anecdotes, something David had become known for among them.

After another two and a half hours' march, the company came to the crest of a rise. A miners' entrance stood out in the side of the large hill, and the town sprawled out from it, becoming less dense the further the buildings got from the mine. The company walked into the outskirts of the town, where it seemed the nicest homes rested, more than likely the homes of the governing individuals of the town.

Soldiers wearing Desanadron uniforms walked through the muddy streets past the company, a few of them recognizing Selena and Hayes, and one or two knowing who Byron was despite his shroud of darkness, giving him brief nods. The town was a protectorate of the city-state that had already begun reconstruction three days to the west.

The company asked some of the locals about lodging, and one kind old couple pointed them directly to the inn. Byron paid the Gnome proprietor, a mottled-skinned fellow with glasses as thick as a hand and a smile as quick and easy as a snare trap, and they each paired up for a room. Shoryu walked hand-in-hand with Ellen, and Byron saw the Gnome smile gently at the couple before burying his nose in a book again. James, Selena and Alex entered a room of their own, while Morek and David Spore walked upstairs to their rooms. Only Byron roomed alone, his chambers at the end of the first floor hallway.

He walked into a well-kept room with a king sized bed, a work desk, and a small eating table. A bookshelf next to the bed contained a small collection of dusty volumes, most of them pertaining to Gnome sciences. He plucked a storybook from the second shelf, sat at the work desk, and lit the candles with a spark from his fingertip. For a while, he stayed awake, but he felt drained despite the quality of Shoryu's offering earlier. He read for a short while before he stretched out on the bed, his bare feet reaching the very end of the footboard. He was asleep in minutes, unaware of the strange black cloud that seeped into his nostril hole from the corner of the room. None of the others of his company were aware either, and each slipped silently into dreams.

The company awoke and met in the main foyer of the inn the next morning, thanking the Gnome for the hospitality before moving out of the inn and north, out of town. The day passed mostly without incident, and, much to their relief, without the dismal, gray wash they had traveled in the previous day. They stopped a traveling fruit merchant at around midday, and enjoyed a simple meal on the move, finally coming to a halt for the evening only twenty miles north of the mining town.

They shared another simple meal, still remaining relatively silent, and Morek volunteered to keep the first watch that night. As the members of the company drifted off to sleep, each had a black mist drift over their eyes. In the darkness, the taciturn Dwarf didn't witness this phenomenon, and thus, was not prepared for its meaning.

* * * *

Shoryu rose in a daze, stretching his arms wide, looking down at the slumbering form of his lover, Ellen Daires. He swung his legs over the side of the bed, and looked out the window of their humble little bedroom in Whitewood, Ellen's home only until recently. He gazed out at the streets of the Elven city, watching the people walk past as he opened the window and breathed the fresh air. He turned back to look at Ellen, only to find no trace of her, not even her scent. Something, he decided, was amiss. Hadn't he fallen asleep outdoors?

He looked out again at the streets of Whitewood. They were abandoned, the carts and animals remaining where there had been hundreds of Elves only a moment before. Where had they all gone? He was dreaming, he realized, pulling on his long, baggy hunting trousers. He cinched the belt in place, grabbing his bow and quiver, strapping them to his back, and sheathing his short sword at his hip. This was not right, he thought. I have never had such control over even myself in dreams. He took one more look out the window, and saw the Elves once again; they were being attacked by an army of Lizardmen and Greenskins, just like his village had been.

"Not again," he whispered, his voice haunted and shallow. "Not again!" He stormed through the cottage, past the familiar chairs and couches, stopping only briefly to call out to Ellen. No response was forthcoming. Bow in hand, he charged through the doorway, and out into a massacre.

At that moment, James Hayes suffered from similar illusions. He stood atop a parapet in Fort Munduka, an Order of Oun outpost in the far northeast. Legions of undead creatures assailed the walls and gates of the walled city, crashing into the fort from all sides. Wraiths floated up the sides of the fort, pulling the souls of Paladins and Knights from their bodies, leaving them wide-eyed, empty shells twitching on the stone. The sun had set many hours ago, and poltergeists, phantoms and even Vampires, the most deadly of the undead Races, stormed the fort from all angles and directions. Even floating in from above, exposed to arrow fire and Paladin magic, they came on without slowing. Yet this seemed more than an ordinary nightmare, James thought. He could feel the sweat on his face, the bruises and cuts of battle as he plunged his silver sword into another Vampire's chest, watching it become so much smoke and ash. Everything seemed alarmingly real.

Had he been sleeping? Had he dreamed the whole experience with Byron of Sidius and the company of Whitewood? No, he thought, clenching his teeth and throwing a burst of holy magic into a phantom. *This* is a dream, though one unlike any he had ever had. The shriek of splintering wood tore through the air, and he looked down to see that the gates had fallen. Hundreds of creatures poured through, cutting down and devouring everything in sight. And there, at the forefront, stood a thing more dreaded than most: a Vampire Lord.

Selena Bradford awoke lying in the middle of a dirt road, somewhere in the middle of a city's outskirts. She lifted herself off the ground, and smelled smoke coming, accompanied by the screams of young men. Her feet took her off on instinct, and she made her way through several back alleys, until she came upon a small courtyard area, where a young girl, no older than thirteen, stood amid a circle of six or seven boys.

One of the boys was running around, flailing, his entire body on fire. None of the others challenged the girl, though each held a short, blunt instrument. Terror filled their eyes, and the girl stood there, her long auburn hair waving from the fluctuation of some inner force. Flames spilled and sputtered from around her eyes. Selena remembered this scene; she had been that girl. Among the boys was a bully she had gotten in trouble. He had enlisted some of his friends to help him get revenge, and Selena had let her anger flow freely, no longer afraid of anyone. She had perfect control of her powers.

But this scene was not right, somehow. Selena remembered panicking when the first boy had burst entirely into flames, her power out of control and out of reach. She had put up a barrier of flames then, and three boys had been foolish enough to try to reach her. The whole incident had been put behind her, and she had sworn to take control of her powers. But this girl turned her power on the other boys, sending fireballs and serpents made of fire into each of them, causing them to scream in terror and pain, thrashing about on the ground, running into each other, and running into innocent guards who had come to see to the problem.

"This is a lie," Selena screamed at the sky, sensing that her dream had become a threat to her. "This is not what happened!"

"Isn't it?" said the girl who had been Selena Bradford. The child stalked toward Selena. She moved like a shimmering mirage, disappearing for a moment and appearing suddenly closer two or three times, her image shaking and vibrating out of focus. In the blink of an eye, she stood before Selena, her flaming eyes burning at the Pyromancer. "You killed them, you know." The girl's voice dropped an octave, becoming a perversion of Selena's own husky voice. The hair turned black and lank, and she become as tall as Selena, staring her in the face with those fire-rimmed eyes, the sockets become empty hollows in which a demonic flame burned. "You let go, burned them all."

The Selena-thing struck her across the face with a hand that stank of death, and Selena went cold where she had been struck. She leaped back, lashing out with her flames, creating a semi-circle of protection to ward against this creature. She sensed something wrong about it, beyond the fact that it was a mirror image gone awry. It was no dream phantasm; it was a demon.

Ellen Daires, meanwhile, had just dashed from the room in which she and Shoryu had been resting. He had gotten out of bed to look out the window, and Ellen had felt a connection that should have been more real. But she was familiar with the Dreamscape and its dangers; she did not think twice before bolting from the room. Shoryu could have been a deception, she thought as her robes flapped loosely about her, but he had felt as real as he could. Had she been sharing his dream? She did not want to risk it, and would find out soon enough at any rate.

As she burst through the door to her cottage, closing the door behind her, she heard the whistle of something flying at her, and brought up a shield of rock in time to block a spear thrown by a Lizardman. She darted away, letting the green-fleshed warrior chase her, dodging more of the reptilian warriors and Orcs as she tore through the streets of Whitewood. She knew this city and would not be cornered unless she chose to be.

Bringing her magic to bear, Ellen spun and sent a hail of dagger-shaped rocks from the ground into the following creature, watching it fall dead to the ground, huge, jagged holes torn through its flesh. But where it dropped, five more pounded after it, accompanied by two towering Trolls, the largest and most dangerous of the Greenskin races.

Ellen backed slowly away, summoning her powers from the earth, forming in her mind the image of a powerful Knight. She sent her magic into the ground, throwing her palms toward the ground to raise an enormous rock defender, a Stone Golem. As it came into being, she felt a sense of security, but a dark shadow darted from the rooftops, a Shadowbeast, leapt down onto the Golem, entering its body through its stone flesh.

Ellen froze and watched in horror, breaking her panic only in time to be knocked flying by her own defender. She felt the pain of the blow as she landed atop a fruit stand, crashing through its boards. This dream, she thought, would try to kill her. She came to roughly the same conclusion as Selena Bradford, who lay in the waking world only a few yards from her through a wall: a demon had infected her dreams.

Byron, who had only fallen asleep shortly before, landed with a thud in the middle of the familiar cemetery. But something was different. His Paladin magic screamed to be released as he got to his feet, looking out at the graveyard. The headstones here were scarred and old, several of them broken, and every single inch of the ground was occupied by bodies. The void-like blackness outside of the fence had a crimson tint to it, a waving red mist that seemed almost to threaten.

"Voice," he called out, drawing the Morning Glory from its scabbard on his back. The entire length of the blade shone a brilliant white blaze, but he heard no response.

Byron stalked through the grounds, keeping his body shifting, his eyes scanning the landscape for any sign of life. But he saw none, and for that matter, as he walked for a good ten minutes, he didn't once see an end to the iron fence perimeter. The cemetery seemed to stretch on in front of and behind him for eternity. The headstones took on a more solid look as he went, and he could not help but look from grave to grave, trying to read the inscriptions.

Each of these he read was from men and women who died during the years of his service to Tanarak of Sidius. He felt a sudden surge of guilt: more than likely, these corpses were his to claim. He brushed the feelings aside, becoming the hardened warrior he needed to be. Creeping through the cemetery like a grave robber at work, he sensed another presence, something still in the distance, something wrapped in the fog that slowly permeated the entire grounds around him. It was sinister, and yet familiar at the same time.

His left hand holding fast on the Morning Glory, his right palm extended to bring his magic to bear, he stalked through the soft, white fog, the blade of his holy sword glimmering ever brighter.

Ahead, in the darkness, something huge, crimson eyes smoking, darted behind a ragged, decaying oak tree.

Byron approached swiftly, determined not to play games with this antagonist. He stopped some ten feet from the tree, looking down at the headstone resting at the head of an empty grave. The engraving stood out as clear as the sun at noon; it read 'here lies Byron Aixler'.

From behind the oak tree stepped a towering figure, equal to Byron in height and size. Even its shape resembled his, and the pulsing light of Morning Glory pulsed revealed the creature to be an exact reflection of himself, as he had appeared under Tanarak's control. A wicked, curved scimitar hung loosely in its right hand, vile green light glimmering in its clenched left fist.

"Greetings, Byron of Sidius," the dark Dread Knight said to himself. "I have come to add you to my collection." It lifted the scimitar into position.

* * * *

Morek Rockmight did not care for keeping watch on his own, and so he had awoken David Spore, who didn't mind one bit.

He didn't sleep much anyway, he reassured the Dwarf.

The two fighters spoke of the old days, back when each had been young and still naive in the ways of the world. They had just finished sharing a laugh at one of Morek's long Dwarven jokes, when they noticed that the members of their company had begun to thrash in their sleep, seemingly out of control.

Unsure of what to do and suddenly feeling the need to be on their guard, they tried to wake the others, but to no avail. Snarls issued from the darkness nearby, and they scanned for any sign of intruders.

David was the first to spot the cat-like movements of a Shadowbeast approaching. He remained silent, nudging Morek to catch his attention.

The Dwarven Boxer strapped on his silver-studded gloves, nodding slightly. "We don't move from the group," he whispered. "We'll let them come to us. The others can't protect themselves in their state. Be ready to take the other side."

David shuffled around the company, seeing two more of the creatures, their movements furtive and cautious.

The first one they had seen charged at Morek, bringing three of his demon allies from the shadows at the Dwarf. They brandished long swords made of the same substance as their bodies, swinging with deadly intent.

Morek ducked and dodged the attacks, shoulder tackling one of them to clear some space, then launching crushing uppercuts at the other two as he evaded their blows.

One of the Shadowbeasts lashed out with a claw as it fell, catching Morek a glancing blow to the arm, blood running from the wound in rivulets.

Damn, Morek thought. *I'm usually more careful.*

David Spore wasn't having the best of luck either. Despite his expertise in the martial arts, he still had only one arm. And he had not thought to grab his mystical sutras when Morek awakened him. The Shadowbeasts tore two long gashes in him, one in his left side and another down his back. His blood soaked the ground, mixed with the ashes of the demons he had managed to kill by collapsing its throat with a well-aimed kick.

Morek beat a couple of the Shadowbeasts to death, his hammering punches making short work of the lesser demons. But he was sweating freely in the suddenly stifling heat of the night, his clothes clinging to his skin, his eyes stinging as beads of sweat dripped into them. He feinted and lunged, hoping to find an opening in which to make a final strike. But the last Shadowbeast remained out of his short arm reach, keeping him at bay with its long blade. Anger and frustration rose in his throat, bile burned his mouth as he gnashed his teeth.

Finally, an opportunity opened as the creature stabbed down at him, missing by scant inches and burying its blade in the ground.

Morek spun and launched a solid blow to the demon's throat, the strength of the blow and the enchanted silver combining to turn the creature to dust. He spat on the ground, grunting at the piles of ashes around him. He looked up to see David Spore roll away from two Shadowbeasts, back toward where he had been sleeping, coming up in a half-crouch. Between his fingers, he held a strange piece of paper. A sutra, Morek realized. He sat down nonchalantly and began bandaging his wound as a flare of light and a hideous scream of pain went up as David activated the sutra on the remaining attackers.

David came over and began working on his own wounds, using a salve to staunch the flow of blood. Still their companions thrashed in their sleep. The Monk could detect the auras of five other demons, though he could not see them. He felt their closeness, and with a gasp as he applied the salve, he realized where they were.

And there was nothing he or Morek could do about them.

* * * *

Shoryu smelled Ellen suddenly, the scent too solid and familiar to be anything else. He had been firing arrows at marauding Lizardmen and Greenskins, unconcerned with what he hit. This was, after all, a dream, and nothing more. He felt the sudden release of a great magic, the same kind that Ellen used. He bolted then, from his sniper spot atop the library to the streets. He found Ellen lying in a heap behind a wall of vines and thick tree roots, sprung from the ground to ward off a lumbering creature of stone. She looked in his direction for a moment, and he saw hope spring into her eyes.

"Shoryu," she cried, and he darted past the defending plants to her side. "My Stone Golem, a Shadowbeast inhabited it." She gripped her lover by the shoulders. "If it gets through my defenses, we'll be crushed."

Shoryu looked through the screen of defending plant life, seeing the eyes of the Golem. No ordinary Shadowbeast had possessed it; it tossed defenders aside like they were paper, tore at the wall of magic that Ellen had generated with increasing success. Shoryu doubted altogether that it was a Shadowbeast at all within the stone flesh of the Golem. An idea had been forming in his mind, however, since he had seen the creature. It was a plan forged in haste and desperation, but if it worked, they would be done with this nightmare.

"Ellen, the walls of stone you can make to protect yourself. Can you make a dome?"

She seemed confused, but nodded her head.

"Good. Make one now, and leave its center of creation visible for me." The demon-Golem had slowed its advance, seeing him now and looking confused.

Ellen summoned her magic once more, fatigued nearly to the point of sleep, except that she knew she could not sleep here, for this was the realm of dreams. Falling asleep would not rest her, and she would not dream. She lay back, leaving a small circle of shimmering force directly in front of Shoryu's line of sight within the protective dome.

The Cuyotai Hunter drew his bow, notched an arrow, and watched the magic of his arrow glow. He looked back and forth from the arrowhead to the circle of the stone dome now being shaken by the Golem's fists. The barrier would not last long, but Shoryu waited until he could match the rhythm of the enchanted arrow to the dome. Listening to the exertions of the demon without, he timed its downswing, and released the arrow from its notch.

Blue light flashed as his weapon's magic combined Ellen's, collecting and pooling together, pushing the demon back with its strange brilliance. The two magics swirled together, and Shoryu and Ellen stood to their feet, hands clasped together, as the magic tore a gaping hole through the Golem.

A scream of fury and pain erupted from the demon as it returned to its natural form, a strange and twisted half-breed of snake and man, its blood spraying black and acidic on the ground. "It, cannot, beeeee," it screamed. "You cannot, destroy, cannot, destroyyyyyy-," and nothing more. The Dreamstalker's eyes turned gray and dead, and its body crumbled like dirt.

"We shall stand together always," Shoryu whispered to Ellen before they awoke from their thrashings.

Morek and David Spore had already started a fire to cook food, and the Dwarf was instantly at their side.

"Are you two all right," he asked hurriedly. The Cuyotai rubbed the sleep from his eyes, remembering the dream as vividly as if it were reality. He looked around at the group. They were all shaking, but appeared otherwise to be asleep. What was going on? Was what had happened to him and Ellen happening to the others as well?

"Don't try to wake them," Morek advised. "I did, and nearly got a face full of fist from Hayes. He's got it particularly bad."

They all sat about the fire, while Ellen and Shoryu relayed what they had experienced.

* * * *

Selena Bradford fought for her life against a perversion of herself as a youth. The demon-Selena had hurled streaks and balls of fire at her, and she could do little more than dodge and block the fury of the magical strikes with her own flame shields and walls.

"You couldn't control the power," the demon screamed at her in horrid delight. "Now let it consume you." The demon struck out with such fury and force that Selena was left no opportunity for a counter-attack. Guilt ate away at Selena, for one thing about the memory had been correct; she had set one of the boys on fire, and he had run into a shop, dying in the building's collapse. Several businesses had burnt to the ground, taking the lives of five more people, and she had been to blame. And all because she could not control her temper and her powers.

One of the demon's attacks ripped through Selena's shield, blowing her back against a wall to an inn. She felt her will to fight slip away; the demon was right. She had been foolish and rash, and innocent people had paid for her arrogance.

But wait, she thought, her mind clearing. She had been barely a young woman. She had been a teenager, and of course she had not had full command of her magic. She stood, wrapping herself in a ring of flames, absorbing the demon's attacks as part of the ring of defense. She had been a child then, but she was a full-grown woman now, experienced beyond measure, the most powerful Pyromancer in most of the lands of Tamalaria.

"I am a sorcerer supreme," she rasped. "There is none who is my equal. Certainly not some half-remembered child who is no longer who I am. Get you back into the Pit, demon."

The demon-Selena growled and down the meteors of the Meteor Strike spell, but Selena shifted her weight and focus, holding the flaming boulders with her ring of magic. With an inward twist, she sent the spell and her own ring of flaming streaks spiraling back at the demon, who stood wide-eyed in horror.

With a ghoulish shriek, the demon exploded as the magic struck him, turning his body into ashes. As she awoke, she found the faces of her friends hovering over her, smiling the smiles of those who are happy to be lacking sleep. Among them were Morek, David, Shoryu, Ellen, and James Hayes, who had conquered his own nightmare rather easily.

"Are we all awake," she asked groggily, half sitting up.

Shoryu shook his head despondently, looking over at the one remaining form who thrashed in his slumber. Selena looked over to see Byron twitching violently in the night. There was nothing they could do for their leader, except pray.

* * * *

Byron squared his shoulders to his dark copy, the Morning Glory gripped in both hands, his legs apart with knees bent to give him freedom of movement. *Anticipate the first strike*, he thought over and over in his mind, a litany to which he adhered often.

The dark Byron shifted right, coming around the open grave. Its eyes glimmered a pulsing crimson, the dark color of settled blood on the ground. With a twist of the hips, it charged at Byron, slashing and hacking from upper left and right angles.

Byron easily deflected the blows, keeping his footing and composure. The copy lunged and feinted, using many of the tactics that Byron employed in combat, with one clear difference; these attacks were foreign to the creature, whereas Byron himself had years of experience with the maneuvers.

The dark copy landed a glancing slash on Byron's left shoulder, and blood ran freely from his split shoulder plate.

But Byron had made a worthy trade, letting the blow strike as he launched a series of rapid, shallow stabs into the copy's chest. Black, thick fluid pouring from the wounds. The copy leaped back ten feet, holding its chest in pain. "It seems our swordsmanship is still the stuff of legends," the black creature hissed at him. "But I shall not be defeated so easily." It waved a hand over the wounds and they disappeared entirely.

Byron prepared for a strike, but the copy faded into the shadows, disappearing completely.

Where had it gone? Byron searched the field.

A sudden burst of dark energy slammed into him from the side, sending him flying into an unsteady oak tree nearby, snapping it in half.

As the upper half of the tree crashed down, Byron rolled away, avoiding a nasty pinning situation. He sprang to his feet, listening as the demon laughed mockingly at him.

"Ha ha ha ha haaa. Where am I, Byron? To your left, to your right, or am I right in front of you?" Its voice echoed through the air, as another ball of energy hit Byron from behind.

He was better prepared for the impact, digging his heels into the ground as he was pushed forward with ease. He remained on his feet, but felt drained and battered, the damage from the dark magic taking its toll.

Shadow magic, he thought glumly. *Much more advanced than my own.*

"Why don't you use the same trick, eh? Make yourself less of a target," the voice shouted, taunting him.

"I would not resort to such trickery," Byron yelled, the sword in his hands blazing brighter still, almost blinding him. "I am not a creature of deception any more. I am not Byron of Sidius." He saw the flicker of movement too late and was crashed into by the copycat, the two tumbling to the ground, armor glinting in the dim light of the cemetery.

The demon was unbelievably strong, getting the upper hand as they stopped, pinning Byron to the ground. Byron's sword arm was held fast to the ground, and he could not get a good shot with the Morning Glory. The demon, on the other hand, began punching him in the face, trying to shatter his skull.

"You will die here, Byron of Sidius," the creature growled as it drooled on him. "I have even gone to the trouble of digging you a grave. In the name of the Seven Hells, you will die." Over and over the demon struck him, being careful to keep the Morning Glory pinned.

Something squirmed inside of Byron, and he felt warmth spread through his body. His eyes filled with holy magic, the pinprick lights becoming huge and blazing as brightly as the Morning Glory. The light repelled the demon, tossing it off of him. He stood and marched to the flailing demon, hacking its left arm off—the wicked scimitar held fast in the detached hand.

Howls of pain rose up out of its throat as it fell to the ground, maintaining its disguise.

Byron stopped right before the creature as it knelt before the open grave. He thrust his palm to its chest plate, and righteous fury filled his entire being. "Go now, demon. Return to whence you came, and never return. Great Oun, of Paradise high. Grant me power, from your seat in the sky. Holy Cannon!"

A riptide of white light blasted forth from Byron's palm, tearing a hole through the demon, yet leaving all else it touched intact.

The life ebbed from the demon's eyes, turning them into hollow, lightless pits in its skull-face. Still it knelt there, dead as could be.

Byron put one heavy boot against its head, and kicked, sending it into the empty grave. As he turned away, stalking toward the opening gates out of the cemetery, he stopped a moment and looked back. "And my name, is Byron Aixler."

Chapter Fifteen
Bait

The company from Whitewood sat about the campfire, the early half-darkness of dawn approaching. Byron had just awoken and joined them, gratefully accepting a mug of coffee brewed from Morek's supplies. The Dwarven Boxer, despite having gone without sleep for most of the night, didn't seem to be in bad shape save a few cuts and bruises.

Everyone had been damaged in their enchanted slumber, the wounds becoming real as they came out of their sleeping encounters. Shoryu was the fastest to heal, his lycanthrope regeneration kicking in as he helped bind Ellen's scratches, being as gentle as a lamb with his love. Yet, once, during his assisted ministrations, he had pinched her arm, seemingly without reason. Ellen blew it off as playfulness, but Shoryu knew that it was a part of his cost of giving Byron his blood.

"So, how did you all fare," Byron asked darkly as he thought once again on the twisted mirror image of himself as he kicked it into the grave meant for him.

"We got by all right," James Hayes said, using a Paladin healing spell on an open hole in his shoulder. "I had the privilege of facing one of my greater fears, a Vampire Lord." He looked haggard and disheveled, and was thinking over the extraordinary changes Byron had gone through during the past week. Had the mighty Oun accepted this dark creature back into his fold? he wondered. If Byron had a shot at redemption, then perhaps James could find forgiveness for his failure to protect Fort Flag. "I didn't come away unscathed, but you should see the other guy," he said in a half-hearted attempt at jesting. No one laughed, as he expected.

"Dreamstalkers," said Ellen in a hushed whisper, barely loud enough to be heard above the fire's crackle. "Greatly formidable demons. We should be grateful we are all in one piece." She clung tightly to Shoryu for support. "If Shoryu and I had not been together, I might not have survived," she said, and all eyes were suddenly on the couple.

"You were together, eh?" Alex squeaked. He buzzed around their heads a few times before landing gingerly on Selena's shoulder. "What were you doing together, if I may be so bold as to ask?"

Shoryu blushed and scratched the back of his head, stammering to get an answer out. A wave of relief and laughter issued from the company, who could always rely on the Cuyotai Hunter and the Ki Fairy to lighten their spirits.

"You needn't answer that," Byron said with a chuckle. "We have a Monk in our presence, and I don't think it would be good for him to hear of such things," he said.

"No, go ahead, and don't spare the nasty details where appropriate," David jested, smiling like an imp. Of everyone, he had received the most severe injuries, his lacerations deep enough to cause him discomfort when he moved. James would heal him before they headed out, making sure to purge any poisons or taints from the Shadowbeast weapons. But for now, he could barely shift his position without pain.

"What happened to you two anyway," Selena asked, taking a bit of her bread and cheese from her pack, giving a small bit to Alex like a parrot. "I thought you didn't sleep?"

"We didn't." Morek spat into the fire. His eyes were getting heavy, and he needed to rest at least a couple of hours before they headed out. "I think the Shadowbeasts were sent as insurance. Vandross didn't want to leave everything to the off chance that we would all sleep at one time. Stupid of him, though, to send so few. Suppose it had been James or Byron on guard? I hate to admit it," he said, growling at himself for saying anything that made him seem inferior to anyone in battle. "But either of you Paladins would have made very short work of them. If David hadn't used a sutra, he might not have survived."

"Well, he did, despite his decided disadvantage," commented Byron as he poured more of the thick black coffee down his throat. "At least for this particular ass-kicking contest he was one-armed and not one-legged." He dumped the rest of the tar-like liquid on the ground. He began packing some of his things, though not all. "Morek, David, get some rest. Any of the rest of you who are still tired, too. I can keep watch, but we head out again at noon. We'll make good time across the plains once we're fully clear of these woodlands."

He looked off into the northern distance, trying to gauge how much time it would take without horses to make the trip to the monastery. Almost twelve days by his calculations, if they had a limited number of interruptions. They had been fortunate to be such a highly skilled troupe: most other adventuring parties would have died in such an attack, if not in Whitewood or Desanadron. But Byron had chosen his companions well; or perhaps it could be said that they chose him. Each had a good reason for sticking by him: Shoryu had the destruction of his village; James Hayes had Fort Flag; Selena, Desanadron; and Morek and Ellen, and even David Spore, the siege of Whitewood. Other than Alex, he had known them all for less than two months, yet they had formed quick and strong friendships and alliances.

Shoryu and Ellen were the clearest example of this. The company could easily be divided into pairs, Byron thought, his mind working through the strategies available to each pairing. Shoryu and Ellen each possessed magic, hers natural, his from his weapon. A mage and a warrior, well suited to each other's talents and abilities. Then there were Selena and James, with Alex in the mix. Once again, a good mage and warrior combination, and a sensible one seeing as how risky Selena's magic could be. Finally, there were Morek and David, two hardened, seasoned veterans of hand-to-hand combat arts. But who was Byron to pair with? He worked just fine on his own, and could mingle with the others as need be. Truth be told, however, he was most keen on Shoryu. He had saved the boy from destruction and despair, to be certain. He was Byron's charge, now. But with the inclusion of Ellen to the group, he didn't feel that obligation as strongly as he had.

As his thoughts turned further to analyzing the young Cuyotai, Shoryu wandered over to him, having tucked Ellen in for a good nap. Byron looked over at Shoryu, taking in the worried look of silence in the Hunter's eyes.

"Not all of us will survive this struggle, will we," he asked, his voice barely a whisper.

"I won't lie to you, my young friend, so no, we won't all survive. I am hopeful that we will all see this through, but I highly doubt it will be so. Why do you ask?" He put an arm around Shoryu's shoulders. The young man didn't seem to mind, and actually seemed put at ease by the gesture.

"I am afraid." Shoryu lowered his head. "I have been afraid many times in my life, but few times with such motivation. I fear for Ellen's safety. I fear that this love between us is only temporary, forged out of need and circumstance."

Byron smiled gently, his jaw slipping slightly on his skull.

"My dear boy, most relationships are thus. My wife and I were married mostly at the behest of our parents, so that they could combine their finances and fortunes. At first, I doubted if I could love her." His twin lights becoming smaller than needle heads, his mind filling with the wonderful memories of her affections. "But I found out rather quickly that she was a very strong-willed girl, and more than competent with a staff. Sit down with me, I'll tell you a story."

Shoryu sat on the ground in front of him, in the tribal fashion of his people, legs folded inward.

"My wife's name was Alice Montegart, and her father was a nobleman once, cast down from high society for rooting around and telling the truth of the corruption of central government. He made his living as a blacksmith, something he was very good at. His business was flourishing, but he didn't have the political power he once enjoyed. Trade agreements became hard to come by for him, for he had been blacklisted by many a city-state for his purported treachery to the governing body of Desanadron.

"My father was Roderick Aixler, an officer of the court and the watch," Byron said, summoning to his mind's eye memories of the towering, muscular rock of a man his father had been. "He was no nobleman by any means, but he was well liked in the courts and in the public, and thus gained the title. He made good money, despite never having taken a bribe in his career, and had on more than one occasion been awarded lands and properties by the Desanadron Parliament. So although he was not a noble, our family had much. One day, after a long and hard-fought arrest of a local thug, my father went to see a blacksmith about getting his armor repaired. It had been dented heavily by the thug and his cronies, but my father himself was in good shape. He prided himself on keeping his belongings in good condition. The man never threw anything out; he'd pay to have things repaired even when that turned out to be more expensive than getting a new one. That's just the way he was. Anyhow, he had gone to Alice's father, on the recommendation of one of his subordinates, who regularly had to use his services.

"They began talking while Mr. Montegart worked, him telling my father of his political woes, and my father speaking much about the stresses of being a watch commander. They shared tales of their works and doings, and became good friends in the days that followed. Mr. Montegart confided in my father that he had a young daughter and an ill wife, and could do little to help either financially. He didn't have enough customers due to his lack of materials, and my father saw the opportunity to help a decent man who had been unjustly tossed into a hard place. He gave Mr. Montegart and his family both money and one of the houses we owned to live in, and even sprung for a healer to tend to his wife, and a tutor to teach his daughter. The same tutor as he had for me, mind you young Shoryu. I often watched Alice playing in the yard from a distance, and I remember thinking even then that she was beautiful. But she was a gruff little girl, my boy," he said, laughing aloud. "The first time I tried to play with her, she kicked me in the shins and ran to her father! He informed her that she had to play nice with me, that some day she would be my bride. Oh, I got a number of beatings from her after that, though in truth, I never fought back for fear of hurting her and getting in trouble with my father.

"A few years passed, and my father told me that Mr. Montegart had not been jesting. He had promised Alice to me as my bride in exchange for my father's kindness. When I was a young man, now trained as a Paladin by my father and members of the Order of Oun, we were wed. It was a soft autumn evening, and the ceremony was small, held in the courtyard of the judgment building. Alice and I had come to a mutual liking of one another, though nothing like love. But as we lived together, I fell hard for her. Her little patterns, her habits, the way she carried herself," he said longingly. "I would do anything to return to that time. Three years passed, and we had our son Jacob. The rest is too painful to speak of." His voice dropped to a whisper. "I tell you Shoryu, family is the greatest thing in the world. I am sorry for your loss of your father," he said, thinking back on the big Chieftain lying dead on the ground as the village burned around him.

Shoryu waved it off, forcing a smile.

"He was not my real father. My true father died in the battle of the Final Push."

Byron remembered a particular Hunter at the Final Push, one with a fantastic enchanted bow and arrows. So, the cycle of time comes around, he thought. Where I failed to protect his father, I must succeed with him.

"Thanks for the story, good Byron," said Shoryu with a grin. "I have greatly enjoyed this time with you, my friend. That makes my next question difficult." He looked up into Byron's face. There was a sadness there, the cause of which Byron was uncertain. "Byron, James Hayes and Bael have both told me that when you destroy Richard Vandross, the bond of magic that ties you to him will dissipate, and you will die. Is this so?"

Byron was taken aback; he hadn't been prepared for anyone to feel badly at the idea that he would pass on.

"Shoryu, I am not entirely sure. But I think that it must be so," he finished, his voice barely a whisper as he looked out at the stretches of woodland.

"Perhaps then, there is an alternative. Some way of stopping him without killing him. Imprisonment in a Paladin outpost, perhaps?"

Byron thought it over for the merest fraction of a moment, knowing that such a thing would only result in the warlock's eventual escape. He shook his head slowly.

"No, young Hunter. Richard Vandross must be destroyed. If there were any hope for redemption, he would already have been saved. There is hope for his soul, if he repents to the gods he has offended, including great Oun. But if not, he is doomed to the Pit; in any event, death will be the only end to his tyranny. Come, let us make ready once more," he said, waking those who had slept another two hours.

The company headed out just before noon, in order to make it out of the Elven Kingdom as quickly as they could.

* * * *

Richard Vandross became so furious that he destroyed about twenty Shadowbeasts, simply because they were there. "Failed? How in the seven Hells did they fail? Unacceptable," he fumed, his voice slipping into the double echo of his rage.

Vilec Roak stood before him as he sat upon the throne, kneeling at the foot of the great seat of bone, waiting for Vandross to smite him.

But he did not; the Human warlock fumed and ranted, but did nothing to Roak himself, taking out his wrath on those foolish enough to poke their heads in on the Shadowbeast Prime and he. "I thought these Dreamstalkers were unbeatable. Garrrgh!" He tossed a bolt of lightning into the high vaulted ceiling, causing the entire mountain to tremble in response to his outburst.

Vandross closed his eye and breathed deeply, trying to calm himself. "Tell me what happened," he said, his voice low and dangerous.

Vilec Roak raised his black head, his feral, yellow eyes glowing with fear. He had to clear his throat for a bit before responding.

"It is unknown how, but the Cuyotai and his Elven mate shared their dream. They share a connection that is greater than flesh, my lord. They were able to overcome their demon, outnumbering it and apparently able to use their powers in combination. The Dreamstalkers gave me this to monitor their dreams," he said, revealing a black orb from his pockets. It showed nothing now, the demons having been destroyed. "I sent a small squad of my men as insurance, in case any of them were of the insomniac persuasion, but the Dwarven Boxer, Morek Rockmight, and their new companion, the one-armed Monk, destroyed them handily."

"In other words, they did little damage to the two of them," Vandross growled. He waved his hand dismissively. "What of the others?"

"Well, the Pyromancer, Selena Bradford, was nearly deceived into her doom, but her command of the fire magic proved too formidable. James Hayes sustained some damage, but his righteous powers kept him alive. And Byron—"

"Don't bother to tell me," Vandross said, clenching his fists in rage. "I suspect nothing short of myself or the Prince of Lies can stand in his way. Damn you Byron of Sidius," he shouted, slamming his fist down on the arm of the throne, breaking it off. He stopped to think for a while, not dismissing Vilec Roak just yet. "Roak, leave me for now. I must think of some more clever way to deal with our undead friend and his companions. Something discreet, something they will never suspect. Perhaps, a false friend," he said, his voice low and level, his thoughts clear. "You are dismissed, general."

Vilec Roak bowed and left the central chamber. The Shadowbeast Prime slunk through the darkness of the mountain labyrinth, his thoughts uneasy and his mind clouded with thoughts of his recent failures. He had been certain that the Dreamstalkers would succeed. Perhaps Tamriel, the huge Renka, was right. Perhaps a large force, solely focused on Byron's company, would be the best way to go.

No, he thought after a moment, passing by a knot of Khan who saluted him. He returned the salute without thought or enthusiasm, listening as one of the tiger-men fell into step behind him. As he made his way to the mouth of Mount Toane, the Khan snapped to attention at his side. "Major Bloodfang reporting, sir," he said, his guttural voice echoing off of the rock face of the mountain. Vilec Roak returned the salute.

"At ease, Major. What's on your mind," he asked, sitting on one of the rock outcroppings.

"Sir, my platoon just returned from Ja-Wen, as per his lordship's commands. I have a report to give, and his lordship seems entrenched in thought. I shall give the report to you, sir."

Hmm, thought Roak. *This Khan is very militant, a good soldier.* No surprise he had worked up to the rank of Major without Roak realizing it.

"Very well, major. Let's hear it." He leaned back on the rock as the Major stood at parade rest.

"Sir! Of the fifteen hundred men dispatched in my unit to Ja-Wen, twelve hundred returned alive. We suffered heaviest casualties from the northwestern quadrant of the city, where a number of elite soldiers laid in wait. They were fierce warriors, sir, highly trained. I removed my men, had them fall back and take a tactically superior position in the northeastern quadrant, where there were fewer buildings for the city's defenders to take easily defensible positions. The decided advantage there belonged to us, sir, but we were routed from that position by defenders come out of the southern quadrants. The city's army has easily tripled in numbers since the first recon on the city only a few weeks ago."

"That's no surprise, really," Vilec Roak responded, bored with this man's report. "Is there anything of relevance in all of this, Major?" The Khan raised an eyebrow, but his eyes told Roak that something had been out of the ordinary in Ja-Wen. "What is it Major?"

"Sir, permission to speak freely?" Roak nodded. "Sir, something truly unnerved me about the city and its defenders. They all wore some sort of armband, a leather item on their left biceps. There were Elves among them, mounted cavalry. They were some of the Black Guard, from Whitewood."

Roak's eyes widened. Already Elven riders had reached Ja-Wen? They must have had the aid of a teleportation hub from the High Council of Whitewood.

"Sir, on the armband, there was the design of a skull, with eyes of white light."

The Shadowbeast Prime's heart skipped a beat.

"Sir, I believe you know whose countenance that is," the Major said in a low voice.

Roak nodded; Byron of Sidius. The Elves had been dispatched to spread the word of the Dread Knight's deeds and his struggle against the armies of Richard Vandross. Things seemed to conspire constantly around his lordship. Roak looked into the past, trying to glean what he could of what he remembered from the time of Tanarak of Sidius. Many things, events in the last few weeks, mirrored that time perfectly, except that Vandross did not yet hold control over any regions outside of Mount Toane, like Tanarak had. But he surely was a more straightforward man that Tanarak, and to his benefit. Vandross didn't have to keep his forces spread out so long as he kept to the tactic of beating a city into submission, and then leaving it to lick its wounds.

But a resistance would form against him, that much was certain. Vandross seemed to be more capable of summoning demons from the Pit than his former master, and this also played to his advantage. He was more charismatic than the dead warlock, and more importantly, still breathing. But Byron stood in the way, and nothing Vandross threw at him seemed to faze him. How could Roak help in this matter? He didn't dare face the Dread Knight alone, or even with a platoon of his very best men, and the Renkas for backup. But now that the Dreamstalkers were dead, there seemed few options left to him, aside from a full frontal assault, and in the open plains that Byron's company would be crossing on their journey north, for they seemed to be heading that way, would be an invitation to slaughter. Vilec Roak would not stand a chance.

It was a matter to stew over for a while, and Roak went to his chambers to do so. But he fell asleep before he could stew about anything.

* * * *

Into the forested foothills bordering the northernmost tip of the Elven Kingdom Byron led his company, James Hayes keeping some relative company, along with Selena right behind him. The rest of the company kept itself evenly spaced and spread out, in the event of an attack. The uneven footing in these hills became treacherous, and several members of the company, all in fact, save Shoryu, slipped and fell at one point or another, before reaching a winding path up through the hills and woodland.

Rows of evergreens stood like sentinels around them, stretching forever towards the sun, trying in vain to touch it. The effect was not lost on Byron; few trees, even in the Elven Kingdom, were as hardy as these. They had been tended to, cared for, by someone or something living in the forest. Ellen, he noticed, had become suddenly apprehensive. "Ellen, do you know what resides here?" he asked her, his voice barely louder than a hoarse whisper.

"Indeed," she said. There were few differences between these trees, and only her trained eyes could pick them out among the group. "An Anudian, one of the Earthly Chosen. We trespass on her territory, Byron. She follows us even now." Her heart turned cold, her skin standing up in goose flesh, fear racing down her spine in a single sweep. Such was the effect of any close contact with the Anudian.

As the company moved forward, they slowed their pace, choosing to be ready if anything hostile approached, rather than try to evade confrontation.

As they passed into a small clearing, a single woman, Elven in appearance, appeared as though out of nowhere.

Byron realized that the woman's skin had turned to bark in patches on her arms and face. Her features were fine and delicate, and she was lovely to look upon, he thought. But an old anger burned brightly in her bright green eyes.

"*Callet ta chock*, intruders," the Anudian growled across to them from twenty yards away. "Who dares to pass through my domain?" Magic flared to life in the woman's hands and eyes, her fury transformed into a clear indication that she would not tolerate their presence long.

Byron stepped forward a few steps, his long strides nearly halving the distance between them. He felt the flux of magic being brought to bear, and made a subtle gesture with his left hand, creating an invisible warding wall against attack.

"I am Byron, formerly of Sidius," said the Dread Knight loudly, his head held high, his tone formal. "With me are my companions, whom I shall introduce my lady." He bowed deeply. "This is Shoryu Tearfang, a Cuyotai Hunter of noble right and mind. Next to him is his mate and our friend," both Cuyotai and Elf blushed deeply, "Ellen Daires, Elven Gaiamancer. Her purpose in life is much the same as thy own. Standing there, with the full plate armor and air of a holy man is James Hayes, Human Paladin, and member of the Order of Oun." Hayes knelt and bowed his head to the Anudian, who actually deigned to smile at the Paladin.

"The lady in red is Selena Bradford, Human Pyromancer. Her passion equals her wisdom and constraint, my lady. You need not fear her flames."

Selena curtsied politely.

"To my right, the Dwarven man is Morek Rockmight, a Boxer and a landowner hailing from Traithrock. Next to him is the Monk David Spore, a spiritual man and, though he has only one arm, a capable martial artist. And lastly, crouched on Selena's shoulder, is our tiny scout, a Ki Fairy by the name of Alex, who has traveled with me far and wide, my lady. We travel from Whitewood to the north, towards a monastery in the mountains of the north. We ask that you kindly grant us safe passage through your lands."

The Anudian seemed to consider this, a small smile tracing over her lips.

"You claim to be of Sidius formerly, creature, yet I sense none of the warlock's taint in you," she said, much to the company's confusion. "You bear a resemblance to the warlock Tanarak's former general, yet your soul, I sense, belongs to a holy man, like your friend James Hayes. A proud Paladin soul," Her voice faded to a whisper.

She stood silently, her magic dissipating then floated toward Byron until she was inches away from his chest, her head level with the symbol of Oun on his breastplate. She reached to touch his cheekbone, and her hand rested there only a moment. The Anudian recoiled suddenly as though stung. "Such pain. Such agony have you suffered in your lifetime, Byron. And such purpose in your actions now, such a heavy burden you bear. No, I shall not hold you and yours any longer here. Go now, and keep well, thou tortured soul. May whatever god you worship grant you mercy in the afterlife, for you have already seen enough of the Hells on earth."

Byron bowed to her, and the Anudian slowly moved away from the company.

The group from Whitewood moved swiftly then, onward north for several hours, until finally Ellen went up beside Byron, who led the group at a half-jog.

"Byron, you have received a deep honor from the Anudian. Her words, though harsh," she said, looking at the ground for a moment, "were words of pity. The Anudian only pity their own, the woods, and the truly worthy." She lowered her voice to a conspiratorial whisper. "What happened when she touched you?"

"She saw into my soul, into my memories," Byron replied after a long pause. He had in turn, received a glimpse of the Anudian woman's torments. She had felt their pain, cried out many nights in anguish, the burning pain of an axe head tearing into her body when men of the axe hacked at the trees who were her children.

Such pain. She took it into herself, in order to spare the trees. She had done so for more than two thousand years; how long could the spirit endure such agony and not become embittered?

But what of his own pains? he thought to himself, watching as Ellen fell back into step with Shoryu. The Anudian had seen him stand by, helpless, while Richard Vandross beheaded his wife and only child. She had looked at the torment of his transformation into the thing known as Byron of Sidius. She had felt his dread as he watched from the private prison of his soul, unable to die, unable to control himself. She had watched his memories flicker past, dark and forbidding. Finally, she could not handle it, and had to leave his mind. But she had left something there, as well. A thought, a single litany that he took some measure of comfort from.

"May the Gods weep for you, Byron Aixler. May they grant you their love and mercy." It had been so heart-felt, that Byron had nearly felt the urge to cry. He choked the urge down.

That evening, they camped near the northernmost border of the Elven Kingdom. Byron slept like the dead.

* * * *

Vilec Roak got out of bed some time after midnight, stalking through the tunnels of Mount Toane. His thoughts were still hazy with sleep, but he remembered with sudden clarity what he had been thinking about before he had gone to sleep. Byron of Sidius, and his accursed company. They seemed indestructible. How could a small pack of mortals be so powerful? There had to be some way to get to them, to cause a weakness. But how would he do that?

An impish grin spread across his lips. They seemed to have a penchant for helping the weak. He could use that to his advantage. All it would take was a single strike, executed with surgical precision.

Once again the nagging question of how to do this raised its ugly head.

Roak was no one's fool, especially not Byron's. He had been silent thus far, a background player in the game of war between Dread Knight and one-eyed warlock. But no longer; he'd begun to form the inklings of a plan.

Like a streak of lightning he darted for the throne hall, finding Richard Vandross sitting in the seat of bones, his chin in his palm, looking bored out of his mind.

"My lord," Roak said, bowing deeply.

The man turned warlock looked up from his unfocused stare to gaze at him. Roak could feel his good eye scrutinizing him, testing his measure as a competent ally. Vandross had become strangely distant, only on this occasion the distance he had gone far enough to take a good measure of time to return from. His good eye flared just once, a flicker of the demonic crimson cast beaming out from his handsome, yet shadowed, face.

"General Roak," Vandross said, the twin tone of demon and man creeping through.

The sound of it made Vilec Roak cringe, inwardly flinching as though about to be struck.

"Come, speak with me Shadowbeast," Vandross said, his voice returning to normal for once.

What had his lord been thinking about? Why did he slip in and out of those states of inhuman tone and mood so often?

"My lord, I believe I have devised a way in which to waylay and injure Byron's company. Perhaps even kill one or two of them."

Vandross laughed harshly and spat at the floor at his feet.

"I want the utter destruction of all of them, fool," he growled, his voice slurring into the twin harmony. "Do not waste my time with anything short of that, Vilec Roak, or you shall find yourself cleaning up after the torture masters of the Hells once again." Vandross's good eye gleamed the color of blood, and his hands became clenched fists.

Roak, though afraid, held his ground.

"My lord, a wise leader does not bull-rush his enemy. He picks him apart, piece by piece, ally by ally, until at last, when the greatest foe of the wise leader looks for aid, there is none for him but the promise that he shall join his dead companions." Roak was quoting the great Tanarak of Sidius.

Vandross's socket returned to normal.

"This is indeed good advice, General. Tell me more." Vandross took a long pull from a liquor flask at his hip.

"Lord Vandross, have you not noticed that Byron and his band have helped all those they can against you? No matter who they are, what they are?"

Vandross nodded, remaining silent, his hands coming to rest under his chin.

"Think of it. After Koreindar, you told me, Byron assaulted you openly. He let you go, because the soul of a Paladin has its limitations. He had no cause to fear you then, as he does now. He went on to help save the Cuyotai whelp,

Shoryu Tearfang. Together, they healed Bael outside of Fort Flag. In Desanadron, they came to the defense of the city along with James Hayes and Selena Bradford. In Whitewood, they met Ellen Daires and the Monk, whose name I have yet to memorize. There also they met Morek Rockmight."

"I know all of this already," said Vandross softly, remaining patient by Roak's measure. "What does any of this have to do with your plans?"

Roak smiled viciously from ear to shadowy ear.

"Don't you see," Roak hissed, his eyes glimmering like gimlets. "All of his companions have been gained through some result of other catastrophe. He'd welcome one more misfortunate man, someone willing to stay close and join his cause."

Vandross ran his hand through his short-cropped beard, nodding his head slightly.

"There are several villages between them and wherever they go at the least," Vandross rumbled, climbing down the steps from his throne to stand beside Roak.

The Shadowbeast felt gladdened and terrified by his lord's closeness; he could not predict when Vandross might become dour and violent anymore. "You would suggest that we send disaster before him, and plant one of our own as a victim, to win his trust."

Roak nodded. This was no small gambit to be dared by a fool. It would require someone of skill, and power. And not a demon; no, the Paladin, Hayes, would know a demon on sight, as might Byron at this juncture. That would be too great a risk. One of their higher-ranking mortals would have to be selected for this grisly task. Someone of power, ability, and great cunning. The latter would be needed in even greater amounts than the former, for all would hang in the balance of the man's cleverness.

"Who would you suggest?"

"I am not entirely certain yet, my lord. But none of the demons will do. We are too easily detected. I shall have to think long and hard about it, my lord."

"You have one day." Vandross's good eye focused completely on the here and now. But though his time limit was harsh, Vandross smiled wickedly. "If even one of them is killed, I shall bestow on you a grand decoration, Roak. Whatever you want." He whipped his head to the side to look directly into the Shadowbeast's eyes. There was maddened hunger there, and something much more deadly. Something murderous. "Monies, territories, whores, whatever you wish within my scope! Just be certain that someone dies besides one of our own." His tone became a whisper. "But it will not be Byron. No, I want the Dread Knight for myself, Roak. I shall slay him as surely as the viper slays the hare. Remember," he said, stalking swiftly away from the stunned Shadowbeast General. "One day. I expect him or her before the entrance of Mount Toane tomorrow to be briefed. Go."

Vilec Roak was left alone once again with his thoughts. Who would be worthy of the task at hand? What single mortal to select from Vandross's thousands?

Byron's company consisted of a Dwarf, an Elf, three Humans, a Ki Fairy, a Cuyotai, and Byron himself, who apparently didn't fit any category. Their skills made them a Boxer, a Gaiamancer, a Pyromancer, a Paladin, a Monk, a misfit, a Hunter, and a Dread Knight. What combination of Race and Class would have a chance against them? He didn't want there to be any common bond between his *victim* and Byron's company. There would be too many questions then. Humans, Elves and Cuyotai were the most common Races of the land, and Vandross's forces had several thousand of them, Illeck taking the place of their good-hearted Elven brethren. The Khan were all known to be fairly loyal as an entire Race to whoever had power, so that too would be an ill choice.

But what of the few Lizardmen that still fought for Vandross, he wondered suddenly. They were said to be assassins all, crafty and dangerous Ninjas and Rogues. None of them had fallen in any of the conflicts they had been involved in. In the utter destruction of Vandross's deployment to Desanadron, they were the only ones to survive that massacre unscathed.

And as far as Byron knew, all of Bael's kinsmen had abandoned his lord's cause. One of them would make the perfect tool for his plan. What was their leader's name?

A half hour later, the Lizardman Ninja moved out of the shadows behind Roak, who had summoned him to his quarters.

How had the man gotten there without him noticing? It didn't matter in the long run. It was a sign of his skill in fact, and one that Roak relished.

The slight and short reptilian assassin looked out at him from behind a traditional black head mask, his eyes small slits in the darkness. "You summoned me, master Roak," he whispered, his voice more of a hint of noise than an actual statement of words. His every action was entirely silent, reserved, and calculated.

"Indeed I did. We have a mission for you, Tal."

* * * *

The sun rose over the horizon, spilling golden rivulets of light amid Byron's company as they awoke from a good evening's rest. The morning was spent in the usual way, walking in contemplative silence, as the morning chill gave way to the late morning warmth of late spring. Down through valleys and over ridges they traveled, until finally they reached the border between the Elven Kingdom and the independent central plains.

Byron had sorely miscalculated their travel time, not having fully accounted for the landscape between himself and the mountains in the far north. Still, they had made decent time. They would travel near and into the outskirts of city-states for the remainder of their journey north, but many days still lie between them and their destination.

Black Guardsmen patrolled the border, keeping those unwelcome from entering the southernmost regions of Tamalaria and their Kingdom. A few of them, Byron noticed, wore a strange black armband of leather, with a white skull embroidered on it. Was this part of their uniform now that the struggle of Whitewood was over?

He led the company openly toward the border, and several of the Elven elite warriors hailed them with wishes of good fortune.

One group even exclaimed, "Hail! Hail good Byron."

Now he understood the armband; it was a symbol of their victory in Whitewood. Was it possible that others outside of the kingdom would wear them, though, wasn't it? Even if the Elves had come up with the idea, would the peoples of Desanadron embrace the cause of Byron and his crew? With a renewed spirit, he led the company directly toward the bordermen.

"Hail and well met," Byron said, trying to smile at the large group of Elven patrolmen. He saluted the tallest of the men, seeing that he wore the insignia of a Major. "Major, may we speak together, as common men?"

The almost feminine features of the Elven Major, his high cheekbones, soft-looking and powdered skin, lent him an air of aristocratic grace. But his eyes told a different story; this man had seen outright war more than once, and had survived some really shitty situations.

"Nay, good Byron," said the man, smiling as he dismounted his midnight-black steed. Looking at Byron, he offered a hand to the Dread Knight. "Let us speak as comrades in a common cause."

Byron shook the man's hand, which was surprisingly strong for one so lithe in appearance and frame. Again, Byron looked into his eyes, and saw not the eyes of an over-educated politician, but the cold, hard eyes of an efficient soldier.

"Anything we can do to aid in your journey, we shall. Pray tell, what would you have of me, sir?"

Byron looked back at his company, each of whom was talking to members of the border patrol.

"We require horses, Major, I won't skirt the issue. We need to travel to the northernmost region of Tamalaria, and we need to make haste. While we travel afoot, the warlock Richard Vandross—" he noted the involuntary cringe of disgust and fear in the Major's muscles, "he shall work against us. He is devious, and he has the power to summon demons. Demons who can travel faster than any running man. Not only this, but they use the magic of teleportation." Byron tried to keep his voice low, so as not to spook the younger, lower-ranking men of the border patrol. "Will you aid us?"

The Elven Major seemed to ponder the undead warrior's need, weighing it against his own duty. But the hesitation was only momentary. The military man was soon shouting to a companion in Elven, a language that, unfortunately, Byron had never taken the time to learn.

The man he had shouted to sprinted over, his chain mail armor clanking together loosely. This Elf didn't seem much older than Shoryu, however, and since Elves lived considerably longer lives, Byron was taken aback by his youth.

"Sir Byron, meet Sergeant-at-Arms Thomas Duradian. He is also our current quartermaster."

"Sergeant-at-Arms," Byron asked, incredulous. "He is barely out of his adolescence!"

"That's true, sir," said the young Duradian, a smile plastered to his face. He had an air of rough and quick experience about him, Byron thought. "But I have already seen a good deal of skirmishes. I am a prized tactician, schooled at the Elven Military Academy for eight years. I graduated second in my class last year, though due to my age, I was not afforded the rank of an officer. I must wait five more years before I am deemed proven of the post of Lieutenant, sir." His words came short and snappish, militant. Had the boy been raised for this post? Byron wondered. It wasn't uncommon in lower class families to raise a child for military service. The city-states and kingdoms of Tamalaria afforded their servicemen a decent living. A child from an impoverished home could be made into a good soldier, and could live better than his or her parents. But often these individuals had short-lived relationships, and families that were torn apart by their service. Divorce was not a common practice in Tamalaria, but it often resulted from military marriages. Byron had been fortunate that Alice had been understanding. Would this young Elf be so lucky?

Byron was brought out of his reverie as the Major began speaking to the young Sergeant-at-Arms. "These folks require horses, Sergeant. How many are there of you, Byron?"

Byron looked back at the group. There were eight in all, himself, James, Shoryu, Ellen, Selena, Morek, David and Alex. But the Ki Fairy didn't need a mount, obviously, and Morek cold easily ride with David.

"Five horses, nothing more," he said.

"Four, Byron," called Shoryu, who had been listening with his pointed coyote ears. "I can take my animal form and run alongside. I am a Hunter, and can run as well as any horse."

Byron nodded to the Major, who sent the young Sergeant and quartermaster off to get the steeds required.

Byron milled about the small encampment with the others, speaking with this borderman and that one, making idle small talk until the horses arrived. He did not have to wait long, thankfully, for he found the conditions of the patrol camp dismal. The men had an air of defeat about them, though why he could not hazard a guess.

"Major," he said, taking the Elf aside as the Sergeant returned with the horses. "Why is everyone so downcast? An aura of gloom lingers over these men."

The Major's eyes turned from bright to dark and depthless in a second. Had the Major feigned gladness for his benefit, or for the sake of his men?

"Byron, word has reached us that Richard Vandross's armies march all over the east, razing entire cities and looting from small villages. While we stand safely on this side of the continent, others suffer at the hands of the warlock. And we can do nothing, for our Queen commands that we remain here to protect our borders. My men wish to fight, Byron. They wish to march into the heart of the enemy and squeeze it. But we cannot disobey our orders. We cannot neglect our duty. Only a few platoons have been allowed to leave for the east, and we await those platoons' return." The Major's tone had gone from simple dissatisfaction to disgust as he spoke, and his hatred of the one-eyed warlock was clear.

This man lost someone, Byron thought to himself.

Lines of pain marked the Major's face. Once more he slapped his fake smile on and motioned Byron's troupe toward the horses. "Here are the mounts you require. They are all fine beasts, and can sprint across the open plains like few others. We have given you our best, good Byron. May Oun protect and guide you."

"And you, Major. Long live the Queen," he called to the bordermen. A loud responding shout of the same words echoed in the distance, and as Shoryu shape-shifted into his animal form, the group rode off into the sun. With the riders fast becoming little more than dots on the horizon, the Major went back to his duties, not noticing a sick Corporal, who had been otherwise silent and unmoving, slink off from the encampment, his movements masked by the stealth and speed with which he darted away.

The Corporal returned to his natural form, his black, oily substance becoming something Human-like, but completely dark. The Shadowbeast spy sent a mental message back to his General, Vilec Roak, who had already laid down the foundations of the trap he prepared for Byron and his troupe.

* * * *

Byron and his company rode at a good clip for the remaining sunlight hours, stopping in the early evening to rest their horses near a stream, and to settle in for the night.

Selena offered them a fire to sit around, and the group sat in relative silence, each lost in their own thoughts. James Hayes, who had become the second-in-command, found his mind floundering for answers. The great god Oun, it seemed, had accepted Byron back into His fold, that appeared certain. So why couldn't he shake his feelings of doubt, of guilt? Why didn't *he* feel worthy anymore? The massacre of his kinsmen at Fort Flag had been devastating, and he had not fallen out of faith, but rather, had plummeted like a boulder. The assault on Desanadron might have been successful, if not for Byron. James could not think like this undead warrior, with his military efficiency, and his own methods had gotten hundreds killed in the city-state capital. Their headstones would forever haunt him, remind him of his lack of ability, of worth. But despite his failings, Byron seemed to trust him to a fault.

But then, the Dread Knight, or Paladin, James thought, trusted in all of them. He had called them all his friends, and held no anger or grudge toward any of them. Byron obviously felt strongly about Shoryu, the young Cuyotai Hunter. When the two of them talked together, James thought of a father watching out for his own son. That made sense, in retrospect; Shoryu, had been with Byron since the beginning of this whole journey. And he was a young man, so Byron's take on the situation might have been a simple matter of an older veteran looking out for a young warrior. But James smiled, watching the two of them jostle each other over some joke the Cuyotai had made, and their manner reaffirmed his first feeling. Father and son, for family was a matter that transcended flesh and blood. Family was about the spirit of two or more people, and no other word fitted properly for the two of them.

James volunteered to take the first watch that night, and as the others settled in for sleep, he stood up and began walking around the camp in a sweeping perimeter. After only a few minutes, he sensed eyes upon him.

Caution came naturally to him as a Paladin, and he brought light to his hand, clenching it in a fist, holding the magical illumination in front of him.

Only a short distance away, a Lizardman in tattered black leather armor lurched toward the company, dragging his left leg as if crippled. Blood shimmered off of his front, ragged wounds bleeding freely.

Seeing that the man bore no weapons, as he fell to the ground in a heap, James rushed to the Lizardman's side, rolling him over and spreading a healing magic over the reptile warrior's body.

The wounds closed, and breath heaved into the man's chest. His eyes darted around, as if seeing still the beings that had attacked him.

After a moment, the Lizardman clutched Hayes's shoulders, hauling himself to his knees, his eyes wild and filled with panic. "They're coming," he rasped at James, sweat pouring over his scaled forehead. He shook the Paladin roughly, getting to his feet. "We must flee! Surely they are demons sent from Al-Hiyus."

James put his hands up, trying to tell the man to calm down, but so afraid was this warrior that he had to slap the man to get his attention.

"Be still, Lizardman." *Al-Hiyus*, James thought. The Lizardman tribes each held their own superstitions, and Al-Hiyus was the deepest pit of Hell for some of the older tribes. "I have friends over there. I shall wake them shortly for a change of shift. For now, come with me to the fire. I'll give you some food and drink to soothe your spirit."

He took the reptilian warrior's arm with his hand, feeling the involuntary jerking of the muscles as the Lizardman spun his eyes. Obviously something serious had attacked the man; he was not as large as some of his kinsmen, but he had the aura of a great fighter about him. Shadowbeasts alone would not leave one such as this man so spooked.

Gently the Paladin led the wounded man to the fire, giving him some bread and dried strips of meat, which the Lizardman tore at as though starving. "Tell me a little about what happened, and give me your name," James said.

"Very well. My name is Phazion Lurik, a member of the Dusanari Tribe. I am a Battle Priest, as was my father before me. Oh father," he cried, throwing his hands in the air. "May your soul rest now in mother Gaia's breast! We were returning from a pilgrimage to the deep southern regions, in the Elven Kingdom. Several villages of our people lie within the kingdom's borders," he said, taking a swig of ale.

James heard Byron moving toward them, sensing the Dread Knight's movements before he actually saw the undead warrior sit across the fire from them.

Lurik, as the man had called himself, stared wide-eyed at Byron for a moment before continuing. "You are the mighty Byron, who aided Desanadron, are you not?"

Byron said nothing, but nodded.

James looked into the pinpricks of light in his eye sockets; Byron was still worn out, but he knew the Dread Knight would not rest now.

"Anyway, we were a small handful of Priests and soldiers, bringing the betrothed of our tribe's healer back to our home in the far north. But along the way, we were attacked by a pack of creatures as black as night. With them they brought a huge abomination. It tore at us without mercy, striking down my father before my very eyes."

Byron looked up at Hayes and both men nodded—they had seen the demon in Whitewood.

"In all of my years, I had always seen my father as this immortal warrior, incapable of dying. Oh, how foolish I have always been." Lurik burst into tears.

James tried to pat the man on the back, but knew a little about Battle Priests; already the man's pride was in tatters. No sense in making the matter worse for him.

Byron abruptly shot upright, his head whipping from side to side. He had heard something in the near distance moving, and whatever it was, it was huge. Had the demon followed this Lizardman? Or perhaps Shadowbeasts had found him. It didn't really matter which, Byron thought, his hand itching to reach for the Morning Glory. But he stayed his hand with an effort. Whatever the noise had been, he realized, James Hayes and Phazion Lurik had not heard it. Neither man had even looked up when Byron moved, and he excused himself quietly from the Priest and Paladin.

Phazion Lurik finally looked up at James, his eyes imploring him silently. *Protect me*, they said to him.

"Do you require our aid, Lurik?" James asked, raising an eyebrow. "We can guide you to your home village safely. I am sure that no one else will mind."

Byron, meanwhile, stalked a short distance away from the camp, searching the night darkness for signs of intruders. There was only the vague sense, however, that something powerful approached. No noise, no movement, made itself immediately apparent.

"Getting paranoid," he whispered to no one. He was ready to turn back and return to the camp when he heard the noise again, and felt something moving through the ground.

Byron tensed his entire body, keeping his hands loose at his side. He would wait to spring on his enemy when it approached.

But there was no sense of urgency, no tension in the air other than his own. Nothing was poised to strike at him.

Slowly, cautiously, Byron turned back the way he had gone from the camp, and saw in the distance what he had felt and heard.

The creature was vaguely humanoid in shape, huge and hulking, and wearing some sort of armor. In the darkness, Byron could make out few other characteristics, but decided to move in for a closer look.

Using the breeze to cover his soft, furtive movements in the tall grasses,

Byron slinked to within twenty yards of the armored man.

It stopped abruptly, turning slowly toward the Dread Knight. Angular, crimson armor shone in a thin shaft of moonlight that broke through the clouds. Round, feral cat's eyes shone yellow through the slit that served as a visor in the creature's helmet. Up close, Byron realized just how large and intimidating this thing was and felt a moment of panic race down his spine as he looked at the wicked blade at its hip.

Just as he was about to remove himself from the area, the creature turned fully toward him. "Thou hast no reason to fear me, Byron of Sidius." Its voice shook the ground beneath the Dread Knight.

How does this creature know me? Byron wondered. *I have never seen him before.*

The colossus moved closer, kneeling some ten feet away from Byron. Even kneeling, the armored creature was a foot taller than he.

"How do you know me, creature?" Byron rasped. His fear had gone, but he still could not speak well.

"I know all peoples, Byron," rumbled the colossus. "My name is Locke. I am an unsuccessful, and as such unnecessary, Keeper. All mortal things have a Keeper, Byron. Know thou the form of thy own Keeper?"

After expelling himself from Vandross's body, Locke had beseeched the Great Gods to give him a new charge, but they had none available. As such, he had been told to roam the lands of Tamalaria, until such time as he was summoned. He might, they said, find someone without a Keeper, who might take him in. Or, as one of the Gods had hinted, he might serve as a sage to all mortal men.

Byron had been thinking of the Voice he heard when he lapsed into the strange cemetery of some of his dreams.

"I know its form. I call it Voice," Byron said, his voice still a whisper. He put his hand to his throat, but did not feel any pain or strangeness there.

"Thou art concerned, good Byron," the colossus said. Yet no words rippled the air, Byron thought. They seemed to be spoken directly to his heart. "I keep thy voice low, that thy friends might not know you speak to mere shadows and spirits of ethereal substance. Thou seest me for thy body and soul exist in a strange place, somewhere between mortality and death. Few can ever see Keepers who have been expelled from their hosts. Yet, thou dost. Tell me, hast thou seen others such as I?"

Byron thought hard on this, but had to shake his head.

"No, I have not."

"Hm, curious. Mayhap there be a reason thou can see me, and yet not others. Yes," Locke said, finally making the connection. Of course Byron would see Locke—his hatred and tie to Richard Vandross would allow this. "Sit with me a brief spell, Byron. There are things I seek to explain to thee, and they shalt make things clearer."

When Byron hesitated, Locke sat, cross-legged, in the grass, trying to think of the quickest, clearest way to explain the Keepers and their purpose to this man.

Damnation of the Realm

As Byron took a seat, Locke began, relating the basic purposes of Keepers, how and why they differed in appearance and how they could change to suit their host. He explained their duties and responsibilities, as well as the laws that governed them.

As Byron nodded, Locke prepared for the response he would get when he made his last statement aloud. "I myself am formerly the Keeper of one you know. I was the Keeper of Richard Vandross." Locke prepared mentally to defend himself against attack; much to his surprise, Byron only grunted.

"Hmm. I imagine you have seen a lot of destruction then, Locke," Byron whispered, rubbing his chin pensively. He was trying to think of what the Keeper might have looked like once upon a time, but as Locke had said, a Keeper's appearance changed in order to either protect it from an unwilling host, or in order to encourage the behavior the host was participating in. Keepers were generally neutral, Locke had said. They often only changed when the host acted against its own best interests, or against the Gods' designs. Locke must have felt threatened to develop a weapon and armor of the caliber he possessed. "But you have also seen the man's thoughts and plans. You know precisely what he intends. Will you tell me?"

Locke considered. If he helped, he would be directly interfering in the world's affairs, something that until recently, he had never fathomed doing. If he did nothing, he was letting Richard Vandross do as he had wanted, which might very well lead to utter chaos for all of the lands of Tamalaria. He had made his decision.

"I shall tell thee all there is to tell. But not tonight," Locke rumbled, standing. "And not directly. I shall speak with your Keeper, and he in turn can relate the matter to you. I trust that is fair enough."

Byron nodded, and reached out an armored hand.

Locke took it in his own, and was almost torn apart by the conflict he felt and saw within Byron's body and soul. Like the guardian of the forestlands to the south, the Keeper was taken aback by the knowledge he siphoned from that single handshake. For a long moment, he stood as if roots in his feet had fastened him to the earth. He released the Dread Knight's hand, and spun violently away, stalking off into the distance with a single image in his mind—the image of Byron standing helplessly by as Richard Vandross slaughtered his family.

But Locke knew something about Byron that even the Dread Knight did not. With this secret in his mind, Locke was able to put aside the image of the former Paladin's pain, and smile inside his helmet.

Chapter Sixteen
Springing the Traps

As the morning sun spread its warm glow like a soft blanket across the realm, the company awoke to meet the new day. Phazion Lurik was introduced swiftly to the members of Byron's party, and the tall Lizardman appeared to have regained a measure of his composure and stature.

Healed and fed, Byron saw that the wounds the man had suffered had been paltry and flesh-deep only. Lurik possessed great strength of body and purpose, he saw, from the way his muscles twitched and flexed beneath his simple white tunics, to the man's carriage and demeanor. As Byron had slept, the Voice had revealed some of Vandross's intentions to the great Dread Knight.

For a while, Byron had despaired; Vandross had slipped from the status of conquering tyrant to power-hungry madman. The one-eyed devil had no plans to dominate Tamalaria. Instead, the Voice had told him, Vandross intended to rend the land asunder, and then turn himself over to the Immortal Rest, in order to arise again in a millennia's time, in order to repeat his atrocities.

This could not, Byron thought, have been Vandross's original intention.

The Dread Knight poured the brackish coffee Morek had prepared down his throat, letting its warmth spread through his stomach and chest.

Byron turned his attention then to James Hayes, who had been seeing to Lurik's needs, offering what succor he could in the forms of more food and drink. The Human Paladin needed something to cling to, Byron realized as he drew the Morning Glory to inspect the blade. This was a false gesture, of course. He simply wanted to observe how his companions would react to this newcomer without interruption, and a hulking Dread Knight, regardless of who he was, generally discouraged distraction with a weapon in his hands. Only Shoryu or Alex would be comfortable enough to approach him as he was, but the Cuyotai was engaged in conversation with Ellen, helping her pack up their provisions, and Alex seemed to be playing a card game with Selena Bradford.

Morek Rockmight and David Spore engaged in conversation with Lurik, and Byron peered at the Dwarven Boxer's eyes as hard as he could without giving himself away. He saw the typical distrust and skepticism of northern Dwarves, knowing that Morek was measuring the worth and nature of this Battle Priest.

David, being a tad more friendly than his Dwarven counterpart, didn't seem to be withholding any judgment. The Monk simply enjoyed what little conversation he engaged in.

As Byron returned his attention to the Morning Glory, a bronze piece clattered to the grass between his splayed feet. He looked up then into Shoryu's smiling countenance.

"Penny," Shoryu said, his tone light and carefree.

"What," Byron asked, picking up the bronze piece. That's right, he thought. People referred to these small currencies as pennies sometimes.

"Penny for your thoughts." Shoryu gingerly lowered himself to the ground next to his undead companion and leader.

Once again Byron was baffled. If he had an eyebrow, he would have raised it in question. Instead, he attempted to mimic the expression as best he could with his animate bones.

"It's an expression among the folk of Ja-Wen. It means I'd like to know what you're thinking," the Cuyotai whispered.

Ellen, Byron saw, was meditating some short way off, gathering her strength for the day ahead.

"Oh." Byron set the Morning Glory across his knees as he sat cross-legged. He clasped his hands in front of him, resting his armored elbows on the thick blade of his weapon. "There is something not adding up about this man, this Lurik," he confided to the young Hunter, his voice low and light. "I am not entirely certain just what that is exactly. He claims to be a Battle Priest."

"Indeed." Shoryu dragged his rucksack over to his side, reached in, and produced a small stoneware bowl. Holding his hand over it, palm down, he produced a sharp claw from his left pointer finger, making a small slice in the palm of his right hand, letting the blood drain down into the bowl. After a moment, he forced the wound to regenerate, closing it as though it had never been. Only a small, discolored line marked the passage of his cut, and he handed the bowl of blood to Byron, who accepted the unexpected gift in one huge fist.

Byron lifted the bowl over his bare skull, then tipped the blood out onto it, the magic of his body absorbing the fresh, copper-scented substance into his body. He felt a hundred times renewed, and thanked Shoryu for his gift with a nod, returning the stoneware bowl to the young Cuyotai.

Shoryu sneered at him, a sort of grimace that held potential violence, and then tucked the bowl away.

Yet again, Shoryu thought, *I come close to losing myself.*

Byron, however, thought nothing of the gesture. He knew full well the risks of feeding off of the Cuyotai's blood.

"Yet he bears no weapons, no religious insignia. He offers nothing more than his word as proof of what and who he is. I do not like to admit such apprehension, Shoryu, but I do not fully trust this man," Byron murmured, shaking his head.

"Perhaps he shall prove himself as we return him home," Shoryu offered, leaning back on his arms as he stretched in the grass, soaking up the vibrancy of the ground and the sky.

Byron sniffed at the air, and found his vacant nostril hole offended. The entire company had collected a good amount of sweat, grime and dirt. They were all due for a bath. Sheathing the Morning Glory across his back, he stood up and moved away from the company in search of a stream. The springiness of the grasses on these plains felt good under his heavy boots, allowing him to move swiftly, freely. For a moment, he forgot about his struggles and conflicts, and simply enjoyed the sights and sounds of the world around him. Tamalaria held beauty in abundance, from the shrill calls and songs of its flitting birds, to the sheen of morning dew on its grasses. Each tree and stone hummed of knowledge gleaned from hundreds of years of silent existence, and the wind whispered of secrets told in regions far from the ear of those who heard it. Had his mood not been so befouled by suspicion, he might have chuckled at taking it all in; but he could not. Byron walked the path of those already dead, and his final destination, he knew, had already been determined. All of the lands' majesty would be lost to him when he felled Richard Vandross, for the tie that held him to this un-life would be severed at last. Whether he fell in defeat, or rose to triumph, death surely awaited him.

After a few minutes, he found a suitable stream for bathing at the bottom of a sloping hill. He would return to the others to recommend a short bathing session, but not for himself. The subtle stench of decay would forever cling to his flesh, for he was, regardless of how much humanity he regained, a member of the undead. No water was pure enough to cleanse him. Turning about, he marched back to the camp to find that everyone had packed up what was left.

"Where have you been?" Morek asked in his gruff, guttural tone.

"I have found a stream, master Morek. I pray none of you takes offense, but you could all use a wash," he said in as dry a tone as he could muster. He attempted a wry grin. "Particularly you two, Shoryu and Ellen. The smells upon you are not just those of travel and work," he said with a chuckle.

Cuyotai and Elf burned red in the face with embarrassment, each suddenly taking a great deal of interest in the ground at their feet.

"Come. I shall show you," Byron said lightly, leading the company downhill. Enjoying the sound of general chatter behind him, Byron stalked over the springy grass until at last he stopped before the stream. As he turned, he noticed that Shoryu, Morek, James, David and the newcomer, Lurik, had stopped a short way up the hill, their backs to the stream. "Is something wrong, gentlemen," he called up. A clearing of a throat from behind him nearly turned his head.

"Ah ah ahh, good lord Byron," Alex squeaked in his 'ear'. "The ladies are waiting for you to retreat a bit."

"Then what are you doing, my diminutive friend," he asked in a whisper.

Alex spread his smile as wide as it would go, nearly splitting his face.

"I believe the young folk call it, sneaking a peek, a-ha," Alex said as he darted away.

Byron shook his head and laughed softly despite himself, climbing the hill to join the men of the company. They all sat with their backs solidly turned to the ladies down at the stream.

"Gentlemen," he said, sitting on a round-topped stone. Poor David, he thought, looking over at the one-armed Monk. David Spore had sat down cross-legged, and had his prayer beads wrapped around his hand, praying for strength. He leaned in to hear what the Monk was muttering to himself.

"A Monk must be pure of heart, a Monk must be pure of heart," the man repeated, a quiet litany against the temptation to look over his shoulder.

Byron almost burst out laughing, especially once Shoryu opened his snout to make things more difficult for the young Monk.

"You know, I must say, from personal experience, Ellen is indeed a beauty beyond compare," he said aloud, though his comment seemed directed at David.

A cold sweat broke out on David's forehead Morek and James chuckled softly, enjoying the young Monk's clear discomfort.

"Indeed," the Lizardman said aloud, looking innocently up at the sky. "I imagine they both are stunningly attractive, though men such as we must surely swear off the sins of flesh. Or at least, we mustn't presume to look at what isn't ours to gaze upon. From what I gather, young Shoryu could look around without fear of reprisal from Miss Daires. Ah, young love," he said, and thus made David chant his prayer louder and more rapidly.

"Is everything all right," Selena asked behind them as she approached, rubbing her hair dry with a small towel.

David heaved a sigh of relief as the other men of the company burst into laughter.

Selena and Ellen looked at them in confusion, then to each other. The women shrugged their shoulders, and sat themselves easily on the blankets they had laid out. "We missed something rather amusing, I gather," the Pyromancer declared as she leaned back.

"Think nothing of it," Byron said to her as the men tore down the hill, quickly undressing and tossing themselves in the stream.

Ellen and Selena did not turn aside or away from them, looking frankly and plainly down at them. "You know, the lads were gentlemanly enough to look away whilst you were down there," he said, trying to sound admonishing, but failing. His tone had too much implied smile in it.

"Well, Ellen has claim to something down there, you know," Selena said as she raised her internal temperature to dry herself.

"And nobody ever said that Selena is a lady," Ellen said, giggling with her Pyromancer companion and the Dread Knight.

Byron suddenly stiffened: something screamed at him to be alert. Leaping to his feet, he whirled and drew the Morning Glory, argent, ghostly flames trailing along and around the blade.

"Good Byron," Ellen whispered behind him. "Is something amiss?"

Byron put his free left hand back to both stay and silence Ellen and Selena. Something was out here with them, in broad morning daylight.

"I'm not certain," he whispered back. "If there is, then someone is either very foolish, or very brave." He winked out the lights in his sockets, effectively closing his eyes. *Feel it out*, he told himself. *Let the power within seek out the wrong.* This he remembered from his time as a Human Paladin, letting his instincts, his soul, carry him to the unseen demons he had fought. When he 'opened' his eyes, he found himself standing in front of a tree.

He sheathed his weapon and scoffed at himself for his paranoia. *Foolish*, he thought. *I'm jumping to conclusions. I need to move, take action.*

He hoped that the men of the company would finish soon, so that they could be on their way.

In the shadows of the oak tree he'd approached, Vilec Roak smiled.

* * * *

They spent the remainder of the day in semi-silent travel, the rolling plains passing by on either side of the company as they rode.

Phazion Lurik, his wounds having been healed, showed a surprising swiftness, able to keep up with the horses and Shoryu as they cantered and trotted along.

Byron wanted to hurry, even to rush ahead to the north, but he reminded himself that so long as nothing significantly stood in the path of the company, they were in good shape.

As the sky faded from bright azure to a dim orange and purple glimmer, the sun fading over the horizon like a swooping bird, Byron slowed the company to a walking trot, making things much easier on his Cuyotai friend and the Battle Priest. Plains-roaming animals kept their distance from the company, barely visible on the outskirts of Byron's limited vision. He had become accustomed to this behavior from the creatures around him, but something in their stand-offishness made him worry. In the Elven Kingdom, he had not been so openly feared by the children of Mother Nature. And Ellen's presence, as both an Elf and a Gaiamancer, should have left them feeling at ease. But as he called a halt to the company's day, the animals continued to stare at the group with apprehension.

No amount of percipience helped him pierce their emotions. Instead of beating his head against that particular wall, he dismounted and suggested that camp be made for the evening.

David approached him as he stalked a short distance away from the company, towards the gathered animals at the foot of a small hill.

He turned to face the one-armed Monk.

"Byron, don't you think we might make some more progress before the sun truly sets," David asked, looking around nervously. "Something in the air does not sit well with me."

"No," Byron said, looking not at David, but at the animals and the sky in turn. He almost felt eyes upon him, like a specter had come at evening's nearing to haunt him with indecipherable hints. "We shall go no farther, Monk, though I agree that there is a wrongness to the area. Something spreads an ill aura about the area. Do what you must to secure us," he said, pointing to David's hip, where he kept his sutras. "We shall keep watch in pairs tonight. Inform the others. I must be alone for a few minutes."

When he turned his attention once more towards the assembled animals, they were nowhere to be seen. A sharp, freezing breeze whipped past, leaving him chilled to the bone, quite literally. The air seemed to whisper rumors of danger and fear to him, and both drawing near. In his mind's eye, Byron saw dozens of Shadowbeasts rolling over the peaceful hills and valleys toward his company, led by a massive demon. His head felt light, as if floating in a tub of some dank water. His vision clouded for a moment, but when it cleared, he saw nothing out of the ordinary. The lush, green grass of the land still stood straight, the trees that spotted the area remained standing, and the bushes and shrubs retained their resilient mien. And yet, he knew, something was wrong with this scene?

Halfway back to his company, he realized what was missing: there was no wind. Not even a hint of swirling air could be felt, and as he looked around once again, he noticed how upright the grass and shrubs were. Nothing, no animal or force of nature, touched them. In the plains of Tamalaria, such circumstances murmured of ill omen.

As he stood in the center of the unfolding camp, he looked into James Hayes's eyes. James nodded knowingly in response, and drew his broad sword.

Shoryu, Ellen and Selena looked at the Human Paladin, clearly noticing that Morek had equipped his silver studded gloves.

David returned to the company, having set up sacred sutras in a wide circle around their encampment. Alex opened his Fairy Space, and floated a heavy spiked mace to Phazion Lurik, an appropriate weapon for a Battle Priest.

Byron drew the Morning Glory, to find that the blade positively beaming with radiance. It was reacting, he realized, to the wrongness in the air and the ground.

Tremors, slight at first, shook the ground beneath them. But they grew in intensity, and the ground rent itself beneath them. The damage within the area of the sutras was slight; outside of the mystic power of David Spore's Monk powers, deep crevices were created in all directions.

From the north, out of a small copse of trees, a small group of cloaked figures approached, a Gaiamancer at the forefront.

Byron peered at them, and Shoryu leaned to him to say, "Illecks, good Byron. Dark Elves."

As they slowly approached, the Gaiamancer summoned forth three Rock Golems, each bearing weapons of stone and wood.

"Everyone, make ready," Byron bellowed above the sound of the tremors.

Thankfully, David had made their area of protection relatively large, giving them some space to work with. If he could, Byron would keep the company within the protection of the sutras. But something in the way Lurik flinched drew his attention from his strategic thinking. "Phazion Lurik, what troubles you?"

"Those men, they were with the Shadowbeasts and the giant demon that attacked my entourage," the Lizardman quailed, anger mixing with fear in his voice. "I shall crush them all."

Without further hesitation, the Battle Priest streaked out of the sutras' protective circle. Leaping and bounding around and over the rents in the earth, Byron Lurik closed the gap with his enemies.

"Selena, Ellen, Shoryu. Stay within the circle and use your magic and arrows. Morek, David, direct left. James, you're with me. Let's go."

With a roar like a lion, Byron led his companions out of the circle, maneuvering around the rifts as Lurik had done, but with slightly less speed.

The Lizardman had already engaged one of the Rock Golems in battle, and was dancing circles around it, tearing into its weak spots with his mace.

For a moment, Byron forgot his distrust of the man, impressed with his prowess on the field of battle. Then, he and James Hayes hammered hard into the second Golem, tearing it apart.

A blast of arctic cold slammed into him, Aquamancy throwing him and the Paladin back.

Byron used his momentum to roll back into a crouch, launching a blast of lightning force from his fingertips. Streaks of yellow, forked force lanced into one of the Illecks, holding him in place as he thrashed and screamed in agony, his body coming off of the ground.

Using his hold on the man, Byron threw him high in the air, smoke trailing after him.

As the Dark Elf fell back to the earth, Byron swept the Morning Glory in an upward arc, splitting the man in half. Blood sprayed the ground, freezing on contact with the air. The remaining four Illecks hesitated, and this spelled their collective doom.

Morek, having approached undetected due to his stealthy movements, launched a fatal punch into the larynx of an Illeck Pyromancer among the group, closing his windpipe. As the fallen man knelt, clutching at his damaged throat, the Dwarven Boxer brought his elbow crashing into the back of his skull, resulting in a crunch of skull and gray matter.

David Spore, once again wound up on the unfortunate end, received a blast of force to the chest. But one of Shoryu's arrows, having been launched at a high arc, blasted through the side of the attacking Illeck's head, leaving a gaping hole where flesh and bone should have been.

Ellen, meanwhile, engaged in magic-to-magic struggle, the Illeck Gaiamancer and she both pressing their palms hard against the ground, releasing magical force into the earth. Beads of sweat ran down her face, and the smell of maple tree sap wafted through the air around her. The exertion appeared to be too much for the Illeck, his skin becoming paler than the normal Illeck, and his arms and legs trembled. A moment later, a man-sized fist of solid packed earth reared up in front of him, snatching him into its grasp.

With a single burst of sound, the man screamed in terror and agony, and then was gone, absorbed into the ground. Blood stained the spot where he had stood, rising up through the soil to turn the grass the color of copper.

As the last survivor of the assault tucked tail to flee, Selena Bradford threw up a wall of hellfire in front of him. The Illeck was too busy looking back for pursuit to realize he was about to run headlong into a flaming wall of death.

Alex fluttered along, hovering high enough that the flame barrier wouldn't touch him.

On the near side of the wall, an Illeck ran for dear life. A few seconds later, a skeleton and a pile of ashes appeared on the other side of that same wall. Through some perverse god's humor, the skeleton continued to move for a few seconds before falling apart. Alex giggled and returned to the Pyromancer's shoulder to congratulate her on a job well done.

The company seemed largely intact, David and James having taken a little damage. Byron made a quick head count, making certain everyone was accounted for. "Well, that went better than I think we could have hoped. But it went a tad too easily for my liking. Alex," he addressed the Ki Fairy almost formally. "Be a sport and do a quick fly-round, make certain there are no others awaiting us for ambush."

Alex fluttered into the sky, flying around and checking the surrounding area. In the fading daylight, he saw no sign of other hostile forces, but he did see what looked like a village about three hours' march away. Rather than report that, he simply flew down and informed Byron that all appeared to be well.

Satisfied with the relative safety of the company, Byron told them to settle in for the evening once more. Things were looking up for them, he supposed. Phazion Lurik had proven himself in battle, and no one had been badly injured. The sensation that someone was watching, testing and measuring him from the shadows persisted. There was nothing he could do about it at the moment, so he chose to ignore it.

The company shared a meal in silence before Byron and James Hayes decided to take the first watch, and the last shred of sunlight disappeared over the horizon.

The sounds of nocturnal animals, wolves baying, owls hooting, arose in the air and replaced the rather dreadful silence that had made Byron aware of trouble in the first place. The sounds of nature gave him some small measure of comfort, an assurance that life proceeded as normal.

There wouldn't be much comfort for the company if they ran into more of Vandross's forces, as it seemed they must upon occasion. After all, the one-eyed warlock was gaining power and ground. He would not be kept at bay forever, that much was certain. Already his cronies had attacked the company, and Byron was still a good four days' ride out from the entrance to the northern mountains.

For a moment, Byron considered James Hayes out of the corner of his eye. The Human Paladin had encountered a great deal of grief recently. He had seen his fort devastated, the city of Desanadron hobbled, and an entire regiment of fighting men and women slaughtered in that great city. His faith in Oun was wavering, that much he spoke of. But beneath that outward doubt, lay another, more personal set of worries. The man had been wounded already, and might very well not survive the final confrontation with Richard Vandross. Surely Hayes wanted a crack at the warlock. Everyone in the company, with perhaps the exception of Phazion Lurik and David Spore, had personal scores to settle with Vandross. For Selena, it was the assault on Desanadron. For Shoryu, the destruction of his tribe. For Hayes, the extermination of his unit. For Ellen Daires, the blasphemous attack on Whitewood. For Morek, the threat of losing a long time friend, Ellen, in a fatal attack on her home. David Spore and Phazion Lurik had their own reasons for coming along, though David had become good friends with Morek Rockmight, and for a Monk, friends were worth fighting for. The greater balance of power also hung heavily in matters. For Monks, balance and order was everything. Richard Vandross would bring about discord and chaos, as vast as he could spread it.

More, however, was at stake for each member of the company. Selena Bradford, was renowned for her particular potency as a sorceress. She had earned the title of Sorcerer Supreme, a title of honor and respect most magic users, let alone female magic users, can only dream to be granted. Her lethal flames were known across Tamalaria. James Hayes represented the Order of Oun, one of the most powerful factions in the lands, with a presence in all territories. Shoryu stood as the last surviving member of his tribe, and so must survive to rebuild the tribe and its honor. Ellen Daires would be his companion in this matter. Morek Rockmight was one of the leaders of Traithrock, the mightiest city in the Dwarven territories. The Dwarves' fealty to the land and its defenses had become the stuff of legends, and Morek would rather die honorably fighting the encroaching evil than let it be said that the Dwarves had no say in the salvation of Tamalaria. David Spore, whom many surely saw as a broken man with only one arm at his disposal, seemed to be aiding them so as to prove his worth to the world. Alex, the diminutive Ki Fairy, appeared to simply be along for the ride. And then, there was Byron himself. He had his own sins to atone for. All the lives he had snuffed out in the service of Tanarak of Sidius. All of the families he had torn asunder. He had tapped into the darkest places of Hell for powers to unleash upon the world at large. And he had let it all happen through his body. He would have a lot to answer for in the afterlife.

Of course, he mused, his deeds didn't hold a candle to the inferno that Vandross would suffer. His would be true and utter damnation.

* * * *

Midnight came, and Byron and James Hayes had swapped posts with Selena Bradford and Morek Rockmight. One magic user and one fighter to each pair, Byron had insisted. It was the safest way.

The auburn haired Bradford rose groggily from her bedroll and sheets, her eyelids sagging heavily and her nose twitching furiously.

Byron snickered to himself at the cat-like movement of her nostrils, to which she only responded with a rather unendearing grimace.

James almost caught a blow to the chin for his troubles, poking Morek in the stomach gently. The taciturn Dwarf rolled heavily over, knocking into James's knees. The stout Paladin fell backward, pinwheeling his arms for balance, only to land flat on his back. Morek rolled up his body, cocking his arm back to ready a damaging blow. When his eyes focused, he saw that it was James who he had assaulted in panic. "Sorry abou' that, lad," he grumbled as he stretched his limbs.

Now, the Dwarven Boxer and Human Pyromancer were the only members of the company awake. They had not spoken much to one another, each preferring the company of others. For Selena, it was Alex or James, and for Morek, it was David or Byron. They shared little in common, and hadn't had

276

much occasion to speak at length. Now, with little more than the wind and the animals to give them audible comfort, they walked in a circle around the camp together, making small talk.

"First time we've really been around each other exclusively," Selena commented as they made their rounds.

"Oi, that it is. But I can't say as it's much of a surprise." He looked up at the tall woman, making note of the way she kept her hands at her sides, her fingers constantly flexing. Heat emanated from her entire body, her magic kept close at hand, ready to be summoned up at any time. If there came a need for it, her power would lash out at anything that threatened the company.

Thinking about it more thoroughly, Morek supposed she could handle her own in any situation. With little effort, in fact, she could probably have laid waste to the entire group of Illecks they had encountered earlier. Yet, for some reason, she had kept her power restrained. "You didn't do much earlier, during the fight I mean. Not to offend, but is there some reason you didn't add in?"

Selena glanced wryly at him, the corner of her mouth twitching.

"My magic is a bit more taxing on my strength than, say, Ellen's is on hers. Touching the very ground beneath her with her palms is enough to gather power. I require sustenance and rest. I hadn't slept well last night, and so had little to offer that would not have totally incapacitated me. I would rather hold back everything than use lesser powers," she said with an air of hauteur.

"A blitzkrieg rather than a siege," Morek asked, raising one bushy eyebrow. He shrugged his shoulders and continued to put one foot in front of the other. He understood her thinking, to an extent. He preferred to pummel his opponents utterly with a single opening to jabbing at them slowly. A single, killer blow would solve most problems, but he also understood that sometimes strategy and technique were the better methods. Selena Bradford, it appeared, didn't have time for tactics and games.

"I suppose you could say that, Morek. Tell me, how long have you known Ellen?"

"About, ten, eleven years," he said, picking up a light rock and hurling it as hard as he could into the distance. The soft, subdued sound of water splashing met his ears. The stream rushed past, however, erasing all evidence that anything had struck its surface. "We first met at a trade conference between Traithrock and Whitewood. The old established trade routes had come under attack for a few years, mostly by Jaft and Khan highwaymen. Scavengers and bandits, to be sure. Those older roads are surrounded by forestland and swamps alike, offering little comfort for wayward travelers or unprotected caravans. Those few wagons traversing those roads are often filled with the rarest of items and materials, and fetch rather a high price in the less reputable cities and townships."

Morek knew this from experience; twice on his trip to Whitewood for the conference he had fought against petty thieves and braggarts, most of whom presented little challenge. "We spoke at length during the meeting in their Council Hall of making the ways safe. Patrols of both Elves and Dwarves were assigned to the protection of the roads, each group containing at least two of each Race. In the territories between our two, the city-states of Desanadron and Palkatel offered up their aid. Thus were the old routes made safe.

"Ellen and I, we spoke afterwards, mostly of the differing natures of our kingdoms. Our opinions were set as in stone, but I tell you this, Selena, we both share a love of the earth. We Dwarves are people of stone and rock, of highest peaks, blanketed in snow. We have a deeper appreciation for metal ores and stone than any other Race, in Tamalaria, or elsewhere."

Selena nodded, appreciating all that the little Dwarf had offered. Rarely did Morek speak at such length, much less of his own people. His tone showed the depth of his love for both his Race and his realm. Although he was outwardly reserved and brutal, Selena had the impression that Morek Rockmight was truly a man of passion.

"For most of my life," she began as the two of them widened their circle around the camp. "I lived in Desanadron. My friends, what few I had, tended to be of the aristocratic and, well, dry sort."

A breeze blew through the night air, bringing with it the scent of herbs from the copse of woods nearby. But something else lingered; a peace of sorts, as though this night would be a truly restful one. As the hours passed, Selena and Morek grew more and more silent, eventually going back to the company to awaken the last watch for the last dark hours of night, and the wee hours of the morning.

To Shoryu and Ellen fell the duty of this last watch. The Cuyotai and Elven girl awoke refreshed and renewed, thankful for a bit of unbroken sleep. They, like Morek and Selena, began walking around the company in a brief circle, their words few at first.

"What do you think will happen to him, if he fells Vandross," Shoryu asked Ellen. In truth, Shoryu wore his worries on his sleeve; there passed no emotion or thought through his mind or heart that Ellen could not read as clearly as the sky.

"I am not entirely certain." Her voice was light and lofty, lined with the softness of feminine tendencies, and yet husky at the same time, shot through with power. "But there are things that perhaps we should not think on. Byron's fate is his own, and we shall aid him as best we may. What is fated to be for him, we cannot interfere in. It is not our place." Her voice softened further still. Though she was not as attached to the hulking Dread Knight, she had become fond of him. She admired his powers, his prowess with the sword, his tactical abilities. But more than that, she liked him for his fatherly presence. He had a close tie with Shoryu, doting on the young Cuyotai like a kindly uncle or older brother, watching out for him. Byron seemed ready to lay down his own life in exchange for the lives of his companions.

"You love him, don't you," she asked suddenly.

"Well, that's difficult to say," he sputtered, awkward. "I feel close to him, yes. He is, in the words of my people, *toa-akhim magto*. It means, roughly, 'guiding elder brother'. He is, as a Human, younger than I. And even as a Dread

Knight, younger. Yet he is much more experienced in the ways of the world. Until recently, I was sheltered in a village of my tribesmen. Being with him has changed my views of the world. Though I have been a well-trained scout, I see every day the most wondrous beauty anew of the world. And I have him to thank."

The Cuyotai pup moved a little in Byron's direction, looking at his still body. "He helped keep me alive when surely I should have died. I owe him a debt that I shall never be able to repay."

The early signs of dawn surfaced in the distance, deep purples and reds giving a hint of daylight.

Two hours later, as the two of them awoke the rest of the company, Shoryu found himself wanting to put distance between himself and this place. His lover's question had set unwelcome thoughts into motion. Thoughts that involved the end of this quest they all had embarked upon, and that led unerringly to Byron's death. The bond between he and Vandross could not be severed, or altered. The terms of the magic did not brook any change in the cost or outcome. That Byron intended to vanquish the warlock despite the inevitable cost to himself spoke volumes about the purity of his purpose, his soul. He would not be turned aside: no matter the cost.

"Hail, Byron of Sidius," called the reptilian Battle Priest from the upper branches of an oak nearby. He had one hand over his eyebrows, keeping the sunlight from his eyes. "I see my town in the far distance. But something is amiss." From a good twenty feet up, Phazion Lurik leaped down, somersaulting halfway to the ground.

Byron marched toward him quickly, measuring his strides in his head, making his movements swift and plain. He intended to test the Battle Priest this day, to reassure himself, if no one else, that the Lizardman was who he claimed to be. If he wasn't, Byron would know; he had seen true Battle Priests in battle, and this Lurik, if indeed that was his true name, had moved more like an assassin than a Battle Priest. Had there been a bit more hesitation in his violence, a slightly less skilled swinging of that mace, more time spent on the ground in combat than leaping about like a frog, Byron would have been none the wiser.

"Phazion Lurik, I have a few questions for you before we address the matter of your home. Something has been bothering me since first we met, and I shall not attempt to conceal my concerns. You are a Battle Priest, yes?"

He hoped that there would be no hesitation on Lurik's part: a good liar never hesitates, or tries to explain things in depth.

"Indeed I am, Byron. I am a follower of Tonari, the great God of Rage," he said. Which would explain his apparent penchant for violence in combat.

Damn, Byron thought. *If he is a deceiver, he is very good at it. Well-read, well spoken, with all of the intellect of a Priest.*

"Why do you not have a symbol of your God," Byron asked, hearing the soft crush of grass as the other members of the company approached to watch this interrogation.

"While my weapon was lost in fear, my necklace I lost to one of the Shadowbeasts who attempted to rip the life from my jugular."

Byron thought on this; there had indeed been marks of claws just glancing Lurik's throat. *Well enough*, he thought. *His home is close, and he will be safe.* For once, someone outside of the company might turn out to be what he appeared. That would be a nice change of pace, at least in Byron's mind.

"Very well, Phazion Lurik. My curiosity and suspicions are satisfied. You are who you claim to be in sooth, and I shall bear you no further illness of heart. Therefore, tell me, what did you say is amiss?"

Lurik shook his head, seemingly sloughing off the interrogation as though it had never occurred, or he was accustomed to such suspicion. Lizardmen were not the most trusted of the Races, and often became bitter and sarcastic as a result; Phazion Lurik, however, was a Priest, and did not lash out at Byron in turn.

"The normal signs of morning life are not present. There are no women gathering in the animals, no men preparing the central fire for the community lunch, nothing!" Lurik threw his hands up in the air, as if in disgust or dismay. "Yet I sense no great evil. At least, not yet. But come." He hefted his few belongings up off the ground. "Your horses are well trained, it seems. We should come upon the village in a couple of hours." A pang of anxiety tainted the Priest's voice, leaving Byron with the sensation that he could not bear to see more of his people harmed.

A Battle Priest is still a Priest, Byron thought as he mounted his large stallion. And as such, the father would be emotionally distressed and battered if he found that his people were either gone, or dead. Either way, it would be the work of Richard Vandross.

"Damn you, warlock," Byron muttered under his breath as his horse began to canter north.

Downhill, toward a copse of trees between themselves and the Upper Plains they rode, Shoryu morphing into coyote form and sprinting ahead to look for signs of ambush.

Byron heard a squeak behind him, and pivoted in his saddle to look back for the source of the sound. It was Ellen Daires, who had just had a squirrel hop on her shoulder. She squeaked again, giggling like a little girl at the chittering face of the little brown rodent.

Byron smiled as he turned himself back around in his seat, shaking his head to himself. A sweet girl, he thought. Shoryu was a lucky young man. Soft, poignant loam wafted through the wooded air, and for the time being, Byron felt at peace. Something inside told him to savor it, for this would be a trying day indeed.

As the company broke through the other side of the woodland, summer heat slammed into him, filling his lungs with humid, fetid air. Already the stench of death hung in the air, and in caution he summoned up a minor degree of both his Paladin and Dread Knight power.

While the Lower Plains flourished with health and beauty, the Upper Plains gave little to sustain life of any sort. It was a wide stretch of blasted flatland, the grasses brown and dry, the trees bent with age and lack of nourishment. Two days exposed to this sort of terrain and environment wouldn't have much effect on the company itself, but the horses would be hard pressed to find sustenance here. The streams, what few there would be, were either protected by greedy and heavily armed landowners, or stalked by creatures that Byron would rather avoid. After all, they had enough enemies for one lifetime.

Byron slowed the company's pace for the sake of their mounts, letting his stallion lead the way on its own accord. The stallion cantered along the flatland easily, shifting its path from time to time to avoid craggy, rock-strewn stretches of ground. The air held a shallow scent of moss and grime, as though the whole of the Upper Plains needed a wash. Byron bounced slightly with the guarded steps of the horse, looking around for some sign of life other than the company. But to his senses, no creature here was large or healthy enough to be discerned.

After two hours of such travel, the company clearly saw the outskirts of the village. It was a semi-modern affair, like the suburbs of the larger city-states. Two and three story buildings stood in the center of the village, one of them with a flag posted atop it, flapping in the humid wind. Little or nothing specific could be seen, but as they drew nearer, Byron smelled decay and smoke: telltale signs of death.

Shoryu stopped short of the first domiciles, morphing fluidly back into the bestial halfway between human and animal. His nose twitched as he scanned the air with his sense of smell. He moved toward Byron and his horse, backing up instead of turning his back on the village. Caution or fear made him draw his bow, and Byron dismounted as he saw Shoryu sweep the homes with both eyes and nose.

"What say you, Shoryu?" Byron whispered as the young Cuyotai Hunter came to a halt.

"Something living lurks here. This is a very civilized city for such creatures, but I have smelled Lizardman flesh and blood. Only one scent continues to move, however. What about you, Byron," he asked, turning to look Byron in the eyes for a brief moment. "What do you sense?"

Byron looked down the cobblestone street leading into the village proper. It could have been a town, he thought, if perhaps the population were larger or the buildings better spaced. But Lizardmen liked closeness.

He let the lights in his eye sockets wink out, 'closing' them, and let his ethereal magic force flow like smoke down the street. In his mind's eye, he saw what the smoke saw, a form of magic called a *sogratec*, also known as a feeler.

Byron urged the *sogratec* to whip up and down back alleys and side streets. Upon finding nothing, he began to retract the magic, when out of the corner of its field of vision, he saw movement. Turning the *sogratec* around, he found himself looking at a small, lithe Shadowbeast.

Surely this creature was not alone, he thought, incredulous that one minor demon could kill all of the inhabitants of the village. During the initial sweep, Byron had sent the feeler into the homes and shops, finding dead Lizardmen everywhere. They had all been decapitated, the heads nowhere to be found. Now, looking at the Shadowbeast, he knew some treachery had been committed.

He drew the *sogratec* back into himself, and opened his eyes. The others of the company stared intensely at him, waiting for an answer, or, perhaps, for an order. He was, after all, their leader.

"There is deception here," he began, thinking through every word he chose. He was well rested, clear-minded, and had been offered a cup of Shoryu's blood that morning to bolster his body. "I have exasperated my feeler, and all that I saw or heard was a single Shadowbeast scavenging about. There is surely something else going on here, so everyone stay alert, and stay together. No splitting up this time, understood?"

They all nodded mutely, James and Byron drawing swords, Shroyu notching an arrow, Morek strapping on his enchanted gloves, and the ladies of the company preparing magic. David Spore kept his sutras on hand, ready to be flung at the first hostile creature he encountered.

As the company inched along, Shoryu and Byron on point, James and Morek looking left and right to guard their flanks, and David at the very back of the group, David stopped periodically to peer into the front windows or open doors of the buildings. Something appeared to be out of balance, unfitting, to his Monk sensibilities. Why had none of the inhabitants been slain outside? Or, for that matter, why were none fleeing for dear life? As they passed by a tavern, he called up to Byron to halt the company.

David placed a single sutra in the doorway, to bar anything from coming in after him. The low ceiling of the serving room creaked as the building settled, the wind outside whipping up into a good current of stale air. Behind the bar, a beheaded bartender slouched against the back wall, a glass still in one hand and a rag in the other. No sign of his head could be found, nor those of the four customers. The woodwork, crude though it was, seemed well fashioned for Lizardmen, natural for their body designs. Still, they seemed out of place. Arranged, as it were.

"That's it," he whispered to himself, his eyes widening with shock. Nothing had been disturbed in the whole tavern! No broken glasses littered the floor, and no one, not even a Lizardman, would have had enough grace to fall so perfectly against the back wall. Judging from the size of the barkeeper, his weight falling back would have dislodged any number of the liquor bottles from the shelves over his head!

"Are you nearly done in there," Morek called in to him irritably.

My God, David thought as he took in the last, and most vital detail, of this scene; there was no blood around any of the corpses. A struggle would have left the place in shambles, bodies in the streets, and blood on everything, to say nothing of the missing heads. Sprinting pell-mell for the door, David exited and removed the sutra in the doorway, letting it crumble as it lost its power.

"Criminey, boy, you look loik you've seen a ghost or somefin," Morek growled at him.

"There's no blood," David blurted aloud. Byron mimicked a raised eyebrow, and the others started looking into the windows and doorways of other nearby buildings.

"He's right," called Selena, returning to Byron with her forehead spotted in sweat. Fear swam through her, a predatory stalker waiting for the right moment to surface for air and cause her a fatal mistake. "These men and women lay dead here only by pose, not by place or time of death. This is a sham, Byron." Looking around, she asked, "Where's Lurik?"

Byron whipped his head around to look. Where had the Battle Priest gone?

At that moment, a piercing wail rose to meet the humid air, an inhuman shout of pain. It was the voice of Phazion Lurik!

"He must have gone off on his own. Damn it all. Shoryu?"

The pup darted to his side, bow in hand.

"You remember his scent?"

Shoryu nodded, choosing mentally to reserve his energy for action, not speech.

"Good! Lead us to him!"

Shoryu pivoted on his heel and sprinted away, keeping his pace slow enough for the others to follow. Something with the heavy odor of blood and ash had appeared as if out of nowhere, the swiftness of its presence causing Shoryu to hesitate a moment before continuing on. It was a vaguely familiar odor, though where he had first scented it, he couldn't tell.

Through empty, abandoned streets they ran, feet pounding, breath rattling in their chests. Byron, Shoryu and James suffered nothing from the run, as they had been trained for long runs. But Selena, Ellen and Morek were not suited for long, drawn out runs. Ellen and Selena weren't physically fit for it, and Morek's stout legs didn't allow for it.

Byron held the Morning Glory close, sweeping the streets with both eyes and ears.

A low rumble shook the ground under his thickly armored feet, and he envisioned something massive moving through the ground itself.

As he rounded the corner of the large buildings with the flag atop it, he saw a crater in the ground where a town square had presumably been.

Standing in the crater, holding Phazion Lurik in one huge fist, was the enormous beast that Richard Vandross had unleashed on Whitewood.

Seeing it again, Byron felt his heart sink into his stomach. The amount of dark power swirling around and through the demon vastly surpassed that available to him; but he had something the demon could never have, the powers of a Paladin. In addition, he was not alone.

Lurik flailed at the demon with his mace, his swings wild and unaimed, panicked.

Why didn't the Battle Priest utilize his own magic? Was it somehow being suppressed by his proximity to the miasma around the demon? It was entirely possible, Byron thought. He had seen such demons before, fought against them in the name of the Order of Oun. But there was another danger in facing these sorts of demons, which lay in the fact that their presence easily masked that of other, lesser demons. There could easily be dozens of other Shadowbeasts nearby, waiting to spring into attack.

"Help me, Byron," Lurik screamed in agony. "For God's sake, help me."

The beast looked from his captive to the Dread Knight, rage in its huge, crimson eyes. Surely the beast had a weakness, perhaps a particularly vulnerable part of its body? Whatever it was, he had to find it, and quickly.

"Shoryu, take aim at its hand. Shoot Lurik free. Morek," he called the Dwarf to his side as a stream of black, foul-smelling fluid shot forth from the beast's free fingertips. Smoke curled up from the scorched ground the bile had touched, leaving a gaping hole in the ground. A warning shot, Byron thought. The blast would only have struck a member of the company if they had charged stupidly into its path.

The taciturn Boxer sped to his side from the right, his stance defensive, ready for action.

"Morek, there are bound to be other Shadowbeasts about," he shouted over the beast's savage roars. "Guard our right flank from that road entrance. Go."

The Dwarf said nothing, sprinting away to perform the task given him.

"Selena. Do the same, over there on our left flank. Ellen, give us a barrier." As he looked at the Elven girl, he saw that she had already erected a tall stone barrier in front of the beast, leaving it low enough for Shoryu to get a clear shot.

"David, try to get close enough to use some of your sutras on it. Everyone, now." Byron sprang into motion, vaulting directly behind the stone barrier in order to prepare a spell.

Sheathing the Morning Glory, he pressed hard against the barrier, feeling the wall shake as the beast struck at it. An earth-shattering scream erupted from Lurik; the beast demon had punched the barrier with the fist Lurik struggled to free himself from.

Shoryu launched a volley of arrows into the now empty hand, still remembering the smell and power of that black substance the beast unleashed. If he could injure its hands before it used that power again, the battle would go more smoothly. Three, four, five arrows flew, each slamming into an individual finger on its left hand.

Blood sprayed from its new wounds, and the rampaged, stamping about and crushing everything within reach. The barrier of stone began to crack and fall apart in small chunks, destroyed bit by bit.

"Byron," Selena shouted to the Dread Knight.

He looked at her, and saw a line of flames raging skyward, the street closed on the other side of it. Shadowbeasts already had begun to scale the sides of the buildings in order to get around the flame wall. How many were there? he wondered. Dozens, perhaps scores of them. They should not have been so swift, so ready for Byron's party; yet, here they came, jaws slavering, black forms writhing to taste flesh and blood.

"Byron, they will soon be upon us. More surely come from all sides to box us in. We need to destroy the town in order to destroy them."

"Do it," Byron shouted, seeing Phazion Lurik drop from the other side of the barrier, looking broken. David Spore was launching sutras, imposing spiritual and physical restrictions on the beast. Its fist lost an edge of brute strength, and its wounds began to fountain blood on the ground.

The demon dropped to its knees as its companions flooded the center of the village.

Morek bounced back and forth, changing targets with the ease of a force of nature. James Hayes shot waves of holy force amongst the ranks of Shadowbeasts, felling them in groups of six or seven. Serpents of fire danced and slithered through the center of demons as they charged the company, released from Selena's mouth and palms. Shoryu turned his focus from the beast to the Shadowbeasts below, leaping atop the highest standing building and rapidly firing on the Shadowbeasts below.

Though they stood sorely outnumbered, Byron's company had enough power to dispose of the demons' swelling numbers easily.

Perhaps he had misjudged, Byron thought. Surely all of these demons could destroy the village, but Byron and his companions stood against such forces with skill.

But as he turned to check on the others, he saw that while Ellen had encased the huge beast demon in a shell of stone wrapped with vines, Phazion Lurik had regained his feet. There didn't appear to be any signs of injury at all; and instead of the mace he had come with, the Lizardman held a long, thin dagger.

As Byron processed possible meanings of this sight, Lurik jammed the blade through David Spore's back, all the while smiling wickedly.

"Daviiiid," Byron bellowed, instantly drawing forth the power he had summoned earlier and focusing it into a small orb of pulsating light. James Hayes had also begun moving toward the false Priest, weapon raised.

"Treacherous bastard," the Human Paladin cried, leaping high and bringing his sword down at Lurik.

The Lizardman dodged the attack with ease, launching a counterattack immediately, kicking Hayes aside.

The Paladin landed a few yards away in a heap, his head cocked to the side from the raw power of the kick.

Byron released the orb of power, and it flew into Lurik's back, causing him to convulse, coughing a gout of blood as the power blasted a hole the size of a bucket in his torso.

The Lizardman fell dead to ground, but he had a smile on his lips even as he struck the cobblestone.

As soon as David's body dropped beside the assassin's, the Shadowbeasts that had survived the wrath of the company from Whitewood withdrew, fleeing in whatever direction offered the most direct route away from their potential doom. A pair of the demons hurled small black daggers back as they fled, scoring solid blows to Ellen's leg and Morek's warding forearms.

The company rushed to David, each dropping their guard in the slim hope that the Monk could be saved. David Spore hadn't contributed much to the group's survival, but they would not leave him to die at the hands of a deceiver.

Byron dropped down beside him, rolling him onto his side and giving him a light slap on the cheek.

David groaned, his eyes fluttering open.

James Hayes had laid his hands on David's side and the area just below the stab wound, letting his healing energy come forth. But as he probed closer to the wound, a powerful force blasted through David's flesh at him, a coiled viper lashing out at him from within the Monk's blood.

Hayes recoiled, his hands on fire with pain. He looked up at Byron with sorrow in his eyes and his heart.

"What's the matter," Byron barked at him.

"Though your tone is steely, I know you are only concerned. Your worry is well placed, unfortunately. The blade was poisoned, my friends. David is lost to us." As he spoke, the Monk's skin turned a sickly green hue, his veins showing black through the skin. The poison had already run its course—David Spore would be dead in minutes.

Byron raced through a myriad of possible explanations for the weapon's appearance in the Lizardman's hand amidst the battle. Surely he would have detected such a weapon; Shoryu would have smelled the toxin; Ellen would have sensed any natural toxins soaked to the blade. Someone should have known.

"By—Byron," David whispered through cracking lips. His skin stretched taut over his bones, the toxin drying his body out in the final stages of its course. "I, I don't have much time, my friend."

Byron brought his face closer to David's straining to hear his every word.

"The, sutras. I keep, one, in the sole, of my sandal. It, will work, for anyone. Even one who isn't a Monk." Blood trailed over the corner of his lips. "It shall, give you, guidance, when you most, have need. I have, been, in most honorable, company. Thank you, all." In a single, final heave, David Spore brought up a gout of blood that sprayed the cobblestone street. He was at last at peace.

James Hayes rolled him onto his back and closed his eyes. Byron crossed David's arm over his chest, and offered up a prayer for his immortal soul. Everyone stood in silence around his limp, blasted form. When at last they all stood around him, they bowed their heads in silence. Afterwards, Byron knelt and removed David's sandals, and pried the sole open on the left one, finding a strangely marked scroll of sutra paper. The language was beyond his ken, and that of the others as he showed it to them.

An explosion of stone shattered the silence around them, the beast finally freed itself from its prison.

Without so much as looking up at it, Byron, James Hayes, and Selena each launched a single beam of their inherent power. The demon roared in pain and rage one last time before it, too, collapsed to the ground in death. The combined powers of the Dread Knight, Paladin and Pyromancer left little more than a broken husk of the demon.

In utter silence they walked back through the village south, to their mounts. The sun hung directly overhead; it was high noon and their company was now one member short. Betrayal had taken David Spore from them. Byron vowed to never again fall for such tricks by the one-eyed warlock.

This concludes DAMNATION OF THE REALM. The story continues in DREAD KNIGHT'S REDEMPTION, Volume Two of the FREEDOM OR THE FIRE series. Buy it from BooksForABuck.com or any of our retailers.